Clemency

Victoria L. Johnson

PublishAmerica
Baltimore

First printing

This is a work of fiction. Names, characters, places, and incidents either are the product of the author's imagination or are used fictitiously. Any resemblance to actual persons, living or dead, events, or locales is entirely coincidental.

PublishAmerica has allowed this work to remain exactly as the author intended, verbatim, without editorial input.

ISBN: 1-60836-622-7
PUBLISHED BY PUBLISHAMERICA, LLLP
www.publishamerica.com
Baltimore

Printed in the United States of America

Being that this is my first book I have a lot of people to thank. I'd like to begin by thanking my mom for her continued words of kindness and support. I'd also like to thank my brothers and their wives; Tim and Wendy, Rick, Chris and Jen, Nick and Corrie and Maria and Chad. They've all helped with their words of encouragement. My sons, Stephen and Kevin gave so much support both on the computer and with love and smiles when I had down times. I'd like to thank Al Opaczewski for dropping everything and helping me with every computer crisis, even though it was always me and never the computer. I want to thank my good friends Felicia Nielsen and Dave Nanez for supporting me, reading the book and giving such great advice. There's also my Aunt Tina who was so excited it was comical. My husband helped with the title dilemma in his own amusing way. Most of all, I'd like to thank my dad. Dad, you are the best. I dedicate this book to all of you as I couldn't have done it without the entire group.

CHAPTER ONE

Ohio, 1845

Josie knew it would be near impossible to sneak out of the old dirt encrusted cabin while Daddy was awake. His angry anguish filled eyes would follow her every move, hatred seeping from the pores of his work thickened skin. His nostrils would flare like that of a horse and sweat would bead upon his forehead before slowly trickling down his face emitting an odor so familiar to her that it churned her stomach, that of Daddy; the Daddy that no longer displayed the love and affection once bestowed upon her, his only daughter. He no longer bounced her upon his knee or bequeathed her with love filled smiles of tenderness or reassuring "that a girl" pats of encouragement as he had when she was a young bouncy child full of energy and happiness. When she was a little girl she hadn't a care in the world other than how to get the mud off her boots before tracking it through the cabin. She supposed that as a young woman she shouldn't crave that childhood affection from her Daddy anymore. Yet she couldn't help but long for it. She longed for semblance of structure within the household and the unconditional love that only family could offer. She needed stability, a strong hand of faith, and something she had just about given up on…love. More than anything, she desperately longed to be loved, needed, wanted, and cherished.

Shrugging as if those emotions aught exist in the first place, she decided she'd just have to wait until night time when Daddy would be in another drunken slumber, loudly snoring, moving restlessly about tossing and turning, covered in sweat while fighting demons in his dreams. It would be then that the darkness would provide cover and aid in slipping quietly away. It was always then, in the darkness, that she yearned to get away from the anguish that burned her heart, tore her soul in two and followed her every footstep during every day, like a haunting spirit all of its own, manifesting at regular intervals, repeating a time in life that can never be relived, yet wanting something so badly that it can't let go.

"Well," she mumbled slowly blinking through a muddled revere, "there is plenty of work to do before nightfall."

She refused to think about how Daddy had wagered her as a bet in a poker game along the river the evening before last. Shame burned her pale cheeks a crimson red. She was unsure if it was shame from being wagered as a commodity and given to some stranger to be used however he chose, or if it was the shame and embarrassment that she had failed her Daddy on some unknown level, the only family she had left. Imagine grown men wagering her in a bet that started off as a meaningful conversation about the two new counties soon to be named and established as Wyandot and Defiance counties! How on earth had a simple conversation and friendly card game mutated into her dreary future? Did her Daddy think that little of her? She knew she often times got underfoot, but was it to that extent? Tears burned her eyes and she furiously blinked them back.

Disgusted with her thoughts she busied work roughened hands by dusting and cleaning the planked wood tabletop, yet her unyielding mind continued to wonder, to fret and worry. She'd been through this before yet couldn't refrain from asking the same questions over and over again; agonizing questions that tore and ripped the seams of her very soul to shreds. Why did such bad things have to happen to such good people? Why did Daddy blame her so? Shouldn't he have offered words of comfort? Shouldn't he have told her they would get through this? Nothing could change the fact that her very own, once loving, once caring Daddy had given her away. He'd just given her away like she had been no more to him than spit on a whittle.

She'd like to think the alcohol caused him to do it. Spirits from the Devil, that's what the preacher referred to it as. Yes, that was a feather of blame she could take comfort in, but not lack of love, or better yet, a vengeful hate. Still she couldn't convince herself that drinking had everything to do with it, for he hadn't been acting quite the same since Momma died two months ago birthing their first and only son, something Daddy had wanted for years, a legacy both he and Momma desired more than anything. Daddy's change of character had been more than dramatic, even though he knew full well that Momma had been experiencing pain, weakness and other various difficulties all along. The baby had lost the struggle for life as well, which Josie secretly thought was a blessing in disguise; considering the way Daddy was behaving. Of course she didn't think that at first and often felt guilty for feeling that way. Although it upset her, she could attempt to understand the reasoning for his drunken meanness and hateful remarks day in and day out, but a poor innocent little baby couldn't. It just wouldn't have been fair to any of them, especially the baby. She loved her Momma enough to know that she wouldn't have wanted things to be like this. She wouldn't want them to be suffering as they were. She would only ask that her family be happy.

Momma was just too old to be delivering babies. Least that's what the doctor had said about it while trying to comfort her and Daddy the afternoon of the burial, as if it was any condolence at all blaming death on age. Memories of that gloomy rain-filled day rattled her mood into a somber dullness causing an ache to burn in the hollows of her chest and pulsate outward. She placed a trembling hand over her heart as if to soften the blow caused by lovely, yet painful memories. Somehow Josie couldn't think of Momma's sweet face, caring nature and petite frame as old. Thirty-four wasn't old! Momma had been beautiful in both looks and disposition, possessing deep colored green eyes, long flowing dark hair, not quite black, not quite brown. Josie was lucky to have been gifted with her Momma's features. Too old? What was wrong with folks? Heck, she was eighteen years of age herself, a spinster according to many, old indeed!

She snapped a rag on the table. The echoing sound matched the bitterness of her thoughts like the sting of a whip hitting tin. Still, life was short, especially in this area where doctors weren't readily available. They were lucky enough to have Doctor Martin drop in once or twice a year. There certainly wasn't any doctor housed in town. Nor was there a preacher. There was hardly a town. Doctor Martin, much like the preacher, traveled the same circuit over and over again, doing his best to help out when needed, often times a day late and a penny short. Frequently, he'd accept apples or tobacco as payment. Once she had mended Doctor Martin's shirt in trade for care to Momma during the difficult pregnancy. Josie felt that her family had always done what they could to get by, same as most folks. She felt certain that the doctor'n had nothing to do with Momma's death. Women died often while birthin'. It was a common occurrence and a typical fear for many young wives. Still she never thought for a moment that it would happen to her own mother. That was the biggest reason why she herself didn't necessarily want a husband and children. Certainly, if daughters were anything like their mothers than she must worry. It seemed a legitimate concern that she too would die in childbirth should she ever conceive and just like in Momma's case, men were never happy with just one baby. Lord help if it was a girl, they'd insist upon more children, insist upon delivering boys, as boys would carry on the family

7

name and grow to be hard workers helping with the land and the farming.

Women had secret little ways of trying to prevent pregnancy, but nothing was ever guaranteed and most herbal remedies worked for years on some women but not at all on others. Of course, men were the ones that actually owned the land. They even owned whatever dowry the woman brought with her to the marriage. It was no wonder men wanted sons. Then, should the man die, the women and children owned not a thing. Suddenly the future looked desolate and uninviting to Josie. Somehow nothing in life appeared to be fair. What exactly was she around for? Cooking? Cleaning? She felt beyond her years in the veracity of life. She also realized that her control had shattered on that gloomy overcast day, when the first shovel full of dirt had been tossed upon Momma's coffin, any semblance of control she thought she possessed went to the wayside like a particle of dust floating in the air, bouncing in the current with no control over its direction, no control of its own.

When Momma did pass on, Josie was left to clean up the mess and allowed little time to mourn before Daddy started in yelling and blaming her for what had happened. At first she didn't allow his hurtful words to bother her, as he was hurting something terrible inside and she understood the ferociousness of his pain. She too felt the desperate reality and gripping fear of losing someone so precious and dear, the ache and loss of knowing that that person will never return and be a part of your life anymore. She too for a short time had doubted her own faith in the Lord, had doubted the reasons and the ways of the world, but she had worked through the cycles of loss. Her Daddy had not.

Her mourning was done secretly and alone in the wee hours of the night as her heart felt as if a big piece of it had been brutally torn out. Losing her Momma left her feeling lost and empty, as if her very soul had been violated. Sometimes it was difficult to breathe. Her Daddy would just holler and get angry when he saw Josie crying. He continually barked that she should have done more work around the house to help out, that this was all Josie's fault. Josie's petite shoulders already carried a world of guilt and regret. She agreed she should have done more of the cooking, cleaning and lifting. She should never have let Momma rub her fingers raw on the washboard early in the mornings or stay up in the late hours of darkness, forsaking much needed sleep just to spend hours sewing and working her fingers to the bone.

She and Momma used to have wonderful conversations while rocking by the fire and sewing late at night. That's what they had done to earn extra money, for another mouth to feed wouldn't be easy and Momma knew Josie wasn't fixing to marry anytime soon. Lord she had plenty to do as it was. To go off and marry would leave Momma on her own with a new baby while Daddy worked all day at the timber yards. Momma claimed it wasn't the first time she'd taken care of a baby. She also insisted she was pregnant, not sick. She'd be fine. Yet Josie loved her too much to up and leave, especially when she could tell; the further Momma's pregnancy progressed, the more frail and ill she became. Her back ached terribly. Her feet were swollen and her color was pale and dull. Well, enough was enough.

She wiped sweaty palms on the dirtied apron tied snugly around her slim waist and glanced about the dull lifeless cabin that seemed so gloomy, never holding the sunshine like it had before. She found it odd that the presence of people one loved not only made a life so full and complete, but also had an effect on the environment in which one lived. What once was bright now seemed dingy and unexciting. Upon the wooden hutch were two mended shirts ready to be returned to the Wilson homestead down the way. She'd walk into town shortly and ask if Mr. Heckle needed any eggs at the mercantile. After that she would deliver the shirts. That would put a few extra pennies in her pocket for there was a basket full of eggs she and Daddy didn't need and folks always paid well for sewing.

Mentally, she scored a long list of things to do before sunset. There was a floor to scrub, chickens to feed, biscuits to bake and packing to do without Daddy finding out. She suspected that if she didn't clean and bake as normal, he would guess that she was up to something. Hopefully, she'd be able to conceal enough food and supplies to survive on her own for a short while. Lacking the experience of traveling alone or sleeping under the stars didn't deter or discourage her plans in the least. She had no clear idea of where she would go or what she would do with her future, but she'd be damned if she'd let some no good boozin' gambler named Ebony C pick her up two hours past sundown as planned. Just saying his name sounded ominous. Shivers trickled down her spine as she attempted to shake off the dreadful feeling of unease. Mr. Ebony C may have won her in a poker game but it wasn't going to happen, not over her dead body was a stranger going to take her away without a fight. With a little bit of luck and a small prayer, she'd be long gone by sundown. Let Daddy give Mr. Ebony C something else in trade. It wouldn't be her!

By high noon Josie had packed soap, food supplies, plates, utensils, lucifers, candles and a few garments in the saddlebags. She then hooked and tied a cooking pot to the exterior of the bags before concealing everything in a large pile of hay near the back of the barn. Next she began brushing the sleek shiny coat of her horse Buster. Buster seemed too good to be true when he just wondered into their yard one day. Momma was certain he was an expensive appaloosa and insisted they, as honest folks, post signs around the settlement giving the true owner a chance to come forward and claim their lost property. No one had ever staked ownership, which made Josie extremely happy for she prayed every night that she be able to keep the horse she had fallen in love with. The animal's gentle nature was a close match to her own for he was a little wild and ornery when it suited his needs. She had decided to name the magnificent creature Buster because he was truly beautiful with a deep black coat and even darker coal colored eyes. The deepness of his eyes always made her think that the soul was just sitting there, waiting to bust out and fly away. Plus, Momma had said over and over, "Get out of the way Buster, I'm trying to work here." So Buster it was.

Daddy had thought Momma crazy for allowing her to keep the animal, complaining constantly about the cost of feeding him each week. Determined, Josie proved Buster valuable and worthy by expanding their small farm crop last spring. Although he wasn't a workhorse, he did it quite well. Without the horse, the oxen would be used for plowing and Lord they were slow tedious creatures. She personally thought they were ugly and found the smell of them quite offensive. Of course the oxen were much stronger and good for plowing land that hadn't yet been tilled, such as what they had to do upon their arrival at the new settlement. Buster may have been less powerful than the oxen but was tremendously faster and perfectly suited for the half acre expanded crop that provided vegetables for the entire family to last throughout the year. It appeared Buster seldom ran short of energy for after a long days work in the field, he'd still be prancing around and ready to run, often times doing exactly that, running for miles with Josie on his back dodging trees and mud holes. The corners of her mouth tilted upwards at the memory. Thanks to Buster's speed, they had extra vegetables to sell at the mercantile. She and Momma had even canned peppers and tomatoes to donate through the church to folks less fortunate. Using Buster also allowed the oxen to recover from the severe mosquito and horsefly bites. The insects circled in frenzied patterns as thick as clouds, constantly attacking the animals with a vengeance, showing little mercy for the welts caused by the endless assaults. Josie always kept Buster covered with a thick quilt she had made herself to lessen the damage to his fine coat and sensitive ears.

Avidly teaching herself to ride, she started off bareback and had a heck of a time even mounting at first. Before long, riding the graceful horse became second nature; for the commanded actions were merely an extension of her own thoughts and movements. Persistently, she worked extra hard along with Momma to do more farming and sewing than ever before, saving up enough money to buy a used saddle. It had cost a small fortune. Now she was glad she had the old worn out leather seat and bags. Even though Buster hated it, she knew it would be useful to carry supplies and leave, as she so desired. Buster was compliant to the saddle, although begrudgedly. They both preferred not using one at all for riding bareback felt more natural and offered a freedom that was exhilarating beyond belief. Quickly, as an afterthought, she fetched another blanket tucking it away as well, then mentally noted a few additional items to grab and pack that would be hard to do without.

Finally feeling that her plans were coming together she lifted two buckets from the floor and walked to the river to fetch water. Her mood was heavy; matching the weight of the filled pails. The river was a quarter mile down a dirt and stone path. The stone had been strategically placed along the trail to help strengthen the muddy path and give guidance to the flow of rainwater, as the heavy rains caused standing water everywhere. This path directed it back down the river. She'd have to make several trips before acquiring enough water for the dishes, stew, cleaning and a bath. A good long soak in the deep warm tub would make her feel much better. Besides, she didn't know how long it would be in her travels before she would be able to bathe again. However, it would be a few short hours before Daddy returned home from a long days work so she had to hurry if she wanted the luxury of a bath.

Daydreaming as she walked, her mind was miles away from the task at hand. The air was crisp and fresh, filled with a hefty fragrance of springtime wild flowers, which grew in abundance along the path spreading across the bank of the river in a rainbow of colors. A warm breeze lightly kissed the hair on her arms causing tiny flesh bumps to form, as she got closer to the waters edge. The stones were hard on her feet since her shoes were well worn with holes, yet she didn't mind. She had her dreams and memories, all of which were held close to heart and cherished for the time, more than life itself.

Her hair curled with damp tendrils as perspiration coated her forehead. Setting the buckets down to ease the aches in the small of her back she allowed a moments rest and wearily glanced up at the sun to estimate the time then wiped the dampness from her face using the corner of the apron. Dizziness swirled through her head lasting only a moment but caustically reminding her of her body's thirst. More than an hour had passed since this tedious chore began, for this was the last trip. Gripping the heavy water filled buckets with blistering fingers and palms she winced from the burning sensation. It took great effort to work her way back to the house and complete the laborious chore. Before dumping the water into the tub she snatched the ladle hanging from a crooked nail and submerged it into the bucket. Coolness pleasantly assailed her senses as the water traveled down her throat quickly reviving her exhausted body to a fresh state of awareness. She then dipped part of her apron into the bucket and rung it out over her face, allowing droplets to trickle down her cheeks and neck. She felt much better.

"Well." Sighing to herself she stated out loud "I may as well deliver the eggs and shirts." Wrapping a rag around her hands she hung two cast iron kettles of water over the fire to warm the bath, then added cornstarch to the sauce that was well under way. Fetching the freshly laundered and mended shirts along with the basket of eggs she'd collected early that morning before the sun was even up, she left the house skipping along the wheel worn dirt and mud encrusted path they called a lane.

The short trip went quickly. Mr. Heckle paid a penny for every egg and the Wilson's tipped her generously for a job well done on the shirts. Josie really thought they paid her extra because they felt sorry for her since Momma had died and all. Everybody in town had heard the whispered rumors about Daddy's drinking binges. Folks regularly cast pitiful glances at her every time they saw her, yet Josie held her head high. She did have her pride; something she cherished in which no one could take from her. And why should she care what people thought anyway? Well the egg money was rightfully Daddy's therefore she would place it in the crock next to his tobacco box in the kitchen. But the dollar she received for the shirts was hers. That added together with the money she'd been saving totaled eighteen dollars. Surely that would be enough to get her good and far from here.

Back at the house she tucked the folded bills into her skirt pocket then quickly set about preparing her bath. Sinking into the tub at long last she shut her eyes sighing in deep content. The warmth from the water enveloped her senses causing her sore muscles to relax. It would be so easy to fall asleep right here in the tub. Ignoring the overwhelming feeling of sleepiness she pinched her nose and gulped a deep breath of air before sliding downward beneath the water to wet her hair. She scrubbed like never before. The pleasant scent of lavender filled the room. The oats in the soap were harsh on her skin causing it to turn a tinted shade of red. She felt the need to not only leave this place but to scrub it off as well. Maybe if she were shining clean no one would guess that she was a poor farm girl running away from a home that no longer existed. A home that was once filled with love and was now nothing more than four walls of unbearable emptiness. *Besides,* she uneasily reminded herself while squeezing water from her hair, *from here on out I'll be bathing in rivers.* She shivered at the unwanted images her mind provoked although the water still held its warmth. She hated fish or anything else that was slimy and slithering. On that thought she allowed herself the luxury of a few more stolen moments meditating in the waters warm depth.

When she was through she quickly cleaned her mess and brushed her long brown hair. It was so thick she could hardly braid it without her slim arms growing fatigued. Daddy would arrive at any minute. She stirred the stew and put two more kettles above the fire thinking that perhaps he'd feel better if he took a warm bath as well. It certainly couldn't hurt.

A pang of guilt along with a flood of memories overtook Josie and formed a tight grip upon her chest causing her heart to ache for all the familiar things she was leaving behind. Memories of Momma and her sitting at the wood planked table sewing and talking for hours before a warm blazing fire filled her. Memories and visions of the flowers and tall grasses that grew ever so thickly in the newly cleared fields surrounding the house, Daddy playing the fiddle, singing and dancing out on the porch on rainy evenings. Pulling her thoughts from a melancholy of recollections she briskly wiped away-unwanted tears before they could finish their trail over her ivory complexion. Her heart ached terribly for it felt as if it had been ripped apart and now healed with a vast hole in it. With just one event her life had changed drastically.

Her reverie was harshly interrupted when the door swung open banging loudly against the wall as Daddy entered looking tired and beat from a long hard day of working in the woods. His presence filled the room, as he was a big man with dark hair, dark eyes and fine chiseled features. They lived in an area that was known as the "Black Swamp." Men labored night and day to clear out the thick forest, allowing more and more settlers to come in, attempting to farm and tame the land. Daddy worked with a group of men that cut trees into lengthy planks to be used for a new and improved road. Josie thought their efforts wasted for men had been working on the roads for years, some had even died in the arduous project, never yet succeeding. The Ohio Railroad had failed and had literally gone under, as much of there equipment disappeared beneath the muddy terrain never to be recovered. The swamp's rough environment swallowed every road that was built eventually hiding it beneath endless mud and sludge. Passage was a chore for the old and young alike, a chore definitely not meant for the weak and frail. However, it was worth the hard work for newcomers. The land was bountiful once cleared and leveled providing an abundance of foods and plants. Their own establishment proved that.

"Hi Daddy. I made you biscuits and stew. While you're eating I'll get the tub ready so you can relax in a nice warm bath."

Daddy looked at her, blinked and focused as if he didn't recognize her at all. It almost appeared as if he'd been crying. Without saying a word he simply nodded his head obediently before slumping his upper body down upon the tabletop as if exhausted. Placing a tin of cider and dinner in front of him before readying his bath she tried to make light conversation only to be met with silence. With any luck, Daddy would fall asleep so she could sneak away soon. If everything went as planned she'd be long gone before anyone noticed a thing, especially before Mr. Ebony C arrived to cart her away like she was some servant filled with gratitude. She grew angry just thinking about it.

"Your bath is ready Daddy." Quietly she began removing the emptied plate and tin cup from the table, automatically cleaning out of habit. Placing the items in the washtub next to the back door and ringing out a rag she began wiping the table. She'd always been a stickler for cleanliness. Messes just drove her crazy for a clean house was something to be proud of. This was one of the reasons she was certain shed never marry. To her way of thinking men were slobs, plain and simple. The only thing messier than men were children and since one led to the other she figured she could do without either. Just look at Daddy. She was always cleaning up after him. To make matters worse, he hadn't shaved in months changing his appearance from rugged and handsome to an unkempt grizzly man. When she was growing up the boys at the schoolhouse were messy too. They always spilled the ink, broke the quills and left things behind when they were done. The day she met a man that picked up after his own messes was the day she would consider marriage. That meant never.

"Josie I have something to tell you." Daddy's rugged voice snapped her mental state to attention. She turned to look at him, taking in the saddened expression, the wrinkles just below the hairline that weren't there before Momma passed on. His eyes were wet and shiny from unshed tears. There was an inner battle he was fighting. Daddy had his pride and men didn't cry in his opinion. That fool hearty battle had obviously been causing him some anguish. He had lost weight lately as well, which was amazing since he turned to the bottle more often than not.

"Yes Daddy?" Her heart felt as if it were suspended in mid air waiting to be put back in place. Her breathing haltered, lungs expanded and full. Perhaps Daddy would fix everything and put a stop to this cackle-brained idea of giving her away to pay a debt. Was she really that much of a problem to him? He'd always said she favored her Momma in looks and actions. Was that why he couldn't bear to look at her anymore? Did she remind him that much of the graceful woman they both missed desperately? She had worked so hard to make him happy; neatly picking up the pieces where Momma left off in every way she possibly could. Didn't he know he needed her?

"Josie I'm sorry. I'm sorry for everything." Silence hung as thick as syrup in the air while they looked into each others eyes groping for the right words to say; yet in the end saying nothing at all for a wall had formed between them that neither was aware of until this very moment, a wall that had erected almost overnight, one that would take a lot of work to demolish.

Finally, Daddy sprung from the table so quickly that the chair fell backwards hitting the floor with a loud thump. He grabbed his hat and placed it solemnly atop his stubborn head before exiting. The door slammed shut ricocheting a heavy finality throughout the room, then the only sound was silence.

Josie was outraged beyond belief. He left. He'd said, "I'm Sorry" and left. What was that supposed to mean? Although his leaving aided her plan tremendously, she was angered by the fact that he wasn't planning on staying until Mr. Ebony C arrived. He was feeding her to the wolves while he went down to the riverfront again! "Unbelievable." She muttered. Was he really that hopeless? The answer barreled its way into her mind like a fierce thunder rumbling through a gray darkened sky. Now that she would be out of the picture all he wanted to do was drink and gamble. Well fine! Huffing to herself she decided to let him drown in his misery. Let him be an oaf. One of these days her Daddy would wake up to find himself a very lonely man but she didn't care.

Bending over she righted the fallen chair with jerky angry movements.

Sniffling she told herself she'd be okay. After all, she had survived worse than this and there were numerous folks out there with a lot less than what she had. Numerous families that had lost a lot more than what she had. Convincing her own self by going through a mental list of accomplishments thus far in her life she briskly placed one hand on her hip, tilted her head skyward and began a silent list. Let's see now, she had conquered this land alongside her family working from dust to dawn for days on end. She had survived sicknesses that no tonic would ever cure no matter what the label read, then nursed and buried dozens of others that weren't as fortunate. She'd grown accustomed to the bugs, mud and filth ever present in this lackluster environment. She'd get through this. She didn't care that Daddy didn't love her anymore and she wasn't going to cry either. Did she hear herself? She wasn't going to cry darn it.

She swiped the tears streaming down her pale cheeks with bitterness than clamped her jaws tightly shut. She then pulled her shoulders back and drew in a shaky breath before looking around the dull neglected house one last time. It was earlier than she had planned to leave, but all the better. There was nothing keeping her here now. Snatching her wool shawl from a rusty hook near the back door she inwardly whispered a silent goodbye to the past and a little prayer of hope begging Momma's forgiveness and guidance. Feeling somewhat better and reassured she squeezed her eyes shut then blinked back unwanted tears refusing to give in to self-pity. Quickly before she changed her mind she made for the barn trying to move with a grace she didn't feel thanks to the rushed circumstances of her secret departure. The ground was brittle for the grass was damp and covered with straw to help soak up the mud.

Without a doubt it was time to go. She could feel it in her heart. There was nothing more for her here anyway, except Momma's grave. Swallowing hard she trudged on until finally reaching the barn. There she quickly saddled Buster while softly speaking to the creature in a way that soothed her own nerves and calmed her fears. Gathering the hidden supplies she slipped a carrot to the horse and double-checked the contents she had packed. There'd be no turning back so she needed to make certain everything she needed was on hand. Once assured a feeling of independence washed over her along with a burst of courage and invincible braveness. Another wall of protection was silently erected around her heart.

"Looks like it's just you and me." She stated to the stealthy animal before pulling herself up and swinging a leg over the saddle. The movement was more difficult than what it should have been for her shoe became tangled in her skirt. Adjusting herself modestly she softly nudged the horses sides and clicked her tongue against her teeth urging the horse to a trot right away.

Her cheeks flushed and blotched to a rosy hue as the cool air mixed in contrast with the heated temperature of her skin. Once around the heavily wooded bend, she took the road out of town with vigorous speed and agility. Allowing anger to fuel her spirit, she raced throughout the star filled night in an effort to span the distance between her past, her future and the wicked Ebony C. Although Josie mentally berated herself the entire time, she was conscious of the effort it took to not look back. Another hollow emptiness to place inside her already damaged and hurt heart.

CHAPTER TWO

When the sun dimmed to an orange hue before fading behind the hills and treetops Josie wondered where she should be heading. She had deliberated and prepared to leave for quite some time but somehow her planning lacked the most important aspect: a destination. Now she wondered if insanity had caused her to overlook such a significant facet for surly she needed a solid plan. If anything it would offer a semblance of security. She was all alone now in a world that was much bigger than she realized for she had traveled miles already and had yet to see a cabin or road let alone another human being. Although she had only considered the dangers briefly in her planning she was well aware that a woman on horseback shouldn't attempt to venture out alone. It just wasn't safe, not now days. Although Ohio provided a fairly calm and settled environment there were threats everywhere. Red wolves were prevalent in the area and posed a grave danger to all travelers, especially when hunger drove the ferocious packs and animalistic instinct took over turning many people into prey.

Indians had been removed from the area yet some still lurked. Shrugging away the concern she rationalized that the Indians didn't much care for the swamp land as they had demonstrated their dislike of the area years earlier when early pioneers tried to charter off land within the swamps regions as a safe haven for the Indians, free from interference of the settlers and the white man's rules. The Indians outright refused. There were other things to fret over such as the men who robbed people while they traveled and the wild cats that could tear a person to shreds in a matter of minutes. Her most worrisome problem was immediately at hand however. It was growing darker and darker as the forest thickened yet again and she found herself slightly confused, losing her sense of direction in a jubilee of greens, browns and blacks for every direction now looked the same. During the day it was easy to use the sun as a guide but night time in the wooded swamp area was more difficult for the stars were hardly visible between the tree branches. Leaves and cocoons hung in thick covers above the grounds clearance.

The air suddenly was damp and heavy wrapping her in a silent chill, a darkness that hung heavy like a layered quilt.

Still determined to come up with a destination, giving Buster free rein trusting his instincts more than hers, she wrinkled her eyebrows together and thought. Should she travel to Michigan? No. It would only grow colder the farther north she ventured and she preferred the warmer weather if at all possible. Should she go to Pennsylvania? No. The state was too political and she cared naught for the dictates of society. Plus, she was just a poor county girl. There was no possible way she could keep up with the latest fashions coming from the colonies. She could journey northeast to Toledo and remain in Ohio. Although she knew that the Ohio and Michigan war had ended she had heard frightening tales about the rapidly growing city with all its industrious noise and pollution. The glass industry loomed large and the waterway brought a lot of traffic with it. She's heard the railroad was setting up there as well. Definitely not Toledo, but it did sound like a fun place to visit.

Why not follow the river and see what new establishment it led to? The land offered a little of everything and yet remained a challenge to those who weren't afraid of endless days filled with laborious task and hard work. Ohio was her home, and a good place to stay if only she could dig some solid roots, planting her life and spirit in another town, one that her Daddy would never venture into.

She knew enough to build her own place and farm her own land if need be. That's what she could do with her money; buy property. An unmarried woman just may be able to get away with it. The idea struck her full force causing a flurry of excitement and a wide spread smile. She also knew full well how to cook, clean and sew. She could always fall back on those skills if times got rough. It'd be the same as what she and Momma had done all along anyways. The best part about the plan was that Daddy would never guess. Furthermore, he most likely didn't care enough to look for her. Ironically, it was that thought that offered a small semblance of comfort in this moment of doubt and worry.

As the hours slowly passed Josie's rear end began to ache with soreness and her eyes burned for lack of sleep along with the constant strain of scanning the darkened environment up ahead. It was time to find a cove or high area of ground to make camp. It had to be a site that offered protection and shelter from animals and nature alike, even more so because the sun would be up soon and she planned to sleep during the day. Traveling at night would be more treacherous and dangerous but the trails were less populated and Josie felt she might not be recognized or remembered as easily. A harboring thought lurked in the back of her mind; less populated trails at night meant that if she did run into trouble, there would be a lesser chance of help arriving. Allowing the worry to pass, she calmed herself by reaffirming the fact that she was her own protector now. She was simply on her own.

The darkened shadows made it extremely difficult to find a safe place to sleep. The blackness of the night hid all the crevices swallowing the landscape, which appeared deep and ominous. One particular shadow seemed to be deeper and darker than any of the others. Perhaps it was a cave. With rising hopes she steered Buster off the beaten path and up a small rock encrusted hill. She grew more and more nervous each time the horse lost his footing for she could hear numerous rocks tumbling and sliding down to the bottom, landing atop one another, forming a pile at the base of a small ravine. She grasped the harness firmly while visualizing the horse as well as herself skidding painfully in the same manner the loosened rocks did. Fearful and uneasy they continued their trek upwards until finally at the top she let out a gust of air filled relief calming the turmoil of fear within. Listening carefully she heard the faint and muted trickle of flowing water from somewhere ahead in the distance. A few moments later the air chilled tellingly. Feeling the coolness of the damp murky shadow as she approached, a flutter of apprehension passed through her stomach.

The cave opening was large enough to allow both her and Buster to enter. Josie remained mounted, planning to escape quickly should the need arise. Once inside the temperature dropped dramatically. The air was damp and stale with a musty scent. She paused a few moments at the caves entrance waiting for her eyes to adjust while whispering a silent prayer of thanks to the good Lord above. She could clearly hear the fluid echo of trickling water coming from deeper within the cave's hollow belly. Good, there'd be water aplenty for her and Buster to drink. She would save what was in the canteen until she was desperate or somewhere that had no fresh or clean drinking water.

Inching her steed forward slowly and cautiously she noted that she was more spooked than the horse that went willingly, which was a good sign. Relying heavily once again on the horse's instincts to warn of danger she nudged gently with her heal. She wasn't foolish for she was fully aware of the fact that caves were home to a variety of snakes as well as bear and cougar. Lord only knew what else they were apt to encounter, but she'd be ready, come what may. They cautiously crept forward a few feet at a time, listening and searching intently for any sign of danger. The magnitude of caution allowed for tedious but safe entry.

Glancing over one shoulder back towards the entrance was somewhat unsettling for the mouth of the cave was still bathed in silvery moonlit darkness. She thought it funny how the darkness outside was so much lighter than the darkness inside the cave. Shaking off a chill she spread fingers open wide while placing her hand directly in front of her face. Try as she might all she could see was black. The inability to see her hand less than an inch from her nose was oddly reassuring. If she couldn't see it, than neither could anything else. She was suddenly struck with the thought that somewhere in the past, she had heard that animals had very good night vision. Her stomach clenched and her hands began to tremble. Did she think that lack of vision reassuring? Ha! That thought bordered crazy. It was certainly not reassuring! It was most unsettling!

Inhaling a deep breath allowed the cool dampness to fill her lungs. She urged the horse on only after assuring her own self that everything felt safe so far. Feelings and gut instinct were all she had to go on. That did not offer her much faith. Just when her mind grew clouded with negative thoughts and self-recriminations, Josie realized they had reached the back wall of the rocked interior. Buster put his head down to drink the water that was flowing in a steady path along the firmly packed layers of stone etched with earth. Granting the horse his leave she dismounted and bent backwards then stood straight to ease the aching in her rump and limbs. Chilled hands felt for the roughness of the saddlebags and with trembling fingers she fumbled to unhook the buckles. Plunging through an array of packed items and feeling for the box of lucifers was frustrating in the least. *Ah there they are.* Once struck the cave instantly filled with the flickering glow of light. She and Buster were alone. There were no furry or slimy creatures around as best as she could tell. She offered up a silent prayer of gratitude.

Cupping one hand around the match so as not to blow it out she carefully worked her way back towards the cave entrance. Although it was warm outside the coolness of the cave clammed and chilled her skin absorbing and expanding the pores to the core of her bones. Close to the entrance the small flame began to burn her fingers. "Ouch." She mumbled while flicking her wrist back and forth in rapid motion putting the tiny flame to rest.

Venturing just outside the caves opening, she gathered what she could of brush and kindling in hopes of building a small fire. Grumbling the entire time because the uneven ground covered with rocks and dirt tore at her worn shoes duly twisting her fine but sturdy ankles. Oh well, she thought, at least her feet were dry. After all, it could've been much worse.

Entering the cave again she halted all movement and once more allowed her eyes time to adjust to the acute darkness. Then she continued forward carefully placing one foot in front of the other poking and feeling with the toe of her shoe each time for even ground. When she was near the stream again she laid the brush on the dirt packed floor forming a cradle to place the kindling and then one large log for a warm yet tiny fire. Striking another match she skillfully set the brush on fire and watched eagerly as the flames grew taking life from nature, slowly heating her skin. The smoke from the burning brush added to the burning of her eyes reminding her of the smudge pots they so often used to repel insects. Soon warmth began to take the chill from the air as the kindling crackled and popped tossing sparks in every direction.

Josie tethered Buster near the water, fed him an apple and removed the extra blanket from under the saddle. Buster's tail swayed with gratitude. Apples were his favorite and she hadn't thought only of herself while packing. Lying next to the fire she decided she was too tired to worry about eating right now. Warm and cozy comfort enveloped her as she drifted off into an exhausted slumber.

When she woke the sun hung high and to the west indicating the time to be late afternoon. Her stomach growled loudly and every bone in her body smarted from lying upon the cold hard surface of rock while sleeping. The fire had completely died yet it was easy enough to see the sunlight filtering through cracks and crevices of her cavernous realm. Bright light streamed in with large rays of sun narrowing as they expanded to the floor near the mouth of the cave. Hemlocks swayed in the breeze as Josie led Buster outside and tethered him to a tree nearby where there was plenty of grass to feed on. "Go ahead boy, dig in." She urged the horse while patting him gently on the side of his neck.

Back at the small stream of clean flowing water she drank heavily before washing her face and hands with the piercingly cold liquid. Then she ran cold fingers through the mass of thick hair upon her head in an effort to tame the wild curls that began to form from the caves dampened interior. Catching her fingers in snarls several times and wincing from the pain she decided to give up for she wasn't trying to impress anyone anyhow. With any luck she'd be alone on her journey until she decided otherwise. *One night down* she thought. *If I can make it through the first night alone, I can make it through them all.* The accomplishment made her proud and happy putting her mind at peace. It also added a bounce to her step and lift to her lips.

Picking berries from a nearby tree she checked for the starred marking on the bottom before popping them into her mouth savoring the flavor of each and every one until her belly was full and she couldn't eat another bite. Her fingertips were stained purplish blue along with a few blotched spots on her skirt. Too bad she couldn't pack a washboard.

Now that she felt uplifted both mentally and physically she vowed to start her new day with a positive attitude and determined stride. The warmth from the afternoon sun bathed and tanned the exposed skin on her arms as she saddled Buster and embarked once again on her journey to a home away from home. Her original plan of traveling only in the dark had altered slightly. She intended to travel as she saw fit. No ands, ifs or buts about it. That phrase reminded her once again of her Momma. It was a figure of speech she had used when she boded no argument from either Josie or Daddy. In other words, it was Momma's final say in things.

Everywhere she looked she saw nothing but trees, entangled in a giant web they grew in a mass as one forest. Giant oaks with limbs spread wide grew in abundance, some of them hallowed out at the bottom creating crevices large enough to fit two full grown men within the heavily barked embrace. There were patches of flat land scattered here and there but they were far and few between with tall grass and berry bushes gathered in clusters amongst the small ponds of muddy depth that nested atop the ground, many having green ringed stalks of horsetail reaching outward towards the sky before dipping faintly and swaying with the breeze.

She wished she had remembered to bring a hat for the sun shown brightly through the treetops and covered patches of openness, blotching her skin red and pink wherever exposed heedlessly causing pain whenever she moved or bumped the twigs and branches hanging from the trees and bramble they trudged through.

Did she dare hike up her skirt in the daylight in an effort to cool off? It wasn't rightly proper but the area was shielded with woods and bushes so surely it wouldn't hurt. If she noticed anyone coming she'd cover her legs right away. Following through with the notion she rolled down her stockings exposing sweaty legs then bunched the skirt beneath her bottom pillowing and adding cushion to the hard saddle seat. The sticky sweat on her skin made her feel dirty and uncomfortable causing her normally happy and outgoing demeanor to alter into an agitated and fidgety grumbling young lady, uncharacteristically removing any beauty in the landscape as they traveled.

She seemed to ride for endless miles before the sun slowly began its descent once more dimming the sky as the ground became less murky. The graceful song of insects filled the air with harmonious cadence bouncing among the treetops as the temperature cooled slightly. Josie permitted Buster a much-deserved rest when they came to another creek with clear water flowing mercifully among its rocky bottom. Bending down and splashing her face and neck with the clean water she drank aplenty noting this was a good water spot as evidenced by several different animal prints in the dirt along the sides of the stream. Her own footprints would now be added to the display as she stood and blotted the dampness from her skin with the hem of her now wrinkled beyond repair skirt.

Leaning against a sturdy walnut cropped with sprouting twigs of witch hazel she nibbled on a salty piece of jerky mentally calculating the distance she had traveled. She was no Daniel Boone but guessed the expanse to be about ten miles or so. The mud and rough terrain had slowed her progress, a heedless challenge proving her journey a determined effort of will and fortitude, all grumbling aside.

Daydreaming peacefully and caught up in her own thoughts she was reluctant to move when she heard Buster snort and prance upon the ground giving alert that something was amiss. Cautiously looking about she thoroughly examined the area noting nothing strange as shivers passed along the length of her spine. Buster continued to prance and snort in horse like fashion displaying a great amount of nervousness.

Josie quickly went over to aid in calming the animal. Maybe there was a snake nearby for snakes always made Buster edgy. She prayed it was that and nothing else. "Okay Buster, just give me a moment and we'll be on our way." Her hands soothingly patted and petted the horse's neck offering calm reassurance.

She had to use a bush before they set off again. Glancing around once more she inspected the ground for snakes and ivy and then the outlying area for wolves. The last thing she needed was a terrible itch on her rump or a scare from some slithering serpent. Doubt crossed her mind and she momentarily thought of mounting the horse and traveling a few miles farther before relieving herself. The fingers of doubt and wariness were diminished by her desperate need to do her thing. All appeared quiet and still, as she could detect no danger within the immediate surrounding of brush and overgrowth.

While stooped she heard a rustling noise emerging from the lilac bush next to her. She saw the bush shake gently. Somewhat panicked Josie tried to hurry and be done with the deed before whatever critter was there attacked her. However her body refused to follow her own heartfelt command as fear quickened her heartbeat and her hands trembled. She stood struggling with her pantaloons as they stuck to her dampened skin in opposition while she stepped away from the chosen bushes and heard a terrible hissing noise that was so unfamiliar to her ears she just had to turn and see what and where it came from. Curiosity driving her need she peeked closer to get a better look when the awful misted spray hit her smack in the face.

"Uhh!" She screamed in mortification as a dreadful odor permeated her clothing and assailed her senses with an unpleasant disgusting taste and smell. "Oh" Josie cried and gagged at the same time as tears blazoned her eyes. Clasping a hand over her mouth, she ran to the small river where she humbly lost the jerky in her stomach, then continued to heave in agonizing disgust. It figured, the one place she decided to stoop had to be next to a skunk that obviously felt the need to protect its territory with the punishment of spray for her unfashionable invasion. She smelled bad. No, bad was and understatement. The stench was utterly revolting. Attempting to control her breathing and not gag she turned just in time to a confirming vision of the beady eyed skunk sticking it's tale in the air before waddling off with a boastful display of dignity. She however, had no dignity left for the episode had robbed her of all self-respect. Tossing an angry oath in the skunk's direction she grabbed Buster's reins and led him further downstream so that she could clean up.

"What are you looking at?" She snapped. "You think you smell any better?" The lousy horse was unable to follow her without snorting and blowing air out his nostrils in several-repeated burst of defiance. "I guess you don't like the way I smell either." She couldn't blame the horse for well she new the sickening odor was neigh impossible to withstand. She could hardly tolerate her own ungodly stench. Thank goodness she hadn't eaten much since the powerful odor caused her to be continuously nauseated and her eyes wouldn't cease watering. She kicked a stone and grumbled at the horse for rubbing in the fact that he had warned her, and she just had to ignore the beast!

A few miles downstream Josie found a decent spot providing adequate depth in the river and a hidden cove just off the hilled embankment where she could wash her clothes and herself as soon as the sun went down. She removed every smelly affected item from the bags and began setting up camp. After this ordeal, she just didn't have the energy to go farther in her travels this day. She solemnly wondered what to do to bathe the horse. She knew what she had to do, but the animal was entirely different matter. Once she had a small fire built she poked some sturdy sticks into the ground to hang her clothes on. The setting sun now cast a golden glow to the sky just above the treetops thinning with a narrow line of deep pink providing a view that was breathtaking. She then noted sarcastically that perhaps it was her smell that was breathtaking rather than the setting sun.

Stripping down to the bare skin she scooped up her odor infested clothing using the garments as a shield to hide her nudity. She waded through the mud to the creeks edge. Dipping a bare and bony foot into the cold water she unwittingly inhaled a lung full of stench then coughed in regret. She hadn't expected the waters icy sharpness and wondered how Buster would do when she brought him in. Step by step she immerged into the brisk coldness pausing when the water reached her waistline, finding that for some unknown reason she could plunge no further. Finally she scrounged up enough courage to take the final step submerging her body completely into the water. Standing shoulder deep, she scrubbed and rinsed repeatedly until she could feel her fingers no more for they shriveled like prunes and were white as snow. Unfortunately her hair still held a trace of the unbearable odor no matter how many times she washed with lavender soap and her clothes weren't any better either. Maybe a good boiling would help. Thank goodness she had thought to pack a spare outfit meaning only to change every few days as she traveled.

By the time she and the horse had been thoroughly scrubbed, her hands were raw, her arms ached fiercely and the entirety of her body was blue from the cold, evidenced by the chattering teeth and pimply flesh. The smelly rags could remain in the water for all she cared. Impatience and fatigue had her mumbling to herself as she released the garments and watched with gratification while they floated weightlessly down stream and out of sight. Good riddance she thought clapping her hands together thoroughly scrubbing her hair one final time with the lightly scented soap before ambling weakly back to the hidden cove and the warmth of the fire.

Putting on new clothes didn't make Josie feel any better, nor did it make Buster quit snorting in dismay when she came near to feed him some treats. She warmed herself for a while by the fire and tinkered with the thought of eating more jerky then smartly decided her stomach couldn't handle it.

A harsh realization startled Josie as she sat up stiff and straight, a shocked expression upon her face reflecting sheer turmoil as the impact of what she had just done hit her like a ton of lead. Gosh darn it she wasn't using her head as was typical of her. "I lack the brains God gave a Billy Goat!" Constant chastisement of her own doing only aggravated the feeling of despair and the overwhelming urge to cry. While she struggled to maintain a calm within she hurriedly packed mud on top of the fire fetching rapid death to the warm flames. Instantly the airs chill assailed her anew for her body was still cold from the icy bath.

She gathered her belongings and mounted Buster in one single fluid movement. Urgency filled her voice, no longer soft and soothing. "Let's go boy!" Tapping her heals into the horse's muscular sides they began to race along the waters edge as if the devil himself were on their heels. She was such a fool. How could she forget? Her eighteen dollars was in the pocket of that smelly skirt she had so graciously let float away. She had to find that skirt. She simply had to. Her entire future depended on it.

Night was approaching rapidly. The sun had almost completely set and Josie wondered where following the stream would take her. As long as she was heading in a northerly direction she supposed it really didn't matter. Keeping a watchful eye out for her clothing she took in the changing and eerie environment. The flowering landscape had melted into a carpet of mud and the woods became a forest blanketed with so many trees one couldn't see past the wall they formed. It seemed there was little difference between day and night in the thickness of the trees, as their branches crossed with one another, spread apart like fingers reaching endlessly into the night sky. Instead of the riverbank being coated with grass, it was now covered with sticks, twigs and a thick sludge barely offering an embankment at all. There were still no signs of any establishments or her clothing.

"Geez, how fast can a river flow?" She wondered out loud not wanting to rest just yet, forcing them to continue their trek through the spooky forest while visions of ghost threatened her grip on reality. She grabbed the reins in a tight clutch and ground her teeth in nervous agitation. There wasn't a road or a trail in sight. There really wasn't anything other than the ominous forest and murky presence of unsettling evil. She could sense that all wasn't right with nature. Someone or something had tainted the atmosphere with an essence of filth.

Shortly after dark fully settled Josie heard a whimpering noise coming from the rivers edge on a slightly sloped and sheer embankment. Curiosity made her want to find out what is was yet freight of encountering another skunk kept her response cautious for the repelling scent still lingered upon her person mockingly keeping the insects at bay. At least some good had come from the ordeal.

Drawing closer to the embankment she tilted her head and listened intently, stilling Buster by pulling back and slightly tightening the reins. Perhaps her mind was playing tricks on her or maybe it was just a sound from the water or somewhere deeper in the forest. Then she heard it again. It didn't sound like a skunk but then she thought, what was a skunk supposed to sound like? The last one was pretty quiet except for the slight shake of a bush.

Dismounting she inched closer to a mound of rocks near the edge of the water. The ground was covered with puddles that had tiny fish swimming in their shallowness. "Great. I hate fish."

Lifting her skirt she stood to cross one puddle on tippie-toe. Although she was careful her torn and holy shoes absorbed the cold water against her will and she began to shiver uncontrollably as an intolerable chill invaded her body robbing it of what little warmth she'd obtained since her bath. Here the coldness was more so intolerable because she'd had enough water on this day to last a lifetime. As she got deeper into the rushing water the whimpering became louder. Apprehension and doubt consumed her thoughts and controlled her movements as she carefully peered down over the rocks, seemingly terrified of what she'd find.

Lying in a shallow bed of muddy water was a dog. A dirty, stinky, filthy dog with an injured leg gazed at her up with eyes that begged for love and looked upon her as if she were and angel. An angel sent from Heaven above and in that instant...they bonded.

"Awe" Josie cooed. "Poor baby, what happened to you?" She could clearly see that the dog had been dragged through the rivers crisp and icy water for quite some distance, fighting for life as it's fur was mangled and matted with blood and muck. Bending at the knees, with her free hand she began removing a few of the rocks that trapped and held the dog's legs halfway between mud and surface. This poor animal was lingering on a teeter-totter of life and death.

Once free she scooped the mutt securely within her grasp before the current had a new opportunity to carry the animal away. Slowly lifting the wet mangy mutt into her embrace she eagerly shared what little body heat she had left for the dog shivered and shook uncontrollably, no doubt close to death from being held hostage beneath the cold water for so long a time. Upon closer inspection

Josie could tell that one of the dogs legs was in bad shape but it didn't appear to be broken. Swathing the animal in baby like fashion with her skirt she calmed its rapidly beating heart with softly spoken words of gentle compassion.

Remounting Buster she continued once again along the river in hopes of finding her skirt and her hard earned money while cradling the dog. Eighteen dollars was a lot of cash to just toss away as foolishly as she had. Once again she inwardly cursed herself for a lack of wits. All of her dreams were to begin with the management of that money. It was solid foundation that was built by her saving every penny since she was a little girl, never indulging in hair ribbons and gumdrops like the other children. Refusing to give up she continued scanning the span of the river for any sign she could find, hoping and praying fervently for a miracle from above. Although she truly believed one had already occurred with the finding of the dog, she pressed her luck in praying for another.

About two miles later Josie got lucky and thanked the Lord in earnest for she spotted her skirt some distance from the mud slicked embankment, held in place by the steady flowing current again a large boulder directly in the middle of the rivers path. She was briefly discouraged but quickly overcame the feeling and prepared to get her feet wet again by removing her shoes and stockings, solemnly reminding herself that this would be the last time today she'd walk in water. However, since the sun had fallen the waters coldness would be more pronounced. She didn't like the idea but was certain she'd live through it and insisted she would reward them all with a fire a soon as the money was retrieved. Perhaps the blueberry stained, skunk smelling skirt would be worth saving after all.

Clumsily dismounting with a bunched up skirt and dog in hand she stepped forward laying the dog on the ground in front of the horse but far enough away where the horse could focus his vision on the dog, then gently kissed them both indicating that they were to remain where they were. She was certain neither understood a word she spoke. Perhaps they could understand the tone of voice she used and the love in her movements.

Placing her shoes and stockings on the ground near the wet and exposed dog she softly whispered "I'll be back," then hiked up her skirt and slowly waded into the brisk water. Sharp rocks and shells assaulted the tenderness of her feet as she cautiously raked the tired limbs along the rivers bottom. The current and mud pulled with a force that was strong and steady. "Ouch," she muttered softly and continued forward concentrating on the task, focusing all her attention on the boulder in order to fetch her garment. Behind her she could hear the loud whiney of the horse and the soft whimper of the dog over the flow of the water. More so she could feel the animals concern and turned to look at them in an attempt to calm them with her eyes.

Once she reached the boulder, she struggled to grip the skirt she was wearing in an attempt to keep it dry and above water while at the same time clutch the sopping wet skirt she'd just found to her chest, not lose her footing, all the while make a great effort to remain as dry a possible while shivering uncontrollably. It was a remarkable feat. Leaving the bitterness of the icy water as long last she stepped onto the bank with chattering teeth and stiff aching feet. The coldness seemed to seep right through to the bones as her teeth chattered loudly together. Whatever feelings the river robbed her of, the happiness of retrieving the money quickly restored.

It was early May so even though the sun warmed the days, the evenings were still brisk and the ground was moderately cold. She was exhausted and could travel no further this evening. As she looked into the eyes of her faithful traveling companions Josie's heart felt their weariness for it matched her own.

"Oh all right, we'll build a fire and call it a night. Would that make you two muddle-mutts happy?" She wasn't about to admit that she had already conceded to a nice toasty fire. Hmm.

With hands upon her hips she thought the decision safe and sound. After all, she hadn't noticed anyone trailing her. In fact, she hadn't seen another soul all day. At that thought Josie became ill at heart as disappointment washed over her like the pelting drops of a ferocious thunderstorm. She so badly wanted Daddy to be searching for her and if not him than someone he hired, anything just to prove he actually cared. A token of the love he once displayed at her expense, a love he once gave so freely but until now, was never cherished.

She felt gravely forlorn and unsettled; her mind was miles away while she gathered wood, built a fire and unsaddled Buster, covering him in the blanket once again. As she placed the dog near the fire to warm up and dry off, her stomach growled loudly.

"Well, that wasn't very lady-like." Cheerfully muttering to herself she began mixing the ingredients for flapjacks. She would share with the dog and hope the meal provided some much needed healing nourishment. The poor thing was most likely famished. As she set about the chore she thought of the future, letting her mind wonder and drift thinking of the many possibilities that lay ahead and feeling happy and hopeful at the same time because she had a lot to look forward to and her dreams continued to grow bigger with each passing thought. The catch was, she told herself, that she had to use common sense and be smart. No more stunts like the two earlier episodes. The lessons of the day would be to trust your instincts and not to throw money away.

After their bellies were full she returned to the river to wash the small cast iron pot and her hair once more since she could still smell the lingering repulsive odor from the skunks defensive spray. Luckily there weren't any people around for she wouldn't want to offend the good folks of the land yet she realized she wasn't the kind of person to trek through life alone. She needed people, company and conversation. The last few days had taught her that. She sorely missed the noise and commotion that came with a settlement, the sound of children playing and women gossiping in muted whispers. Hopefully she would come to a town soon. She was already running low on supplies, which was no small surprise. Life would be much easier with a few candles and some more soap.

When finished she returned to the fire and kneeled down to check her new pet. He seemed to have perked up a little since eating and once dry she realized that he was only a puppy, a very big puppy at that. She wasn't certain what kind but he had unusually large paws, a sign that he'd be big once fully grown. He was definitely under fed and mistreated. Whoever owned him should be ashamed of the way they cared for the dog. Josie believed that folks should show kindness to all of God's creatures, not just themselves. To her it was a basic fact in life, something a person should know through proper upbringing. Well she'd be doubly kind to make up for the previous owners lack of attention.

Gritting her teeth to bite back the anger that ebbed its way to the surface, she began tearing apart strips of her now dry skirt and retrieved the missing money from its pocket. Thank goodness she had the cash in hand once more. Although still damp, she folded the bills into a wad and tucked them safely into the pocket of the clean skirt, making a mental note not to make the same mistake twice. This money was her livelihood, a foundation for her new independence.

Focusing on the dog once more she closely inspected the injured leg and cleaned the open wound with soapy water before using the scraps of fabric torn from her skirt to wrap the limb. She caringly swaddled it in as many layers as possible. This would prevent the dog from chewing and gnawing at the injury during the healing process. That was something that Daddy had taught her when she was just a little girl. Once finished she sat back to inspect and admire her handy work. The dog began to vigorously lick her face displaying a special admiration for the care given.

"Well you need a name little one." She laughed then watched while the dog hopped around the fire searching for more scraps of food. A name quickly came to mind. "That's it." Jumping up she snapped her fingers with excitement. "We'll call you Hops."

The dog whimpered as if to disagree putting both paws over his eyes.

"Well, you seem to think you're a rabbit, hopping around the fire. Although I must admit you're awfully big for a rabbit and clumsy too." She giggled as Hops tripped over his own oversized paws then proceeded to lap at her face with his tongue like one would a sugar stick.

Later as Josie lie next to the fire on her blanket she marveled at how close the stars seemed to be, a bright twinkling contrast to the black backdrop of the sky. She took notes of the North Star and used its glow as a guideline, giving direction of travel the next day. She was hoping to get an early start and was glad she now had the dog to keep her company and boost her spirits. He'd be a good companion, not that Buster wasn't. The more the merrier.

Without warning the day's events caught up with her as she lie upon the blankets covered ground so close to nature and within moments drifted into a deep sleep.

When Josie woke she instantly sensed that she wasn't alone. She also realized that she hadn't been sleeping all that long. Goosebumps formed on her flesh and chills went down her spine for she had a sinking feeling that someone was watching her. She could feel it in her bones. She remembered how uncomfortable she felt traveling through the forest earlier in the evening, how the shadows seemed tinged with wickedness: like something dirty had come through and left a tainted mark upon the forest.

Lying as still as possible she thoroughly scanned the area immediately surrounding her campsite. Clouds moved across the sky covering the moon causing the shadows to become deeper, more ominous. Or was that just her imagination? Who was out there? She couldn't see anything at all causing her frustration level to rise in a rapid crescendo and her heartbeat to increase. Nothing in her little camp area had been touched or moved and the fire had burned down to small glows of smoldering embers barely radiating any heat at all. Dampness filled the air and clung the ground in tiny droplets of dew. Morning was only a few scant hours away.

Buster snorted as if warning her of a presence. The dog's ears pointed straight back with awareness yet he was too lazy to lift his head and move from the curled comfort of her feet. Some watchdog she thought to herself as her nervousness escalated. She hadn't heard a sound yet sensed danger in every shadow. She had never thought of it before but she had no weapon to use as protection. Gosh, how could she be so foolish as to take off by herself without a weapon, unescorted, and without so much as a gun? Was she crazy? Peas for brains, that's what she had. Her eyes were now fully dilated and adjusted to the darkness but it didn't make the shadows any easier to decipher.

"Who's there?" She whispered as she stared at the cluster of pine trees where she thought she saw looming shadows move in her peripheral vision. "Show yourself." Inwardly she prayed it wasn't a bear or wolves but immediately distinguished the thought. Bears and wolves wouldn't be that quiet as if waiting out her next move.

"What are you doing with my dog?"

The harsh words startled Josie and caused her to jump. The dog remained at her feet and began to growl and snarl, baring teeth. She still couldn't detect any movement from the forest of shadows as branches swayed with the wind. She was sure the voice came from the patch of trees to her right.

"I'm sorry. He was hurt. I just fed him and tended his wounds." She responded and swallowed a mouthful of trepidation.

"Well, well, well, looky here, its seems we have a proper young lady before us Neb."

Josie jumped again only this time she sprung to her feet then quickly bent and grabbed a stick. That statement was made by a second voice to the left. How many were there? Was she surrounded? Panic set in as she held the skinny little branch with both hands in front of her, waving it slowly from side to side and shifting her weight from one foot to the other. The stick and the dog were her only defense against at least two strange men.

"Looks like you've got yourself into quite a pickle little lady." Said the man referred to as Neb.

Josie lifted her chin and turned to face the pine trees, "Don't you know it's rude and improper to approach a lady in the middle of the night and scare the wits out of her? Show yourself this instant or I'll, I'll..."

"You'll what?" Said Neb. "Put that stick down. You look like a damn fool and besides, it won't do no good since I have a gun."

Josie swallowed hard but did as was told. The man named Neb stepped from the shadows. Her eyes immediately took inventory. He was tall, about six foot or so. His clothes were torn, tattered and covered in dirty grime and something shiny. Upon closer inspection Josie gasped out loud then cupped a hand over her mouth trying hard not to gag. He had blood oozing from a wound on his head. It formed a trail down his shirtfront all the way to the cuffs of his trousers, flowing so thickly that she could see its shimmering path in the darkness.

At that moment a gun cocked and clicked right next to her ear as the other fellow grabbed her around the waist and spoke in an even tone. His breath touched her cheek when he talked and she once again had to control the urge to gag. Hops growled and bit several times at the man's leg. Showing a mean streak, the man kicked the dog with a solid thud landing the mutt on the other side of the campsite. The dog whimpered and remained still.

"My brother needs some tending himself. Now I'm sorry for being so improper and all but this here's an emergency. We gotta' get fixed up and be on our way. If you're a good girl I might only shoot you once."

"Randy, let her go." Neb ordered as he fell to the ground with a loud thump.

Josie reacted instinctively lunging forward to help him. She began barking out orders for Randy to rekindle the fire and fetch some water. Taking only a moment to pat and calm the dog she kneeled and inspected the wound on Neb's head as best she could. It was really bad. In fact, Josie was sure she was looking at a dead man.

"How is he?" Randy asked roughly while setting a pot of water next to her.

"He's not good. I'm going to need more water than this. I'll have to rinse the wound a lot before I can see well. Then I'll know what to do."

They worked in silence for a lengthy amount of time. While heating fresh water on the fire Josie cleaned and scrubbed Neb's hair. He was very pale and the moonlight wasn't enough to provide adequate vision. The wound was deep and right on the temple. She could stick her finger in it. No wonder it wouldn't stop bleeding. Up until now she had controlled her stomach but she was very close to getting sick and forced herself to focus on what she was doing while slowly breathing in and out to settle her squeamishness.

"How'd he get this?" She asked a short time later and was met with complete silence. "Look, I need to know if there is something in there or if I should just cauterize it now."

"He was shot." Randy glared at her. "If he dies, I'm killing you."

"What? I had nothing to do with this!" Josie's mind was racing a mile a minute now. Disbelief and rage consumed her. This guy was crazy.

"He was alive when he met you. If he dies now that means you kilt' him. Now quit yackin' and fix him."

"I can't just fix him. I'm not a doctor. I'm not a nurse. I don't even have tools to work with. OUCH!" She was hit directly in the chest with a wooden box. It fell to the ground scattering contents all over the grass. The glow from the newly built fire allowed her to see it was a medical kit.

Forgetting the bruising sensation on her chest she stooped and collected the materials. There were several items consisting of; alcohol, catgut sutures, rags, whiskey, a bottle of pain powder, two beeswax candles, bandages, tape and some kind of gadget the resembled two forks hooked in the middle.

"Where'd you get this?" It looked like it was stolen from some military troop or something and she couldn't help but inquire.

"You ask too many questions." Replied Randy. He sat back, cocked the gun once more, and aimed it directly at her before repeating his earlier words. "Git busy."

Taking a deep breath Josie complied. Now that the sun was slowly rising she could see the end of the misshapen piece of lead that was in Neb's head. Dousing the wound with alcohol she worked the shared chunk out with the forklike gadget. Thank goodness Neb was out cold. At least he wouldn't feel all the pain she was inflicting. She worried about the severe amount of blood loss. In fact, she didn't know that people had that much blood in them.

Concentrating, she next set about stitching the wound and cleaning up his blood stained face. When she was done she rung and twisted the boiling hot rag then quickly laid it atop Neb's freshly stitched forehead using the gadget instead of her fingers.

That stirred him a little and he began to groan in painful agony.

Josie looked at Randy who hadn't moved or flinched the entire time. "You'll have to get him someplace safe to rest. He'll also need his bandages changed soon and some broth or soup would do him well."

Turning she began gathering up her few meager belongings and packing them away. This Randy guy made her really uncomfortable and she wanted to be on her way as quickly as possible. He had a dark evil aurora about him. She had the distinct feeling he could be Satan himself for he was of a larger build than his brother, towering over her height by more than a foot. She also sensed that without Neb's guidance, he'd explode. She housed no desire to be anywhere near him if and when that happened for she was positive, without a doubt, that Neb wouldn't make it.

"We're gonna' have to put Neb on your horse. Our horses are about a quarter mile up wind from here, real close to town." Randy was finally moving and helping to collect several scattered items.

"There's a town nearby? How come you didn't go there for help? Surely there's a doctor better qualified than I am!" Josie was flabbergasted. It was inconceivable that they didn't get proper medical attention when it was so close at hand. "Besides, I refuse to go anywhere with the likes of you."

"Shut up!" Randy yelled and backhanded her with so much force she fell to the ground landing roughly on her rump, biting her tongue. Tears filled her eyes yet she blinked them back as a burning sensation warmed her cheek and jawbone. Standing, she pulled back her shoulders, held her head high and looked Randy directly in the eyes.

"Now let me warn you." Her tone was dangerously low and steady and her eyes burned with hatred. The dog stood at her feet, ears pointed back, growling lowly. "If you ever lay a hand on me again I'll kill you. Do you understand that? Don't ever underestimate me mister. It may cost you more than you can afford." With that she flung her hair over her shoulder and turned to finish packing her things.

"And what would you do to me little miss priss?" The question was little more than a growl as he stepped towards her clenching his fist purposely cracking his knuckles in anticipation of throttling her.

Holding the medical box Josie turned in a flash and threw it at his chest as hard as she could.

"Ouch." Randy was taken by surprise. The little spitfire she-devil was feisty.

"That's what you get you big ox. What's good for the goose is good for the gander."

Basking in the glory of catching him off guard, the moment was short lived as the big ox pointed the revolver at her again and barked is own orders to hurry her along. One good thing Josie could say was when they left they were heading north.

CHAPTER THREE

Randy displayed no semblance of concern for his brother and insisted on riding at a faster pace than what Josie was comfortable with. The constant trot of the horses joggled and bruised her body. She could just imagine what it was doing to Neb. However, when she voiced her trepidation she was once again met with silence and a hateful glare. Then Randy whipped the horse ordering it to speed up in a wicked display of authority and opposition to Josie's request on Neb's behalf.

She was nagging and persistent in her demand to stop and rest. She'd absolutely had enough. Randy was growing more and more agitated but Josie put her foot down and demanded a five-minute break chancing his anger for the sake of Neb whose entire face was caked in the mud that had kicked up from the horses trotting hooves. Her head was pounding and her rear end was as sore as a pincushion. Not only was the saddle extremely uncomfortable as it chaffed her inner thighs mirthlessly raw, but sitting in front of Randy was unsettling and nerve wrecking for he kept sniffing her hair and neck as if she were a piece of meat, then cursed out loud each time she moved in an attempt to ease her aching legs and back.

Josie needed to check on Neb. Even though she didn't know him personally; she worried over his condition and the severity of what might happen. Presently he was slung over Buster's saddle and looked every ounce of dead. She was certain she was looking at a corpse and was very afraid of the consequences should that be the case.

Her hands trembled as she felt the injured man's cold and clammy skin for a pulse. It was faint but it was there. She silently breathed a sigh of relief while tapping her head, chest and shoulders in the ancient symbol of a cross. His head was bleeding again and she found it impossible to rouse him no matter how hard she tried. In a way, the mud had formed a clotting clump and her prying fingers had misguidedly loosened what was acting as a cork. She should have left well enough alone. She placed the palm of her hand to his head again and applied pressure.

Uncertain of what to do she turned to Randy and asked. "How much farther to town?" She hoped her voice didn't betray her uncertainty.

"We'll be there within the hour. What's your hurry? You got ants in your pants?"

"Are you daft? No, I'm worried about your brother. I think the ride is literally killing him. You have to slow down. All this trotting and galloping is causing his head to bounce around and bleed even more. I know you're smart enough to realize that he can't afford anymore blood loss."

"We'll be there soon enough. When we arrive I want you to book the room for yourself only. Don't tell anyone we're with you."

"Why? What are you hiding Randy? You should contact the local doctor and get some professional help. Your brothers life may depend on it."

Her prying questions grated on Randy's nerves. "It's none of your damn business what I'm hiding and you'll do as you're told or I'll shoot your horse and that damn ugly mutt that's now following you around instead of us. They may not be much but looks to me like they're all you've got."

"But I can't just get one room. That means there's only one bed. Are you crazy?"

"It'll give you something to think about big mouth. Now shut your trap and move."

Josie sulked and fumed proving to be as difficult as possible until the town came into view. A big sign read *Providence-population over 100*. More than one hundred people in one town, wow! They probably had a real school and a real store. Excitement began to flutter in her mind. She could see the main street lined with boardwalks and horses tethered to poles designed for just that with large water filled troughs in front of them. Women were wearing bright colors and carrying baskets and packages of all shapes and sizes. It was a busy town even though the thoroughfare was strewn with puddles of mud, the boardwalks seemed to be swept cleaned on a regular basis.

The largest building stood at the outer edge of town right off the main road, painted pale yellow yet dingy and gray in spots from the dirt and dust that covered its exterior. A firmly packed dirt walkway lined with tiny violet flowers led to the front door. Overhead hung a sign that read *vacancy*.

Josie's stomach lunged as they approached the back of the building. Randy cocked his gun, handed her a few bills and nodded for her to do as ordered. Josie walked around to the front entrance feeling as if the weight of the world was upon her shoulders. Her carriage held a hunched over posture, a mere reflection of her thoughts and concerns. She convinced herself she would stick around just long enough to make certain Neb got proper treatment. It was an unconscious effort to feel that she still had control over herself and her future. After all, in a place like this, it'd be easy to slip away, alone that was. However, she needed her horse and she wondered how Hops was getting along on his leg, poor thing. She had momentarily forgotten about him; shame on her. He'd been toddling along throughout the wee hours of the morning. Keeping pace with the horses trot. She silently vowed to love the animal to no end once this was over.

As she entered the dim interior of the hotel she lifted her head, a smile appeared firmly upon her face. Approaching the front desk she cleared her throat. "Excuse me."

"Yes ma'am. How can I help you?" This from a man she could barely see across the polished countertop which stood at least four feet high. The man was very short. Only the top of his head was visible to her due mostly to the hat he wore.

She'd never seen anyone so short before in her life. It was hard not to stare. In fact, she didn't even know what to think. Settling for simple amazement she responded. "I'd like a room please."

Stepping up onto a stool the man looked at her and replied. "It's a buck and a quarter a night and it must be pre-paid. We do not serve meals. There's one bathhouse for the ladies and one for the gents; same goes for the outhouses. There are towels in the rooms and more in the bath area if you need em'. Housekeeping cost extra. There's a water basin in the room. The water hole's out back." He pointed behind him but Josie couldn't see his arm all that well for it was short and stubby like the rest of him.

"How many nights you plan on stayin?"

"Oh at least three I think." Josie handed him the bills and signed the register gulping down a spoonful of apprehension while waiting for the correct change.

The gentleman peeked at her signature then looked at her again. "Single and alone are you?" He didn't wait for her reply. "You'd best be careful round here. There are all kinds of freaks on these streets. They come in off the Maumee River all the time. You never know what kind of folks may get off the next riverboat. Just be careful is all I'm saying. My name is Hank by the way. It's a pleasure to meet you."

His friendly warning came a little too late, Josie thought as he handed her a skeleton key to the room that would be her dungeon for the time being.

"Rooms by the back door on the second floor. Stairs are to your right. Let me know if'n you need anything at all.

"Thank you." She replied quietly thinking the placement the room very appropriate, being near the back door and all.

Relaying the information to Randy she helped tie the horses to the railing out back then went ahead and located the room and waved an "all clear" signal out the shuttered window.

The bed was small and placing Neb's big body in it only made it appear even smaller. She quickly fetched a pail of water and a towel before returning to the room. Upon her entrance Randy shut and locked the door behind her. Glancing at him she noticed how tired he looked.

"I'll tend to Neb if you want to rest."

"You'll kill him for sure if I'm not watchin."

"Now that's simply not true. I'd never intentionally hurt or kill anything." As an afterthought she added, "except oxen." Pausing for a moment to let her words sink in she met him eye to eye. "Look, you have my word that I won't hurt Neb or leave while you're asleep. I promise this one time only. Now get some sleep. Maybe it'll wipe some meanness away."

Randy seemed to be taken aback by her promise. However the next time she looked at him, which was only moments later, he was fast asleep in the chair. The gun was cocked and ready in his hand. Neb slept fitfully once his bandages were changed, offering little resistance except for the dead weight of his limbs. Although he was pale his temperature was on the rise and his skin clammy and chilled. Josie kept dunking a washcloth in the water basin and wringing it out over his mouth, pressing down on his chin with her thumb. He needed fluids desperately, without them he didn't stand a chance of surviving.

She still had some change leftover from earlier and wondered if it was enough to buy some soup and juice. She didn't want to break into her own stash of money or give Randy any cause to suspect she even had it. He was the one responsible for Neb. Let him pay to feed the man. He should thank her for fetching the food.

Quitting the room Josie wondered down the boardwalk until she came to a mercantile. There she purchased a jug of cider and a bar of soap as quickly as possible keeping her eyes averted to the floor. Then she crossed the dirt packed street carefully stepping around the piles of horse dung and puddles working her way to a place called "The Cookin' Kettle." It sounded nice. There was a help wanted sign hanging just below the blue and white-checkered curtains that ran along the length of the window at eye level. She couldn't get over how beautiful those curtains were trimmed in lace. Someday she'd have house with curtains like that in the windows. Yes, someday she would have a house with pained glass windows! Imagine that. There she went daydreaming again.

Upon entering her senses were overtaken by the pleasant aroma of roast beef and potatoes along with fresh apple pie. Her mouth started to water and her stomach growled vigorously. She boldly placed an order for chicken soup, two biscuits and one slice of apple pie. She'd give that to Randy although he didn't deserve even a morsel of it. Maybe he wouldn't be such a grump. A bell rang and silverware clanked and clattered as orders were shouted towards the back of the room giving the atmosphere a busy but friendly environment.

"Do you have utensils I can borrow?" She asked the friendly looking waitress, crossing her fingers behind her back in a gesture of hope. "I promise to bring them back tomorrow, clean too. I'll even sweep the floor in exchange for their use."

"You've got yourself a deal. What's your name honey?"

"Josephine. You can call me Josie."

"My name's Hanna Louise. What brings you to Providence Josie?"

"Well truthfully I'm not at liberty to say right now. But I can say I need a friend and I'm trying to make the best of a bad situation."

"Well." Said Hanna inspecting Josie from head to toe before judging her good in nature. "If you need anything at all just holler. I can spot a kind heart from miles away. We'll see you sometime tomorrow with a broom in your hand." With that she winked and returned to work.

Retracing her steps back towards the hotel, Josie felt her spirits lift somewhat. She liked Hanna and thought it'd be fun to sweep the floor for a while. It actually gave her something to look forward to. Plus, the smells in that restaurant were heavenly. Her mouth watered just thinking about it. What would it be like to actually eat a four-course meal there? She wondered absent-mindedly pretending as she walked that she was returning to the restaurant rather than the dreadful hotel room. The hotel room was the last place she wanted to go, but she had given her word, although it was a promise offered foolishly, she did have her pride and would honor her word rather than run. There was something about Neb that made her feel almost responsible for his life. She knew if she didn't return, he would die for sure. She may be his only hope. Yet it was more than that. It was a purpose of sorts. Everybody had to have a purpose in life. Right now, she felt her purpose was to help keep Neb alive. If that was what the good Lord wanted her to do, than so be it, she'd do it. Perhaps that was why she felt obligated to go back and aid in fighting for his life. She was meant to. It was as if some invisible hand was guiding her in that direction. She couldn't understand it so there was no use pondering it.

The sound of Josie's footsteps lithely ascending the stairs must have woken Randy because he started grumbling as soon as she entered the room. "Where the hell have you been? God damn it, you made me a promise." He bellowed so loudly the walls dully vibrated.

"I didn't break my promise. Neb is perfectly fine and I'm still here…against my will of course." She couldn't help it; she just had to get that little remark in.

Randy stood and was across the room faster than Josie could blink. He smacked her hard across the face then grabbed her by the throat, easily backing her against the wall as she hung like a rag doll, the movement effortless on his part.

Josie had one hand holding the sack of food and the other over his wrist, trying desperately to ease the weight of her body hanging from his tight grasp. His fingers were squeezing her throat, bruising and cutting off her air supply. She was truly frightened as dizziness paraded through her senses.

Suddenly Randy seemed to smell the odor of soup and pie permeating the bag. He loosened his grip and asked. "Where'd you go off to Josie?" He eased her down in silent descent but still didn't let go.

"I got some cider at the general store and some dinner for us all. I even got you a piece of apple pie. I was hoping it'd put you in a better mood." This was said in a meek rasp for it was difficult to talk. Her voice was forced and croaky, the hand around her throat hindering the full use of her vocal cords making it impossible to swallow.

He released her so fast she sagged to the floor gasping for air, feeling lightheaded and rubbing the bruises around her neck. Her head was spinning in a wild array that had her slightly swaying back and forth as she regained oxygen and a sense of balance. Keeping her gaze focused on the floor tears filled her eyes with the reverberating change of emotions from hurt to a raging anger that steadily mounted to a point that made it difficult to keep her actions in check.

The feeling scared her to no end for she had never before in her life harbored so much hatred towards one person that she actually wanted to physically harm them. Refusing to let Randy see her tears she desperately blinked them away gathering her thoughts, collecting her wits.

That big ox needed a good butt whippin'. It was too bad she wasn't big enough to do it. One thing is for sure, she thought pondering quietly, she had to get away before he killed her, which she was certain he would eventually do. Unfortunately, she was too wrapped up in thoughts of saving Neb that she overlooked the important fact that her own welfare was at stake. For now, she felt it was best to think things through and come up with a solid plan. If she was so easily able to get away from Randy once, she should be able to do it again. She also longed for a way to get even with Randy, teaching him a lesson once and for all, then silently lectured herself for the thought. She'd be lucky to just get away alive. Well she knew the burden of getting even wouldn't make her a better person, it would only lower her to his level but surely it would be worth it.

Josie picked the bag up from the floor and began pouring soup into a cup for Neb. She'd attempt to get something warm and healthy into his system in hopes of nurturing him along. She then readied a platter for Randy begrudged that she had to do so. Handing it to him she offered little more than a sour expression and a tart flip of the hair. The ass didn't even say thanks, which was exactly what she had expected from someone as rude and improperly mannered as he.

Neb only swallowed a small amount of soup and Josie had to rub his throat to get him to do that. Nibbling on a biscuit while pouring small sips of cider into his mouth she wondered if Neb was anything like his brother. For some reason she didn't think so. She raised and fluffed the pillow beneath his head then checked and cleaned the bandages until she was content with the way the wrappings looked. It would have to do for the time being.

"I have to return these utensils to the restaurant tomorrow and sweep the floor there. It's a deal I worked out with the waitress in exchange for the use of the silverware."

"Is that where you got the pie?" He asked in earnest not knowing what to think about Josie's thoughtfulness towards him and his brother.

"Sure is. There's some real nice people in this town."

"Who you been talkin' to Josie?"

"Only the waitress." At his angry stance she added. "Don't worry I didn't mention anything about you, I promise." He visibly relaxed with her words and Josie breathed a sigh of relief wondering again what he was hiding. Obviously he was a very bad person. He must be hiding a lot. Shivers ran down her spine. She knew she was in over her head. These men were not the type of men that she and her family would normally consort with.

That night she slept fitfully on the floor while Randy used the only chair the room provided. Neither of them had any pillows or blankets. Neb needed them more and so they gave willingly and made do without. Josie let Hops in the room, thankful that Randy didn't refuse her the one comfort from the drafty floor upon which she lay. Pure bliss came in the form of warm body heat radiating from the dog, as he lay curled up sleeping at her side.

Throughout the night Josie kept a diligent watch over Neb giving him spoons full of cool water and sponging him often in an effort to keep his fever down. She felt like she was fighting a losing battle. He still hadn't moved a muscle although his breathing was more regular now, not as shallow and labored as was during their ride earlier that day. She wondered what would become of her patient once she was gone. Would Randy give him the care that he needed or would he shoot him like one would an injured horse? Somehow, she didn't find the thought comforting. Either way the outcome was gruesome.

Peeking over at Randy she realized his gun was on the floor next to his chair, one arm draped limply over the side of the chairs wooden armrest. His large knuckled fingers hung a hairs width from the guns barrel. An idea too good to resist bloomed in her mind as a smile slowly formed on her face. He couldn't possibly be such a menace without that gun. Could he? She carefully acted on her thoughts before she had a chance to change her mind. Very quietly she crawled over to where Randy slept and inch by inch reached for the gun keeping her eyes glued to the sleeping man's face the entire time, willfully watching for any sign that he would wake bringing doom down upon her. Sweat beaded her forehead when she finally felt the coolness of the guns metal, grasped it carefully and pulled her hand back slowly. Tip toeing across the room towards the door she winced and halted each time the floorboards creaked looking to Randy for movement while calming her rapidly beating heart. She was sure it was beating so loudly that its sound alone would waken the tyrant. Turning the doorknob ever so slowly she slipped through the crack when it was opened just far enough, quietly trying to muffle the click of the latch while shutting the door behind her.

As quickly and quietly as she could, she hurried down the steps to the outhouses out back. Filled with trepidation and excitement her fist softly knocked on the door with the sign that read "GENTS," when no reply came, she slowly pulled the door open cringing when it loudly squeaked and groaned it resistance then blindly tossed the gun into the open hole on the bench. She could hear the plunk and splash when it contacted the raw sewage in the tank beneath the wooden floor.

Feeling triumphant and chuckling to herself, she quietly snuck back into the room and lay down upon the hard floor curling into a ball on her side then gently pulled Hops into her embrace. She had a terrible time controlling the urge to giggle and almost woke Randy several times before wiping away the tears that formed in the corner of her eyes from too much laughing. Just picturing his expression in the morning made her feel good. Calming her gusto she settled down and sought sleep and comfort at the end of a very tiring and trying day, reminding herself that Neb was the reason she once again, placed herself in jeopardy. Neb would live if she had anything to do with it.

Before sunrise Josie tended Neb, saw to her own needs, tended the animals, cleaned the utensils and laid some leftover jerky and cider out for Randy. Slipping out the door she walked to the restaurant inhaling deeply the fresh air, so fragrant with the tantalizing aroma of flowers, bacon, horses, and wilderness that one could almost visualize the surrounding scenery without even opening their eyes. She was fully aware that she would have to return. If she didn't she was certain Randy would do something drastic to the horse, the dog or both. The thought was devastating.

Strolling down the boardwalk she studied the storefronts and shops to see what was what and memorized the names and locations of each establishment. There was a general store, a small post office, a mill, a blacksmith and a sheriff's office. Her mind screamed as her lightly patted footsteps faltered before stopping completely. A sheriff's office, hmm, she could get help. Hopefully they would take her seriously. Biting down on her bottom lip she pondered and wondered if they would try sending her back to her Daddy. Surely not once they heard what her Daddy was going to do to her. After all, this was the Americas and Polk was the president! He was an honorable man.

Stopping just outside the sheriff's office she craned her neck scanning over a remarkable display of posted signs pegged on the buildings exterior. There were reward signs, lost and found signs and a variety of wanted signs; some offered rewards for people both dead or alive while others offered money only if they were alive and healthy. One sign in particular caught her interest sending chills down her spine, taking the wind right out of her lungs. In large black bold print it read '**Wanted dead or alive'**. Below that was an inked sketch of Neb and Randy. Reading further Josie learned that they were the notorious **HURLEY BROTHERS** wanted for **bank robbery, horse stealing** and **cold-blooded murder.** Josie was horrified. No wonder Randy didn't want people to know they were there! Everything suddenly made sense and anger once again seeped its way into her blood turning her pale cheeks a blushing red. Surely, being held by outlaws such as this would merit some immediate attention without having to say a word about her Daddy.

Making up her mind she opened the door to the jailhouse and stepped inside. The room was dark and damp beseeching a dreariness unsurpassed by the windowless creosote stained walls, which burned her nostrils. Cobwebs clung in the corners trapping the rays of sunlight that did manage to pass through the small holes and notches in the wood framed room. It smelled like stale cigar smoke and sweat amongst other things. On one side of the room was a row of three small cells with solid strap iron doors and matching strap iron shelves holding a single blanket for each opposite the cell openings. The entire cubby was made up of narrow strips of iron measuring about two inches in width. An iron bench filled the far wall with a bucket tucked beneath it. Even the floor of each cell was made of the iron straps that rested atop the wooden planks of the establishment. All three cells looked exactly the same and she could just imagine what the buckets were used for. Thank goodness they were all empty, assuring her this was a peaceful town despite the fact that it was hot and unpleasant in the small room. It definitely wasn't a place she'd be longing to spend her days and nights in.

A young man wearing a wool button-top hat and matching vest whistled loudly as he cleaned the inside of the cell closest to the far wall clearly in good spirits not minding the chore.

"Excuse me young man." Josie said quite loudly.

The boy jumped proving he hadn't heard her enter then turned towards her, a surprised look upon his face. She accurately guessed him to be about twelve years old.

"I'm sorry. I didn't mean to scare you. Is the sheriff in?" She placed a hand over the bare skin at her neck in an effort to hide her nervousness as well as the finger shaped bruises.

"No ma'am. He's gone off scoutin' for some outlaws we heard were nearby. He'll be back by sunset." The boy scanned her from head to toe making mental notes of the bruises and marks she so painstakingly tried to hide. "Can I try to help you?" Big brown eyes looked up showing a concern and understanding that exceeded his youthfulness.

"I have some information the sheriff may be interested in. It's regarding one of the postings outside. I believe I need his assistance so I'll try to stop back this evening, if I can manage to get away that is." Bowing politely, a gesture of respect to the boy, she smiled then turned and fled as quickly as she physically could without drawing attention to herself. That jailhouse-combined sheriff's office made her nervous, belaying a premonition she couldn't shake. That coupled with the sinking feeling that something terrible was about to happen, lurked overhead like a dark cloud. Absent mindedly, she sent up a silent prayer for Neb's life. *Dear God, let's take this one day at a time. Please.* She had the jitters. She didn't know why but she couldn't shake the uneasy feeling creepy up her spine with each step she took. Every nerve in her body jangled like a bell hanging around the neck of a cow in a field.

Crossing the street she went directly to the restaurant in search of Hanna, intent upon returning the silverware and sweeping the floor as promised.

Hanna's face bellied her shock at Josie's battered appearance. "Honey what happened to you?"

"Oh." Replied Josie waving her had in the air as if it was nothing at all. "I had a run in with an ox, so to speak."

Hanna's face betrayed a puzzled look as she handed Josie the broom and looked up when the tiny bells hanging above the restaurants entrance door chimed the arrival of another visitor. It was part of her job to greet the guest as they entered and show them to their seats. However, the man coming through the door looked anything but pleasant and had Hanna hating her job and fearful in no time. One glance in Josie's direction confirmed that she was upset too. The poor girls face was two shades dimmer than gray. It had gone white as a ghost.

Gulping back her sudden queasiness then grabbing the broom handle in a grip so tight it turned her knuckles ashen she simply stated, "there's the ox."

Hanna tossed a studious look toward the man now surprised by the sheer size of him for he was huge, not just tall but big boned and very muscular, towering a full head size above most men. He looked familiar yet she couldn't quite place him. Uneasiness pricked the back of her mind for she was certain she'd remember seeing or meeting a fellow of this stature. She would mention the man to Sheriff C. Mean looking' guy, that was for sure since the daggers shooting from his eyes were placed on Josie and were terrifying enough to scare a grizzly away. Turning to Josie she asked blatantly. "Is he the one responsible for your appearance?"

Tears filled Josie's eyes as she thought of what she'd been through in the last couple of days and the fear of what was yet to come. "Please don't tell him you know. He'll kill my horse, my dog and probably me. Then I'll have no way of escaping." Her eyes now pleaded silently with Hanna, wordlessly begging for the confidential admission to be kept secret for now.

As Randy moved closer Josie began briskly sweeping the polished wood floor trying to ignore Randy's threatening presence while Hanna went to intercept the big guy offering him a seat. So this was Josie's ox. The man sure was a crab. He stunk too.

"Can I help you sir?" Hanna asked in her sweetest voice while batting her eyelashes in an attempt to distract him. In no time she had him seated near the door. His gaze never wavered from Josie and she felt helplessly sorry for the girl.

"Yeah, I'm looking' for my wife. She'd be the one sweeping your floor. You tell her we're leaving right away." He glared coolly at Hanna sending chills down her spine, chills that were beckoned by the hint of murder shining brightly in his eyes. Ugly and ruthless the man didn't appear to have a decent bone in his body.

"Well, have a seat." Hanna said praying her voice didn't betray her new friend. She didn't want him to know Josie had confided in her. "I'll fetch some water and inform your wife of your wishes." She efficiently placed a glass of chilled water in front of Randy then swung around to deliver his message to Josie.

Randy sat glaring at Josie while she briefly talked to the waitress, then ignoring his wishes she continued sweeping the floor stubbornly refusing to look at him. That little bitch stole his gun and now made a fool of him by outright disobeying his orders. Oh, he was boiling mad. Cracking his knuckles he removed a cigar from his shirt pocket and leaned back in the seat flicking a lucifer along his boots, lighting the tip. Inhaling deeply he allowed the bitter taste to fill his mouth and lungs. He was done messing around with the little brat. It was time for little miss priss to learn a lesson. Her acting all high and mighty was gonna' stop for he was ready to knock her off that pedestal she placed herself upon.

Josie was sweeping the isle by Randy's table now in short rough strokes that scratched through the air while fuming inwardly at his attitude and her predicament. She ordered herself to think but her brain refused to cooperate and the strokes of the broom grew harsher.

While her back was turned Randy flicked ashes on the floor where she had just swept. "Um Josie, looks like you missed some here."

Glancing in his direction, a puzzled expression traced her features. She didn't think she had missed anything but there it was, dirt on the floor, plain as day. Back tracking her steps she swept the area again making sure to get everything this time before moving on, working her way towards the rear of the restaurant. That big oaf, couldn't he see she was doing this as payment for the use of utensils last night? He didn't complain then, when he ate the piece of pie he surely wasn't worthy of.

"I said you missed some here!" Randy's loud voice bellowed startling Josie and causing her to jump as she turned around once again and peered at the floor near his table.

Looking from Randy to the floor comprehension slowly dawned in her mind. Fury mounted as his harassment continued with a nasty look aimed directly at her. That big ox was flicking ashes where she had already swept. She narrowed her eyes at him and marched back over to his table. Before he knew what happened Josie snatched the cigar out of his dirty hand and dropped it in the glass of brownish colored water Hanna had ever so sweetly placed in front of him. After that, she spun on her heel, flung her braid back, squared her shoulders and marched to the rear of the restaurant intent upon finishing her job. Halfway across the room she heard heavy footsteps and the fierce vibrations of the floorboards as he approached from behind. Turning around she yelped as Randy forcefully grabbed her around the waist and effortlessly threw her over his shoulder.

Pain filled her midsection when his shoulder punched into her abdomen as she landed with her dairy-air facing the ceiling, blood rushing to her head. Pounding her fist on his back she demanded. "Put me down!"

Randy made for the door and she hollered breathlessly. "Help, please." To her mortification he continued on and no one stepped in his way or even attempted to stop him.

"Hanna please help me." Josie begged on a sob, desperation evident in the sound of her voice.

"I'm sorry Josie. Being that he's your husband, there's nothing I can do." Hanna's face looked grim with worry as she resolutely stepped back.

"He's not my husband damn it! Look at the posting across the thoroughfare." Josie was so angry. "Oh please, somebody help me." She grasped at the framework to the doorway as they were exiting. Once her fingers contacted the solid wood she clutched on for dear life yet there wasn't enough strength in her fingertips to allow a good grip.

"Now damn it Josie stop." Randy said as he tried to twist and exit, attempting to pull Josie with him caring naught of what she hit. Her fingernails were split, now pulled back and bleeding from her struggle to resist exiting the safe haven of the eating-place.

They were making a terrible scene and a crowd was beginning to gather on the boardwalk in front of the restaurant. Randy decided he had to do something quickly to end the situation and quit the commotion. His natural meanness surfaced as he forcefully flung and bent his body forward then quickly straightened up causing Josie to flip backwards out of control, hitting the back of her head on the edge of the boardwalk railing just opposite the doorway. He heard a loud crack when her head made contact. Randy felt an excited little flutter run through his veins along with a stirring in his groin. He was swiftly gratified at the sound. There wasn't a single person within a twenty-foot radius that didn't hear the gruesome noise. Josie's eyes rolled to the back of her head as her body went limp.

"That's better." He mumbled as he scooped her up and walked back towards the hotel. The little bitch, he'll show her. He'd break her like a wild horse. If anybody paid attention to what she had said, he'd kill her. He was going to kill her anyways as soon as Neb was better. He'd just have to do it sooner rather than later.

He had walked about ten paces when silence came over the crowd. Randy heard the cock of the gun and knew immediately it was pointed at his back. He stopped walking and stood still, stiff and rigid as his muscles tightened. If'n he had his gun the son of a bitch behind him would be dead already. Unconsciously, his fingers tightened around Josie bringing about new bruises although she was out cold and couldn't feel it.

"You'll put the girl down, raise you hands in the air and turn around real slowly." The man's voice rumbled low and calm. The town's people held their breath. "I'm Sheriff C. You'll do as I say or die where you stand. I have no qualms shooting you in the back mister."

Instead of putting Josie down gently he dropped her like a sack of potatoes.

Raising his hands in the air he falsely acted as if he was going to comply but then at the last moment ran like a madman between two buildings and out of sight. A few of the town's men made hast to catch him.

"Let him go." Sheriff C directed. "I can't arrest the man for causing a scene or beating his wife." He walked over to where Josie lay. She looked like a beat rag mop. Old worn garments clothed her body. Holey shoes barely covered her feet. He could tell she was familiar with hard work by the calloused appearance of her hands and nails. She had black and blue marks all over her small delicate body.

He bent over to pick her up. Yep, she was tiny. The girl couldn't weigh more than one hundred pounds. He carried her effortlessly up the road towards Old Doc's office. Many of the town's people followed him.

"Whacha' gonna' do with her Sheriff?" Asked one of the men in the group.

"Yeah, we don't need trouble like this in our town." One of the ladies added.

"I'll take care of her now get on with your business everyone." Sheriff C informed the group. "Let's not make this worse then needs be." Although he projected a positive attitude about the situation, he felt as if something wasn't right. He was missing some very important detail here. This was his town, these were his people and it was his job to keep the peace, to keep everyone safe. Why did he suddenly feel as if he let the little lady in he arms down, even though he'd never seen her before in his life?

The crowd slowly dispersed until only Hanna and Joey remained. Hanna looked at him and began to speak. Her features were ebbed with worry. "She's a real nice girl Sheriff but I have to say something doesn't add up. She came into the restaurant last evening and bought some pie and soup. She borrowed utensils and promised to sweep the floor in return for their use. She was a little beat up then but I didn't think much about it. The area itself has a way of doing that to people. This morning she returned looking terrible and claimed that man was threatening to kill her horse, dog and her. He's an awfully big fellow to be hittin' on that little girl." She grew angry just thinking about it.

Joey piped in. "Yeah, she was at the office this mornin' Sheriff, asked for you. Said she had some information for you. She was all nervous though." Joey's voice proved his excitement at being able to provide valuable information to his idol.

"Thanks for the help Joey." Ruffling the boy's hair he looked at both of them and nodded. "Does anybody know where she's staying?"

"Hank talked about her checking into the hotel on the edge of town. He said she was real nice and polite. He thinks she's hiding someone in the room." Hanna replied. Hank was Hanna's brother. He was a midget and although he worked at the hotel, he relied heavily on Hanna for a lot of things. He was a good man and seldom spoke out of place so Hanna knew his concern was real.

"I'll take care of everything from here. Just keep your eyes and ears open. Let me know if anything else happens." With that the Sheriff walked up the steps leading to Old Doc's porch. He tried the knob while balancing Josie in his arms. It was locked. Finding a note tacked to the doorframe he quickly ripped it down and read: *Out at the Patchin Farm delivering twins. Be back tomorrow.* Great, what was he going to do now? Thinking through his dilemma he stuck the note back up for others to read. He'd just have to take the girl back to his place and try to care for her until Old Doc returned.

With that he turned and crossed the rutted road. His place was only a few doors down somewhat closer to the river that ran along the outer edge of town. He stayed in town so that he could keep an eye on things and always be close by when trouble arose. For the most part Providence was a quiet little town. He liked it. Most folks did once the land was cleared and they grew accustomed to the wet humid environment.

Entering his small cabin he walked to the bedroom in the back kicking the door open with his foot. He gently laid the girl on the down filled mattress then lit the candle on the night table. As the flame grew and flickered to life he studied her face. It was hard to distinguish dirt from bruises, all of which covered her pale skin. First things first, he went to the kitchen area and began boiling water, then he drug out a heavy wooden tub used for bathing. The tub was luxury item as most folks bathed in the river. He made it himself for he was of a larger build than most men and he enjoyed bathing nightly. This custom built tub was longer and deeper than the ones sold at the General Store.

He started a fire in the hearth that took up one whole wall in the living area of the small cabin. The fireplace was not only used for heating the cabin, it along with the stone hearth was where he cooked all his meals as well. Closing the wooden shutters on the front interior window he placed the tub before the warm fire. He'd see what this girl looked like and if she came to with a warm bath. He wished she could give him the information he needed, as he was impatient to have the answers to many questions but first he'd go by the hotel and see about fetching her horse and dog. Hanna had insisted these animals meant a lot to this girl and Hank would be able to tell him what animals appeared upon her arrival. Putting another pot of water above the fire to boil, he grabbed his hat and quietly shut and latched the front door. Surely the girl would be fine unattended for a short while.

Finding the dog and horse wasn't a problem at all. Getting the horse to move proved to be more difficult than anticipated. It seemed as if the horse could smell the girl on him and kept nudging him with its snout. Finally he decided it would be easier to ride the animal rather than walk in front of it. The dog followed as if it too knew he had possession of its owner. Both animals looked as if they could use some water and the dog was limping immensely. His heart went out to the dog for it was a pitiful site and appeared to have been poorly abused. He must have pegged the girl wrong. He didn't think she was the type to abuse or mistreat animals. The horse appeared to be well cared for if not a little hungry. He'd have Joey give it a good rub down later on along with some carrots.

He secured the horse to the small lean-to behind his cabin then walked to the office and directed Joey to comb, feed and water the stallion before tossing a quarter to the boy. Eagerly, Joey smiled and got busy right away. He was always so anxious to please and a smart young boy to boot. One would never know he'd been orphaned at a very young age and lived on the streets ever since. The boy was like a sponge, always reading, writing, learning, and soaking up as much knowledge as possible. He wanted to be the next town sheriff. There was no doubt in Sheriff C's mind that he would be.

Hauling the saddlebags over his shoulders and whistling to the dog, the Sheriff quickly returned to the cabin and felt a peaceful calm come over him as he entered the normally empty house. After placing a bowl of water on the floor by the door for the dog he finished filling the giant tub with water so hot he decided to inventory the saddlebags while it cooled. He searched through the bag's contents for answers or clues as to who this girl was and why she was with that jackass. Nothing in the bags revealed any useful information. She didn't even have a change of clothes. What little food she did have would hardly last another day or two at best. Releasing a sigh of frustration he raked his fingers through his hair.

The dog wasn't any help at all for it continued to tug and pull at his pant legs demanding some playful attention. He went ahead and entertained the dog for a few moments petting him gently then flipping him around and about in playful gestures. His efforts made a life long friend for when he attempted to exit the door the dog seemed torn between staying and going whimpering loudly with indecision.

The general store was just a short walk across the street. He'd go and purchase some shoes, a dress and a nightgown. God knew the little lady lying helplessly in his bed needed something to wear. He'd do that right away so that when the bath was complete she'd have clean garments to put on. Not caring what the colors were and knowing that gossip would spread rampantly, he purchased his items and was back in no time. Now the water felt perfect, not too hot, and not too cold.

Standing over the bed he gently removed the girl's shoes and stockings then promptly dropped them into the trash bucket. He had no qualms about disposing of her clothing into the trash. The garments were little more than that. If she needed replacement clothing after this, he'd provide it himself. Then he began to remove her dress taking care not to further injure or hurt her. His huge hands felt clumsy as he fumbled with the garments.

Once she was completely undressed with the exception of pantaloons, he couldn't help but study her. She was the most beautiful creature he had ever seen portraying a delicate but sturdy build and a perfect cream-colored complexion. He breathlessly inspected each and every black and blue mark on her body. Not only was her face and neck covered, so were her rib cage and both wrists, some of the bruises now turning to an ugly yellow in color. Hurting for her, he couldn't help the fierce anger that swelled within him for he was obligated to uphold the law but would like nothing more than to kill the man that had done this to her. He wondered if it was her husband that left the telltale marks of abuse, or for that matter, if he was really her husband. God's teeth, if this girl belonged to him, no harm would ever come to her.

Wrapping her in the bed sheets he gently carried her to the tub with little effort, as her petite frame was nothing of a burden. Once he had her completely submerged in the warm water he supported the back of her head with one hand and began lathering a cloth with the other. That's when he felt the huge bump inflicted by the episode on the boardwalk. If he wasn't angry enough before he certainly was now. He would kill that bastard for the bump protruding from the back of her head was the size of an apple. A really big apple! No wonder she was out cold. He only hoped that it didn't cause any permanent brain damage. He had heard stories of people who never returned to normal from such blows as this, or people that had gone berserk and stayed that way.

Carefully he continued to wash and rinse her hair, which was a chore itself since it hung past her waist, and he only had one free hand to use. It's length managed to catch and tangle on everything. Then he began to soap and clean her body. He mentally tried to remain aloof and wash her because it was a duty that needed to be done. A simple act of kindness as one would care for a patient on a sick bed. That was probably why he was in law enforcement and not in the doctoring field. Keeping a doctor-patient perspective on things didn't keep a certain part of his anatomy from acting on it's own accord. He was firmly aroused and she was absolutely beautiful. On that thought he quickly finished and lifted her from the tub. Laying her on a blanket he had spread over the floor, he briskly dried and wrapped her hair tightly in linen. Then wrapped her body in the blanket and returned her to the bed where he combed her long dark hair and dried her tattered body as best as he could for he was unskilled at such practices. The pantaloons remained wet but it would have to do. It almost felt as if he were caring for a small child. He must have been too harsh because she whimpered as if in pain and he immediately felt bad. Covering her he blew out the candle stood to his full height and left the room.

Out on the porch he sat on the swing stretching his long legs fully in front of him. Exhaling a heavy sigh he put his head back and shut his weary eyes, replaying the episode from earlier that day with the guy and girl in front of the restaurant. It was a horrible image as over and over his mind envisioned the scene. Something nagged at him but he couldn't place what it was. Then he remembered what Joey had said about the girl's earlier attempt to contact him. Did this girl know something or have some type of information that would help him in his profession, and if so, what? She had said something in the doorway of that restaurant but he couldn't hear what it was at the time. He knew by the tone of her voice it was a plea for help but his instinct told him it was something more as well. That was why the man roughened her up. He wanted to shut her up. He was hiding something.

Deciding that must be the case, he got up and walked to the jailhouse. Standing outside the one room establishment, he read and studied every single poster. Finally, on the last one he found his answer. "**Wanted dead or alive— The Hurley Brothers**". Sketched on that poster was the man from earlier. His stomach knotted into a tight ball and his head began to throb.

"Damn." He cursed himself for foolishly letting the outlaws get away. The brothers were wanted for murder. What was wrong with him? He knew every poster and every sketch even though this one didn't look exactly like the real guy anymore. Several days of beard growth and not bathing had changed Randall Hurley's appearance drastically.

He'd gather up a few good men and have them scout the area for a trail. He himself would check the hotel room. Maybe the guy was still there.

Inside he opened the desk drawer he retrieved his guns then securely holstered them on the leather belt around his waist. He sent Joey out with messages to be delivered to four of his best men asking them to meet him in one hour. Leaving the office he strolled to the hotel. If he was lucky the fellow would still be there and he could jail him right away. He really didn't want to leave the girl while he was out following a trail for days on end. That could take weeks or longer. His senses were on full alert as his mind absorbed every detail of the bleak surroundings. He inspected every shadow, movement and noise.

Upon his arrival at the hotel Hank supplied him with a duplicate room key and directed him to the stairway in the back of the establishment. He quietly took each step one at a time pausing often to listen for movement from inside the room. Once he got to the top step he carefully pressed his ear to the door. Nothing. Trying the knob, he found the door unlocked and pushed it open with his boot, cautiously sheltering his body with the doorframe. As it creaked open he recalled an earlier encounter with a bullet and winced at the dreadful memory. He had no desire to be hit again. As always he was careful and waited a few moments. Still hearing no sound, he took another silent and cautious step into the rented room and found it empty except for the man lying deathly still atop the bed. What the hell? Guardedly, he took another soundless step towards the bed and then paused. Still there was no movement. Advancing further he stopped alongside the bed clutching the loaded revolver, ready to fire if needed.

The guy lying there was the other Hurley brother. There was little doubt for it was evident in his facial features and the uncanny resemblance to the sketches of the poster. Whether the guy was dead or alive was a good question. Feeling for a pulse he discovered that he was alive, just barely. What the hell was going on here?

Returning to the office he urgently instructed two of his men to carry the other brother to the jail cell. Joey put some blankets down on the bench and left a note for Old Doc to check the guy out upon his return. He personally didn't care if the man lived or died. If he were anything like his brother he'd only destroy what others had worked hard for. Then, glancing around at the dried bloody bandages he felt a stab of guilt. Regardless of his injury, the outlaw had to be lock up. However, there was always more than one side to every story, then somewhere in the middle was the truth.

Next he instructed his four guys to try and pick up Mr. Hurley's trail and to remain split into two separate groups. He, himself, would stay in town. His guess was that the other Hurley brother wouldn't go far. The two things he wanted most were his brother and the girl, both of which were here with him so he expected a return visit. He'd put money on it if he were the gambling type. The puzzle was slowly coming together. Soon, he'd have his answers. Soon.

"Be careful men." He stated clearly. "This Hurley fellow is dangerous and won't think nothing of killing you. Remember to stay together in pairs and circle the town about three miles out, especially by the river. He's out there. I can feel it." The Sheriff's words hung heavy in the air. "I don't want you camping out there. Come back each evening and update me. It's too dangerous to chance him surprising anyone while sleeping. You can head out early each morning. Take extra bullets too. If you see him, shoot him. We don't need to hear anything he has to say. Everybody got that?"

The men eagerly shook their heads as they loaded up and headed out for the rest of the day. He went back to the cabin to check on the girl. She was exactly as he left her only awake now and bundled in the sheet shivering uncontrollably.

"Hi." He said. "How are you feeling?"

Josie thought his voice low and soothing. "I'm not sure how I feel." She answered truthfully, teeth chattering and chin quivering. "I guess I hurt all over. What happened?"

"You took a real bad blow to the head. Can I get you anything?"

"No." Josie shook her head back and forth immediately regretting doing so as pain exploded in her temples. Wincing as the pain pierced her skull she pressed her fingers to the pressure points in an attempt to dull the sensation. She shut her eyes and took a deep calming breath. When she opened them again she saw two of everything.

"My," she asked softly "what's wrong with me?"

"I'm not sure." The Sheriff replied. "You'll feel better in a few days. That I can guarantee. Do you think you can answer a few questions for me?"

"Well." She said feeling a great deal of comfort from his presence. "I'll explain everything to you if you promise not to lock me up behind bars or send me back to my Daddy." She couldn't take her eyes off the polished badge pinned to his shirt pocket and swallowed hard.

Why on earth would he want to lock her up? "Did you do something wrong?" He couldn't help but ask. Perhaps she was privy to the deeds of the Hurley brothers and aided them, he didn't realize he had spoken out loud until she responded thoughtfully.

"No, not at all. I just don't want to go home, truly. You see, my Mom died and I'm eighteen now so I thought I'd try it on my own. Daddy hasn't been the same since Momma passed on and I was only trying to get further north."

She had the prettiest green eyes, reminding him of clouded emeralds. "So let me get this straight, you ran away and that is how you met up with the Hurley brothers?"

"Yes. Actually I came by your office earlier today but you weren't in. I needed help. Oh my…" She exclaimed trying to get up. "I have to get Buster and Hops!"

"Oh no you don't." He gently pushed her back down. "If you're referring to the horse and dog, I've taken care of them. There're fine. I promise." With that he whistled and Hops came running awkwardly into the room attempting to jump onto the bed with his thickly bandaged leg in tow. His efforts proved fruitless for his springy jump wasn't high enough and he scrambled backwards onto the floor.

Laughing, the Sheriff gently commanded. "Why don't you start at the beginning and tell me everything." As he spoke he lifted the dog onto her lap.

Josie did. She told him all about her Daddy and the Ebony C guy. She told him about running away, the cave, the skunk, her money, Randy, Neb and the nice waitress. When she was done she looked up at him. He was smiling warmly at her with a handsome face and sparkling eyes that crinkled like crowfeet in the corners. His teeth were perfectly straight and healthy which was unusual. She looked into his deep dark blue eyes.

"What's so funny?" It was a sad tale and he was smiling.

"Well." He chuckled while looking back at her. "What's your name?"

"Josie." She replied meekly then straightened with pride. "Josephine Grace Edwards." Why was he looking at her like that? "What's your name Sheriff?"

"Well, that's the funny part." He said while forming another easy smile. "My name is Ebony C. My full name is Ebony Christian Coy." He shrugged his shoulders. "Folks call me either Ebony C or Sheriff C. You can call me anything you want." He stopped to let his words sink in. She had a stunned look on her face. God she was pretty, breathtakingly beautiful in his opinion.

"Well then that would mean you're the guy I'm running from. Boy isn't that funny?" She laughed nervously and wrapped her arms around herself pulling the sheet up to her chin. Disbelief was written plainly on her face.

"Please don't cower form me Josie. I would never hurt you. In fact, I'm going to get the son of a bitch that did." It amazed him at how quickly his mood had changed and at how vehement his words were. He squeezed his fist at the thought of anyone hurting Josie. Josie. He liked her name too. What shook him the most was that he meant what he said. He was going to get Randy Hurley, and he would uphold justice. Not because he was wanted dead or alive, but because of the marks upon Josie that he was looking at right now. He would avenge Josie. That shook him to the core.

She began to relax again feeling safe and content with his words of comfort. "So Sheriff C, what was it you wanted from me in the first place?

"Well, I was playing cards with your Daddy while on a trip to see some friends. Really I was chasing postings, you know…trying to hunt down the bad guys…undercover so to speak. He mentioned how you and your Momma made extra money sewing and mending shirts. I needed some shirts mended. He told me you'd do it to pay off the dollar he owed me for the card game. I was to come by a few nights past and drop the shirt off, but I didn't get the chance, as I've been busy as all get up around here. It's not like I'm in the neighborhood often."

"That was it?" She couldn't believe it. Her Daddy didn't sell her in a card game? Ebony C needed sewing done? Her head started spinning again. "I don't believe this." She mumbled. Her poor Daddy, he must be a worried sick. "What have I done?" She looked down in shame. "I've made a pickle of everything."

"Don't worry Josie. I'll send word to your Daddy that you're okay and under my protection. Really, you've only traveled about fifteen miles since you left home. Why don't you try to get some rest while I make something for us to eat?" Humor danced in his eyes as he turned to leave the room.

"Christian." His name rolled off her tongue and stopped him in mid stride. No one had addressed him by his God given name in years. It sounded nice purring from her dainty lips.

He turned. "Yes Josie?"

"Thank you." She whispered as her eyelids grew heavy and she sank back into the soft mattress. He looked at her for a moment before leaving. She was something else.

He wasn't the greatest cook in the world but he cut and fried potatoes and a slab of deer meat. He didn't have much to drink either so he put together what he could. On the tray he arranged a glass of water and a tin plate filled with salted meat and buttered potatoes. As an afterthought he added utensils and a wildflower from outside. A smile spread wide on his face when he shyly delivered the assortment to Josie. She slowly sat up and tried to be cheerful. The aroma of the food smelled absolutely wonderful and her stomach growled ferociously causing her cheeks to burn red with embarrassment.

"I'm sorry." She said. "It's just that I haven't eaten much lately."

"Well we're going to fix that." His reply was sincere as he set the tray on her lap.

Josie tried to display proper manners and eat slowly but for the life of her she couldn't. She gulped the food down with vigorous ambition throwing all manners to the wayside. The food tasted wonderful. When her tray was empty she told Christian exactly that. Once her belly was full she found herself sleepy and had trouble keeping her eyes open. It was daylight out yet she couldn't understand what was wrong with her.

Christian sat watching her expressions, growing more and more worried with each passing moment. Unlike earlier that day, she now had developed black marks beneath each eye and across the bridge of her nose. He knew the marks weren't there when he bathed her earlier.

"Josie, I've purchased you some pajamas, or whatever women call them. I'd like to help you into them and tuck you in for the night."

She nodded and weakly complied not seeming to mind the fact that he saw her nearly naked. Once done, he covered her up and turned to leave. There were a few things he needed to do before the day was done.

"Christian?" Josie whispered weakly.

"Yeah sweetheart?" The endearment came naturally.

"You won't leave me will you?"

"Never. I promise. Now you just get some sleep." With that Josie was out. Her body was trying to fight a battle and recover from its battered state.

Christian decided the things he had to do weren't that important and began cleaning up the main room. He began picking Josie's old clothes up off the floor where he had dropped them earlier and remembered her story. Reaching into the pocket of her skirt he pulled out a cluster of folded bills. Turning, he threw the old skirt into the trash bucket atop the shoes and stockings he'd tossed there earlier. Next, he put her hard earned money into the pocket of the new mint colored dress he bought for her. She'll look beautiful in this he thought. Returning to the bedroom he sat for hours just looking at Josie and watching her breathe memorizing the softness of her features. Falling more and more in love with her with each passing minute. Yet, he didn't recognize it as love, he recognized it as need. He needed her. That was all he knew.

He would route a letter to the judge tomorrow morning explaining the entire weeks events and ask that he come to town and organize a trial. The judge was two days away and he was certain he'd have Randall Hurley in custody by then. He had to get this over and done with fast for he was having a difficult time controlling his own emotions. He tried to never get personally involved with any case. With this young chit, it was neigh impossible. For some unexplainable reason he found he was unable to control his emotions. He was overly protective of Josie and drawn to her like flies to pie at a picnic. Christian fell asleep late that night on the hard floor near the fireplace. His dreams however were haunted replays of Randy hurting Josie. Repeating nightmares that had him blustering in his sleep.

Josie woke in a sweaty panic. It was hard to breathe for the room felt stifling hot. Her body ached all over and her head was pounding with the worst headache she'd ever felt in her life. Her bedclothes clung to her damp skin. Lying still for a moment she looked around slowly remembering where she was and what had happened. The effort caused her head to throb even worse. She stared at the wood beams planking the ceiling overhead. Her stomach knotted tighter. She silently directed herself to lie still and breathe evenly hoping she'd feel better in a few moments. After inhaling several shaky breaths she began to relax a little. She must have had a bad dram although she couldn't remember dreaming. Turning her head to the side she peered out the one small pained window in the room, into the darkness beyond. Closing her eyes she began thinking how she was cushioned in Christian's bed. She inhaled his scent for it smelled like him with a pleasant wooded spicy aroma. Opening her eyes she looked out the window once more. Warnings of shocked alert fired to every nerve in her body. She had to be seeing things. It was only her imagination, she was sure of it. She squeezed her eyes tightly shut and then opened them again. The frightening image was still there. It was Randy. He was watching her through the rustic little window. She knew that mean ugly face all too well. Gone was her security. Gone was her mental stability. Gone was the safe nest of comfort she had spent hours reveling in. Her chest tightened to the point of pain. She could no longer breathe rationally. Every breath was a painful movement as her chest muscles fought for up and down movement.

"Go away." She rasped as she reached blindly for something to throw at the window. Her efforts proved worthless when he disappeared with the thought. Josie painfully pushed the blankets off and swung her legs over the side of the bed groaning as pain rippled through her midsection. Her mind was working fast. Weapons. She wanted a gun. She needed protection. She had that blinding need to physically harm Randall Hurley before he did more harm to her or anyone else for that matter. Walking painfully across the room thinking more clearly now that she was upright; she searched her surroundings. The glowing embers from the dying fire lit the main area just enough to rob the shadows of their darkness. She saw Christian's blanket covered form lying on the floor and scanned the room for his gun-belt. Where was it? She had seen it earlier. She had to find it. She stepped closer to the fire and looked around again, her heart drummed rapid beats against the walls of her chest.

"Where are the guns?" She whispered frantically to herself. "Where are the guns?" Where are the guns? Where are the guns?" Her words were spoken louder with each question repeated again and again until finally her voice was shrill and panicked. "Where are the guns? Where are the guns?"

Christian jumped at Josie's fear filled voice. Instantly he was up and at her side wrapping strong solid arms around her trembling form, engulfing her with his strength. "Why do you need the guns Josie?" He tried to calm her by whispering in a low even tone. Josie was acting crazy, like she had lost her mind. Perhaps the blow to her head did cause permanent damage. If figured he'd fall for a lady that had lost her wits.

Her voice was now heightened and shaky. "I need the guns because Randy is outside. He was watching me through the window." Even her movements were fear filled and agitated. The blind panic in her voice wrenched at his heart. He believed her. She wasn't crazy just frightened out of her mind. Christian's body stiffened as anger hit him full force. Damn, how could he be such a fool? Randall Hurley was more unpredictable than anyone could imagine.

He guided Josie to the rocking chair in the corner of the room greatly concerned with her being out of bed. "Now you just sit here sweetheart and don't move."

He hurried to put his boots on and grabbed his gun-belt off the floor by where he had been sleeping. He checked the revolvers for bullets by taking one finger and spinning the metal drum above the trigger. The sound seemed to sooth Josie.

"I'll be right back." He told her as he lightly brushed a kiss upon her forehead. "Don't unlatch this door for anyone. If it's me, I'll knock three times fast, and then three times slow. Got that?"

She shook her head up and down in silent answer and wrung her hands together while rocking back and forth impatiently.

Rising to his full height he soundlessly stepped across the room and left to check around the cabin's exterior. If Randy were out there he'd leave a trail. It'd be easy enough to find in the daylight but right now he had to make sure the guy was gone. His eyes searched the darkness as he examined every shadow. There were a lot of places for a person to hide both near town and within the surrounding woods. There were so many shadows and shapes it was hard to discern one object from the other. An uneasy feeling remained with him as he continued to the opposite side of the cabin. There was nothing there. Randy was gone. Just like that the uneasy feeling disappeared. One more trip around and he felt certain the outlaw had retrieved back into the woods. He'd have the guys search and follow the trail tomorrow.

Josie sat in the chair attempting to calm her own self. What had gotten into her? She leaned forward holding her head in her hands. Her stomach coiled tightly with the movement and suddenly she had another problem. Quickly running for the door briefly forgetting the aches an pains just moving caused, she fumbled with the latch before finally swinging it open and completely disregarding Christian's instructions to stay put.

His silhouette came into view as she covered her mouth with one hand roughly pushing past him. Stepping onto the porch with bare feet she swung to the side and fell to her hands and knees. While tremors wracked her body and seat beaded her temples, Josie heaved again and again. She lost her dinner ungraciously over the side of the porch and into the damp grass below. In the back of her mind she was remotely embarrassed yet Christian's hand gently rubbed the small of her back and offered a world of much needed comfort.

Moments later her body calmed and she wiped away the tears in her eyes. Sitting on the edge of the porch Christian wrapped his arms around her once more and pulled her exhausted body back to rest against his chest. Placing his chin on top of her hair he talked in a mellow tone calming and rocking her to sleep once more. He soothed and rocked until the sun peeked over the treetops and the birds began to sing their songs of promise to anyone that would listen.

CHAPTER FOUR

The sun was high in the sky the next day when Josie received a visit from the Old Doc. Her first impression matched Christian's referral of the doctor one hundred percent. The man was old. It took him a long time to work his way across the room. Josie quickly learned that although he was slow and moved like a snail, Old Doc has a very strong voice and an opinionated mind to match. His first insightful words to her were, "What the hell happened to you? You fall off the back of a wagon train?"

Josie giggled. She couldn't help but instantly like the man.

"Hmm." The Doc speculated. "Must have addled her brain, let's take a closer look shall we?"

Josie sat very still while he looked into her eyes with a light, felt the back of her head, checked her pulse and took her temperature. He then continued to examine her ribs, her feet, her hands and her belly with cold calloused and speckled hands.

"Well?" Asked Christian who sat patiently off to the side. "Is she going to be alright?"

"Of course she's going to be alright boy. What's wrong with you? Can't you see she's tough as a fiddle?"

Josie giggled again but when Christian shot her an exasperated look she burst out laughing holding her arms over her rib cage to minimize the pain.

"And in good spirits too." The Doc added. "She's got a very serious concussion which may be the culprit that caused her to get sick last night." He turned back to Josie. "I recommend you don't get out of bed without help young lady. You'll be dizzy for several days. You also have a couple of cracked ribs best as I can tell. That'll take a while to heal. Now there's not much we can do for them there ribs other than wrap your midsection real tight. I'll leave you some powder to mix with your drink at night. It'll help you sleep. You'll need to stay in bed for at least three days. Doctors orders mind you, young lady." This was said while shaking a speckled finger in Josie's direction. "I expect you know how to follow directions." Piercing her with a threatening glare he added. "Oh and eat more. Dear God girl you're as thin as a piece of licorice, wind will blow you away next time a good storm comes through."

Christian stood and pulled a bill from his pocket. "Thanks Doc." He said in a voice filled with concern while handing over the money.

"What's wrong with you boy?" The Doc replied again. "I can't take money from the town's Sheriff. I might get arrested or something." With that the old man winked slyly at Josie and slowly took his leave shuffling to the door while mumbling something comical about the sheriff when he was young.

When the door finally shut behind him Josie giggled out loud once more. Christian stood looking exasperated which made everything seem even funnier. The expression on his face was the same as one would find on a lost and helpless puppy.

"What are you giggling at?" Laughter danced in his own blue eyes as he strolled nimbly towards her.

"Oh nothing much, I just think he's cute that's all." She smiled up at him as he sat on the edge of the bed.

Christian was beside himself. All he could think of was how beautiful her smile was. Her bottom lip was slightly fuller than the top. Perfect for kissing, he thought.

"Uh, Christian what's wrong? Do I have dirt on my face or something?" Josie began to fret nervously and sat up straighter adjusting her nightgown at the neck. Yet he continued to stare.

"I was just wondering how the hell you can think of Old Doc as cute?" He replied in a husky but questioning voice as their eyes locked and he slowly inched closer to her, his hands sank into the mattress with the movement. Looking into her eyes he felt a force he had no desire to resist. His lips caressed her so briefly and so softly that Josie wasn't sure the kiss even happened.

Was this really the way a kiss should be? She wondered for her eyes were shut yet she strongly sensed that he was waiting for something, perhaps a signal from her, some sign or movement that would assure him the attraction was reciprocated. This was too much as his face was merely inches from her own. She could feel his warm breath mixing with the very air she breathed. Opening her eyes she met his gaze and ran her hands up his back to rest them atop his shoulders. She felt the smoothness of his muscles beneath her palms and shamelessly wished his shirt were off, then she began to run her fingers softly through the hair at the nape of his neck gently messaging in an effort to touch and feel the man before her.

Breaking the silence with a smile she asked. "What's wrong with you boy?" Her words crackled and her voice mimicked Old Doc's. "That's no kiss. That's a peck. I'd like a real kiss please." Nodding she pulled his head towards her and found no resistance as Christian was more than happy to comply.

This time, when their lips met Josie knew she was being kissed senseless. As their tongues danced, a pleasing tightness rippled through her body. Not realizing what she was doing, she pressed closer to Christian releasing a delicate moan as her nipples felt his body through the thin fabric of her gown. Christian brought one hand up to cup a firm breast causing pleasure to wash over her in fluid waves. She dissolved even further into him.

He couldn't believe how willing Josie was to be touched. It was as if she melted in his arms. Her breasts felt tight and firm as his thumb brushed back and forth across her nipple causing it to pucker and harden. He became thoroughly aroused and nearly lost control wanting only to bury himself inside Josie. He could hardly catch his breath and had to gasp for air as the kiss deepened further.

What was he thinking? Her poor body had to hurt. The thought had the effect of cold water splashing on his face. It doused his control and brought his senses back to reality. He gently pulled away groaning with frustration as he did so.

"Oh no, what'd I do? Christian please don't stop. I like kissing." Josie pleaded in her innocence as a tingling sensation flushed throughout her body.

Oh sweet heaven the little imp liked kissing! He ran his fingers through his hair trying to think straight. He couldn't think straight for her words only enticed him more. "Honey look at you. You're all black and blue. I know you hurt. I just don't want to hurt you worse. Not to mention the fact that we've only known each other for two days!" His frustration continued to build as his body was denied release. He wanted her in ways he never wanted any other woman before. He couldn't help but visualize all the promising positions he could place her in. His muscles tightened and he snapped his knuckles for control.

"But it didn't hurt. I promise."

Christian didn't know what to say so he simply turned and left. He had to get some air and cool down. He had to place some distance between him and Josie, or else he'd do something he'd surely regret on the morrow. Lord knew if he stayed in the room with her another minute he'd roughly rip her clothes off and devour her like yesterdays dessert. He was very close to losing control of his functions. Just two days! He'd known her for less than two days and she had him wrapped around her little finger. He'd grovel at her feet if he could just bury himself deep within her core. He had to stop thinking these thoughts right now. Perhaps a good swim in the river would help cool him down.

Christian stayed away as much as possible the next few days. His intentions were to allow Josie time to heal while sorting out his own feelings. He posted the best men he had to serve as guards around and near the cabin, making certain Josie was protected and watched at all times. He had a tremendous amount of work to do and a judge due to arrive by stagecoach any day now. Neb Hurley hadn't improved much but was still alive and held under lock and key at the jailhouse. He was seen to several times each day by both Old Doc and Hanna. Old Doc grumbled and complained about the conditions in which he had to treat his jailhouse patient yet reported improvement each and every day. It was a miracle and nothing short of it he claimed.

Christian's goal was to catch Randy Hurley quickly, have Neb Hurley recover and hopefully the two brothers could be tried as the same hearing. He knew it was a long stretch but it was a plan nonetheless.

Josie was hurt and confused by Christian's behavior and obvious effort to stay away but found that she had to concentrate on healing and getting better. Hanna stopped by every day after work and brought her some leftovers from the restaurant for nourishment. Her visits were brief yet Josie looked forward to them whole-heartedly. Their friendship flourished rapidly and she began to think of Hanna as the sister she never had. She loved her dearly. And she swore, the green beans from the restaurant were the best she'd ever had. Through Hanna, Josie learned who everyone in town was, what farms or establishments they owned, and caught up on all the gossip, which she had never took part in before. However, being new to a town and stuck in a bed made the gossip kind of story like and fun. She did feel guilty and promise never to repeat any of it once she was out and about.

As the hours blended into days Josie's bruises faded to a dull yellowish color and her body began to regain energy. On the third day in bed Josie decided she couldn't stand the idleness any longer. She had grown grouchy and bored without any activity to keep her mind busy. Christian was off working and not speaking to her. She had long ago quit wondering what she had done to offend and cause him to stay away from his own home. Hanna wouldn't be by until evening time and Josie swore she'd go mad if she didn't get up and move her aching muscles and stiff limbs. Since there was no one inside the cabin to monitor her, she decided to go against the doctor's orders and do some cleaning. Although Christian did a fair job at picking up after himself, the place needed a good scrubbing. Besides, she thought, it was the least she could do to pay him back for his hospitality and kindness. After all, hadn't he been staying away from his own home to accommodate her? She really didn't know what she had done wrong and what had transpired between her and Christian was the one secret she would not share with Hanna. So, before she got better and left to go stay somewhere on her own, the least she could do was something nice for Christian as a way not only to say thank you but to apologize as well. She hoped he would appreciate it.

Mamma always said to do unto others, as you would want them to do unto you. Feeling somewhat comforted by the thought she began with the bedroom. She thoroughly dusted, removed cobwebs and scrubbed the wood floors on her hands and knees working until her fingers were raw and her nails dry and cracked. Her movements were slow but consistent for determination powered her soul as she hummed a bouncy tune. Her aching ribs caused a moderate amount of pain but the overwhelming urge to move and be useful won the battle within, silently urging her to continue. Once the bedroom was complete she began sweeping and cleaning the main room. The repeated strokes of the broom caused tiny dust particles to float in the air, only noticeable where the sun streamed in through the windows and cracks in the walls. Tomorrow she would wash and hang the bed linens as a final touch.

By evening time the little cabin owned by Sheriff C was shining and sparkling like new. It smelled of fresh cedar and the floors were clean enough to eat off of. Josie however looked and felt exactly the opposite. She had been fine all afternoon but for some reason she was extremely exhausted now. Pain hit her chest and stomach in fitful bouts allowing her no reprieve from its grip. She swallowed her powder in her drink per Old Doc's orders. She could hardly take a deep breath as she wondered back off to the bedroom easing her sore body onto the bed and falling into a deep slumber the moment her head hit the feathered pillow.

Hanna arrived with scrumptious smelling soup shortly after and walked in eagerly looking forward to a good chat with her new friend. She was surprised by the cleanliness of the cabin and knew instantly that Josie had performed the miraculous deed. Concern overcame her surprise when Josie failed to respond to her coaxing tone and little pokes and prods. Leaving the soup on the night table she resolved to covering her friend with a blanket. Nodding to the gentleman posted on the porch as guard, she hurried down the steps to the edge of the street. She was more than a little worried now. She was downright upset. Josie had worked all day and no one noticed or said anything, which meant she could have been hurt or kidnapped by that terrible outlaw and no one would be the wiser until nightfall, until her visit for crying out loud! What good did it do to post watchmen if the watchmen didn't watch? Well…she was miffed to say the least.

Entering the gloomy staleness of the jail, Hanna let the door slam loudly behind her. The sound vibrated throughout the room. The Sheriff had his feet propped and legs crossed on the edge of the desk yet swung them lazily aside upon her fashionable entrance. He looked just as tired as Josie did with stress lines lightly drawn across his features and dark circles beneath his eyes. This piqued her curiosity. What was really going on between the Sheriff and Josie? Although Josie hadn't come right out and said anything she could tell the girl was taken with the handsome sheriff. Then Hanna was struck with a wonderful idea. If her gut instincts were correct, instead of lecturing the Sheriff on his poor treatment and absent-mindedness of Josie's care, she would simply voice her concerns and allow fate to take over. If he was really and truly smitten with little Josie he'd go home right away and all would be fine. After all, there was nothing wrong with a little meddling was there?

"Hanna." Curtly nodding Sheriff C stood and removed his hat. "What brings you here? Is there trouble at the restaurant?"

"No." She replied flatly than looked him straight in the eyes and tossed out the bait. "I just saw Josie and quite frankly she didn't look good. In fact she was too exhausted to visit with me this evening, wouldn't eat, wouldn't even wake up. Something's very wrong." She projected her words mystically, enabling them to hang inexplicably in the air. Then she covered her mouth with her hand to hide a smirk of satisfaction as the Sheriff grabbed his hat, jumped over the desk and literally ran past her to exit. She stood by the door laughing and feeling giddy as Sheriff C's silhouette meshed with the darkness.

After a few moments her smile faded to a thin line as she noticed Neb Hurley's still form lying on one of the cell benches. Slowly and cautiously she approached the wrought iron door to the cell. His coloring was a pale cream yet his features were so strikingly handsome it took her breath away. Starring passionately at his face she had to remind herself to breathe. It was obvious that Old Doc had been there treating his injury, skillfully picking up where Josie had left off. The big guy hadn't moved a muscle in days setting the folks around town to wondering what the judge would rule. How could any civilized person hang a man that wasn't even conscious? Perhaps he would never fully recover from his injury. Perhaps he would die. Longing for the ability to see into the future Hanna decided then and there to bring hot soup to Neb Hurley on the morrow. After all, good and bad folks alike had to eat. Folks that were hurt needed more nourishment than those that weren't. That was a fact she knew from experience. Swishing her skirt she did an about face and marched from the room locking the door behind her, knowing the Sheriff would have done the same had his head been on straight.

Christian's long strides led him home in no time yet it seemed to take forever. It was amazing how many thoughts could go through one person's head in such a short period of time. Before his footsteps landed upon the cabin's front porch his heart was beating erratically and his stomach was turning summersaults while his mind spiraled through a tunnel of emotions, each one causing his imagination to grow more and more fierce. Seeing the man he had asked to stand guard sleeping soundly on the porch swing only caused his apprehension to flourish. Clearing his throat he towered over Angus and peered angrily down at him.

"Ahem."

With a startled jump Angus sat up. Embarrassment quickly burned his features a bright red visible even in the darkness.

"Go home Angus. You're worthless when you're tired." Anger drifted just beneath the surface of the Sheriff's gruffly controlled voice. In a dismissing motion he turned to go inside.

He knew immediately upon entering that his home had been cleaned and polished from roof to floor. There was no fire in the hearth or candles glow to aid his vision yet his sense of smell was assailed by the overwhelming aroma of soap and pine. With his nerves on edge he made his way through the dark to the bedroom. Lighting a candle he placed it on a table near the window. One look at Josie was like swallowing a shot of green whiskey. It burned fierce yet calmed his senses at the same time. She had apparently worn herself out by working too hard. A glance around the two rooms confirmed his suspicions. The place was clean that was for sure. It also had Josie's touch to it now. Her presence seemed to envelope every inch in some small way. Some objects were moved and a few pieces of his hand made furniture were placed around the rooms differently. Rugs from the porch had been laid in front of the hearth and doorway giving the cabin interior a warm cozy affect. Adding to it was the dog curled up in the rocking chair, which now faced the fireplace and had a folded quilt hanging over its high back.

So, he thought to himself, this is what it would be like coming home to Josie every day. It was an unexpected thought, for Christian usually found women to be insensible and expensive. He tolerated them because his proper upbringing demanded so and they had the ability to relieve his sexual tension from time to time. Yet Josie was different. She was spirited, strong and caring. Most of all, she felt good in his arms. Shaking his head he decided it was nonsense. He didn't believe in love at first sight. Hell, he had only known the girl for a few days now. There was no way he could determine her character in such a short amount of time. Furthermore, why did he care? He didn't. His brain was addled, he reassured himself, because she was the maiden he happened to rescue. This he surmised while pulling the quilted blanket off the back of the rocking chair and spreading it over the floor at the foot of the bed. He didn't know why but he felt an uncanny need to be in the same room with her tonight. His thoughts were jumbled as he drifted off only to rise at the crack of dawn. He was on his way to work before Josie woke to face another day.

"Morning Angus." Josie said to the gentleman posted on the porch. Opening the door all the way she let Hops out and allowed a deep breath of fresh air to permeate the belly of her lungs.

"Ah Ms. Josie, I have specific orders from the Sheriff today." He replied a little chagrined. "You're not to be working and cleaning like you did yesterday or the Sheriff will have my hide, said so himself."

She saw a brief flush pale the coloring of his skin before looking down. His refusal to look her in the eyes became clear. She was temporarily awed by the thickness of his mustache. It was kind of funny looking. Giggling she assured him. "Don't worry Mr. Angus. I'm only washing the sheets and sweeping the porch today." At his dismayed glare she added. "I'm worse than the Sheriff you know." Raising an eyebrow and trying to look her meanest she continued. "I'll not only have your hide, I'll box your ears first." At that she flippantly went back inside to get ready for the day and cause Angus as much grief as possible.

Later as she was sweeping the porch she heard a commotion further down the main street. "What's that?" She asked Angus.

"Stagecoach. Must be the judge."

Josie watched the stage's grand entrance from a distance somewhat excited because she'd never seen one before. The towns' people quickly gathered around on the boardwalk eagerly waiting for the dust to settle. Their chattering voices could be heard from afar catching every onlooker's attention. She couldn't imagine why folks would want to gather around for the ground had dried up a lot the last few days and dust kicked up everywhere. The entire ordeal was quite messy.

Millie hissed and complained about the miserable journey non-stop. Why, they had been halfway across that stupid planked road when another horse and wagon approached. Since the road was wide enough to allow passage of only one wagon or coach at a time, they had to unload their belongings and stand knee deep in mud alongside the planked road while the driver steered the coach off the road into that muddy trench next to it. They couldn't quit the planked road while the wagon was fully loaded for fear that it would sink because the load was too heavy. Once the other wagon had passed they were able to reload and continue on. When she voiced her opinion on the matter the driver reminded her that this was a pretty decent spot for the paths to cross. Some areas had mud so deep it could swallow a person whole, never to be seen again.

Still the episode put her in a foul mood that failed to improve even an ounce during the last two days of the journey. She hated traveling. The inside of the coach was filthy. She doubted the upholstery had ever been cleaned. Their fellow travelers hadn't bathed in weeks, possibly even months. The ride was rough and the air was stagnant. It was an awful way to travel. She'd rather ride on horseback but father had insisted that this was easier. The only reason she agreed to come along with her father to this God forsaken territory was because of the tall handsome Sheriff C. She wanted the Sheriff as a husband and Millie McQuade always got what she wanted. Her mother had seen to that. Pressing at her curls with gloved hands she prepped her hair and straightened the pleats of her brown travel dress before pinching her cheeks for color.

Moving to exit once they were completely stopped the coachman awaited with his chubby hand held high, ready to assist her down onto the dirt packed street.

"Don't touch me you imbecile." She snapped.

The coachman, seeming the least bit perturbed, returned to the front to unload the tower of travel cases.

With great effort she placed her best smile upon her face and turned to the Sheriff. In a sultry voice she lightly spoke. "Why Sheriff I didn't even see you there. Would you mind helping a lady down?"

Holding out her hand and batting her eyelashes offered Christian no other alternative lest he make a spectacle of himself. Gritting his teeth he stepped forward. Her voice sawed through each and every one of his nerves. Millie was a fill-in schoolteacher a few towns south, hoping to have her own class in the future. He felt sorry for the children that had to sit in one room and listen to her whiney voice all day long. Once her feet were planted firmly on the ground he began to pull away but she refused to let go clasping his elbow firmly and pressing her partially exposed bosom into his upper arm. He hated it when Charles brought his daughter with him.

Following in Millie's steps, Judge Charles McQuade stepped from the coach forcing Millie to release the Sheriff's arm or suffer her father's wrath.

"Christian my boy!" He exclaimed while hugging and patting Christian's back like one would a son. "Truly it's good to see you."

Christian nodded while breaking the embrace and stepping back. "It's good to see you too sir. We've got lots to talk about. Shall we visit the restaurant first and allow you lunch and a moments rest?"

Once again Millie took advantage of the opportunity and pressed against the Sheriff as they walked across the street. She sashayed her hips provocatively and focused on stealing the man's heart.

"Humph." Josie exhaled placing her hands on her hips and squaring her shoulders in a defiant gesture. She was a little more than miffed by what she had just witnessed. That strawberry blonde hussy was hanging all over her Christian. Well what did she expect? There she stood berating herself. A man as good-looking as Christian was bound to have women aplenty, swooning over him everywhere he went. That particular woman just happened to be beautiful and surely never did an honest days work in all her life. Josie was certain she couldn't even compare. Suddenly she felt ashamed and belittled. What a fool she had been. No wonder Christian pulled away from her the other day. No wonder he had ignored her and remained absent. Goodness, she had nearly acted like a harlot. Here he had beautiful women hanging on his side on a regular basis! Josie's cheeks turned bright red at the thought and depression took over. Between that and her sore body she felt terribly miserable.

When Hanna came for her customary visit once the restaurant closed for the evening she was in a sour mood as well. One look at Josie and she silently put her own worries aside in order to comfort her friend. Josie looked pathetically depressed and worn down. In fact, Hanna thought she looked as if she needed a hug. And so she sat on the side of the bed and pulled her friend towards her. This also helped to settle her dower apathy as well. She could feel Josie trembling.

"Shhh. Go ahead sweetie. Let it out." Hanna cooed in a warm caring voice.

A few softly spoken words were all it took before the damn holding back the tears suddenly crumbled and Josie wept uncontrollably, her body racked by heavy sobs. She cried over her Mamma's death and that of the baby. She cried remembering her encounter with Randy Hurley and the brutality she had suffered at his hands. She cried for Neb and his injury along with the harm they most likely caused others. She cried for herself and the uncertainty of her future but most of all she cried because her heart was broken.

When her tears were spent at last she pulled away from her friend noting the large wet stain her tears had left upon the shoulder of Hanna's blouse. Trying to apologize she suddenly began to laugh instead for she now felt foolish. She should be counting her blessings rather than crying over them. After all, a lot of good things had come out of this crazy brained journey she had traveled. She had made a new friend and gained a faithful pet. Expressing her thoughts to Hanna they both began to feel much better.

Hanna explained about her problems. "I've had a terrible day too thanks to that no good Millie McQuade. I was running around like a chicken with its head cut off. I swear that girl is never happy, always complaining she is. I often wonder if she ever gives herself a headache. Lord knows she causes plenty of them!"

"Who is Millie McQuade?"

"Why she's Judge McQuade's daughter. They arrived just this afternoon. I have to tell you Josie; she has her eye on our Sheriff. Funny thing is he can barely stand her." Hanna stood and peered out the tiny window gazing at the stars.

"Is she the pretty lady that got off the stagecoach?"

"Josie honey the woman would only be pretty to a man if she were a mute." Hanna nodded as if to finalize her statement and placed her hands on her hips. "Once she finds out our Sheriff has an adorable young lady coddled under his roof she'll be blowing in for a visit like a tornado. You just wait and see."

"Are you sure Christian can't stand her?" Josie's wrinkled forehead and pouty lips portrayed her doubt.

"Let's put it this way honey, he'll be sleeping here tonight. I guarantee it. He'll probably be home early too." At that both girls laughed together and bid farewell until the next day.

To Josie's relief Hanna was right. Christian did come home early and Josie's heart felt as if it had wings. Although he seemed somewhat stressed and appeared a touch peeved, she was determined to prove herself good company.

While he relaxed in the rocking chair warming by the fire, Josie snuck out onto the back porch. There she lifted one of the wood boards planking the deck and lowered a bucket down into the hole beneath. Once the bucket filled with water it became a heavy burden for her to struggle with. It certainly didn't help any that it had a few small holes in it. Pulling on the rope she hefted the bucket to the fireplace trying to cover the holes with her fingers as she did so. Then poured the murky water into the boiling pot.

"What are you doing?" Christian bellowed startling her as she was pouring, causing her to spill some of the water over her bare feet.

"I was heating water for your bath."

He was dumbfounded and unsure of what to say. Every time he turned around she surprised him with yet another eager display of kindness. So, he simply settled for a thank you. Walking up behind her he stilled her movements by grabbing her wrist and taking the bucket from her hands. "Josie please." He paused and swallowed causing his Adam's apple to bounce. "Sit down. I'll finish getting the bath ready. You can go first. I have to feed the horse and dog. I'll also burn the smudge pot. You can have a little privacy." His words were soft and filled with kindness.

"Wha...what about you?" Her uncertainty wavered in the air.

"I'll bring in more water and bathe when you're done." Noting that she still wore the nightgown he had given her four days prior, he remembered the mint green dress and shoes. He smiled and attractive wrinkle lines tweaked the corners of his eyes. Suddenly he was happy and full of energy announcing unexpectedly, "I have a gift for you."

"A gift?" She nearly yelped. "I've never gotten a gift before. What is it?" Lithely jumping up and down she clapped her hands in front of her displaying the same excitement one would expect from a child on Christmas Eve.

"Well now it's a surprise. When we're both finished cleaning up I'll give it to you." He couldn't help but smile at her behavior. When she gave another yelp he laughed and added. "Only if you're a good girl."

"Oh, pox on you. I'm always good." Thus she smiled and started shoving him on his way earnestly hoping he would hurry.

Once she was done she waited in the bedroom offering the same privacy given her. Upon hearing his voice she sprung from the bed and pestered him in a joking manner.

"Okay, Okay." Christian cried once she began tickling his midsection. "I'll give it to you." As she sat in the rocking chair he handed her a long narrow box while hiding the other behind his back. "Go on." He urged just as excited now as she was. "Open it." He couldn't wait to see her reaction. He wanted to see her smile. He wanted so badly to make her happy. He suddenly realized that making her happy would ultimately make him happy. He'd never had that with any other woman before and he silently wondered what was happening to him.

She swallowed hard removing the box lid gently before placing it on the floor next to the chair. As soon as she saw the dress her eyes became huge and her sudden intake of breath broke the silence that had settled over the room. She didn't pull the dress out of the box right away as Christian had expected. Instead she sat there balancing the box on her lap, stilled by a wave of emotion. Her fingers gently caressed the fabric and circled the smooth delicate buttons stitched down the front. The dress was so beautiful she could hardly believe it was for her. She had always sewn her own clothes and any garments not hand made were usually given to them by neighbors or friends. Hand me downs from one generation to the next. Finally she stood pulling the dress from the box letting its length tumble to the floor. Holding it beneath her chin she swung around watching the flare of material span wide as she twirled. It was like a fairy tale dream come true. Truly she felt like a princess and she hadn't even put it on yet. "Oh Christian it's absolutely lovely."

Producing the smaller box he added. "One more."

Josie stopped spinning about and held her breath. Folding and replacing the dress carefully back into the box it was received in; she reached out and grasped the second gift nervously before opening it. This time tears streamed down her cheeks as she removed the brown leather shoes. The sole of the shoed were thick and a laced leather pattern ran above it to form a delicate beaded design. Looking up at Christian she cried. "I can't accept these gifts. I'm sorry. They are gorgeous and I find myself unworthy." Looking to the floor she waited for his reply.

"You do yourself great injustice by thinking that you're not worthy of them. This outfit was made for you Josie. It'll break my heart if you refuse." He was met with silence causing him to fret for she still wouldn't look him in the eye.

Suddenly she jumped up on top of the rocking chair. Before the motion could throw her off balance she flung her arms around his neck and planted tiny pecking kisses all over his face. "Thank you. Thank you. Thank you." She repeated over and over again.

Oh these kinds of pecking kisses just wouldn't do. He grabbed her face with both hands and placed his mouth firmly over hers. He kissed her soundly. Her senses were on full alert and her body began to heat. He told himself that he had to maintain control. This was just a kiss. Now, he wanted a date.

Ecstatic that she would accept the gifts he pulled away slightly and placed his hand on her waist to steady her so that she wouldn't fall. "Josie, would you do me the honor of joining me for dinner tomorrow at the restaurant? Dressed in this outfit of course."

A flicker of uncertainty passed through her. She had never eaten at a restaurant before. In fact, she had never even been in one until she arrived here. What if her table manners weren't proper enough? Her eyes must have betrayed her concern for Christian smoothly reassured her.

"It'll be fun. You don't have to worry about a single thing." He could tell she still had doubts. "Don't forget, I'll be right there." As her eyebrows rose he could tell she was contemplating her answer. He smiled and added the final touch. "We'll get a big piece of apple pie for dessert."

At that Josie smiled and said, "How can a girl refuse an offer like that? I only hesitate now because I'm not certain which is better." She paused momentarily. "You or the pie. I've smelled the pie. It smelled and looked absolutely heavenly. You on the other hand…well let's just say there's room for improvement."

His head shot up and he caught the wicked little smile on her face. She was trying hard to look serious, deliberately teasing him again. "That's it." He yelled and began to chase her around the cabin while holding out his hands and wiggling his fingers. "Do you know what these are Josie?"

"No." She giggled while backing away from him circling the rocking chair.

"These," he said moving his fingers even faster, "are tickling monsters. Everything they touch they attack and tickle."

Quickly he dived catching her off guard and tickling her so thoroughly that tears formed in her eyes. Finally, he let her go so they could both catch their breath. Josie had to hug her midsection for her ribs suddenly began to smart.

"Guess it's time to call it a night." His voice sounded full of regret.

"Well yes." Josie stated flatly. "After all, if I'm to have dinner tomorrow with the handsome town Sheriff, I'll need my beauty sleep." She batted her eyes to add gesture to the joke.

He couldn't resist. "Oh come on now Josie, you'd have to sleep for a month."

"Why you!" He was teasing back and she knew it. "No good, cackle brained…" Her voice trailed off as she went to the bedroom and tucked herself in for the night.

They were both happy for it turned out to be a very pleasant evening.

CHAPTER FIVE

The following morning the sun shown bright in the blue sky spreading it's rays of warmth like a blanket heating the land. Clusters of fog hung near the ground in low lying areas clinging to clumps of bushes and high grass land, refusing to release its hold to the warmth of daybreak just yet. Josie began her day in earnest anticipation of the evening to come.

Christian had left earlier that morning taking Hops with him. He claimed he would pass the day scouting the perimeter of town and outer edge of the woods for Randy, hunting for evidence left in his wake. Josie couldn't imaging what evidence would be left. It seemed to her that most of the animals that roamed the wooded swamp at night such as; wolves, rabbits and deer, not to mention the bugs plus the weather would surely would have a hand at altering any evidence or trail Christian was looking for. His job must be very frustrating.

She spent a large portion of the morning cleaning and refused to eat anything so as not to spoil her appetite for the evening to come. She was more than a little excited and fantasized about the dinner hour the entire time she was cleaning. She couldn't help it as her imagination got the best of her. It certainly slowed her down as she was daydreaming more often than not and caught herself constantly grinning, standing still and fantasizing once more. She would simply shrug, scold herself and get back to work. Around noontime she poked her head out the cabins front door and spotted Angus sitting on the steps leading from the porch.

"Mr. Angus, would you mind if I joined you for a few minutes? I could sure use some fresh air."

"Suit yourself." He replied just before spitting onto the ground near the bottom step. Josie looked away pretending she hadn't noticed the unbecoming habit. He was purposefully trying to offend her. She couldn't blame him. She had been a little tart and ornery towards him, purely for the sake of fun. She felt they had formed a somewhat unique friendship. It was the type of friendship that was meant to befuddle, amuse and irritate each other as well as grow and flourish.

The mosquitoes and other insects were growing thicker as the season warmed and the rains increased. A buzzing noise filled the air growing louder as a small swarm neared the edge of the woods. Come evening time, the song of katydids would be heard everywhere. Josie found the music from these strange insects comforting and could sit for hours listening to it as it calmed her nerves and bounced from tree to tree. Try as she might, she could never pinpoint where the noise exactly came from, it just filled the air as if by magic.

"I'd better get the smudge pot started so ya' don't git eatin' alive." Grunting, Angus ambled up off the step returning shortly with the pot, leaving a trail of gray smoke in his wake. Once the smudge filled the air the mosquitoes thinned out and were kept at bay.

It was still early in the day but Josie was as restless as a bee in its hive. "Do you have a wife Angus?"

"Nope." He spat again then wiped his mouth on his shirtsleeve. "Ain't nobody that can stand me." His tone indicated that she should already know this.

"Why's that? I mean, what's wrong with you?" She was curious and refused to be baited. She could always see the good in people. One just had to look harder for some than others. Of that she was certain.

"Just look at me. I'm old, grouchy, hairy, ugly and I have no manners." He nodded to emphasize his point. She focused on his beard and waited for something to crawl out of it. Nothing did.

"Well." She replied after carefully contemplating his words. "You're not that old. Now look at Old Doc, that's old. As far as hair goes, it isn't anything a comb and a string of leather wouldn't fix." Shrugging her shoulders she went on. "In fact, I'd bet you'd look down right handsome with your hair pulled back and your beard combed."

"That's right nice but I still have bad manners and I'm too old to be a changin' my ways." His tone was convincing enough. He was definitely a man set in his ways. It appeared to Josie that he tried to keep folks away from him. She got the distinct impression that he didn't want anyone to get too close to him.

"I'd agree." She said enthusiastically offering her brightest smile. "There's no reason to change a big teddy bear like you. Maybe what you need is a lady that's too old to be a changin' her ways." Her quote matched his, with a little more sauce in the voice.

"I'm not talented in any way. I reckon it don't matter none." He was trying to change her opinion of him and she knew it.

"You sure do spit good." Her quick reply had them both laughing. She was in such good spirits and Angus was good company, even if he resembled a big brown bear.

When Josie re-entered the cabin she sensed right away that something was drastically wrong. Goosebumps dappled the skin of her arms and a chill trickled down the length of her spine. An ominous presence had taken over the cabins warm interior. Seeing the sunshine streaming through the wide-open back door confirmed the inner suspicions. She could have sworn she'd latched that door last night. She was certain she hadn't touched it since. In fact, she remembered dusting it earlier. Quickly she wondered if Christian had by chance unlatched it before he left but doubted he'd be that careless regarding her safety. Automatically, she began backtracking her steps, smartly making the decision not to go any further into the cabin alone. If it was Randy, she knew perfectly well what he would do to her. She could feel her body begin to shake and mentally calmed herself. Wounds that were healed suddenly began to hurt all over again. Breathing deeply she reached behind her and once more opened the front door. As she backed over the threshold she made an effort to keep her footsteps silent. Her eyes busily scanned the main room for any sign of movement.

"Angus." Her voice wavered in a loud whisper. She didn't like this one bit. As of this moment her safe little haven no longer existed. In an instant so much had been stolen. Gone was the feeling of security. The absence of that security shook her to the core. Although she hadn't taken Christian's home and protection for granted, she didn't realize until this very moment how much she actually needed it, how much she had actually gained from its comfort, and how much she actually needed him.

"Need something Josie?" Angus was standing behind her now, peering over her shoulder. The problem was evident for he immediately noticed the door and the tell tale signs that it had been pried through the crack and the latch had been lifted. He muttered a few choice words, unfit for a lady's ears, and then gave direction. "Stay close now. You hear me Josie? I need to think for just a second here."

She couldn't find her voice to talk so she nodded her head up and down instead, hoping he would understand that she was currently paralyzed with fear.

Angus found himself in quite a predicament. First off, he wondered what happened to the fella' guarding the rear of the property. It couldn't be good. Now he worried about little Josie. He couldn't very well leave her on the porch while he investigated. She would be unguarded and vulnerable. He couldn't take her inside with him while he had a look about. That'd be like stepping right smack dab into the middle of a trap. His brain kept working the scenario this way and that until finally he had a solution. Placing his back against the doorframe he whispered to her. "Okay Josie girl, this is what I want you to do. Walk down them steps quietly. When you get to the road, run like your tails on fire. Stay in the middle though and go get help from the Sheriff. Do you understand?"

Once again she nodded while gathering up the long end of the nightgown she still wore. Lifting the hem to just above her ankles she did as was told and prepared to run.

"When you get to the Sheriff's office, tell him what happened. Let em' know I'm waiting for back-up." As he spoke he pulled back on the bolt of the rifle, a loud click resounding through the air. "I'll watch you the whole way. Now git."

His nod emphasized urgency and Josie took off like lightening. Her quick light footedness was powered by fear as adrenaline rushed through her veins. She ran faster than she had ever run before. Terror fueled her speed and agility. When she reached the deck of the Sheriff's office she looked down the road to the cabin. Angus still stood in the doorway, one booted foot planted inside the cabin, the other on the porch, both hands grasping the rifle, ready to fire if need be.

Pressing down the lever on the handle with her thumb, she entered only to be disappointed. Old Doc sat in the cell tending Neb Hurley's wound. The rest of the place was empty. Her stomach clenched as an overwhelming sagacity of panic fought to take control of her senses.

Before Old Doc could mutter a word she turned and fled across the street, into the restaurant. The place was packed full with conversation so loud she could barely hear the doorbells jingle overhead. Knowing that Angus could only wait so long caused panic to briefly rule her actions. Not being able to spot Hanna she cleared her throat and yelled. "Excuse me."

Silence immediately fell upon the room. There was not an empty seat in the place and all eyes were looking expectantly at her now. Looks of grave contempt flowed from many of their faces and whispers began to ensue.

Boldly she continued. "I'm sorry to interrupt your meal folks. Um, my friend Angus is down at the Sheriff's cabin. Someone broke in and he needs help." Swallowing the lump in her throat she added for good measure. "Please."

Several men got up and immediately went to help with no questions asked. Josie once again swallowed her nausea and held her head high. A dozen or so people stubbornly remained glaring meaningfully at her. Their distrust was evident in the sheen of their eyes and the tone of conversation blooming faintly in the background. Unsure of where to go from here she politely begged their pardon, bowed and turned to leave but was halted by Hanna.

"You can't go back there Josie. It isn't safe. Follow me."

Pulling on Josie's arm Hanna silently led her to the rear of the building and down a narrow path of steep lye washed steps. Once at the bottom they were met by an even more narrow wooden door, barely large enough for a child to fit through.

"This is the old pantry." Hanna explained. "You can hide in here until we know it's safe for you to come out." Pulling open the door and stepping aside she motioned for Josie to enter. "I know it's small but not many people know it's down here. It wasn't very convenient so the owners built a new one on the main level. I'll fetch ya' as soon as I can. I'm the only one that has a key. Don't open this door for anyone Josie and you will be safe." Shaking her finger while looking into Josie's deep green eyes she continued. "If it's not me or the Sheriff, well you dare not answer."

Josie nodded then hugged her friend. "I'll stay put. I promise. I won't make a peep. Don't fret Hanna, please don't and thank you for your help. You are a true friend." She squeezed Hanna's hand as she left and then huddled onto a stool as she heard the lock click into place finalizing her time in solitude.

As she sat there in the dark her mind did nothing but wonder and worry. She was terribly concerned about Angus and Christian. She could only imagine the outcome of Randy Hurley's visit to the cabin that afternoon. What was he hoping to gain? He'd created nothing but havoc. It also proved he was still in the area. Obviously he refused to leave without his brother, but why stick around when if caught, surely the sentence would be harsh? Possibly even death. It had to be a delusional revenge he was seeking for his actions grew bolder by the day. Her biggest fear...one of these times he really would catch her. She'd have to be prepared to fight for she'd grown weary of hiding and was now fully aware that there was no safe place at all. She was convinced that even surrounded by armed guards, she'd not be safe from the likes of Randy Hurley.

She'd have to take some of her money, go to the mercantile and purchase a weapon. Something she could hide on her person but use as protection if needed. The question in her mind was, could she actually use a weapon against him if needed? She truly felt she could and that fact chilled her to the core. What kind of person had she become? At this point in time was it a need to persevere? Or was she simply full of hate? She sent a prayer up to the good Lord for guidance in this matter for she was more confused than ever. She was full of doubt and questions that she simply didn't have answers for at this point in time and sitting alone in this little room only made her think about things more and more. It certainly didn't seem to help matters any.

Feeling even more like the victim she sighed placing her elbows on her knees, resting her chin upon fisted hands. The hours slowly crept by while she developed ideas to help aid her in the upcoming yet predictable battle for freedom from Randy Hurley. She plotted, planned and relived each nightmarish moment in his company until she could think no more and did nothing short of give herself a headache.

The sound of the door opening startled her as a stream of soft amber light filtered in from the top of the stairway. "Josie honey, it's me."

"Christian." She jumped up as the door opened all the way and flew into his arms once she clearly recognized his tall silhouette.

He held her close as if to reassure himself she was unharmed but Josie would have none of it. She had been confined to that small pantry for too long. The narrow stairway did aught to relieve her willfulness for open space and fresh air. Pushing her way past Christian she stormed up the steps muttering angry words of hatred toward Randy with each and every stomp of her feet.

"Why that no good…" Stomp. Stomp. "Pot bellied…" Stomp. Stomp. "Brainless…" Stomp. "Gutless." Stomp. Stomp. "TURD!"

Yanking open the door leading outside she deeply inhaled fresh air filling her lungs to capacity while placing her hands on her hips. The sun was just beginning to fade turning the sky into a beautiful array of yellows, pinks, oranges and blues. Standing still she shut her eyes and continued to breath deeply. Then turning to Christian she said. "The good Lord sure did create a beautiful world. It's too bad it's tarnished with rats like Randy. Randy the rat, that suits him just fine." She nodded and spun around on her bare heel. "When I get my hands on that dung filled ox I'm going to…" She thought hard. "Kick him in the shins. That's what I'm going to do."

Christian couldn't help but laugh. She was definitely spirited, like a fireball in the night. "Come on Josie girl, let's get ready for dinner." Reaching for her hand he clasped it and pulled her along the back trail to the cabin, chuckling as she continued to mutter all kinds of names to describe Randy Hurley. There was the main thoroughfare through town, and the walkway to all the establishments out front, but behind all the shops and buildings were back trails. These trails allowed folks an alternate route without walking through the mud that usually encrusted the main road thanks to all the horses as well as the sheer amount of foot traffic.

They found that the cabin was once again spotless and the back door now had several planks of wood nailed across it, guaranteed reinforcement against another foul attempt.

The first thing Josie noticed as she approached the bedroom was that the pretty little paned window had been boarded shut as well. Anger instantly embedded itself in the core of her being. Returning to the main room she approached Christian.

"I refuse to live like this." His back was to her and she saw his broad shoulders stiffen at her words. "Perhaps you should take me to jail and lock me up." Her voice was filled with bitterness.

"I wouldn't wish to do that." A blatant reply, as if she should know better.

"You may as well. I feel like a prisoner, smell like one too."

Christian would have offered comfort but he himself was too upset. Josie didn't seem to comprehend the seriousness of the situation. His home had been violated and she was in great danger. "Tom Hawkins, the man posted to guard the rear of the cabin, was found dead Josie. His throat had been sliced." He really didn't want to tell her the gory details but she needed to hear it. It was for her own good he demised as her face visibly paled. Hopefully she wouldn't swoon. No. Not his Josie. She was too strong for that.

"He left behind a wife and four children to fend for themselves." He was shaking now. "Angus was assaulted, hit on the head and knocked out cold. You were very lucky, circumstances being as they were, that you were on the front porch when Randall came in. I'm certain if he had gotten his hands on you, well, it wouldn't have been pretty Josie. And...you were very smart to back out right away. Angus told me all about it."

She winced automatically placing her hand over the egg-sized lump that still protruded from the back of her head. Poor Angus, she thought, knowing exactly what he was feeling right now. "I...I'm sorry. This is all my fault." Blinking back tears she realized that only one thing would help the situation. She had to leave before others got hurt as well. The hard working people of this town didn't need all this trouble. The trouble she had brought with her upon her arrival. Folks had been killed because of her. Children has lost their father because of her. She had to make it right for she owed them nothing less.

"Where's my horse?" She asked.

"Oh no you're not Josie. You are not leaving." Anger flashed in his eyes.

He could read her thoughts too easily causing her to fidget where she stood. "I didn't say I was leaving. I just want to know where my horse is." Lifting her chin she stood her ground feeling every inch the woman that she was for his eyes raked her up and down lighting fires in their wake.

"I'll hog tie you to my side if I have to. You will remain here under my protection. Is that clear?" He was filled with rage and venting on her yet he couldn't stop himself. She was acting like a fool and too damn stubborn to admit it.

Refusing to speak she stood crossing her arms defiantly in front of her midsection, tapping her foot in irritation. She was not a prisoner and refused to be trapped because of some stupid ox's evilness.

Finding his patience wearing thin Christian snapped. "Look, you can forget about dinner tonight. I've no desire to converse with a stubborn headed rag-mop." He instantly regretted his words wishing he could take them back yet knowing he couldn't. He was the grouchy one. He was battling with his own insecurities and inadequacies. He was deathly afraid that he couldn't protect this little slip of a girl, even while she was in the envelope of his own home. Lashing out at her would solve nothing and probably drive her away. She was already feeling guilty. He could see it in her facial expressions. Now he'd added to her burden and belittled her self-esteem and all for no good reason that he could explain other than he was an ass.

Josie turned in a flash but not before Christian saw the pain in her eyes and the sadness of her features. Agony etched along her jaw line, proof that she barely held her emotions in check. He had no way of knowing how insecure she was because of Millie's arrival, or how badly she felt for the trouble she had brought with her. Still, his words were out of line and he knew it.

Well it was for her own good he thought although the soundless reminder was of no comfort. He busied himself by building a fire, angrily shoving kindling between and under the larger logs. He was angry with himself but not yet willing to admit it out loud. He had to cool down a bit. A bath would help. Aiming for the back door he cursed then stopped in his tracks. Darn it all, suddenly everything in his life was more difficult than what it used to be. He'd have to use the front door. So be it, he shrugged. A little extra work wouldn't hurt him a bit.

He needed to work off some steam anyways. Maybe he should split some wood first and pile it up on the porch. That would burn some anger away while the bath water was warming.

Josie heard him leave and then return with water. When he went out to get another bucketful she flung open the bedroom door, raced across the room and snatched the kettle. Quickly returning to the bedroom, she poured the semiwarm water into the washbasin. With her heart beating rapidly she replaced the kettle above the fire, ran back into the bedroom and hook latched the door shut. There was no time to spare for at that very moment the front door creaked open again and Christian strolled towards the fireplace.

His footsteps stilled and she clasped her hand over her mouth in an effort to keep from giggling. Leaning with her ear against the door, anxiously awaiting the next movement, she couldn't help but smile. Her smile faded however, when she heard his footsteps approaching the bedroom door. Quickly, before she had a chance to change her mind she grasped hold of the handle, lifted the eyehook and flung the door wide open catching him with his fist in mid-air ready to knock. Before he could mutter a single word she raised her own hand in the air and begged.

"I'm sorry. This is your home and I have no right to complain about anything. I appreciate your hospitality and your protection. Please forgive me."

Clearing his throat he attempted to speak but found himself at a loss for words. The woman was constantly throwing him for a loop. She was always doing the unexpected causing him to grovel at her feet. She had a radiant beauty that shown from within and he just stood there, mouth agape like a love sick puppy.

"I just wanted to wash up." She claimed meekly raising her eyebrows then looking to the ground.

"I'm sorry about what I said. It isn't true. I'm just frustrated and upset right now. I had no right to take it out on you." There, he was man enough to apologize when he was wrong. That should count for something.

"Forgiven." She rocked from heal to toe and smiled.

"Would you consider accompanying me to dinner Ms. Edwards? I find all the food in the house has been stolen." Hope filled his eyes as he awaited her answer.

"Why certainly but I stink." This was said in unladylike fashion while sticking her nose in the air and puckering her face.

He bowed low sweeping his arms in a circular motion gesturing towards the tub. "Madam." His low voice rumbled. "Your bath awaits."

"Why thank you." She curtsied. "You are too kind." Their foolish words had them both laughing as the evening brought forward a new beginning in their relationship.

Christian waited restlessly while Josie finished getting ready. It had only been minutes yet it seemed like hours had slowly dawdled by as he paced back and forth across the main room floor trying to relieve some of his anxiety. He so badly wanted tonight to be special. Rubbing sweaty palms along the sides of his trousers he mentally debated his dilemma of weather he should wear his gun belt or not. Deep down inside he knew the guns were a means of protection for Josie as well as himself. He was also Sheriff and held duty in the highest regards. His occupation demanded he always be prepared for any situation. Still, a certain part of him considered this an official date and a true gentleman would never escort a lady with guns slung around his hips. Some ladies of society would view it as a disgrace to Josie. That's ridiculous he commented inwardly. Josie wasn't the type of woman to care about the terms society dictated. This he decided was the final factor as he buckled the stiff leather belt harboring two holsters and loaded the revolvers before tucking them both securely into place. Running his fingers through his hair he began to pace once more wondering what had come over him and what in the world was taking Josie so long?

On the other side of the door, Josie nervously paced back and forth, nibbling on her fingernails until there was nothing left but raw skin. Suffering from a mixture of emotions she wasn't sure how to act and what was expected of her tonight. So much was completely new to her. The unfamiliarity of it all vastly diminished her security in herself and the world around her. Much to her surprise, she felt something odd when slipping the new dress over her head and shoulders. Discovering her money in the pocket left her awed and speechless for she had completely given up all hopes of finding her missing cash. She had thought the money long gone believing it had fallen from her skirt when Randy was tossing her around at the restaurant. She had thought one of the citizens of the town lucky enough to find the money and be able to provide for their family a little bit better for the time being. She had hoped they appreciated their good fortune and used the money wisely.

There was no mirror to aid her in prepping for this first official dinner in a restaurant and a special date with a man she truly wished to impress. She had brushed her hair until it hung in dark shimmering waves down her back. Refusing to place it in the customary bun, she wrapped it at the nape of her neck with a piece of ribbon that had been used to tie the gift box her dress came in. The sheer volume of hair bound neatly, hung down the center of her back and lightly touched the small bow at the base of her spine. The dress was absolutely lovely and fit perfectly accenting her curves snuggly along the bust and waist. The moderate neckline was cut into a square shape causing her collarbones to show and slightly protrude, evidence of her recent weight loss. Flaring slightly at the hips the material was trimmed along the hem and cuffs with stitched embroidery of the same color giving the overall appearance an elegant but subtle affect. It was by no means plain, nor was it extravagant. It was absolutely perfect. Pinching her cheeks for color she opened the door and stepped into the great room awaiting Christian's open scrutiny with caustic trepidation.

Upon hearing the click of the latch Christian looked up and instantly forgot all worries for they were washed away by Josie's beauty. He stopped pacing and smiled broadly at her appearance before whistling out loud and shaking his head in adoration. "My my, Miss Josaphine, you have to be the most beautiful creature to walk the earth tonight."

Her cheeks burned red at the compliment and she inwardly chastised herself for pinching them in the first place. He couldn't have said anything nicer to her and she beamed with appreciation. "Well thank you Sheriff Coy." She bowed and broke out a smile meant for him and him only. She liked the way his eyes seemed to devour her, roaming from head to toe causing her blood to warm her entire body as trickles of excitement began to flutter in her belly.

"Shall we?" Offering his arm in gentlemanly fashion he couldn't help but wonder how it was he was so blessed. Josie was absolutely stunning with a radiance and beauty that was topped with innocence and a carefree attitude. He found himself mesmerized by her every move.

They strolled leisurely to the restaurant, window shopping and laughing the entire way. Once inside Hanna greeted them with a wholesome yet inquisitive smile and some offhanded remark about how nicely they cleaned up. She then led them to a booth near the back offering as much privacy as possible. The booth's high backed seats and thick cushions helped diminish the noise surrounding them. Once seated Christian nodded his approval in answer to Hanna's speculative look and was met with a discreet little wink and a wicked smirk.

They both ordered Shepherd's pie, biscuits and tall glasses of fresh chilled milk. Josie swore she was hungry enough to eat a cow and said as much to Christian. However, she regretted her words as soon as Hanna placed the meal in front of her. There was so much food piled on the platter that her eyes nearly popped out of her head from astonishment. The aroma that wafted from the plate was heavenly and had her mouth watering before the blessing was complete.

"I'll bet you a dime you can't eat all that food." Christian's devilish smirk matched his words as merriment danced in his eyes and dimples formed at the corners of his mouth defining his handsome face causing Josie's pulse to flutter wildly .

"Okay, you're on." Without any further hesitation she dug in. He probably wasn't aware that she hadn't eaten much at all these last few days. On further thought she realized he was fully aware of her eating habits. That was why he placed the bet in the first place. Well that was just fine with her. She'd take that dime and spend it on him. A look of mischief settled her features as they continued to eat in compatible silence listening to the hum of conversation and clanking of dishes in the background.

Once the meal had completely disappeared he winked at her while sitting back. "Good girl. I knew you could do it."

"You're lucky we are in a public place or I'd tan your hide with the thickest whipping stick I could find." Her voice was light and the teasing was taken well for he knew she'd never whip anything or anyone.

"How about dessert?" Hanna's voice interrupted their easy banter.

"Josie quickly replied "no" simultaneous with Christian's "yes", confusing Hanna more than anything. The young waitress threw her hands in the air and rolled her eyes heavenward.

"I promised the lady apple pie." Looking at both girls he raised his dark eyebrows and continued. "I can't break a promise. It's against the law. The fines are stiff."

"I've never heard of that." Josie rebuffed laughing at his nonsense, liking the way he moved uncomfortably in his seat. "I'm stuffed like a turkey as it is. If I eat another bite this dress will split at the seams and pop right off." She looked down the front of herself as if to check the dress right then and there. Smoothing the fabric with her hands she couldn't help but be happy.

"That settles it then." Christian said loudly. "I have no complaints about the dress popping off."

Hanna giggled and Josie turned beet red as she hid her face in her hands before lightly kicking him under the table.

"Ouch. That wasn't nice Josie. Hanna, we'll take two pieces of fresh apple pie to go please." Turning to Josie he explained. "She'll wrap them in table napkins. We'll take them home with us to eat later."

Josie's thoughts stuck on that one simple word; home. How nice it would be to share life with him and spend each evening like they had the last few days. Truly he was a good man. She surely liked the way those guns looked holstered on that belt, hanging low around his hips. She continued daydreaming with her chin propped on one closed fist until her thoughts were interrupted by a thick sultry voice that bore the equivalence of a swift sharp slap across the face. The sting was harsh and lingering.

"Sheriff Coy what intrigue, dinner with an orphan?" Millie's eyebrows arched and her pert little mouth rounded while waiting for an answer to her question. Anger lay barely submerged beneath her fluent control and false pretense.

Before Christian could reply Josie sprung out of her seat offering a delicate hand in a friendly gesture. Josie had decided to give the girl the benefit of the doubt, and very badly wanted to be liked. "Hi. I'm Josie Edwards. Pleased to meet you."

Millie refused to shake Josie's hand much less respond politely. Acting as if Josie were the plague itself she stuck her nose in the air, primly turned her back on the girl and spoke directly to Sheriff Coy. "Please tell me you haven't eaten yet. You could join father and I at our table. Father has so much to discuss with you." She sounded winded, as if she had been running for quite some distance.

Josie winked at Christian just as he was turning to respond to Millie's invite. She then smugly stuck her tongue out at Millie's back. Caught in the act, Christian shot her a warning look as she plopped down hard on the bench, crossed her arms and focused on the wooden table top.

"Josie meet Millie McQuade. Millie, please meet my good friend Josie." He looked directly into Josie's eyes while talking, warming her insides and causing Millie to bubble with hatred.

"Why yes, Josie" Millie exclaimed forced to turn towards Josie once again with a smug look covering her face, "I've heard so much about you and your inappropriate attire while trolluping through town. It appears the rumors are wrong perhaps?" Millie's eyes scored Josie from head to toe in a very distasteful manner. Challenge and vindictiveness gleamed from the depths of her slanted cat like eyes.

What a witch! Josie thought to herself. How could Christian associate with, think highly of, or even see anything in this woman? She was so nasty and full of loathing it made a person want to take a cautious step back when she approached. Shrugging her shoulders Josie finally resolved to pity. She kind of felt sorry for Millie for certainly it couldn't feel good on the inside when one was that unhappy and miserable. Of course, she didn't know anything about Millie but obviously something in her past must haunt her dreadfully today.

"Yes. Yes. I have been around and about in a few different outfits but…" Josie carried on flippantly waving her hand in the air in a bye the bye manner. "Christian does have such good taste in clothing. How could people help but notice?" She felt bad suddenly for using Christian as a weapon in this personal war with a girl she didn't even know. What was wrong with her? Opening her mouth to apologize she halted.

Loosing grip on her anger Millie stomped her foot, reached for Josie's half full glass of milk and promptly poured what remained over Josie's head. Slamming the glass back onto the table she patted her hands together as if to dust them off on a finishing note and turned towards Christian. "When you're in the mood for proper company, call on me." Sticking her nose upward she sniffed loudly then rigidly stomped over to her father's table and sat down pertly as if nothing had happened.

Hanna, who was watching inquisitively from across the room, rushed over with towels in hand and began to assist Josie in cleaning up her face and dress. Clucking like a mother hen she cooed and soothed with warm words of comfort.

Christian was pissed. There was no other word to describe it. He swore he would never speak to Millie again. That spoiled little brat needed a spanking. Someone should have done it a long time ago. Tonight she had shown her true colors. There was no mistaking her vehemence and unsettling nature. Reigning tight control over his anger, he fought desperately to ignore the urge to walk over to Millie and slap her silly. Looking to Josie he slid out of his seat and bent to gently kneel at her side. His gut ached at the hurt she must be feeling and the dark expression in her eyes. He so badly wanted tonight to be a special experience for her. Clasping her hands in his while looking up into her watchful eyes he opened his mouth to speak.

Josie halted his words by putting a hand up in the air in a firm and direct signal. She refused to let him apologize for someone else's actions and poor behavior. Instead she calmly offered a weak smile while lifting her chin and speaking softly. "I bet I look like a complete milksop right now." Pausing she included Hanna in the exchange. "Get it? Milksop?" Josie began to shake with laughter as tears formed in the corners of her eyes.

Hanna and Christian both stared back slack jawed in dumbfounded surprise, unable to believe that Josie was laughing in earnest after what had just happened.

"It's okay really, I'm fine, besides I happen to like milk." Her smile was a solemn effort to ease the tension in the air.

Before she could say anything else Christian grabbed the back of her head, bunched her hair up between clasped fingers and pulled her to him. Their lips locked in a harsh and desperate meeting of desire that caught them both off guard. Neither of them could help but respond adding fire to the kiss, causing it to linger longer than it should have.

Hanna beamed with happiness. Millie's actions sure did backfire. Moving to leave and return to duty she scowled at several peering onlookers. Of coarse it wasn't proper for a couple to kiss in public, especially if their courting wasn't formally announced, but this was an exception. Triumph lit her smirk as she passed Millie.

"Looks like the Sheriff found himself a lady friend." Judge McQuade remarked approvingly to his daughter while scooping a piece of roast into his mouth then chewing hard as his jaw snapped with each rotating bite. He was completely unaware of Millie's role in the evening's events.

Peering over her shoulder towards the booth Millie stifled an angry scream and fought for control over her emotions. Kissing in public was just atrocious! He'd surely catch some type of disease or illness from that filthy little tramp. She hoped they choked. Oh she would get that Josie Edwards if it were the last thing she ever did!

CHAPTER SIX

Slowly blinking his eyes in an effort to open them fully, Neb found great difficulty emerging from the hazy darkness ensnaring his soul. Focusing on any image was nye impossible for everything appeared heavily shaded, a cloudy mixture of both light and dark tones. His body felt as if it were anchored to blocks of lead for it wouldn't respond to the commands his brain set forth. Concentrating solely on his fingers he sent every ounce of energy he could muster to his hands desperately urging the muscles to move, causing his fingers to twitch ever so slightly.

If Hanna hadn't been sitting where she was, she may have missed the movement altogether. Leaning over and tapping Old Doc on the shoulder she quietly pointed to Neb's hand and whispered. "He moved. His fingers twitched."

Old Doc reached a cold speckled and trembling hand out feeling Neb's neck and forehead. His voice strained while informing Hanna. "Pulse is strong…fevers gone…I suppose anything can happen now."

It was difficult for Old Doc to talk in soft tones, a mere token of his age, yet he made the effort out of respect to a patient that had so far miraculously beat the odds and remained alive. He and Hanna continued to watch for any sign of Neb's recovery. Their hopes mounted to sheer excitement when together they witnessed his eyes rolling and fingers twitching once more.

Hanna automatically placed her hands around Neb's and leaned closer to talk softly in his ear but Old Doc stood up rather swiftly halting her intentions by placing a firm hand on her shoulder. Confusion ebbed her expression as he wordlessly ambled across the room and reached for the Sheriff's long barreled rifle, which was propped in a darkened corner behind the desk. Checking to see it was properly loaded, he then shuffled in snail like movements to the door. Opening it and sticking his head out he promptly whistled a preplanned note, indicating a need for assistance. Joey appeared from the shadows anxiously awaiting Old Doc's commands.

"Let the Sheriff know he's needed here right away. Neb Hurley's come to."

Shaking his head vigorously up and down, Joey took off running possessed with the agility of youth. Excited that the adults in the community needed him and eager to carry out their commands hoping to please the Sheriff more than anything. He wanted to be a Sheriff someday.

Turning back towards the cell while remaining close to the door the old man pointed the long end of the gun then nodded his approval for Hanna to carry on as intended. "We have to be prepared for the worst Hanna. You never know." He cautiously explained as the words intended meaning hung unspoken in the air.

Tears filled her eyes causing them to glimmer, deep pools in the dim light. Her olive complexion was as smooth as fine porcelain while shadows of doubt danced across her features. Peering down towards Neb's face she silently willed him to open his eyes before coaxing him with the sweet song of her voice. "Neb Hurley my name's Hanna. Please open your eyes and look at me."

Neb was sure he heard the voice of an angel, a light beautiful sound, as if the voice itself had wings, it fluidly graced the air leaving a fragrance of temptation. Reaching toward it he longingly needed to grasp the link leading from the darkness. There it was again, that beautiful sing song voice.

"Open your eyes sweetie. You can do it." Hanna urged sensing his ability to hear her words. "I'm here for you Neb. Come on darling." She soothed while gently rubbing a circular pattern atop his large hand with feather light fingertips.

Grogginess clouded Neb's senses as his mind whirled through a kaleidoscope of colors, traveling away from the darkness and returning to reality at long last. Fully opening his eyes and focusing on the sights and sounds around him, he lay motionless feeling for the first time in days as pain flowed in stream like currents from the top of his head to his shoulders before finally subsiding in a burning sensation only to begin the pattern anew. This first realization bid him to lie still for his senses warned that something was very wrong. Then, as if a flash of lightening struck through his blurred memory, he recalled his last few moments of consciousness. He groggily remembered the robbery that had gone bad because of his brother's poor attitude and hotheaded inability to follow directions. Visions of a frightened young lady, standing alone holding a stick, flashed through his mind. She had helped him. She had saved his life. With the onslaught of another flash he saw Randy hit the young woman hard across the face with staggering force. Waiting for more, Neb was sorely disappointed to

96

find that he couldn't remember anything else. His mind had gone blank.

"Welcome back Neb."

There it was again, the angel's voice, sweet and soothing. Turning his head a notch to the right he concentrated on focusing his sight, trying hard to overcome the fresh onslaught of pain. Squeezing his eyes shut, then opening them again, he swore inwardly. There sat the most beautiful and radiant angel he'd ever laid eyes on. He must have died and gone to heaven. No. No. That couldn't be right he told himself. His actions in life damned him to a hot fiery hell and this beauty surely wasn't to be seen in hell. He moaned aloud while attempting to sit upright.

"No. No, just lay still there." Hanna's voice soothed. "You don't want to hurt yourself now do ya'?"

Neb tried to reply but couldn't. His words wouldn't form as directed. The only sound that escaped his mouth was a rough animalistic grunt.

Hanna stood up and briskly left only to return momentarily with two blankets and Old Doc's handkerchief, which she had quickly snatched from his shirt pocket and "tskd" him into silence when he opened his mouth to voice objection. Folding the blankets she very carefully placed them beneath Neb's head and upper body allowing him to sit in an upright position, something a little different than laying the way he had been for days. Folding the hanky she carefully wiped away a trickle of saliva that had run from Neb's mouth to his chin when he had attempted to talk.

"There now, is that better?" She really didn't expect an answer.

Neb discovered that the right side of his body wouldn't respond as he wanted it to but the left did so without too much difficulty. He quickly shot out his hand and caught Hanna's wrist as she moved the hanky from his face. The surprised look on her face confirmed his action as completely unexpected and startling.

Hanna held her breath for a brief moment unsure of what to do. In her peripheral vision she saw Old Doc stiffen as he stepped away from the door, holding the rifle higher so that it's aim was pointing dead center of Neb's forehead. She cringed at the thought of him being shot again and begged with pleading eyes to be released. The look of pure panic and fear in Neb's eyes had her heart sick immediately.

Instead of letting go Neb repeated her actions of earlier. With his thumb he lightly traced a pattern of circles on the sensitive underside of her wrist. He heard a gasp of shock along with a strong intake of breath displaying her surprise at his touching response. She then relaxed as if somehow knowing he wouldn't hurt her. They both peered deeply into each other's eyes for they were merely windows to the soul. His lay bare, open and exposed for her to read.

The brief exchange was shattered and Hanna nearly jumped out of her skin when the jailhouse door roughly smashed open and the Sheriff hurried in with a disgruntled Josie in reluctant tow behind him.

Christian wasn't all that happy to be interrupted this evening. After dinner he and Josie had returned to the cabin where she bathed and cleaned up once again while he laid out a long undershirt and breeches for her to wear. The clothing swallowed her petite frame but at least her skin was covered. He had imagined better things to do with her tonight than visit the jail.

"What's going on?" His voice clearly betrayed his agitation.

Old Doc had had enough action for one evening. He gruffly muttered something about a heart attach while shoving the rifle into the Sheriff's hands. Shuffling towards the door he took his leave without saying another word.

Hanna smiled and explained the situation to Christian and Josie while holding Neb's hand the entire time. "I'm going to feed him some soup now. It's okay, really, you two can go. I'll be fine."

"No Hanna, we are not going to leave you here alone with an outlaw." Christian's words served as a cold harsh reminder of Neb's prior actions and role in life.

"He didn't kill anyone." Hanna passionately argued in Neb's defense.

"How do you know? Look at the wanted posters for Christ's sakes Hanna! You're placing yourself in danger." Christian couldn't believe it. Hanna sat there looking at this guy like he had moved the earth for her.

"Randy is the bad guy, not Neb. I know it in my heart. I see it when I look into his eyes. Now I've said my piece and that's that! And don't you dare curse the Lord in my presence again Sheriff." Turning her back on the couple she read Neb's confused expression. He must finally realize he's in jail, she thought.

Christian looked to Josie for help. "Josie you just say the word. Tell me this man hurt you. Tell me the truth now." He grasped her shoulders and gently shook her back and forth in an effort to yield the words he longed to hear, a confession of brutality. "I swear I'll kill him now." Releasing her, his fingers tightened a firm grasp around the butt of the gun.

Shaking her head Josie placed a hand on Christian's upper arm to add sincerity to her words. "No Christian, this man never did me any harm. I only tended his wound. Randy's the one with the iron fist. I only pray Neb isn't as monstrous as his brother."

Christian's broad shoulders visibly relaxed and he rubbed his forehead with his fingers, attempting to ease the building tension.

Approaching him from behind, Josie began rubbing the back of his neck and shoulders to aide in calming his tightly strung nerves and tense muscles. "Let's sit down and work through this, shall we?" With one eyebrow raised higher than the other she glanced from Hanna and Neb to Christian and back again.

"Okay, okay." Christian reluctantly agreed while pulling a chair from behind his desk and placing it near the open door to the cell. He then dragged another chair from alongside the first one, scuffing the floor, leaving a trail dust as well as a lighter scratch mark upon the floor. With a single tilt of his head he indicated for Josie to sit as he did the same, keeping his hand cautiously on the rifle the entire time.

They sat for a few moments in silence before Christian looked directly at Neb and asked. "Are you Neb Hurley?"

Neb, propped in an odd position, met Christian's gaze levelly and with extreme difficulty nodded up and down.

"Are you kin to Randall Hurley? Is he your brother?"

Again Neb nodded slowly. It was evident to all that any faster movement would cause sharper, more undo pain. Even though he displayed tremendous improvement, every one of them knew his injury was severe and could still be life threatening.

Josie asked the next question. "Neb are you tired? Would you like us to return tomorrow?"

Slowly, with more concentrated effort, Neb shook his head to signal a negative response. He then held up his left hand and moved it about in the air.

Josie and Christian looked to each other in puzzled confusion, shrugging their shoulders simultaneously.

"Write." Hanna stated eagerly. "He wants to write his answers."

Christian went to the door, whistled for Joey and kindly asked him to fetch a slate board and piece of chalk from the schoolhouse. He then directed the boy to stop at the hotel before returning and ask for Judge McQuade to join them at the jailhouse as quickly as he could.

Joey fervently took off anxious to impress the Sheriff. Christian sat back down in the dusty chair. While waiting for the orders to be carried out, they sat in eerie silence fiddling their thumbs, looking about the room and contemplating their own thoughts.

Hanna helped Neb eat his soup then fetched fresh water to rinse it down. When the door finally did creak open and the Judge appeared with slate and chalk in hand, Neb's meal was through and the mess had been cleaned.

Christian, as the town's Sheriff, briefed Judge McQuade on the turn of events while Josie sat motionless, examining the stranger before her, trying to decipher his character. She quietly mused and wondered how such a successful and obviously strong willed man could father a venomous creature like Millie. Mayhap she was being unfair in passing judgment based on Millie's actions. The Judge really did seem an honest and fair fellow. He probably gave everything he could to his daughter, like every father longed to do. Unknowingly, he had created a monster.

The sound of another chair scrapping across the floor roused her from impervious thoughts as she once again turned her attention to Neb Hurley who was at that particular moment in time, starring directly at her with a grave and serious expression upon his face. Chills traveled down her spine as apprehension pricked her senses. She automatically leaned over placing herself closer to Christian, needing the comfort and strength he so easily projected.

Christian responsively draped a protective arm over Josie's shoulders. His jaw tightened into a firm line as he directed a blatant and distrusting gaze on the prisoner. "Neb, I think it's time we made our introductions. Sitting next to you is Hanna Bailey. She's been helping to take care of you since your arrival here." Motioning to his left he continued. "This is Judge Charles McQuade. He'll be in charge of your case as well as your brother's. I'm Sheriff Coy, the one that brought you in and booked the charges against you and this here," he nodded in Josie's direction squeezing his arm more firmly around her shoulders, "is Josie Edwards whom I believe you've already met."

Earnestly trying to write using the thick stubby piece of chalk, Neb moaned an odd pain induced sound then reached into his pant pocket pulling free a small and delicate item. Scribbling something more on the slate he then stuck out his left arm offering the slate and trinket to Josie.

Cautiously she accepted both with nervous trembling hands. Looking down she read the written words aloud. "Thank you friend." Opening her hand she closely inspected the shiny token of his gratitude. It was a breathtakingly beautiful piece of golden amber inset into a skillfully detailed pewter backdrop. Designed to hang from a chain as a pendant, the piece was genuinely gothic in appearance and held the significance of a family heirloom.

Holding out her hand to give it back was not a lighthearted ordeal for in her heart of hearts she had never seen anything so beautiful, nor had she ever worn much less owned a piece of jewelry. That was something perceived for only the rich and well to do. This fine work of art was something Neb should cherish, not her. "Please. I accept your gratitude but I cannot accept such a treasured piece."

When Neb refused to hold his hand up and receive the pendant Josie dropped it in his lap.

"I can't Neb. I just can't."

Still Neb didn't reply. The black orbs of his eyes remained focused and almost angry like as he continued to stare, not blinking or moving at all, causing Hanna to fret and worry.

Christian stepped in by asking a few yes or no questions related to the robberies and his brother, ending his portion with a final question that had them all holding their breath. "Have you ever killed anyone?"

The slightest nod of Neb's head indicated the answer was yes causing Hanna to whimper placing one small hand over her mouth. Disbelief shown on all their faces for Neb somehow seemed vulnerable and innocent laying there the way he was. He had silently and solemnly won their trust.

"Who'd you kill?" The Judge inquired refusing to let it rest at that point.

Scribbling on the slate again the chalk ticked and tacked while wearing low before snapping from too much pressure. They were all silent while waiting for Neb to grab another piece and finish. When he was done he shoved the board towards the judge and shook it up and down until it was removed from his hand. He was obviously disgusted by the written words and impatient to let go of the slate.

Judge McQuade's grim expression revealed nothing as he contemplated the words and pondered his reply. One could never be too quick to judge a man, yet one could never be to quick to trust a man either. He had very mixed feelings about this one and his instincts refused to be of any help at all. One thing, he decided, always proved the truth and that was time itself. Time would tell all.

Looking to the others he explained. "Neb claims here that he killed his stepfather for beating his mama to death. He also claims that this fellow would have killed Randy if he hadn't shot him." Turning his gaze to Neb he spoke in an inquiring manner. "I assume Neb, that this happened when you were younger?"

An up and down bob of the head confirmed that he was correct in his assumption.

"Oh now come on!" Christian's voice portrayed extreme aggravation. "All someone has to do is come up with a good sob story and everybody gets all teary eyed. Facts are facts. This man and his brother robbed banks, stole horses and hurt a lot of innocent people along the way. Let's not forget the Hawkins widow and how on earth she's going to provide for four youngins' on her own."

"That may be." The Judge's voice boomed filling the air, startling the girls. "But we will uphold the law. That means Sheriff, that he will be held in custody and treated humanely until the trial when all evidence is laid upon the table. At that time I will pass judgment, not you."

"Need I remind you sir that I do uphold the law every day in order to protect the good hard working folks of this community. I will also remind you that he has been treated humanely while in this jail. You can tell that by the fact that he's still alive and doing so well. He has been visited and tended to on a daily basis and I take great offense to any implication otherwise." The hard line along Christian's jaw portrayed his anger at being placed in doubts eye by the judge.

"I'm sorry son." Shaking his head from right to left in heartfelt admission he continued. "I didn't mean to imply anything derogatory. Fact is, I'm just as baffled and frustrated as you are. In truth, I don't rightly know what to do about this whole situation. I guess that's why it's so important to find his brother and bring him into custody as soon as possible."

"I agree with you there." Christian stood, leisurely stretching to his full height and shaking off his anger. After patting the Judge on the back of his shoulder he crossed the room, rubbing his chin with his thumb and forefinger deep in thought.

As Josie watched him she noticed the shadows from the flickering candle flames were dancing erotic patterns along the filled split log wall. Her forehead wrinkled in puzzlement. She could have sworn the shadows grew brighter by the minute. Time seemed to halt as she fixed her gaze on the wall, studying the flickering shapes and shades, hearing nothing of the conversation around her. Hmm, she thought, must be something outside. Acting on impulse she got up and slowly crossed the room while still watching the shadows, blindly reaching for the door handle.

"What are you doing Josie?" Christian couldn't help but ask for he had no idea why she would want to leave.

"Something's wrong. It should be getting darker outside, not lighter." Pulling on the heavy wooden door to open it she stepped over the threshold onto the boarded porch outside. Filled with alarm, she frantically spoke out loud. "Oh dear Lord, Christian please hurry!" Motioning for him to come look she swung her forearm in circles. "What do we do?" Then she quickly covered her mouth and nose because the odor from the burning building was sooty and acidic and the burning sensation was felt instantaneously.

Stepping up behind her he was embraced in a stunning moment of awe for across the street flames darted wildly, reaching for the sky, billowing from the frame of the restaurant, lighting up the entire town with a brilliant glow of orange, red and yellow. He instinctively yelled. "The restaurant's on fire!"

Adrenaline flowed through the Sheriff's veins as he fired three random shots into the night sky signaling for help from the towns' people. "Hurry everyone, we have to form a line. Bring your buckets. Hurry now."

Running across the dirt packed street over to the restaurant he tried to see through the doorway, checking for any sign of people inside. It should have been closed and empty but he needed to be certain. Edging his way forward the heat singed the hair on his arms and the whiskers on his chin. There was no way anyone could enter through the front. His eyes burned from the smoke and soot continually tearing up and clouding his vision as he worked his way along the side of the building towards the rear. Tunnels of black smoke poured from the windows and doorways hanging in the dark sky like a thick wool blanket. People all around were placing handkerchiefs and scarves over their nose and mouths to avoid breathing the sooty ash residue floating without direction in the heated atmosphere.

Christian wiped the sweat from his brows and forehead. Reaching the back of the restaurant he felt sickened by what he saw. If anyone had been in there it was impossible to help him or her now. The rear entrance and stairway was completely burned and at this point simmered with black bubbly soot and fire red embers. Several timbers of wood used as support beams lie on the ground smoking and gray. Clearly this was where the fire had started for this portion was ravished and done, the flames no longer affecting what was already burnt and destroyed.

Working his way back towards the front of the building while trying not to get scorched from the intense and unrelenting heat, Christian was amazed to find every man, woman and child working together in unison, synchronized in a unified battle to end the mighty flames. They had formed three lines leading to different water holes in town. Several buckets were passed back and forth in a well-organized and efficient manner, effectively dousing the flames. Searching among the crowd he spotted Judge McQuade, Hanna, Angus and Josie all working their fair share, hefting heavy water filled buckets from the water hole beneath the jailhouse porch. Some folks were even fetching water from the horse troughs speeding up the dousing process. A few of the bulkier men had gone into the woods and filled an entire tub with watery muck from the floor of the swamp area.

Minutes stretched into hours as the exhausted community refused to give up, laboring well into the early hours of morning before the flames could be seen no more. The damage had been contained to the restaurant and sighs of weary relief rippled through the crowd as they slowly began to disperse. All were thankful the fire hadn't spread or taken any lives, yet angry that it had happened at all.

Looking around for Josie, Christian mentally noted that Millie was most likely the only person missing. She hadn't shown up to help put the blazing flames to rest. He cringed with disgust thinking of how selfish and lazy Millie was, placing herself on a pedestal and projecting a superior attitude that claimed she was better than most. Of course she would feel it beneath her status to help commoners and get her hands dirty. He had to shake off an overwhelming anger and try to get some rest. It had been a long night.

Later that morning, almost towards noon, many people set their own chores and household activities aside to show up in the blistering sun and heat only to sweat and labor for hours on end cleaning and removing mound after mound of debris and rubble left by the fires destructive wrath. They would have to wait a few days for the bulk of the pile to cool as most of it was still smoldering and too hot to work with. But they could at least get started and work from the outside in. Right now, the hardest part was watching out for the children. They were a curious bunch, and the burn site was a dangerous place for them to be. The parents had their hands full and most did the right thing by leaving the children home, in charge of the chores there. Even that backfired as the youngsters worked doubly hard. They got their chores done at home and still wondered into town to help. Mischief was the farthest thing from their minds but somehow that was always where the youngsters ended up, getting into trouble.

Christian, Angus and Judge McQuade sifted through the fallen embers and massive piles of ash and debris trying to determine the cause of the blaze. It was the rear portion of the building that had been damaged most severely and showed signs of more extreme burning. The fire more than likely worked its way from the back to the front of the restaurant, making it too late to save anything once the bellowing inferno was noticed. Standing with hands on hips Christian walked towards a torn piece of cloth hanging from a half dead tree. The tree had been singed and scored of all it's leaves from the heat of the fire, most likely blazing from the back entrance. He thought it odd and slightly disturbing so he took care in folding the red material and pocketed it for inspection later.

Hours later, sifting through more rubble, he finally found what he was looking for. A soot tarnished brass candleholder lie near the spot where the old pantry once was. The candleholder itself was taken as evidence. Christian took note that the candleholder was an expensive piece. Not many families in this area could afford items of that degree. He also took note of the puzzled look upon the Judge's face that quickly shifted to paleness when he inspected the candleholder. Briefly discussing the findings with Judge McQuade, the men rationalized and debated before finally settling on the final determination that this was to be named officially as the cause of the fire. After double-checking the evidence they went to the street and announced their findings to an impatient crowd. This time everyone was there including Millie. Although there wasn't a speck of dirt on her body or a hair out of place, her face as well as many other solemn faced individuals peered up from the group with expectant looks. They needed resolution, answers and a final outcome.

Clearing his throat, Christian spoke loud enough for all to hear. "It looks like the cause of fire was a burning candle left unattended in the old pantry that was no longer used."

Murmuring voices were heard throughout the crowd as everyone spoke and whispered at the same time. Finally, the noise dimmed as one man addressed the Sheriff on behalf of many.

"Sheriff C, the only person that's been in that old pantry of late was Josie. Everybody knows that Josie was hidden in that pantry all day yesterday."

Swallowing a lump of apprehension, Christian mentally replayed the prior days events. It couldn't be. "That would be impossible." He explained to the villagers. "I myself got Josie out around three o'clock in the afternoon. She was with me from there on out. This fire started around eight o'clock at night. It doesn't fit right."

A lady yelled out. "The candle may have burned for a few hours before catching fire to something. How does that fit Sheriff?"

Josie felt her knees getting weak. This couldn't be happening. It just couldn't be. Rubbing her temples with shaky fingers she found herself standing alone now with angry glares cast upon her from every direction. Her undoing, however, was the confused and doubtful look upon Christian's face. He doubted her. He believed them. Then she thought of something and spoke out fervently. "I didn't have a candle. I sat in the dark. Really it's true. Sheriff, you know it's true. Hanna you do too." With a pleading look her eyes jumped from face to face making eye contact with every individual that she possibly could.

Hanna spoke out in her friend's defense. "I know she didn't have a candle. The restaurant doesn't have candles."

"Well." Christian spoke again, silencing the crowd. "Unless someone actually saw Josie with a candle in hand we have to start looking for the real culprit."

Millie's voice shrilled and raised a few octaves above the noise level of the crowd. "I saw her with a candle. Does anyone want to question my word?" Millie didn't have many friends within the group but they saw the opportunity for her word to benefit their accusations and ran with it.

Another flow of sound and angry voices rippled through the clan. Apparently the whole town agreed. Josie had been tried right there in the middle of the street. She had been labeled as guilty. Raw anger set her jaw firm. How could the Judge stand by and allow this to happen? What about justice and a proper trial where the evidence was to be laid upon the table? Sarcasm dripped from the thought. So great was her anger at the moment that it brought tears to her eyes.

Holding her head high she looked to Christian for answers. What was she to do now? How far would he let this go? "Owe." Someone had thrown a stone at her, hitting its mark square in the center of the forehead instantly leaving a large red welt.

Others followed the example and before she could fully comprehend what was happening the crowd had gone crazy throwing stones and dirt at her. Many women were yelling and screaming as loud as they could, urging others on with their brutality. A few of the men, including Christian, desperately tried to bring the crowd under control but the commotion proved too much for so few to handle.

Someone shot a gun into the air momentarily pausing the assault on Josie.

The Judge's voice boomed over the crowd. "I have evidence that Josie is not the culprit and I expect you folks to uphold the law. Lynching is not the way of the law! I'll not stand for it!"

The crowd was still riled but began a collaborative rebuttal by drilling the Judge with questions that he wasn't yet prepared to answer. Yet the Judge had voiced his concern in an effort to save Josie from unjust treatment due to an out of control group that grew violent with the need to feel justified for the wrong that had been done to their own as well as their community. His lack of response only refreshed their anger.

Christian had his suspicions but was concerned both for Josie and for the Judge. He knew that both were in precarious situations and he had to tread lightly on both accounts in order to help each one the best way he could. It was hard right now to stand aside and control the crowd when all he wanted to do was hold and protect Josie. That would only vex the crowd even more and make the law appear to be one sided. For both his sake and the Judge's, he had to refrain from doing that.

Turning, Josie hurriedly walked away lifting her chin, holding her head high and refusing to flinch at several severe and accusing glances. Once she reached the cabin she hastily gathered her few meager belongings as tears ran freely down her cheeks. In the shed she easily found her saddlebags and blanket. Carelessly filling the bags she shoved supplies and clothing in them, strapped it to Buster and rode off disappearing into the murky forest of gloom and never ending mud. How fitting she thought, for the swamp and its dreary environment matched her mood completely. She had a panicked feeling and the need to hurry nearly engulfed her. So angry and hurt was she, that she not once sparred a look over her shoulder, not once did she feel the urge to look back, and not once did she consider all the dangers lurking about or how she would survive even a single night in the swamp.

Giving the horse free reign and relying on his instincts as usual for footing, she sat crying for hours, not knowing or caring where she was or where she was going, wallowing in self pity and feeding her sorrows. She absent mindedly petted behind Hops ears and took what little comfort the dog had to offer. At least she wasn't alone, she had her horse and dog. They seemed to be true friends for they had stood by her since the beginning of this adventure. Tried and true; they were certainly better friends than any person could ever be.

Christian had little time for worrying for he was too busy fighting and calming the maddened mob to chase after Josie. He had hoped that she would stay inside the cabin, using common sense, awaiting his return. In the pit of his soul he knew all too well she'd leave. Since when did women ever use common sense? Several hours later, when things were finally settled, he returned to an empty cabin confirming his suspicions. She was gone. He felt drained as fear and anger clutched the very center of his being. It was as if a piece of his heart had been torn right out. All that was left in its place was an empty void. A hole in the center of his chest cavity.

Trying to shake the empty feeling he told himself that Josie was trouble. If he were smart he'd wash his hands of her right now, this very minute, while the opportunity was within reach, before she cost him his job and ruined his life altogether. Yet his gut instincts told him he was wrong. He was very wrong. He roughly realized he missed the dog and horse too. He shook his head and mumbled beneath his breath.

Torn between two different thought processes indecision proved unrest and Christian grew agitated. It was easier to be angry with Josie than to feel anything else. Staying mad at least kept him from worrying. It also kept his heart from aching. Really it was just too much to think that he actually loved her, therefore he chose not to. What on earth was she thinking? Taking off like that with no one to protect her other than a lousy dog... that would get her nothing but hurt for God's sake! Obviously she wasn't thinking. He was good and bound to wring her neck or tan her hide when he found her. At least he'd bend her over his knee and give her a good spanking. The girl had to learn to use common sense! If she didn't he'd surely go crazy soon.

While packing supplies and food he gave Angus directions and explained to the Judge that he was going out alone to search for either Josie's or Randy's trail, whichever he found first. He was certain one would lead to the other. They were both out there and the only thing left in town Randy might want was his brother. Christian was sure he'd search out Josie before he'd return to fetch Neb. Hate was a terrible thing. Look at what it had done to this town. It had turned good Christian folks into a hardened mob. It had been an ugly thing to watch and Christian prayed he'd never witness anything like it again as long as he lived.

By nightfall Josie realized the stupidity of her actions and completely regretted her decision to leave on an angry whim. She had been thinking for quite some time now, trying to sort out ways to prove her innocence for both her sake and Christians. She also knew now that she loved him. With all her heart and soul, she loved him. The thought didn't scare her as much as she thought it would. Instead it burned like coal in a steam engine, giving her fuel and energy to fight anew, leading her to a destination she secretly desired. She pushed on relentlessly.

She had no smudge pot and the mosquitoes feasted on both her and Buster without comprimise. Clicking her tongue she pulled on the reigns encouraging the horse to backtrack. It seemed the animal was smarter than she for it acted happy with her resolution, snickering and bouncing it's head up and down before breaking into a trot with renewed energy. The hooves sloshed in the mud causing a wake upon the ground.

Josie pulled on the rolled up blanket and effectively draped it over her, the dog and most of the horse. It would serve as a small barrier to aid in the ongoing attack from the feisty mosquitoes until they ended their feasting for the night. It had once again grown eerily dark in the wet forest and the path of visibility was led only by the silver glow of moonlight. Growing rather spooked by the uncanny shadows and creepy noises, she fought for control of her own minds imaginings. The suction noise from the mud's opposing force on the horse's hooves played on her nerves like fiddle strings strung too tightly. At any moment she felt as if she would snap and break, loosing hold on reality.

The horse grew tired and weary, well she knew for she felt it too, so they stopped alongside a fresh water stream to rest and drink, allowing a moments reprieve from the monstrous shadows set within the swaying of the tree branches and the ebony color of the night.

Cupping her hands together she filled them with cool water and drank quickly before the fluid could seep through the cracks of her fingers. No matter how tightly she pressed her hands and fingers together, the water eventually leaked through. Finding it a fascinating concept, she lingered in thought. The twig that snapped behind her was hardly enough notice to react. A cold hand clamped over her mouth as a lean muscular body pressed along her backside.

"Shh."

"Christian?" His name was spoken softly rolling from her lips as she turned into his embrace, wrapping her wondrously soft arms tightly around his midsection, locking her fingers behind his back. Although she was unable to see his face in the dark, her body knew it was he and began to warm upon contact with his tall frame.

"I guess I have to keep you chained to my side now." His condescending voice was music to her ears for she thought she'd never hear it again.

"Not unless you want to be stoned." It was a hearty reminder of the reason she had fled in the first place, unwittingly accusing him of not believing her.

"Are you okay?" He ignored the unsaid accusation.

"Yes. I'm fine. I've been through worse than that before. I'm just tired and I want so badly to go home."

"Where is you're home Josie?" He really didn't understand what home she was referring to. Did she say "home" meaning back with her daddy or did she mean "home" with him, where she belonged?

"I guess, if truth be told, I don't know. I only wanted to be with you, surrounded by your things, in your cabin. That's why I started to double back."

Once again Christian didn't know what to think or how to feel. She had stumped him with her unrelenting devotion to him. Anger had driven him like a madman venturing on a dangerous journey through this mud-infested hellhole. The entire time he planned to shake her senseless when he caught up with her. Now that she was in his arms he was flooded with a savory feeling of relief and content. Randy hadn't gotten to her first, which was his biggest fear. She was tattered and torn but in one piece. That's all that really mattered. She had even doubled back to be with him once more. And for what purpose? He wondered. He had let her down. On that thought he stood stiff and tense, still unsure of his emotions while his brain and heart fought an unrelenting battle with each other. But when her hand reached up and touched his cheek, it was his undoing.

Pulling her closer, they kissed passionately until her knees nearly buckled and her insides rolled in turmoil. She couldn't help but respond for she knew she loved him without a doubt and inwardly swore she would never leave him again. Still there was a need to hold back for she was uncertain and afraid that he didn't feel the same. He was an honorable man, most likely fetching her out of duty. Well she had already caused enough trouble in his life. Why throw love in his lap now?

The horses began to snicker and prance about displaying an alerting show of nervousness, alarming them to danger and bringing the kiss to an abrupt halt.

"Come on Josie get back on the horse fast."

"What's wrong? Is it Randy?" Looking about she tried to discern the shadows and see what was upsetting him and the horses.

"No." He said with a grunt while boosting her up and helping to cover her with the blanket once more. Welts had already started to form on her arms and face from the viscous insects bites.

"Well then what is it?"

"Wolves." He mounted quickly grabbing the reigns to Josie's horse. "We'll have to hurry back and attempt to outpace them. On this terrain, it'll be difficult."

The ride back was quiet and fear filled for the wolves stayed a short distance away but were close enough to upstart the horses making them more unpredictable than usual. They had both been jostled once or twice by the bucking and rearing behavior of the animals when the wolves would circle and get too near.

"Pesky creatures." She mumbled after having her teeth jarred and her rump bruised once more. "Why on earth did God create them?"

"They serve a purpose I'm sure." Christian couldn't resist the chuckle that came out as a soft undertone.

A few hours later they arrived back at the cabin tired and sore from a journey that only led them full circle, back to the beginning and in each other's company. Christian actually led the horses onto the front porch tethering the leather reigns to the railing near the door. The wolves had followed them home and were sure to create a problem eventually, seeking out the horses, hungry for flesh. Christian would have to sit the night out on the porch, offering what little protection he could. He knew that food was what the wolves wanted, but if they got it from here, they'd keep coming back for more.

"Josie, make sure you don't let Hops out tonight. He'd just fall prey to the pack." She nodded and hugged the dog closer, thankful once again for all that she did have.

"Thank you for collecting us Christian. I don't know what would have happened if you didn't."

"I don't want to think about what would have happened. I'd rather thank God that it didn't. You worried me Josie. Please don't do it again."

"I will never leave you again Christian. Not on my own free will. Not unless you ask me to. You have my word on that. You have my heart on that."

"What the hell does that mean?"

"Never you mind for now. Good night Christian."

CHAPTER SEVEN

Josie insisted on helping to clean the mess from the fire even though many of the community members shunned her and displayed their hatred openly on a daily basis. She had been called obscene and vulgar names repeatedly and eventually began to turn a deaf ear on all of them, surmising that these people had a right to feel the way they did. After all, they were human and needed to place blame somewhere.

Often, Josie worked next to Hanna, one of the few faithful friends she had, preparing soups and rolls to serve the folks that worked for hours on end, late into the day. When some of the women adamantly refused to eat the food Josie's blistered and roughened hands had prepared, she moved over towards Angus to begin working by his side withstanding harder, more intense labor, work that was considered much too dirty and difficult by many of the local women. She loaded up wheelbarrow after wheelbarrow full of wood, rock and debris only to cart if off to the edge of the forest to be dumped. Refusing help or aid from anyone when sparingly offered, she'd simply state that she could do it herself. She regularly skipped meals since it was nearly impossible to be served food that someone hadn't spit on for the women were very unforgiving, holding grudges for days on end. Many of them clustered around the Widow Hawkins, forming a click of hatred solely directed towards Josie, and even the Sheriff and Hanna now that they had openly befriended her.

Josie did make certain she drank plenty of fresh water throughout each hard day of endless hours laboring with sore muscles and bones while the tips of her fingers grew raw, and bled much of the time. Most of the men wore gloves but her stubborn pride wouldn't allow her to ask, much less beg for a pair. She refused to take anything else from these people, vowing that from here on out she would only give.

Two weeks went by before the ground was cleared and the remnants of the fire could no longer be seen. It was finally time to begin work on the new restaurant and excitement fluttered through everyone's veins at the prospect. Josie didn't know anything about constructing a building but she had attended a few barn-raising parties when she was younger. She always thought it amazing when the framed sidewalls were erected and a structure was built seemingly overnight, as if it was meant to be there all along. Once the foundation was laid and the red bricks spanning a two-foot climb upward from the ground and outlining the entire diameter were set, the work was called to a halt. She was somewhat relieved and felt a well-needed rest would work wonders on her aching limbs and spine. Relief didn't dwindle her curiosity any though. She couldn't understand the reason for the setback but was too timid to ask for the animosity between her and the other women had only begun to settle. She had no desire to go barking up the wrong tree now.

Angus walked her back to the cabin as was customary each day now. Once she was delivered safely inside, he'd wait on the porch until Christian returned from scouting out Randy's trail only to be disappointed as yet another day passed without a capture of the area's most notorious and wanted outlaw.

Tonight proved to be a special treat since Angus insisted on helping her to build a fire in the stone pit behind the cabin and aided in hanging kettles of water above it to warm for a bath. The nights were much too hot to burn a fire indoors as June was rapidly leading to July and the humid damp air tended to cling to a body, making the heat that much more unbearable and bathing more necessary than ever.

When Christian returned he waited on the porch out of respect for Josie, allowing her the privacy she needed, listening for her tender voice to drift outside with an "all clear" to enter. Tonight he was exhausted and extremely agitated. The heat as well as the terrain had gotten the best of him. Randy's trails led in circles, often disappearing completely causing him to pull his hair and curse out loud. Never one to give up, he'd go back out the next day only to try it all again and hope for better luck.

A short while later he was inside the cabin's dimly lit interior eating Rabbit stew that Josie had prepared solely for his sake, smelling her fragrance as it lingered in the air, causing him go grow more and more unsettled by the minute. When finished eating, he tidied up his own mess, removed his boots and sat in the rocking chair stretching his long legs out in front of him, meaning to rest for only a few moments but falling asleep right away.

Josie lay in the bedroom tired out from her own days work, sleeping lightly while the candle burned on the night table casting shadows throughout the room. A loud knock at the front door caused them both to jump and their heartbeats to run rapid. She moved to answer and see who the caller was but Christian motioned with a glance and a flick of his hand. She waited patiently as he retrieved a revolver then nodded for her to stand behind the door out of view from any outside visitor. Obviously he didn't want her to answer the knock but wished for her to remain near, another kind display of protection.

Cautiously opening the door, inch by squeaky inch, he immediately stepped back motioning for Josie to come forward and see for herself who stood on the other side of the threshold. She had to look down to greet their caller for he stood no more than three feet high and held a tin cup full of change in one chubby little hand. Dirt smudged the tip of his nose and a cap, with one tiny button stitched to the caps top, it covered unruly blond locks of hair while shorts that sagged below his knees only made him appear smaller. Looking beyond the boy, there was a group of children gathered along the street's edge, quietly being hushed and controlled by their schoolteacher.

When stooping to look into the young boy's eyes, Josie wore a big smile that was truly genuine for she dearly loved children. "Hello there. What can I do for such a handsome young fellow?"

The boy looked down as his pudgy cheeks turned red and began to fidget with the big brown buttons on the cuffs of his shirt.

Josie allowed him a moment to get over his embarrassment, keeping her smile in place while examining his chubby hands and cheeks. A pang of longing settled in her stomach.

Finally the young boy looked up and spoke. "Our school is selling tonics and collecting donations to help Mr. And Mrs. Kettles rebuild their restaurant. You see, they ran out of money and they lost everything in that fire."

"Yes, yes I know." Josie replied as her mind worked a mile a minute, replaying the events and cruelty she had suffered from many of the town's people including Mrs. Kettles. Yet, she truly wished for them to get back on their feet again. After all, she thought, wasn't the restaurant where she had her first and most disastrous date?

"What's your name young man?"

"Christopher."

"Well Christopher, can you wait her just a moment while I fetch my donation?"

He nodded up and down enthusiastically; smiling broadly his brown eyes twinkled brightly.

Winking at Christian she stood and went to the bedroom and with unselfish determination retrieved all of her eighteen dollars. Shrugging her shoulders she wondered and rationalized the need for the money silently. She wasn't using it and the Kettles needed money more than she did right now. She'd just have to work a little harder and earn more.

While Josie was busy fetching her money Christian opened the door and handed Christopher a dollar bill. The boy's eyes grew big and round. Avidly thanking the Sheriff, Christopher informed Christian that he was the first to place paper money into the collection. Thus was said with pride and Christian beamed with a sense of peace knowing he had put it there. He beamed that was, until Josie marched back and kneeled down to look at the boy once more, putting the entire rolled up wad of eighteen one dollar bills into the tin cup. She was filled with a great sense of gratification in doing so and hoped God would smile upon her for the deed. The bills slid apart spreading and filling the circumference of the tin causing the boy to yelp wildly and jump with excitement.

"Gee thanks ma'am. That'll buy gobs of new stuff for the Kettles."

The teacher approached from behind and Christian retrieved one of his own tins offering it to the boy in hopes they would continue to collect. Upon seeing the cause of the boys inappropriate outburst, the teacher, unfamiliar to Josie, bowed politely thanking her with sincere appreciation then left pulling on the boys jacket, tears gleamed in her eyes as she bestowed God's blessings upon them.

Little Christopher wasn't to settle for a mere verbal "thank you" and tidings from the schoolmarm. He ran back and flung his arms around Josie's still bent frame, eagerly kissing her cheek before shying away, hiding his face behind the teacher's skirt.

As they left Josie shut the door, leaned back against it and smiled. Christian stood not far off looking at her, studying her features and watching with an intensity she'd not seen before, catching her off guard by covering her hands with his larger more calloused ones.

Not fully understanding why he offered this small token of affection, she peered up with an inquiring look. "What's this about? You're not jealous of Christopher are you?"

"No. Not really." He smiled at her teasing remark. "It's just that I think you're beautiful and I like what you just did. I like it a lot. You're a good woman Josie Edwards. Don't ever listen to anyone who says otherwise."

Feeling slightly uncomfortable with the flattery, she shifted onto one foot and inhaled a deep shaky breath, an effort to control the flood of emotions his comments had evoked to surface. "Thank you. I needed to hear that more than what you could ever imagine. You have no idea how difficult these past few weeks have been for me. I've tried constantly not to listen to all the negative remarks that are said about me."

"Oh believe me Josie, I know what's been going on around here. I can't say that I like it because I don't. There are good people here Josie. I know you'll win them over. How could they not…" He gulped catching his words before they were completely out. He almost said, "love you", but didn't. Instead he ended with; "like you." Shaking his head to clear away the wondering thoughts he added. "Come on, it's late. Let's get some shut eye while we still can."

With the dawn of a new day came rain. The rains were terrible. And he winds so strong that all the animals had to be sheltered inside sheds and barns. Heavy thunder and ground shaking lightening kept the street empty as it filled with muddy water, soon flooding over the boardwalks and slowly seeping beneath door cracks working an unwelcome path into store fronts and shops, keeping the owners busy while trapped indoors for the day. They endlessly mopped and wrung water from rag after rag, dumping bucket after bucket of water back out into the pouring rain.

It was a gloomy day but Josie wouldn't allow herself to feel under the weather. Standing at the pained glass window looking out she daydreamed. The winds flung twigs and debris onto the porch and the tiny squares of cut glass set into the window frame shook and rattled a rapid tin-a-tin-a-tin beat while the raindrops pelted the roof with a much faster rat-a-tat-tat rhythm. The sounds of a good thunderstorm always calmed her and offered comfort as she relaxed and listened to every noise.

"What do you want to do today?" Christian asked as he approached her from behind, placing his arms around her waist; resting his chin atop her oat and berry scented hair.

They both stood watching the storm, sharing a peaceful moment of silence before Josie answered. "Truly I have no idea what to do. It's a lazy day but sure to pass more quickly than we want it to."

Even the dog was lazy for he lay warmly curled on the rug near the front door until a good gust of wind blew through the crack blasting his back with unwanted coolness. The indolent dog then got up and shook his hind leg as if to brush off the cold before sticking his stubby tail in the air and leaping onto the seat of the rocking chair.

Josie laughed at Hops. He was growing each and every day so that he barely fit into the chair's cushioned seat any longer, yet the silly mutt couldn't figure out what the problem was. Suddenly struck with a thought she spoke out load verbalizing exactly what had crossed her mind. "It was very nice of you Christian, to open your home to me, Hops and Buster. We must be a grave invasion to the privacy you once had. I promise as soon as Randy is in custody and locked securely behind bars, I'll leave you to your privacy once more. If that's your wish that is." She said it as an afterthought but prayed daily that he would ask her to stay.

He was stunned to hear the words come from her mouth and his heart raced as alarm set in at the thought of her leaving. Confused with his response he crossed over to the fireplace mantel noting there wasn't an ounce of dust upon it's highly polished wood thanks to Josie. "My life was empty before you and your pets came along. I'm actually glad to have you here. It's not so bad." Winking he asked on a whim. "Are you afraid to get wet?"

"What?" Her look was pure confusion. The questions had obviously thrown her off guard.

"Let's get out of here."

"And go where?" She stood with arms hanging limply down her sides, puzzling over his insistence to get out when they hadn't had a days rest since she'd arrived.

"Come on Josie, put a smile on the pretty face. We're going shopping."

"Shopping for what?"

"For you."

"Oh no." Pulling away from his grasp, shaking her head she persisted. "I don't like shopping for me."

"How do you know? Have you ever shopped for you before?"

"No. I've never shopped at all."

"Well then, I don't want to hear any opinions from you until you have."

"But Christian, I don't have any money remember?" Spreading her arms and shrugging she pointed a meaningful glare at him to emphasize the point.

"I have plenty of money and I'm tired of seeing you in that same green dress and dingy night gown. They used to look nice but now they're worn thin and stained."

She couldn't argue that fact. Plus, she had lost more weight of late causing even her stockings to pool loosely about her tiny ankles. Meekly, in a soft quiet voice, she asked. "How will I ever pay you back?"

Knowing full well she wouldn't go if he flat out told her she wouldn't have to pay him back a single penny, he replied with a misleading answer, crossing his fingers behind his back as he did so. "We'll work that out later. Don't worry. "I'm a nice fella to owe money to. I don't spit fire or have horns you know. We'll work something out, I promise."

Exhaling a laugh she complied. "Oh alright, but we won't get carried away with this and by the way, you do have horns. They're just invisible."

"Really?" A dark eyebrow shot up as he placed an evil look upon his face and stomped intentionally towards her. "We are going to the mercantile and you will enjoy yourself or else…" Letting his playful words hang in the air he quickened the stomping pace, getting closer at a surprising rate.

"Oop!" She shrieked running away from him towards the door.

"Josie you need a coat."

Turning she blinked her eyelashes several times matter of factly and mocked a snotty rich filled tone while placing her hands on her hips. "Daaarling, I don't have a coat, but if you insist I'll charge one of each color to your account."

"Good try you little brat." With that he tickled her lightly before grabbing his hat and placing his hands on the small of her back, gently urging her out the door and across the street to *Hayward's Mercantile and General Store*, trying desperately to keep both of them dry by holding his own coat over their heads.

They arrived wet and wind blown from the short jaunt in the bitter storm yet it was obvious to several people within the store's warm interior, waiting out the storm, that they made a very handsome couple and seemed to get along quite well with one another.

"Good day Sheriff." One of the men tipped his hat in acknowledgment of their gusty entrance.

"Miles." Christian replied nodding and tipping his own hat in return then reaching for Josie's hand pulling her towards the back of the store to where the women's clothing was neatly displayed along with a variety of knick-knacks.

Filling the back wall was a large bellied stove used to heat the place. Since the storm brought cooler temperatures, a young man stood shoveling coal from a cast iron bin next to the stove into the open door on it's front. Although the walls inside the store were washed white and kept clean, the wall and ceiling directly behind and above the stove were blackened with residue, signs of the carbonated stain often seen when coal was used for burning rather than wood.

Josie couldn't help but be awed for there were cloth shoes, wood shoes, leather shoes, slippers and boots. Hanging from taller racks were swaths of fabric in various materials, some of which Josie had never seen before, and colors so bright they put a rainbow to shame. There were pre-made dresses in all different shapes and sizes as well as dressier gowns and Sunday outfits and pinafores. Cotton skirts, night dresses and stockings were boxed neatly, labeled and sorted by size and color. Most of the pre-boxed items were limited to white and ivory with a variety of lace and trims.

What struck her most were the bonnets, lots of them. Some comprised of solid colors. Some had designs that matched a few of the dresses, but her favorites were the bright colored ones with tiny flowers etched into the fabric. They reminded her of springtime, fresh air, sunshine and molasses.

"Get one." Christian urged in a carefree manner.

"No." She said still sorting through the array of colors and sizes only partially paying attention to his words. "Besides, I could never choose just one. They're all so pretty."

"Then I'll choose for you." Before she could protest he snatched a solid light colored yellow bonnet from the rack knowing that it's soft tone would blend perfectly with her complexion and offset her large emerald green eyes.

Sidetracked once again Josie stood looking around at all the store had to offer.

"Josie."

Jumping slightly she turned back towards Christian delightfully smiling. "I was just looking around. I've never been in a place like this before. What's upstairs?" She had to ask since the steps were also in the rear and were decorated tastefully with small rugs and potted plants.

"The owners live up there. That's why the pot bellied stove is here below the draw vent. It heats the upstairs as well." He pointed to a hole cut in the ceiling that had been covered with wire.

"Oh." It was a pert reply, as if she finally had all the answers she needed. With a sweep of her arm she set her mind to the task at hand. Sifting through the many dresses hanging on display she found several she liked then minimized her selection to two. Both went well with the yellow bonnet and were fairly plain, proving practical for everyday use. She added to the pile two undergarments, two pairs of stockings and one more nightdress before briskly announcing "I'm done."

"Oh no you're not. You can't spend ten minutes picking things out and expect me to be happy. Have a care Josie, you don't want to upset me in front of all these kind folks in the store." Pulling her back to the dress section he grabbed her shoulders turning her towards him. "Stand still." He commanded firmly before turning and hollering over his shoulder towards the front of store. "Mr. Hayward, is the Mrs. about today?"

Mr. Hayward didn't have to answer for Mrs. Hayward suddenly appeared in the stairway, smiling as she descended the steps. "Sheriff C, how nice to see you today."

"Mrs. Hayward." He acknowledged with a grin. "You look lovely as usual."

The older lady's cheeks warmed to a pretty pink at the compliment. Her raven black hair was pulled tightly back in a dramatic bun, thinning her features and effectively narrowing her face. The burgundy gown she wore was trimmed with white lace and looked beautiful on her. "This must be your Josie." Mrs. Hayward hugged Josie like her Mamma used to do then stepped back keeping her hands upon her shoulders. "Welcome to Providence dear."

Josie was touched. She couldn't help but think about the woman's words. She had referred to her as "your Josie", meaning that Christian had spoken of her. It was a sentimental thought causing her to blink back tears before replying politely with a half smile and a meek voice. "Thank you." She instantly liked Mrs. Hayward for she was warm and friendly but most of all she was motherly.

"What can I do for you two lovebirds?"

Now it was Josie's turn to blush as Christian stood next to her turning a shade brighter himself. "Josie needs a wardrobe for she's very limited right now. Can you please help her to spend my hard earned money?" Winking, he continued. "She has the tendency to be conservative."

Chuckling whole-heartedly, Mrs. Hayward said in an assuring tone. "My dear boy, we'll have no problem doing that. Now shoo. Go on, be gone with you." Brushing her hands through the air like a broom she shooed the Sheriff up towards the men lining the stools near the front entrance, then quickly returned to Josie. "Now," she sighed. "Let's get started shall we?"

Selecting several dresses, skirts and blouses Mrs. Hayward led Josie upstairs to a changing room, instructing her to come downstairs and model each outfit before moving on to the next.

Josie felt like a princess for the first dress was a pale lavender with a tight fitting bodice and draping skirt. The low cut squared neckline made her appear older than she really was, flattering her figure and heightening her color. As she stepped off the landing she heard Christian's sharp intake of breath and noted Mrs. Hayward's approval by the sparkle in her eyes.

"Lovely my dear, just lovely. I've often wondered who would buy that dress for none of the women around here would do it justice. It certainly looks charming on you. Now come forward, let's see if it needs to be altered or hemmed." Mrs. Hayward continued to fuss over Josie while Christian sat atop his designated stool winking and nodding his approval for each gown or dress he liked.

Before she was done Josie had a peach colored dress, lavender, yellow and blue. She had two new brown day skirts and linen tops as well as petticoats, hoses and gloves. Christian insisted upon a purse, two more bonnets to match the dresses and knitted wool stockings.

Mrs. Hayward added a lovely hooded cloak; high healed laced boots and a pair of slippers. Josie was physically worn out by the time they were through and fretted over the final bill.

"If you say another word about money," Christian barked in a harsh tone, "I'll add something else to the pile." His eyes held a hint of danger, proving he was serious.

Josie snapped her mouth shut, biting her tongue with controlled effort. He had already added hair ribbons, soaps, perfumes and lotions while she was changing outfits upstairs. What more could she possibly need? When Mr. Hayward announced the total sum, Josie practically choked then proceeded to feel lightheaded and dizzy. Paling visibly she swayed and reached for the countertop to help balance herself. Her shopping adventure had cost Christian a small fortune. She'd be indebted to him forever. Shame was an overwhelming feeling and she suddenly regretted feeling so giddy when trying on each dress.

Christian worried, casting a glance in her direction he tried to understand how difficult this was for her. She obviously had lacked for money while growing up and what seemed like a small amount to him was monumental to her. He had plenty of money and reassured her with a smile and a joke. "I was saving it for a rainy day." Squeezing her arm he grinned and winked hoping she would feel better. The crease in her brows said otherwise.

"I'll get a job." Josie vowed fiercely. "Mark my words. I'll pay back your kindness twofold."

Shuffling through the rain they both carried a burden of packages back to the cabin dropping them into a heaping pile upon the floor once inside. Josie's heart swelled with gratitude as she sorted through the boxes removing tags and placing her new items in the bedroom closet, watching Christian from the corner of her eye while he built a small fire and hummed an old tune.

The clouds still blocked out the daylight and the rain continued it's pelting dance upon the slated rooftop while he stood starring into the fire, lost in thought, a million miles away. A pleasing warm scent from the burning of cherry wood filled the air.

Josie's mood was serene as she watched him, wanting to pay him back in some way for his kindness, loving him even more for what he had done for her today. She quietly approached him and boldly stepped between him and the fire. He had made her feel like a queen today, worthy of the best, comparable to women like Millie. He had made her feel pretty. She had never in her life been treated with such dignity, admiration and respect. She longed to stay here, with him, to live out this fairytale dream forever.

His eyes snapped to attention for she had a look upon her face he had never seen before. Was that desire he saw in the depths of her eyes? "Hey." He spoke lightly. "All finished putting things away?"

"Yes." She purred but didn't move. Longing and desire surfaced from the core of her womanhood causing every nerve in her body to become sensitized, as if she were floating on a warm cloud, waiting to fall. Looking into his eyes she slowly reached upward, placing her arms around his broad shoulders, spanning his neck with a hug.

"What are you…?"

He was unable to finish the question for she fell into him pressing her curves boldly against his muscular body, covering his open mouth with hers, kissing him with every ounce of desire she possessed. Opening her heart she gave all, taking a chance, holding nothing back, inviting him to take what she offered, inviting him to feast upon her desires and needs, making them his own.

He was lost, unable to think of anything except her body pressing against his. His own body responded swiftly to her actions as he wrapped her tighter in his embrace, kissing her more deeply, evoking a response from the core of her being. She felt like heaven to him, not just a toy or a need. This was Josie, the woman he…instantly he broke the kiss, needing air, fighting for control over his betraying body and thoughts.

Josie however, refused to relent. She knew what she wanted and wouldn't be deterred so easily. To her this was a moment of truth of sorts, for she knew he wanted her too. She had felt his hardness, giving her courage, encouraging her to continue, offering her a semblance of power, making her feel womanly, a new experience for her.

Running fingers through an untamed mass of hair while turning away, he stood silent and rigid, trying to tame his desire and hide his arousal. She had no idea what she was doing, at least that's what he kept reminding himself of, rationalizing her behavior and the boldness of her actions. She was young and inexperienced in the ways of men. It was up to him to resist, that's what he intended to do. The problem was he wasn't sure he could.

Intending to explain his feelings to Josie he turned back around, gulped and swallowed hard. All coherent thoughts went to the wayside in a flash. Oh Lord, he was going to break. She stood proud and beautiful, clothes pooled at her feet, firelight cast upon her bare flesh adding a bronze glow to the nude perfection of her body. With head held high she starred into his eyes, reading his response.

"God you're gorgeous." His eyes took in every curve; every freckle and every hair, imprinting her image upon his memory for this was a sight he'd not soon forget. Feeling discomfort at the rise in his body temperature, he scolded himself for building the fire. His blood was heated, flowing freely through his veins, adding color to his tanned skin. He determined that this would be one of the most difficult things he'd ever have to do.

Placing his hands upon her shoulders he squeezed his eye shut summoning deep within for self-control and will power. Breathing intensely he swirled his thumbs in a circular pattern on the bare skin of her shoulders before looking into her eyes. "Josie." The words stuck in his throat, refusing to work their way out. Clearing his throat and swallowing he continued with difficulty. "We can't do this."

Her mortified expression caused him to falter, wondering if he'd gone insane…lost his marbles so to speak. Any other man would have taken her by now, not caring who she was or how she felt.

"It wouldn't be proper Josie. Don't you understand?" His voice carried a pleading tone. "Folks are already spreading gossip about your staying here without proper supervision." His eyes roamed the entire range of her compliant body and he groaned softly. "If we do this, it'll only prove me a bastard and you a harlot. Is that what you want?"

His words were like a slap in the face to her. Although she didn't fully comprehend their meaning, she shook her head back and forth flushing bright red from head to toe. Tears pooled her eyes as she bent to gather her clothing, wanting only at this moment to bury her head in a hole. Wishing she could erase the past ten minutes from her life, cringing at his reminder—that her actions were those of a harlot. It seemed every time she turned around she was acting unladylike. No wonder she hadn't many friends, she thought. No wonder he rejected her advances. She would always remember this shame filled moment for she had never been so embarrassed or humiliated before in her life.

"Josie look at me."

She couldn't. She refused to allow him to see her indignity. Clamping her teeth together she purposely looked away from him, clutching her garments about her midsection to hide the nudity she so foolishly presented and concentrated on holding back the flood of tears that threatened to break the small barrier blinking provided.

"Awe, come on Josie, this is hard enough as it is. Look, I think you're beautiful. Actually, you're stunning without your clothes on. I must be crazy not to make love to you right here, right now. But I respect you and I know you deserve more than a quick roll in the sack. You deserve marriage and children and…and…" pausing in mid sentence he wondered what he'd said that was so funny at a time like this. Josie stood in front of him now, laughing mirthlessly. What the…why was she happy all of the sudden? "What? What?"

"Say it again." She demanded, face shinning with a bright smile.

"Say what again? Josie have you lost your mind?" His forehead wrinkled with a puzzled expression. First she was all upset, now she was laughing. For the life of him he couldn't figure her out and it irritated him to no end.

"Say the part about me being beautiful. Say it again please."

Looking intently into her eyes he replied with whole-hearted sincerity. "Josie you are beautiful. So damned beautiful…" His words trailed off as he inhaled deeply and his radiant eyes studied every inch of her body once again.

"More beautiful than Millie?" Her voice shook inquisitively as she tried to rein control over her emotions.

"You are much more beautiful than Millie both inside and out. I promise."

To finalize his statement he yanked her roughly to him, planting his mouth firmly on her lips, kissing her senseless, tasting her sweetness with his tongue, as if she were some divine feast. He ate hungrily before pulling away; depriving himself of the greatest feast he'd ever been offered.

"Should I move out?"

"Propriety would demand so but I kind of like having you around. I mean, you don't smell that bad. You cook decently. It's edible. I haven't died yet from your food." With a devilish smirk upon his face he added as an afterthought. "Cabin's nice and clean too."

"Oh you." Punching him playfully on the upper arm, she couldn't help but worry about the nagging reminder that the people in this town really didn't like her. "Christian, can I beg a favor of you?"

"Anything for you Josie."

"When you leave for work tomorrow, can you instruct Angus to take me into town? I have a few things I'd like to look into. It won't take long, I promise."

"I'll grant your leave as long as you promise to stay close and follow his orders."

"Absolutely. Thank you."

"Now put your clothes back on for Pete's sake, before I change my mind about being a gentleman."

CHAPTER EIGHT

Josie was determined not to give up on Christian yet. She knew she loved him and was willing to do whatever it took to make him love her. She was sure he already felt something for her. After all, he did say she was beautiful. Smiling to herself she finished putting a lunch together for him. The sun was barely sprouting its morning rays over the treetops. The air was warm and fresh.

Christian was looking forward to tracking Randy Hurley today. With the heavy rains the previous day his tracks would be easier to find and follow since foot and horse print were hard to hide in the mud. Reaching for the door latch he was halted by Josie's sultry voice. Lost in his own thoughts he hadn't even realized she was up yet.

Sauntering over to him with nothing on except a sheet wrapped and knotted snugly above the bust line, she smiled smugly handing him the pouch containing a nice homemade lunch. "My contribution to the town's Sheriff. There's enough there to feed three men if need be. Good luck scouting today." Rising on her bare toes she brazenly planted a kiss on his whisker-covered cheek.

He groaned out load trying to hide the effect her actions had on his betraying body. "For Christ's sake Josie put some clothes on before Angus sees you. I don't understand. I buy you all kinds of clothes yet you walk around in a ten cent sheet!" His jaw tightened into the now familiar firm line that characterized his struggle for control.

She relished in his gaze with a smugness beset by a girl awakening to womanhood. His words were harsh yet she smiled knowing he was frustrated, feeling giddy because she was the cause of it. Giggling, she saluted smartly and replied with a brave "Yes sir."

Yanking open the door he had one foot out before he threw caution into the wind and blindly acted on instinct. She had already kept him awake all night. Images of her nude body appeared every time he shut his eyes making sleep impossible. Stepping back into the cabin's interior he slammed the door shut, grabbed and pulled Josie urgently to him, kissing her smiling lips, pulling her body more firmly against his, squeezing her tight little bottom and rubbing his thigh between her legs. As the kiss deepened he felt Josie's body become placid, almost melting in his arms. He knew the exact moment her passion filled body surrendered. Pulling away abruptly he tipped the edge of his hat as she staggered backwards momentarily thrown off balance by the intensity of her desire. "You shouldn't play with fire Josie. See you tonight." Winking, he opened the door this time proceeding through without looking back. Nodding to Angus, he gave the directions Josie had requested and warned. "Keep a watchful eye on her man. The little nymph is bound to cause trouble in some way, shape, or form. I swear she'll be the death of me."

"Oh the nerve of that man." Angry words echoed the stomping of her foot as she turned and began cleaning her mess from the lunch preparations, fuming all the while at Christian's arrogance. Why did men have to be so difficult? Were all men like him? She couldn't stop the flood of questions his behavior caused her inquisitive mind to develop. Maybe Angus could enlighten her a little.

Braiding the long locks of hair spanning down her back she busily prepared for the day, choosing a simple skirt and blouse to wear. She didn't want to appear too fancy for her walk into town, yet just the starchiness of new clothing made her feel like a new person. She felt worthy. Self-respect was something Christian had taught her. She felt she owed him so much more than she'd ever be able to repay, so much more than just money.

Stepping onto the porch and smiling brightly she informed Angus that she was ready.

"Where are we goin?" He asked gruffly.

"To find me a job, if that's at all possible."

"Oh. Okay then, where to first?" He offered his arm and she gently hooked her hand upon his elbow.

"How about the general store?"

When they entered the storefront Josie was filled with delight for the memories of her shopping adventure the day before were pleasant.

"Well Josie dear, how are you today?" Mrs. Hayward immediately bustled forward embracing her in a warm welcoming hug. "What can I do for you? Is something wrong with one of your dresses?"

"No. No not at all Mrs. Hayward. I've come to imply upon other matters. Do you have a moment?"

"Why certainly dear. Come on back. Angus, Josie will be in the back with me. Oh don't give me that grizzly look! She'll be fine."

Once in the back they had a little more privacy, away from curious looks and big ears. Mrs. Hayward turned, pinning Josie with a peculiar look, offering one hundred percent of her attention. "Now dear what do you need?"

"Well, um…" Licking her lips and twining her fingers together in a display of nervousness, Josie wasn't sure how or even where to start. "I owe Christian so much, and I'd like to pay him back. He mentioned last evening how improper it is, my staying with him and all. He claims folks are talking. I'm not sure how to feel about that but I need a job to earn some money. I need to find another place to stay but that's only half the problem." Pausing to breathe then urged on by Mrs. Hayward's expectant look and slightly raised eyebrows, she continued. "I think I've fallen head over heals in love with the man. I was hoping you could guide me as to what to do. You see, I'd give anything for him to love me too."

Patting her hand for comfort, Mrs. Hayward smiled and carefully replied. "My dear you've come to the right place. I think I can help you with all but one of these matters. But, I'm certain you won't have to worry overmuch anyways."

"I don't understand."

"Well do you know how to sew and clean?"

"Yes. Yes I do." Josie nodded emphatically as eagerness bubbled to the surface.

"I can pay you twenty cents a day to do cleaning and mending here for me. It's not much and it'll be slow earning. Beneath the staircase is a tiny room with a bed and a small bureau. You may stay there. It will be considered part of your weekly pay but…" She held up a finger as if to halt all thoughts in Josie's spinning mind. "I will only comply if the Sheriff himself tells me it's okay."

"Oh Mrs. Hayward!" Josie's bubbled up anticipation broke free. A smile spread from ear to ear as she leaped forward and hugged the older lady. "Thank you. Thank you. Oh I promise to do a wonderful job for you. You'll see, there won't be a single ounce of dust or dirt anywhere."

"Like I said, I expect the Sheriff's approval first, but we'll plan on you moving in and starting Monday. How's that sound to you?"

"Wonderful. Thank you again Mrs. Hayward. I promise you won't be disappointed."

"Oh and Josie, about him loving you, he'll come around dear. You'll see."

Josie couldn't help but be happy. Lifting her skirt just above the ankles, she skipped across the street and back to the cabin causing Angus to grunt in dismay at having to walk faster in order to keep up with her.

As they climbed the steps to the front porch Angus asked. "Why are you bouncing around like a little sprig?"

Turning she plopped spiritedly down on the top step then scooted over motioning with a wave of the hand for Angus to join her. "I'm just happy today Angus. How about you? Aren't you ever happy?"

"Nope. Can't say as I am." Looking away he stuffed a pinch of tobacco beneath his lower lip.

"Well that's too bad. I think everybody should be happy every now and then." Silence spanned as they both sat shoulder to shoulder, lost in their own thoughts. The sun peaked high in the sky, warming the air considerably.

"Angus?"

"Humm."

"What qualities do men like in women?" It was a very serious question. She had thought the words over carefully before asking.

"Well let me think here." Scratching his head, stifling a cough he replied. "She's gotta cook good."

"Yeah. Okay."

"It's always a plus if she's mute."

"Oh Angus you're rotten!" Shoving him playfully her smirk promised retribution. "I got a job today so I can start paying Christian back for all he's done for me. I've got a place to stay and…"

"And you've got company." The tone of his voice dripped with distaste as Josie looked beyond the path to see who was approaching.

"Oh puppy dog tails." She moaned with dread tucking her face in her hands, slumping her shoulders and pouting. "I wonder what she wants."

"I expect you'll find out right soon." Angus's look was filled with apathy as Millie approached them.

"Hello Miss Millie." Josie said standing to greet her unwanted visitor. "What brings you here on such a nice day?" She had to hide a smirk of satisfaction as Angus spit right close to Millie's foot, causing the girl to turn red with anger and take a step back.

"I've come bearing apologies. Is there some place we can talk offering a little more privacy, a clean floor and some shade?" Millie's mood was smug and her reply curt and controlled in an even tone. Her words were mock disrespect to

Angus. All of which he deserved, Josie thought, since he couldn't seem to control his spitting habit of a sudden.

A ting of guilt spread through her as she swallowed a dose of apprehension while looking directly into Millie's eyes. "I guess we can go inside if you insist."

"I'm insisting." Millie replied. "The sun is a trifle hot this afternoon." Pulling a fan from her reticule, she spread it fully then began flicking her wrist back and forth allowing the faint breeze to kiss her face.

Josie knew her own smile was fake and felt her face muscles cramping from the effort. The tongue must be a mighty muscle, she thought, for she wasn't sure she had the strength to hold it. Opening the door she nodded for Millie to cross the threshold.

Millie's very presence within the cozy cabin was a violation to the moments and memories of her most intimate thoughts. It was comparable to placing a rattlesnake atop a bed of roses. Attempting to dismiss the ugly thoughts from her mind she focused on Millie's face, trying to read her expression, trying to decipher truth from lies. "Well we're inside now so talk. What do you want Millie?"

"My goodness." Millie batted her eyelashes feigning surprise at Josie's bluntness. "You're not very pleasant today."

"That's because you weren't very pleasant the first time we met."

"I'm sorry Josie." Puckering her lips into a pout Millie silently counted to ten before calming herself down enough to speak. The rude little bitch acted like she owned the place. "I already told you I've come to say I'm sorry. Can you please find it in your heart to forgive me? We can start over if you'll accept my apology." There, she thought, that wasn't so bad. But was it convincing enough?

Josie must not have thought so. "You know Millie, I wish I could but I'm beyond that point. If the milk wasn't enough to ruin a friendship, the accusations in town regarding the fire were. No, I do not wish to start over with you. What's done is done. I think it best if we simply stay away from each other."

Slowly walking around the room, inspecting it's clean interior, Millie thought of her reply as she pulled a necklace from under her sleeve and slipped it onto the mantel before turning to face her adversary once more. Trying hard to divert Josie's attention she sauntered back to the front door. "Well I can't say that I blame you for not forgiving me. I am a spoiled brat from time to time. I however, am the better person for I have apologized none the less. You really should reconsider. You don't want to have me as your enemy. Trust me."

Reaching for the door she tossed another snide remark over her shoulder. "By the way, I like what you've done to the place."

What was that supposed to mean? Josie couldn't shake the feeling of dread left in Millie's wake. Something bad was going to happen. She could feel it in her bones. A knock on the door pulled her thoughts free from a knot of emotions. "Who is it?" If it were Millie again, she'd bolt the door rather than open it.

"It's me, Old Angus."

Relief flooded through Josie as she opened the door gaining him entrance. In a beaten voice she invited him in, informing him that she needed to be cheered up.

"Are you okay?"

"Yes I'm fine. Thank you for asking. I don't trust her and I can't help but wonder what the real purpose was of her visit today."

"What'd she say?"

"She said she was sorry but I don't believe her one bit. She's up to something. I'm sure of it."

Angus was quiet for a minute before asking. "Did she touch anything?"

"No I don't think so. She just snooped around a little."

"Okay Josie, you're right. There's a reason for her visit. Now let's retrace her steps and see if we can figure out what it is."

"That won't be too difficult. All she did was walk over here to the…Holy Saints and Angels!" Putting a hand over her mouth she gasped for air before placing a shaky palm above her heart, feeling faint as its rapid tempo increased.

"Gosh Josie." Angus said peering over her shoulder. "Looks like you're in another pickle again."

"Angus!" She bellowed flabbergasted and shocked. "What are we going to do?"

"We?"

"Yes we. You're in on this too!"

"I'm not sure I like that but let's have a look see here." Lifting up the necklace he inspected it carefully. "Hmm."

"What?" Her curiosity was overwhelming as she bounced up and down heal to toe. Impatiently awaiting his expertise.

"I know exactly to whom this necklace belongs to."

"Who? Who?"

"You sound like an owl. It belongs to Mrs. Hayward. See their family mark is right here." He held the necklace up showing Josie the display of garnet stones with a fancy *H* scrolled on the back.

Josie felt horrible. In fact, she felt down right sick to her stomach. What a terrible thing to have happen. That Millie McQuade was evil through and through. "Angus, I didn't take that necklace. I swear on my mothers grave I didn't take it."

"I know you didn't Josie. I'm just not sure what to do. Sure do wish Sheriff C were here. He'd know exactly what to do." Standing in one place he rocked from one foot to the other revealing uncertainty.

"Oh never mind him. Here, give me that." She reached out and quickly snatched the necklace from his fingers.

"Josie whatcha doin? Hey! Come back here young lady. Where do you think you're going?" Angus leaped forward trying desperately to keep up with Josie's angry strides as she stomped out of the cabin. He'd never seen her angry before but the look in her eyes as she crossed the street and marched bravely into the storefront would have scarred the devil out of any man, much less a woman. He almost felt sorry for Millie.

As soon as they entered the store a rumble of low voices hushed as the room became completely silent. In the back stood a small group of people. Millie was the center of their attention.

"Ah Josie, maybe you should hold off for the Sheriff. Let's not do anything foolish her now girl." Angus's voice betrayed his worry and concern as well as fear of the Sheriff's anger should he not watch over Josie well enough.

Josie heeded no warning for she was boiling mad. She almost couldn't think straight. Hatred and anger embraced her heart and soul causing her to loose check of her emotions. Marching towards the back, the circle of people stepped aside creating an isle way leading directly to Millie and Mrs. Hayward. Holding her head high, Josie approached with a mad fearless look in her eyes. "Mrs. Hayward, Millie stole this from you and planted it in the Sheriff's cabin. Angus is witness to it all. I'm here to give it back." She heard Millie's gasp as she held out the necklace, dropping it into Mrs. Hayward's shaking hand. The older robust lady's face appeared stricken and confused yet relieved at the same time.

Millie's hissing voice grated on the silence. "Why Josie you're a thief! Nobody here will listen to your..."

Josie didn't let Millie finish her sentence. Stepping quickly she punched Millie square in the eye as hard as she could. Stumbling backwards, knocking over a display table, Millie landed roughly on her rump, skirts up over her knees, feet in the air as she began to cry. The welt from the assault showing immediately upon her face turning purple in color, changing her features from pretty to pitiful.

Without a word Josie walked back to the entrance, past a gaping Angus who stood slack jawed in astonishment. Before they were both out the door the people within the store began to applaud, clapping and hollering for Josie had done something they had all wished would have been done ages ago.

Mrs. Hayward smiled and stated. "That's my girl."

"Josie!" The door banged open causing tiny chunks and crumbs of mortar to fall from between the planks of wood along the wall, leaving disappearing trails of dust in their wake. The noise resounded throughout the cabin interior causing both Angus and Josie to jump in surprise at the abrupt interruption.

"Geez Christian, you nearly scared the tar out of me. She was so engrossed in the game of checkers she hadn't even heard the approaching footsteps on the porch. Standing to stretch out achy muscles she began folding the burlap material they had used and marked as a playing board while Angus gathered the wooden pieces he had proudly created himself with a carving knife and pine branches.

Christian's look was livid causing Josie to fret for she had never been on the receiving end of his wrath before. His eyes pierced her, angry orbs that shot daggers right through her heart. "I can't leave you alone for one damn minute can I?"

"What are you talking about?" This couldn't be the same man that had kissed her so passionately this morning before leaving.

Angus quietly put the rest of the game away before slipping into a shadowy corner awkwardly awaiting his boss's dismissal. Silently he observed the battle about to unfold between two of his favorite people. He would step forward if need be, however he was certain of two things. The first was that Sheriff C would never harm Josie no matter how barmy and upset he was. The second was that Josie was tough enough to put the Sheriff in his place. Instantly his face lit up with the realization that is could be quite a show of entertainment. He mentally began calculating the odds then placed an imaginary bet with himself on who the victor would be.

"You know damn well what I'm talking about. Don't play daft with me!"

"No. I don't know what your talking about so why don't you explain?" With hands on hips she flippantly batted her eyelashes while mentally reviewing her day. Maybe he had met up with Mrs. Hayward. Could he be upset about her job? Surely he'd be happy for her.

"Are you crazy? What the hell is wrong with you? Why would you do something so foolish?"

"What do you mean foolish?" She was yelling now, matching his voice level. Feeling the veins tighten in her neck from the strain. Placing her arms down along her sides, squeezing her fingers into tight fist for the second time that day she remarked. "I was only trying to pay you back."

"Pay me back! Pay me back? How the hell would punching Millie McQuade pay me back?" This was ridiculous. The entire incident was almost unbearable.

Of a sudden Josie seemed to lose her voice for she couldn't talk past the lump that had formed her throat.

"Well answer me damn it!" He had to clench his fist and grind his teeth together to keep from hollering even louder. When it came to her, he found himself unable to rationalize or even behave in the same upstanding manner he once had. When it came to her, he was always loosing control.

Feeling uncharacteristically timid and slightly embarrassed at her weakness and inability to control her temper when encountering Millie, a flush spread its warm touch along her face and neck as she fixed her gaze upon her feet.

"You know Josie, I thought you were better than that. I thought you of all people, would never hurt anyone or anything." There was no longer regret reflected in his tone, only disgust. "I guess I thought wrong."

His condescending words weren't lost on her. Remaining silent, she concentrated on breathing evenly for the churning of her stomach created a feeling of growing nausea. She fought the urge to flee before loosing her lunch.

"God damn it Josie! What the hell were you thinking?" Unable to hold his emotions at bay any longer he grabbed her shoulders, roughly shaking her in an effort to evoke an answer, not just any answer but one that would magically clear up this entire mess, one that was just short of a miracle. "Answer me."

Sobbing, her words came out in an uneven tone. "I wasn't thinking. I was just angry. She can hurt me but I won't stand by and watch while she hurts others that have shown me kindness." Her face constricted in a feature of pain for his hands were squeezing her shoulders so hard she was certain there would be marks left long after the sensation of the contact had ended.

Christian read the pain on her face and released her shoulders only to pull her to him for the second time that day. He enfolded her in a stalwart embrace, resting his chin atop her faintly scented hair, breathing her scent and blinking rapidly to hold back unshed tears, tears that would only demean his manhood if ever discovered.

Josie sensed his unease more than felt it. Unable to see his face, she was instinctively aware of the exact moment that his mood transformed from anger to despair. A peculiar feeling prickled along her spine sending unease throughout her system like a brisk wind fluttering through the leaves of a tall tree. Pulling away to free herself of his hardened embrace, then peering up to look at his facial expression, she attempted to accurately read his features. Dread filled his lovely eyes while determination set rigidly along his chiseled jaw line.

"I'm sorry Christian. I didn't mean to cause you more trouble. Honestly I didn't."

"I don't know what to do Josie." Holding her hands while looking into her emerald eyes he silently willed forward a vast amount of strength for the both of them. "For the first time in my life I find myself doubting my own actions and beliefs. For some reason you seem to bring out the worst in me."

"What do you mean by that?" Her brows drew together and her forehead wrinkled in confusion. "I think that you're wonder…"

"Josie." Harshly interrupting her, the words poured from his mouth, rushed and hurried, they were dispelled like an evil curse. "I have to place you under arrest."

Stunned into silence she snatched her chilled fingers from his warm grasp for it had suddenly turned cold. Her mouth opened in genuine disbelief before snapping shut causing her teeth to clank painfully, She pursed her lips into a firm line. The room began to sway while shadows faded into blurred clouds in her peripheral vision. Oh dear Lord. Ordering herself to be strong and mentally repeating that she wouldn't swoon, she shook off the feeling of weakness by pulling her shoulders back, standing tall and lifting her chin in a defiant gesture. Looking straight into his eyes she stretched her arms out towards him, hands clasped together, waiting to be shackled.

"You do what you have to do Christian. I'm adult enough to face the consequences of my actions. I won't, however, apologize for I'm not sorry for what I've done." Her words were short and clipped, fronting a bravery and boldness she didn't feel on the inside.

Christian admired her strength as well as the respect projected towards him. His job was hard enough as it was without having to arrest the woman he lov…cutting the thought short he cursed out loud then stiffened rigidly as he heard the cock of a gun coming from a shadowed corner of the room. Craning his neck to one side his body followed filled with warning signals, growing agitated with the situation. "Angus, what the hell are you doing?"

"I'm sorry Sheriff but I draw the line at you cuffing the little lady here. No sir, I can't allow it. Devil have your soul if you do."

"Do you realize that you're breaking the law now? What do I have here? A bunch of criminals?" For Christ's sake put that thing down. I'm not going to cuff her but I do have to arrest her. I'm sorry. I have no choice. Millie filed a formal complaint and got the judge to sign it. It didn't help any that she's got a black eye and the judge is her father. Josie will have to go to jail and come Monday, we'll have a public hearing."

"Monday!" Angus roared. "You're gonna let her sit in jail for nearly a week?" Taking a step forward, squeezing his fist, cracking his knuckles, murder danced in his eyes. He growled. "Why I aught to…"

"Settle down now Angus. There's no need to raise hell here." Damn his best friend, won over and gone trader, all for the likes of Josie. There had been a lot of times when the two of them were alone together. Maybe Angus was smitten with her. The thought roared with frustration and darkness as it gripped his soul, draining him of a feeling he couldn't put a name to. In a worse mood now than what he was in before, he barked out orders with a look that dared defiance. "Put that gun down now or it'll become the towns property and I'll tan your hide myself. Come on Josie. You are under arrest for assaulting another human being. There's not a damn thing I can do about it so shut your trap and get to walking."

Ooh, she was more than a little upset with both herself and him. Stomping her foot and shuffling out the door she couldn't help but grumble. "You call Millie a human being? You must be daft." With swinging arms she madly marched briskly along the street towards the jailhouse leaving both Angus and Christian behind. Feeling as if all eyes were upon her when in fact there were very few folks out, she lifted her chin even higher. The musical sounds of frogs and crickets hung heavy in the air but did little to calm and soothe her pride. Ascending the steps leading to the jail's porch she slammed the outer door in Christian's face then went mirthlessly to the far cell before slamming the cast iron door shut, locking herself in.

At Neb's inquisitive look she bellowed. "Hello and excuse me. I'm just a trifle angry right now. I'll have to count to ten." Plopping her derriere roughly onto the squeaky and unstable bench she folded her arms over her chest as Christian stepped through the door. "Maybe I should count to one hundred."

With a somewhat blank look upon his face Neb angled his body weight onto one elbow and replied. "Ma…ma…maybe you sh…sh…should c…count higher d…d…dan dat."

Looking over to him she caught a twinkle in his one good eye and smiled before laughing. "I think you're right. Thank you Neb." With that she pulled her knees to her chest then turned facing the wall, giving Christian the silent treatment.

CHAPTER NINE

Strolling back to the cabin, Christian was in the foulest mood he'd ever been in. That hadn't gone well at all. But what did he expect? He planned to gather a nightgown for Josie along with a few other supplies. If she had to be locked up he was going to make sure she was as comfortable as possible. He also had every intention of staying with her the entire time. He had never dreamed the day would come when he would have to place a female behind bars and the amenities at the jailhouse were not designed for the needs and privacy of a woman. If Josie didn't hate him now, she certainly would real soon.

He couldn't help but smile at the spirit and determination she had whole-heartedly displayed, showing her true character for what it was while marching down the street to the jail, chin up in proud defiance. She sure was something. Most women would have taken to tears and pleading, but not his Josie. She held her head high. He solemnly realized he had expected nothing less and admired her even more for her gallant behavior. He also accepted the fact that she was "his Josie" for that's what he had come to think of her as. God help anyone that tried to harm her or any man attempting to call on her. He'd wring their necks with his own two hands.

Clenching his first and cracking his knuckles, he gathered the things he thought she would need and walked back towards the jail. The hour was growing late and light filtered from some of the windows along the boardwalk casting shadows into the street. Many shops were closed or in the process of closing and he could hear the twanging screech of a fiddle being played off in the distance. The music floated on the air, more than likely strung as a lullaby to put little ones to sleep. An image of him and Josie tucking children in for the night flashed through his mind causing desire to bubble to the surface, diminishing his reservations and uncertainty. For the first time ever he allowed himself to contemplate having a family and loving a woman deeply enough to cherish her for the rest of his life. He could only see Josie as that woman. She'd be wonderful.

He just knew it. "What the hell am I thinking?" He quietly mumbled to himself and shook his head to clear his mind.

"Evening Sheriff." The sultry voice caught him off guard, his awareness instantly on edge, thoroughly irritated that the little chit in front of him had violated his thoughts.

"Evening Millie." With a firmly set chin he looked across the street intending to ignore the girl and return to Josie as quickly as possible. Unfortunately, luck wasn't with him tonight. For that matter, luck hadn't been with him all day.

"I'm glad you were kind enough to put that wild cat behind bars before she hurt someone else or even a child!"

Stopping dead in his tracks he stiffened rigidly before turning toward Millie, dark eyes blazing with hatred from the fire that burned within, igniting fiercely with her words. Millie didn't know him well enough to measure the level of anger which was evident in the firm set of his jaw as well as the controlled tightness of his stance, the way he stood stock still, convincing himself not to strangle her.

Stepping into him and placing a gloved hand upon his elbow she added provocatively. "I do believe Sheriff, you are a hero. However can I thank you?"

"I am far from a hero Millie, and you are far from being the innocent angel you'd like everybody to believe."

"Why Sheriff, what are you saying?" She gasped, innocently placing a hand over her heart, as if hurt and betrayed.

"I'm saying that the underhanded way you set Josie up has not escaped my attention. I'm not a fool Millie. You should heed my words as fair warning."

"Obviously you misunderstood my good intentions."

"No. You misunderstood mine. I don't like thieves and underhanded liers."

"Well, neither do I Sheriff. Neither do I. That's why I did what I did. I'm only trying to help protect the fine ladies and gentlemen of this town."

"Protect them from what? A harmless woman with a big heart bears no threat to this community!"

"I strongly disagree. She is more than harmless! She's the devil's own spawn!"

"Oh really?" His eyebrows shot up. "And who is she going to hurt?"

Millie's silence wore thin as he adamantly put everything together in his mind. The pieces fit like the spokes on a wooden wagon wheel. Millie saw Josie as a threat because of him. Now what was he supposed to do? Should he add fuel to the fire in an attempt to see what Millie would do next, or should he down play his care and concern for Josie and pretend she didn't matter to him in the least? Either way, the only one to get hurt would be Josie. He couldn't let that happen.

"Just stay away." The tone of his voice projected a fierce threat as he yanked his arm away from her hand.

"Stay away from who Sheriff? You or her?"

"Don't be foolish now Millie. I already told you point blank that I don't like thieves and liars. Especially ones with black eyes."

"Ooh!" Stomping her foot didn't make her feel any better as she stood open mouthed staring at his back while it faded into the darkness. She had thought that making Josie look bad would solve her little dilemma with the Sheriff. Now, she was miffed that it hadn't. Well she'd just have to come up with another solution to the problem or, she thought clapping her hands together to free her gloves from dust, I'll just have to get rid of the problem altogether. A wicked thought raced through her mind and she quickly began to devise and plot against Josie forming a plan that would work to her benefit. She would have her Sheriff, no matter what.

Quietly slipping into the jailhouse, Christian lit a few wax candles since the room had grown dark and gloomy. He had never thought before about how it would feel to sit here in the dark, all alone and fretful of the future and/or what may or may not happen. He reminded himself that the men held in the jail before had done things wrong and deserved to sit in a cell rotting away a little with each passing day. Josie didn't deserve this. She had wronged no one except Millie and Millie had deserved it no doubt.

Glancing over at the object of his thoughts only made him feel like a cad for Josie appeared a lone flower in the middle of a dry dessert. She sat with her back against the far wall, arms crossed angrily in front of her. She looked so small and beautiful he could hardly keep himself from saying exactly that.

"Josie I um, I brought you some clothes and a few other things."

She looked away refusing to meet his eyes or even to acknowledge hearing his words at all.

"Please Josie, don't make this any harder than it already is."

Silence.

"I understand. If you decide you need anything at all, I'll be right across the room." The woman was exasperating to say the least. Kicking off his boots and laying his head upon the desk he was close to dozing off when he heard Josie's velvet soft voice.

"Good night Neb Hurley. May God smile upon your dreams."

"N…n…night Josie."

He knew she was just trying to raise his hackles and he couldn't blame her one bit. He felt terrible. His last thought before falling asleep was vowing to take better care of the one thing he cherished most in his life—her.

"Good morning Hanna."

"Morning Millie. What can I do for you today?" The restaurant had just recently re-opened and it felt good to be back to work. Of course everything was new and sparkling clean from the tabletops to the new cash drawer. The biggest and best surprise ever was the new pot bellied stove and tiled ovens that would now be used to cook all the food. The tiles were white with black spring shaped handles and amazingly efficient. Hanna was so happy that even Millie's presence wasn't going to bust her bubble.

"I'd like a job Hanna."

"What?" Hanna was shocked, almost speechless. This couldn't be possible. The Judge's spoiled rotten daughter, miss 'I'm better than everyone else' wanted a job? It was truly unbelievable. She peered out the curtained window up at the sky.

"What are you doing?" Millie asked.

"I was looking for light from the heavens, angels, demonic beasts. Surely this has to be the revelations. Is this your idea of a joke?"

"No. No please. I'm serious. I really want to work." Seeing Hanna's doubtful expression through raised eyebrows Millie continued. "I've been evaluating myself so to speak and, well, frankly I find myself lacking. I can see why people don't like me." It was a down right lie and a small part in her plan for revenge. She desperately needed the job in order to carry out her wicked scheme. She let that desperation fill her voice and begged with sincerity. "Honestly Hanna, how would you like to be me? It isn't any fun. Trust me, I know. I really think a job doing something more than just grading slates is the first step to the new me."

Hanna didn't know what to say. The girl seemed sincere. Maybe she was right. A job was exactly what she needed. Well she'd give her the worst one and see how she did with it.

"Okay Millie, I'll let you work here but the only position open right now is for a dishwasher and cleaner. The general appearance of the restaurant and its cleanliness will be your responsibility." The corners of her mouth twitched as she tried to hide a smile while watching Millie's features change from a horrified expression to mild acceptance.

"When can I start?"

"How about first thing tomorrow morning…say 5:00a.m.?"

Millie gulped back her natural retort. "Sure. Thanks Hanna." Five o'clock in the morning, she thought as she walked back towards the hotel; she hadn't ever been up before 10:00 in the morning. This would be difficult but worth it if everything fell into place. Plus, father would be proud of her as well. Maybe he would forgive her for the little stunt she had pulled. He was right upset with her as it was. A job could only influence her positively no matter who was around.

Josie awoke sore and ruffled from passing the night on the small bench in the cell. Every bone in her body ached as she moved to stand, blinking back tears of a new dilemma. She could see Christian sleeping soundly with booted feet propped on his desk. His head slumped to one side as he snored softly. His features were softened and appeared to be much younger while caught in a peaceful slumber. Anger rose rapidly taking over her thoughts and she could hardly contain it as she wrapped delicate fingers around the cold iron bars locking her in.

"Sheriff C wake up."

When he continued to sleep without even stirring she grew slightly frantic. Shaking the bars with all the might she could muster forth and swearing inwardly she repeated the plea. "Sheriff wake up!"

Christian jumped wondering what was so urgent-causing Josie's distress. His hands automatically felt for the guns holstered at his hips as he stood surveying the room. Nothing appeared out of sorts. It was still dark outside but sunrise was only moments away. Usually he was up and about by now but last night he had watched over Josie for hours and wasn't blessed with the release of sleep until morning was near. "What is it? What's wrong?"

"Sheriff please open the door."

"Josie I can't." His jaw tightened and twitched in aggravation as he took heady note that she was addressing him as Sheriff once again and not by his god given name. It didn't settle well for reasons he couldn't explain.

"Please have a heart." Her voice begged.

They were now standing face to face; only the bars prevented him from pulling her close, smelling her hair, hugging her tightly.

"I have to use the outhouse." Just putting the problem to words embarrassed her.

"There's a pot in the cell Josie. Use that."

"I can't." She hissed as her face registered shocked horror. "There's no privacy. A woman needs her privacy for such matters."

He was silently thinking of what to do, mentally hatching one solution after another.

"Please. You can tie my wrist. Just walk me to the cabin and allow me to wash and change. I won't be a problem. I promise."

"Josie honey I can't do that." The Judge is right upset about this whole situation. It'll be my job." His gut clenched as he fought an inner battle to forgo any concerns about being Sheriff and do what was right by Josie.

"Don't call me honey you big oaf. Don't ever call me honey again! That's some silly stuff that bees produce. I'm not your honey and I'll never be sweet to you again." After a moments silence, except for the tapping of her foot, she asked. "Well, what do you suggest I do?"

"For starters, I can leave and guard the door while you use the pot. Just holler when you're finished."

"What?" This was terribly humiliating. Her cheeks turned a crimson red; as it was dark he could still tell her face was flushed. "I've already explained. I can't go there. Even if you gave me privacy Neb is next to me and Joey would empty the pot. That's terribly embarrassing. It may not matter to a man but it certainly is demeaning to a woman! For God sakes allow me to keep some dignity!" Crossing her arms in front and tightening her jaw she stood with both feet apart while looking directly at him, awaiting an argument.

"I'm sorry Josie. I can't treat you any differently than any other person that's been housed in this jail. It could open the door for all kinds of problems."

"That's just nonsense Sheriff C and you know it. You're just being a jack in the box trying to prove your authority over me." Golly she was mad. He was being pig headed. Well he could try all he wanted to. Dignity was dignity and she was born with plenty of it. Raising her chin even higher in a dismissive gesture she talked in a calm and low voice. "Never mind. Just go away Sheriff. Just go away."

Plopping back down on the bench she quietly simmered in anger while turning her back to him, facing the wall. He was a stubborn box head. Worst of all, she thought, was that she had fallen in love with a complete ass.

Thinking quickly Christian left the jailhouse and fetched some clean linen from the cabin. Upon return he shoved them through the bars towards Josie. "Here these should help."

When she didn't move or look at him his anger snapped. "Fine. So be it. You'll have no privacy at all because of your own foolish pride. Hasn't it gotten you into enough trouble already?" Moving to walk away he bit his tongue. Women! He could certainly do without the headache.

"Wait."

That one word halted his steps. Apparently she had changed her mind.

"I'd be grateful for the linens."

He couldn't help but smile. No matter the circumstances, Josie was no fool. Unfolding the linens he made a makeshift curtain for her. She could pull it to the side and hold it in place by wrapping the length through the bars. This allowed her to see out or, she could leave it hang straight down, offering a semblance of privacy. He had assumed she was satisfied with the idea until she smartly ordered him out.

"What do you mean out?"

"You have to go outside. I can't do my thing with you listening."

Rolling his eyes and begging mercy from the lord he left as requested wondering if all women were as fickle about such matters. Then he remembered that not all women were put in jail and felt a waterfall of guilt was over him.

A short while later Hanna brought breakfast over as was customary. The restaurant had always provided meals for the prisoners based on the leftovers after all others were served. This caused breakfast to be served around ten o'clock in the morning, lunch was around three o'clock, and dinner was always very late, usually around nine o'clock at night.

Josie's stomach growled but she refused to eat. To her way of thinking, if she ate or drank, she would eventually have to use the pot again. Although it was God's will that a body work the way it did, she had no desire to relive the humbling event again anytime soon.

Christian grew angry for he couldn't force Josie to eat and so she had gone an entire day without sustenance. Come nightfall, he simply asked what he had to do to get her to eat and was much surprised at the directness of her answer.

"Let me use the outhouse. That's all I ask."

"Fine." He agreed flatly. "Do you wish to use it now?"

"I would be relieved to use it now." She batted her eyelashes and smiled primly, reminding him of the battle he'd just lost.

The few minutes of offered privacy was a grave joy to Josie but when the iron bars slammed shut once more she was all the more aware of her environment and felt like a caged animal. The walls seemed to be closing in on her and she felt she couldn't breath normally. The heat of the night was almost unbearable. Christian had propped the door open with a wooden wedge, providing a small breeze of fresh air—but not nearly enough.

By morning Josie had had her fill of the small enclosed quarters and wondered mirthlessly how a body could continually pass a nights sleep on a bench as hard as this; a strap iron bench none the less. It may as well have been made of stone for she was certain her backside couldn't ache any worse. Surely there were red markings permanently indented on her skin from the nail-heads that had been hammered flat into the narrow strips forming the seat. It was now her second morning and she was sure to burst and go berserk at any moment.

It was dark and gloomy in the room and a musky scent impaled her senses when she moved the linen to one side, draping it through the iron bars. Christian was nowhere to be seen. Fuming at his arrogance she ascertained that he most likely passed a peaceful nights sleep in the comfort of his own bed. She supposed, in all fairness, she couldn't blame him for doing so. After all, she had occupied and slept in his bed for weeks now while he was left lying each night on a hardwood floor. If that floor felt anything like the wrought bench, she couldn't blame him for being grumpy all the time and actually felt sorry for not thinking of his comfort and disposition before this.

Lost in thought, she combed through the snarls and locks of hair with nimble fingers then wound a thick braid and tucked it beneath the nape of her neck. With crescendoing agitation she briskly wiped her face using the hanging linen then sat back down. Pouting was never becoming to her nature and was slowly put to rest as her temper swiftly formed an unyielding burst of anger. A disarming madness overcame her every thought as she stood and yanked as hard as she could on the cast iron rails, shaking the frame with a blinding bout of fury. An animalistic groan erupted from somewhere in the back of her mind and it took a moment for her to realize it was she that made the noise.

"What's w.wrong Josie?"

It was Neb's voice and the insanity doubled upon hearing it. In a frenzied haze, all she knew was that she couldn't stand being locked up, caged like an animal with barely any light or food or company. Tears poured down her cheeks, dripping from her chin in steady flow. She began to violently shake the bars again.

"Josie p.please, my head h.h.hurts." Putting hands over his ears, Neb searched for reprise from the relentless pounding inside his head.

As the words were absorbed Josie inhaled a shaky breath and slumped down to the floor. It didn't seem to matter any longer if she sat on the floor or the bench, they both felt the same; hard, filthy, not a fit place to keep any human being; not her and not Neb. No one should be behind these bars except a cold-blooded killer. Filled with shame and concern for Neb, she wiped the tears from her face with the back of her hand several times. She could feel the swollen puffiness around and beneath her eyes.

"I'm sorry Neb. I didn't mean to make your head hurt. Is there anything I can do to make it better?"

"No." There was controlled anger along with the telltale quiver of pain in his voice.

"How can you stand it in here Neb? I feel like I'm going crackers."

"I just shut m...my eyes a.and im.imagine a d.different p.place, a h.happy p.place with b.bright sunshine and a.angels."

"Oh Neb, I'm so sorry. I forgot for a moment that you were here in the same room with me. Will you ever forgive me?"

"Yes. It's n.not so b.bad. Everyday I g.get b.better. This j.jail has b.been a h.healing p.place for m.me. I've d.done a l.lot of think...ing. The S.Sheriff, h.he's n.nice."

"I don't think he's very nice. I think he's a big toad."

"I th.think h.he l.loves you."

"I think I love him too Neb. But, you see where it's gotten me. If he really loved me he wouldn't have locked me up. He would have thought of some other way to go about this."

"Sometimes a m.man's hands are t.tied. J.just l.like m.me and Randy. I l.love him. He's m.my b.brother. L.look where it g.got m.me. I c.can't even t.talk r.right anymore."

Seems to me, we're like two peas in a pod. We're both helpless, stubborn and behind bars."

"Yep, and w.we b.both have g.good hearts, b.big m.mouths and...and l.love."

"Who do you love Neb? Is it your brother?"

"N.nope. Hanna. S.she's m.my angel." through this mess."

A few hours later, when Josie slid along the length of the bars to the floor and began to cry again, Neb snaked an arm through the bars on the door and grasped Josie's hand, squeezing it with silent comfort. Falling into a fitfull sleep did little to ease her worries as she held tightly to Neb's hand; her only link to compassion and sanity which she direly needed.

Christian carefully balanced the food-laden tray while attempting to open the door to the jailhouse. It was a balancing act made worse when Hops ran between his legs, throwing him off balance, almost causing the tray to spill. The dog went directly to Josie and eagerly lapped her face through the bars. Christian took quick note of her position on the floor and swallowed a lump of anger when her fingers untwined from Neb's only to reach through the bars and pet the dogs head. Watching her movement, he realized that she would probably never touch him gently like that again. The dog was more likely to gain her love and affection than what he was. Placing the tray on his desk, he carefully sorted the contents, giving Neb a larger portion of food than Josie. Then he stiffly delivered the tray to Neb, nodding roughly in acknowledgement to his piercing eyes and accusing stare.

Feeling as if he were silently being scolded, Christian ignored Neb and delivered the other tray to Josie. Stepping into the cell he shut the door behind him and sat down on the bench placing the tray to the side. Josie stared silently at the floor, plainly ignoring his presence while still petting the dog.

"Come on Josie. You need to eat. We'll go to the cabin once you've eaten. There you can bathe and change. I promise you'll have your privacy."

Her look of despair and trust was equivalent to a punch in the gut. She had been crying. Now he really felt like a rake. No wonder Neb was holding her hand when he came in. Neb had offered Josie comfort in his absence. Feeling as if his heart had been tied in knots, he watched as she nibbled on a hard-boiled egg held by trembling hands.

"What happened?"

"Nothing."

"Why were you crying?"

"I wasn't."

"Liar."

The flat out accusation had her feeling like a child. "I just lost my head for a minute. That's all."

"No one's hurt you?"

"You have. This whole town has." The reply was quick and harsh. It smarted with truth. She shouldn't be here.

"I was up all night long trying to figure out a way to get you out of this cell. It's driving me crazy Josie." He ran frustrated hands through his hair before burying his face in his palms. "Still, there's nothing I can do."

"Then get Judge McQuade to come here and talk to me. He's a fair man. Doesn't he have the authority to let me out?"

"Yes he does. I've already asked him to visit. He's busy poring over some legal documents drawn up in 1830. Apparently there are a few problems regarding borders between counties. He'll be here in a few days. Unfortunately, that's the best he can do."

"That's a long time Sheriff." The stiffness in her voice harbored a dismissal tone.

"I know it's a long time Josie. I'll do whatever I can to make it easy. Cheer up. I'll even stay the whole time if you wish it. I promise."

"What about Randall Hurley? Don't you want to go and find him?"

"Of coarse I do but what he wants most is sitting right here in this jail. You and Neb side by side in the same building. That's all he could wish for. If he's still out there that is."

"So we're sitting ducks?" She stood angrily crossing tense arms over her breast, tapping one foot in agitated rhythm, a rapid cadence to her mounting fury.

"Well yes, I guess so."

"Do you have a plan?"

"No."

"Do you have any idea how dangerous that man is? Do you have any idea what a madman like him could do?"

Christian raised a hand attempting to speak but found he couldn't get a word in edgewise for Josie continued in a fit of temper.

"Do you have any idea what I'll do to you if you allow my friend Neb to get hurt?" Her voice grew louder with each question. "Do you know what I'll do to Randy if he so much as hurts you? Well, I'll tell you. I may as well get used to these bars for I do not believe myself capable of self-control. First I'll kick him. Then I'll punch him. I might even bite, hit and knee him where it counts."

"Josie please." Christian chuckled. That was his Josie. It felt good to talk to her like this, to perform a battle of the wits on an even level.

Laughter filled the room and both Josie and Christian looked over to Neb, whom was laughing so hard tears filled his eyes.

"What is it Neb?" Christian already had an idea.

"I f.feel s.sorry for R.Randy too. J.Josie will k.kick his b.butt b.bad."

After a few moments of shared laughter Josie was taken to the cabin as promised. She silently told herself she would get through this. She just had to have strength and faith, faith not only in God, but in Judge McQuade and Christian as well. Deep in thought on the return walk to the jailhouse, she was surprised to note what a beautiful day it was.

"What do you want to do to pass the time Josie?"

"Well, can I have Angus visit the jailhouse?"

"Why?" He was irked to no end. Here he had clearly explained that he would stay with her and yet she asked for his friend instead. He was slowly loosing faith in the fact that Angus was his best friend and wouldn't steel Josie right out from under his nose.

"Yesterday he spent hours carving checker pieces for me. I was in the middle of teaching him how to play when you barged in and insisted on locking me up like a criminal. Anyways, I'd like to finish what we started."

"He's got other more important matters to attend." His irritation hadn't subsided any. She hadn't even asked if he knew how to play.

"I guess there's a lot of more important matters at hand than me."

"I didn't say that."

"Yes you did."

"No I didn't."

"Than what did you say?"

"Well calm down now Josie. I'm only saying that…"

"That what?"

"That I'm jealous. I'm jealous because you have stronger affections for Angus than what you do me."

Stopping in the middle of the street, uncaring of curious onlookers and passerbies, she turned and looked up into his ocean blue eyes. He towered a good foot above her own height. "Now Christian Coy that's just nonsense. I have brotherly affections for Angus. I have naughty, sinister affections for you. Lord help me, affections that I myself can't explain. One minute I want to punch you, the next I want to hug you. Now I fully expect to explore these feelings once I get out of the pickle I'm in. I adore you Christian even though you are the most irritating man God put on this earth. Now what do you have to say about that?" Throwing hands upon her hips, she stood awaiting his reply.

He was stunned, shocked, happy and giddy. He felt like a young boy in school. She did that to him. She made him feel good and whole. "Marry me."

"What?"

"You heard me." A few folks had gathered on the boardwalk along the storefronts openly listening to the conversation. Christian could feel many eyes upon them. Gossip would spread like wildfire, letting everyone know that Josie, whom was to be behind bars, was not. When looking back into her adoring eyes he decided to stake his claim right then and there. Grinning half-heartedly he clasped one delicate hand in his while bending down on one knee. The boyish grin on his face caused handsome dimples to deepen making him appear younger than he was. "Marry me Josie. Please."

Her breath caught in her throat and she went a full minute before inhaling. Nervously looking around she drew in a few shallow shaky breaths and wiped the sweaty palm of one free hand along her skirt. The longer Christian remained down on one knee, the more people began to accumulate, seemingly coming out of the woodwork itself. All of them bearing witness to the daring proposal.

Bending slightly forward she whispered. "Christian what are you doing?"

"I'm asking you to marry me."

"Why?"

"Because I love you. I could be happy with you for the rest of my life. I like who you are and what you are Josie, and I don't want to let you go."

Blinking back the tears that began to form and blur her vision, she straightened and looked around once more. Smiling broadly at Christian's sincerity, she shined from within. "That's the nicest thing anyone has ever said to me. I would be honored to be your wife Sheriff Coy, once you bail me out of jail that is."

He started to rise but her voice halted his actions with a chilling calm.

"Under one circumstance of coarse."

Peering around yet again Christian was certain the entire town had now swarmed along the streets edge. "What?"

"The next time I stand before you in nothing but goose bumps, you'd best not turn me away. Do you understand what I'm saying to you Sheriff?" A wicked smirk pulled at the corners of her perked lips.

Rising to his full height Christian wondered in awe at how she had, with a few simple words, saved her reputation while brazenly flaunting the sexual awareness between them. Yanking her roughly to him, he kissed her smiling lips before replying.

"Nymph. I look forward to next time."

A bright red coloring settled over her features as the full impact of what had just transpired settled in the pit of her tummy.

One person began to clap and before they had reached the jailhouse steps, the entire crowd was applauding their engagement. Some of the younger men were hooting and hollering, carrying on carelessly as people slowly began to disperse.

Millie was furious. Hanna stood next to her just outside the entrance to the restaurant smiling broadly. Stomping her foot, she turned and went back inside to the washroom. Grabbing a scrub brush, she began briskly scrubbing the inside of several dirty pots and pans. As her anger grew she worked harder and harder, breaking several of the bristles off the brush completely. A voice from behind made her jump.

"You have to be careful Millie. I know you're trying to do good and clean the pots but those brushes are made with horsetail."

"So, what's that supposed to mean Hank?"

"Silly woman. Horsetail is poisonous to people if eaten or swallowed. Make sure you rinse the pots well and you'll have nothing to worry about. We wouldn't want the customers getting sick."

"Thank you Hank. I didn't realize that. I really am trying you know."

"Sure Millie. Were is my sister?"

"I don't know where Hanna is."

After Hank left Millie smiled to herself. Thanks to Hank's information, Josie wouldn't be too difficult to get rid of after all. And once Josie was out of the picture, she would be there to offer her condolences to the Sheriff. She would help comfort him as much as he needed in his time of sorrow. With any luck, before he knew what had happened, she'd have him hook, line and sinker.

Quickly, she grabbed one of the dry scrub brushes still hanging above the washbasin. At the counter she grated the edges into tiny pieces and mixed in ground pepper and salt. Wrapping the pile into a linen cloth, she hid it away in her skirt pocket before continuing on with her work. A smile lit her features as she thought over and over of the planned outcome Josie's death would bring. When Hanna entered the room with another stack of dirty dishes, Millie smiled broadly and asked. "Aren't you just tickled with the Sheriff's proposal to Josie? I think it's absolutely wonderful."

"Why Millie McQuade, you really have changed."

CHAPTER TEN

Later that evening the restaurant was packed full of patrons. The savory scent of roasted beef permeated the air and the evening cash drawer was sure to turn a profit the likes of which hadn't been seen in a long time, for the people seemed elaborate in their spending, ordering full dinners of roasted beef or chicken along with churned potatoes and vegetables lavished with gravy on the side.

Hanna was practically dead on her feet for she had served a tiring day, waiting on one family after another, trying earnestly to make each and every one of them feel special and enjoy their evening out. Most families chose to stay home of late, often too tired and weary after a long hard day of relentless chores to venture into town for dinner. Normally treating the family to a meal at the restaurant was either done in celebration of some magnanimous event or as a treat for overcoming some type of family crises. Either way, many folks were there for one reason or the other and there was no reason to tame the fires burning in the stoves or close the doors while the money was pouring in.

The Hummel's were celebrating their tenth wedding anniversary and had brought their seven strapping children in with them. Seven ornery hell-raisers, Hanna thought as she was hit in the face with a pea, launched by their eldest son and followed by collective giggles from the rest of the clan.

"Now see here Marcus Hummel," Hanna scolded the ten year old in an even, yet sinister tone. "I'm certain your parents would have no objection to your remaining after we close to help scrub clean the floor. You children had best mind your manners, all of you...for I have lots of dishes to be washed as well. That is if'n you don't behave and allow your Ma and Pa to celebrate." Winking to the parents she added, "I'll be back shortly with dessert and some more linen napkins for little Suzy."

Returning to the heart of the kitchen with an armful of dirty plates, Hanna leaned back against the door momentarily and sighed in exhaustion. Ringlets of hair framed her face, the wild tresses no longer restrained in the bun atop her head.

Millie looked every bit as exhausted and disheveled as Hanna felt, yet still managed a small smile while relieving Hanna of the heavy burden stacked within her arms. Shifting back and forth to manage the overbearing stack, she walked back to the cast iron dish basin and began pouring fresh water into the sink to allow the plates to soak.

"My hands have turned to prunes from washing so many dishes. If you don't mind, I'll make the trays for the jail mates and deliver them for you tonight. It'll give my skin some time to dry out."

"I'd be grateful Millie. Thank you so much. Do you know where everything is?"

"Come now Hanna. I've worked here for neigh on a week. I can handle everything, I promise."

"Thanks Millie. You're a godsend. I really don't know what we would do without you now. You've spoiled me into not working so hard."

Once Hanna had disappeared through the door, yelling for the cooks to fill more orders, Millie pulled the bundled napkin from her pocket and placed two clean trays out in front of her. A gleam of wicked anticipation sparkled in her eyes as she piled food atop each plate, and then sprinkled the crushed and finely mixed poison atop Josie's tray, garnishing it like one would by using salt and pepper. She purposely stacked the other platter with so much food there would be no mistaking whose tray was whose. Adding two glasses of mulled cider she covered the tray and hastily left to deliver the feast. There was no way of hiding the smirk upon her face or explaining the cause for it once she entered the jail. The Sheriff looked upon her with suspicion and curtly asked why she was delivering the food rather than Hanna.

"I'm just helping Hanna out. The restaurant's extremely busy tonight and she's running around like a chicken with her head cut off."

"Well I guess that means you need to get back right away. Thanks for helping out." He tipped his hat in dismissal.

The Sheriff's crisp words accompanied by his rigid stance in the entryway as he held the door open, hurried her on her way. She had never been rebuffed and treated so rudely before in her life. Well she wasn't going to let a little thing like that ruin a perfectly good evening. Later she would be lying in bed dreaming sweet dreams; Josie would be as sick as a dog and hopefully on her way to the afterlife. A feeling of triumph rippled through her in small waves of gratification. All the hard work at the restaurant, all the times she had to bite her tongue and act polite, getting up at the crack of dawn, it would all be worth it once Josie was out of the picture. Even school didn't begin this early. Most kids had chores to perform and a lengthy distance to walk just to get there.

"Come on Josie. Up and at 'em. I've got a lot to do today starting off with a letter to Governor Bartley. I know he's busy dealing with fugitive slave laws but I'm hoping he can help us with your case."

The linen hadn't been dropped and Christian could see the limpness in Josie's form as she lie on the bench facing the wall. Unease pricked at the back of his mind unsettling his nerves and spreading cold fingers of dread along his spine.

"Josie, sweetheart, come on."

Concern etched along chiseled features when there was still no reply. The nagging feeling of unease persisted beyond reason. Snatching the ring of keys off the desk, he unlocked the iron bars and yanked the latch handle with so much force that permanent indents were punched in the wood along the wall where the handle had hit.

Quietly speaking Josie's name again he gently tapped her shoulder then shook it with more force when there was still no response. His heart beat fiercely and his hands shook when he rolled her over, gently placing her so that she lay in a supine formation.

Her face was a haunting powder white with large black circles rimming the underside of her eyes, which were sunken in and closed. Pale blue lips were cracked and dry while her cheeks were cold and clammy to the touch. The hollowness of her features would have him believing she was dead except for the slow shallow rise and fall of her breast and the rattling sound that came with it.

"My god what happened?" Asking the question out loud to no one in particular helped naught. Josie's features wedged a block of wariness to the situation, confirming the fact that something was very wrong. People in this area got sick all the time. Swamp fever and malaria were common ailments, but Josie wasn't shaking and didn't have the telltale odor of the sweat that accompanied Malaria. Quanine was served on the table with every meal. Folks used it to put over their food like salt. It usually helped keep the chills and sweats to a minimum. With Josie in jail, he hadn't even thought to serve it to her. Guilt washed over him in waves.

"Neb, are you feeling okay?" With eyes scanning up and down, he searched for signs of illness or a clue that something was affecting Neb as well. Although the prisoner appeared unkempt and burley, there were no traces of any fever, shakes or sickness upon him.

"I'm fine Sheriff. W…what's wrong?" Neb slowly shifted forward on the strap iron bench. Sitting up fully for the first time in days. He stared directly into the Sheriff's eyes, reading apathy and concern aplenty.

"You're speech improves with each passing day Neb. I'm glad for it, really I am." Shaking his head back and forth he paced then continued. "Josie's sick. I'm going to fetch Old Doc. Better yet, I'm taking her to him. Something's terribly wrong."

"She was fine before we supped last night. That's th…th…the last I said anything to her. S.she told me the f.food didn't agree with her."

"It was the same type of food as always wasn't it? I didn't notice anything different."

"Except maybe the d.delivery person. It wasn't my Hanna. B.big disappointment if'n you ask me."

Cursing under his breath Christian scooped up Josie's lithe and unresponsive form. The heat that assailed him upon contact increased his worry tenfold. He was there when the food was delivered and didn't think anything odd about it. Millie was nice enough, yet doubt lingered in the back of Christian's mind. Why would Millie even be working? There was no reason for it, not to mention the fact that it was so unlike her.

He kicked open Old Doc's office door causing a heavy thunk to resound throughout the room. Christian gently deposited Josie like a wilted flower atop the small bed cushioned in the rear corner of the room. The panic and concern he felt within was evidenced by the heaviness in his voice.

"Something's bad wrong Doc. I think we need some quanine here and some cool water. Maybe some clear black rainwater will help. Hell I don't know." Sweeping frustrated fingers through his hair, Christian continued to pace the room, clearly beside himself with worry.

Feeling Josie's cheeks and forehead the Doc slowly conducted a silent yet thorough examination of the newly arrived patient. A little perplexed, his forehead wrinkled as a frown formed his face mirroring Christian's worry and alarm.

"Well it's definitely not the Ague. How long has she been ill?"

"Just now noticed it. She was fine last evening."

"I'm going to need your assistance young man. First let's get her cleaned up and into some fresh linen. Get out the goose grease and start fluffing them there pillows. Make it snappy our little one's having a hard time breathing."

Christian did as was bid while the Doc washed Josie's body with fresh lukewarm water and lye soap. The goose grease was mixed with a small amount of kerosene then liberally spread upon Josie's chest. She was then swaddled in a large woolen cloth before being covered with a nightshirt and tucked in comfortably.

"Wormwood on whiskey, that's what she needs." The Doc huffed.

Christian stifled a cough of disbelief. Wormwood on whiskey was every man's worst nightmare. It eased just about every ailment brought upon a man, but it was not a concoction meant for women. It tasted bad for one and was strong enough to light a fire beneath a mule.

"Why not vinegar bread or elderberry? I don't understand."

"Are you the doctor in this town son or are you the Sheriff?"

Christian was stunned into silence by the Doc's disgruntled words. He had known the Old Doc for a long time and never once had the man ever shown a hint of anger or a pinch of rudeness. Here he was now razzed as a peacock. Staring into the Doc's eyes he searched for answers that remained unspoken.

"It's not normal son, for someone to get so deathly ill so quickly. Frankly I'm worried to the bone. I've already ruled out the Ague. It's not a cold or flue. To put it plain and simple, in my professional opinion, I believe she's been poisoned."

"What? That's hair-brained! Who would want to poison Josie?"

"Well now let me remind you, I'm the doctor. You're the Sheriff. I'll do my job caring for our patient. You do your job and find out who the hell did this."

"How do you know she's been poisoned?"

"Well son, there've been entire families wiped out in days by the ague. Swamp fever's common in this region. Folks fear it so much that I've seen families pack up and leave their loved ones behind as soon as the sickness sets in. They don't even wait around to see if the person lives or dies let alone offer any help. The diseases of this area are so contagious folks react first and think later. I've outlived the symptoms more than once myself. Josie's illness is unique. Her skin is dry and burning but the fever's mild. Her nose is running but her lips are dry and cracked. She's not coherent which isn't normal either. Yes I'd say it's some kind of poison.

I just don't rightly know exactly what. Saw a case similar to this years back. A young girl accidentally ate some Jimson Weed not knowing it was poisonous. She thought it looked tasty I guess."

"And?"

"And what?"

Rolling his eyes with impatience Christian asked calmly. "What happened to the girl? Did she make it?"

"Afraid not son. But let's keep a positive outlook on this. Our girl's strong. She'll fight, that's for sure. You just work on finding out whose gone and done this. Attempting to kill someone is down right evil. Folks in this town will be right upset knowing someone like this is prowling around our fine community. Better find answers right away Sheriff. The sooner the better."

The first thing Christian thought to do was re-trace his steps. He knew Millie had delivered the food to the jailhouse and couldn't shake the inkling that she was involved. If his suspicions proved correct, Millie was in a world of trouble and a greater danger to Josie than he had imagined. The more he thought about it, the more certain he was that Millie McQuade *was* the culprit. He'd have a heck of a time trying to explain this one to the judge. He knew right off that no matter who was to blame; he'd have to gather a ton of evidence. Proof of the devious behavior.

As the door bounced shut behind him dust particles floated freely in the air. "How are you feeling Neb? Any different than earlier?"

Standing to his full height of six feet two inches, Neb grasped the strapped bars and looked directly into the Sheriff's eyes. "I'm fine. How's J.Josie?"

"She's not doing well at all. The Doc doesn't even know if she'll live through the day. She's been poisoned. By who is the mystery."

"It'd be that b.blond haired h.hell-cat that was here last n.night. Not a g.good bone in her b.body. Can tell when you l.look into her e.eyes. Reminds m.me of my b.brother. Ashamed to say if the t.two of them ever g.got together, the w.whole w.world would be in t.trouble."

"Yeah, well I was thinking along those same lines. I'll have Hanna bring you some breakfast. Maybe later I'll take you for a walk on over to see Josie. You could stretch those muscles a mite."

"I'd be r.right grateful Sheriff."

Hank and Hanna sat together at a table near the front of the restaurant, deeply involved in conversation when Christian's gruff voice penetrated their easy banter.

"Plotting you two? Why is it so slow in here?"

"I don't know about plotting anything," Hank shot back, a puzzled look upon his face. "It's slow now but yester eve was busy as all get up. Seemed every family in town had cause to celebrate. We actually ran out of beef. Can you believe it? First time that ever happened."

The news was relevant to Christian. No wonder Hanna was too busy to deliver the food to the cellmates. "Hanna, did you prepare the yesterdays food trays for supper yourself?"

"You mean the trays that go to the jail?" Seeing his nod she confirmed his worst fears. "No. Millie volunteered to do it. I trusted her to do the job right. Please don't tell me Neb and Josie never got served last night."

"Worse than that. They did get served. Unfortunately, the Doc and I believe the trays may have been laced with poison. Did you or anyone else see Millie prepare the plates last night?"

Both Hank and Hanna shook their heads back and forth in a fervent gesture of negativity.

"Is Millie here now?"

"No. I sent her home due to lack of customers this morning."

"I'd like to check out the area where she would have gotten the trays ready."

"Sure no problem Sheriff. Right away."

Hank's features were solemn and pale as he stood watching the Sheriff examine every aspect of the cleaning area leaving no dusty corner untouched by trained assessing eyes. The scrutinizing task lasted more than an hour.

"What's this?" The Sheriff asked as he held out a dry brittle handful of thistle like brush he had scooped from the floor around the trash pale.

"That's scouring rush." Hanna remarked. "We use it to scrub pots and pans clean."

Hank cleared his throat and began to put the uneasiness that had been laying heavily on his mind to words. "Look, Millie scrubs the pots and pans clean but I made a comment to her in passing a day or so ago that may help solve this entire mystery. Before I go any further Sheriff, I want you to understand that I never meant any harm to your little lady."

Christian nodded for Hank to continue, cracking his knuckles as the tension built.

"Right after you proposed to Josie in the middle of the street, well, we all came back into the restaurant to carry on with our work. Millie was scrubbing the tar out of those pots and pans. It didn't seem natural that she be so hell bent on cleaning like that. I'm sure she was angry with you proposing; after all, she stomped in here like the devil was pulling at her feet. I told her to be careful and rinse those pots real well. The scouring rush is good for scrubbing and cleaning but it's actually made with horsetail."

Both Hanna and the Sheriff stared at Hank with blank looks upon their faces.

"Horsetail grows aplenty in these parts. It's poisonous. Real poisonous. If you eat it you can get real sick. Bad sick if you know what I mean. I didn't think much of it until you came here this morning. You see Sheriff, Millie perked right up after I told her that. *She actually smiled.*"

"That's not enough Hank. It doesn't prove a thing. I need something absolute." Christian was growing agitated. He wanted to get back and check on Josie and at the same time he wanted this entire mess solved. He wanted to kill whomever had poisoned Josie. Short of that, he didn't think he'd be feeling himself anytime soon.

"Could be that that doesn't prove much or could be that it does. Think about it," Hank continued "later that evening we were real busy. Millie volunteered to take the food trays to the jail for Hanna. She prepped them and everything. Perhaps you should search for remnants of rush on the floor and in the cracks of the counter planks. Couldn't hurt, All this appears a little strange to me."

Christian had a growing suspicion and was ready to dig his heals in but knew he'd need more than suspicion alone to put the judge's daughter behind bars. He needed solid proof. Facts that couldn't possibly be explained away in some other fashion. Cold hard facts that wouldn't leave a doubt in anybody's mind.

"Okay, so if someone wanted to poison another using this scouring rush, how would they do it?" He was clueless in the kitchen and didn't have an inkling of where to begin. Searching an environment he was unfamiliar with had him feeling insignificant and frustrated.

Hanna took the lead; walking over to the washbasin she pulled a small bundled object from the nail peg above the sink. It resembled a husked broom and Christian realized it was a scrub brush made of dried bundled rush. "If it were me Sheriff, I'd simply shred it into a fine grain powder. Kind of like at the pepper mill."

"Do you have anything that would do that here?"

"Yes we do." Bending down, Hanna removed the handled and bowled base of the contraption they used to chop salt blocks into finer pieces. It worked fairly well on the salt as it was kept on the table at all times in the swamp region. Folks believed that the consumption of salt helped to minimize the swamp chills, shakes and fevers that often festered in many newcomers to the region. Hanna would bet that this self made tool would do a great job at grinding the wiry rush into a powdered grain like substance.

Plopping it on top of the cutting board, she gasped in disbelief upon noticing the powdery residue that already existed and lined the bottom of the bowl. "Golly, what's this?"

Quickly Hank stuck one finger into the bowl swiping up some of the residue. Bringing it to his nose he sniffed then rolled back onto the heal of his boots. "Smells like rush to me."

Christian nodded. "Let's wrap it so I can show Old Doc and use this as evidence. Hanna, once I'm done, why don't you show me how you would grind this rush up. Let's see if we get the same results, results similar to what we just found."

A few moments later a grim faced Sheriff left the restaurant and walked determinedly to the doctor's office. Eager to share his findings, he was hoping with all his heart that the Old Doc would find a remedy for Josie's deathly illness. Hank's departing words rang in his head and filled his heart with hope. "If it's any help Sheriff, I've heard of people getting mighty sick from consumption of scouring rush, but I've never heard of anyone dying from it."

Two days later Christian had compiled enough evidence against Millie to try her for the attempt against Josie's life. Furthermore, he found that Millie had not only tried to harm Josie once, but twice! The fire at the restaurant was a terrible thing. Possibly it got out of hand and went further than what Millie had anticipated, but none the less, she had set it in hopes of harming Josie's reputation. She was hoping that he, the town Sheriff, would be upset with Josie's carelessness and send her away. Millie had carefully set the whole thing up, and almost managed to get what she wanted. Thank God he had decided to go after Josie that night. Thank God Josie had decided to double back.

He had written to the judge who was currently on his way back, requesting approval to search his daughter's hotel room. It was there that Christian and Angus had been faced with an overwhelming abundance of evidence. The first would be Millie's diary, which told everything in Millie's own handwriting. Second was the red dress hanging haphazardly in the closet. It was torn near the hem and the material along with the tear pattern matched the snagged piece of cloth Christian had found while investigating the fire scene. And last but not least, they had found an unlaundered skirt with ground up rush remnants in the pocket. Christian ground his teeth together. Two women in the town's jail in one week were atrocious. He only hoped the small town of Rapids, across the river, didn't hear about all this. It would be a terrible embarrassment, not only for him but for the judge and the community as well since Rapids had a newspaper and all.

He thought of his good friend Judge McQuade. How was it the lord cursed him with such a vile and viscous daughter. The judge himself was a caring and wise man. Christian only prayed that someday, when he had children, they didn't grow up and treat him as poorly as what Millie did her father.

Thinking along those lines brought a vision of Josie to mind. Cracking his knuckles, Christian walked forward in a hurried pace. Josie was still quite sick. She was breathing steady and her color had improved from a sickening blue to a pale white. The fever had gradually subsided and the dark circles beneath her eyes had slowly flushed and vanished but she hadn't yet regained consciousness.

Old Doc had been pouring broth and water down her throat but Christian knew that wasn't enough. At least for him—nothing regarding Josie would ever be enough. There was a certain helplessness that came with not being able to protect her. She had been in his jail, under his care and was still harmed. Anger distorted his features as he continued forward towards the restaurant. Millie, to the best of his knowledge, didn't know that he was aware of her deeds and wrong doings. If it wasn't for the Judge, he'd strangle her himself!

The sun was just peeking its face over the lush treetops, casting golden rays upon the peaks of the horizon when Christian stepped over the threshold of the restaurant. It was early morning and he planned to intercept Millie at the beginning of the day, when there were fewer folks around to witness the arrest. In the cleaning room, she was just donning an apron. Glancing up she saw him enter and a genuine smile flitted across her face.

"Why Sheriff, what a nice surprise at such an early hour."

"Just stop it with the niceties Millie. I'm here to place you under arrest. Now you can come quietly with me or you can cause a scene. Either way, you'll finish out your days in this town behind bars." He stood over her allowing a shadow of intimidation and danger to fill the air.

"Now that's just nonsense Sheriff. Why would you be arresting me? I haven't done anything out of sorts."

She attempted a nervous step backwards but the strong clench of the Sheriff's fingers clamping a firm grip around her upper arms, holding her in a vice like stance just off the floor with her toes barely touching the ground hindered her attempt to back away. He knew he was bruising her and his grip would leave marks; she could tell by the look in his eyes that he didn't care, that he wanted to hurt her.

The deep calm tone of his voice set off a warning alarm within her mind as unspoken and barely concealed anger sizzled beneath the surface of the Sheriff's hard fought control. "I'm through playing games with you Millie. You know exactly what you've done. I refuse to spell it out for you. A word to the wise though, I'd keep quiet right now—or else…"

The threat hung in the air, its meaning ringing with fury. Millie smartly complied and allowed herself to be shackled and jailed without further protest. She did know exactly what she had done. She only now wondered if Josie was alive yet or not. She hadn't heard. Too bad she couldn't simply ask. No, she didn't have the guts for that. Either way, she knew the Sheriff hated her, a cold hard fact she had to face. As he glared meaningfully at her she realized she had seen that look before. She had seen it many times. Her own mother looked upon her with similar eyes of hate, filling her with self-doubt and ugliness. Sitting silently she wondered what to do next. It seemed she had run out of options and she had run out of people to love as well. In a trance like state, she awaited the next moment when someone would look upon her as a hated object.

The Judge returned to town late that evening. The first priority on his list was to speak with Sheriff C. He found him at Old Doc's office nursing Josie by cradling her hand upon his lap. He sat quietly at the bedside whispering a reverent prayer.

"Sshh." The judge breathed into one raised finger then motioned for Christian to remain seated while he removed his hat. "Please don't get up for my sake son. Just tell me everything from start to finish."

Christian watched the features of his friends face change from one expression to another as he recounted the happenings in Providence over the past week. He felt sorry for the man as he appeared to have aged tenfold upon the realization that Millie had been so outwardly hateful. Christian didn't envy the position his friend was now placed in. It was his daughter that he had raised and loved. His little girl that he had once bounced upon his knee every morning and had tucked into bed every evening with a prayer and a hug. His one and only child. The one and only that he had doted upon, spoiled and cherished above all else, save the law. Now, the recourse of that love slapped him in the face with the awful truth that somewhere along the course of their lives, something or some step had been missed, for Millie truly seemed to lack a heart or the ability to feel remorse for anything. It was a very sad fact.

Removing a tin flask engraved with the letter "M" from the inside pocket of his gray coat, the judge released a long pent up sigh of indignation as the amber liquid burned a path to his stomach, filling him with warmth and calming his nerves.

"Well son, there's something I should tell you, not that it matters now, but I've done Millie a grave injustice. One of unspeakable ill repair. In the wake of that, both I and Millie have hurt a lot of people."

Christian nodded waiting for the confession to continue, wondering what it would have to do with the situation at hand. How would it help him and Josie? The silence stretched on like wings of a thunder cloud, full and waiting to relent.

"You see, my wife, the missus, is barren." At Christian's blank look he explained. "She can't have children, never could. But I wanted a child, insisted on an heir. What man has any worth if he can't produce a heir to carry on the family legacy?"

Again silence clouded the air and the judge took another swig of courage from the flask. "To make a long story short, I had an affair or more like a brief liaison, with a young girl I hardly even knew. I used her to conceive, carry and birth a child of my making. Then I forced my wife to take care of that child. I forced her to nurture the child and lie to all our friends and family. I forced her to be a mother and to live a life that perhaps she wasn't made for. God knows she's a good woman and she's done her best I'm sure."

The silence grew even thicker around Christian. It hung like fog clinging to the air, dampened by disbelief and loyalty. The loyalty of two long time friends forced to deal with an ugly truth.

"Well, in my defense," the judge went on, "it wasn't really an affair, more like a one time encounter. The girl was young and gorgeous. I could hardly resist the temptation laid before me. Lord help me but she made me feel like I ruled the world. I must confess. I fell prey to the devil's own work. It should have been a sign, an omen, but I didn't see it that way. Lead us not into temptation, but deliver us from evil." The judge quoted and tapped his head and shoulders in the ancient symbol of a cross. "A few months later that young girl came back to me, claiming to be with child. Well, there was no way to bid waiver to the situation. I supported this woman; kept her well I did, without the missus finding out. But then, well Ruthie, that was her name, she got sick towards the end of her pregnancy. She died giving birth as so many women do."

Christian reached quietly for the flask of whiskey, needing a healthy dose himself.

His insides churned as he continued to listen.

"I was there for the birthing since I had asked Ruthie to summon me as soon as her pains began. I made her a promise just before she died and that was to take care of her little angel. Well, I don't rightly know how she knew it was a girl but she did by golly. She was right. And what a beautiful little angel we had. As soon as I looked into that baby's eyes I fell in love with her. I made up my mind right then and there to do right by the child. I wrapped her up and took her home."

Another swallow of strength from the flask had the judge on his feet slowly pacing to the window, looking out at the stars twinkling brightly overhead. Then turning to look at Christian he sighed resolutely and sat back down.

"You can imagine Mrs. McQuade's reaction to the news. She was none to happy I tell you. And heartbroken at that. She had trusted me and I let her down terribly. Of coarse she wanted to leave, to go back to her family in Pennsylvania but I begged her to move away with me. To start a new life. To be a family. You see, folks in a new town would have no idea that the babe wasn't legitimate and well, you ken that I'm a very lucky man. My wife forgave me. It wasn't overnight mind you. It took years. But she forgave me none the less because she loved me. And I think she did the best she could to teach Millie the proper way of things. I did too; for all that it's worth. But the motherly love wasn't there and I truly believe that when Mrs. McQuade looked upon Millie, well she would constantly be reminded of my unfaithfulness. I do believe that from time to time, her feelings would get in the way of her ability to love Millie unconditionally. I'm confession to you son, because all this has led to here and now. This particular point in time with no way of turning back the hands of time."

"I don't really know what to say sir." Christian remarked unsure of how he should think and feel at the moment in light of the judge's story. Uncertain of how he should react.

"You're like a son to me Christian and I respect you. Hopefully knowing all this will help you to understand Millie, to be compassionate and to help me decide what to do next. I mean for Christ's sake how am I supposed to sentence my own daughter fairly?"

"We'll make it through this together sir. Somehow, we'll make it all work out. One day we will look back on this whole entire situation and remark that it was a turning point for all of us."

"I hope so son. I hope so."

Randy climbed quietly onto the roof of the jailhouse then stretched himself out as flat as he could so as not to be seen. He had been watching the Sheriff all afternoon and knew that he wasn't around at the moment. His heart beat rapidly as he lie quietly speculating his plan one last time. The sheriff would be back soon to check on the jail mates before turning in for the night.

The cells were made of strap iron on the floors and sides. That left only the roof accessible to a break-in attempt. Luckily the moon was high in the sky and the stars shown brightly making it easier to see in the dark. Although he wanted to rescue his brother, Neb was too heavy to lift and haul through a cut opening in the roof. He'd settle for Josie figuring that since the sheriff was sweet on her, she'd make a good ransom. A decent trade for his brother. He'd have a little fun with the bitch first. If everything went as planned, he make a clean getaway. A getaway from this swamp infested region. He was sick and tired of stealing food and hiding out all the damn time. He was sick and tired of being bitten repeatedly by the mosquitoes.

As predicted, the sheriff came bye, saw to the needs of the jail mates and then locked up for the night. As soon as his departing form blended with the shadows Randy got to work. He slowly cut through shingle and tar before finally hitting solid pine. Removing a small hatchet from a bag of supplies hauled up earlier, he made quick work of the wood and chopped right through sending splinters and chunks of debris down upon Millie's head.

Millie had thought there was an animal on the roof and tried not to get spooked by the sounds it was making overhead. When she realized the animal had chewed right through she made to scream. However, the sound never made it past her lips since the animal fell right through the roof and landed squarely on her mid-section, promptly knocking the wind right out of her. Before she knew what was happening, a rag was shoved into her mouth and she was struck soundly on the side of her head.

Once she fell limp, Randy tied the rope securely around Josie's waist then climbed up the iron-crossed rails back out the hole. Pulling on the rope, he fought slightly with Josie's dead weight as he hauled her limp form out of the opening. He rolled her to the edge of the roof and then roughly lowered her with the rope. When she was about three feet from the ground he dropped her and then jumped down himself.

The jarring drop caused Millie to come to. She began to struggle earnestly with her captor but he roughly wholluped her again knocking her unconscious once more.

Randy hauled Josie over his shoulder and carefully made his way to the edge of town, circled around to the opposite side of the main stretch and then merged with the shadows as if the woods swallowed him up. Here he followed a trail that led to the river. He waded knee deep in the direction of the mill further east near the town of Rapids. It was about a quarter mile away but a good plan. He'd been dodging the Sheriff by doing just this for quite some time now. If the Sheriff had any sense at all, he'd had hired an Indian tracker to help him out. It seemed there wasn't a single trail those damn red skins couldn't follow. Although there were very few of them around any more.

Finally reaching the mill, he hobbled around to the back to retrieve his horse, which was hidden in a small copse of lilac bushes directly behind the building. He flung Josie's form across the saddle then mounted pushing her upwards and taking off into the night. Although it was dark, he had been living in the environment for several weeks now and felt comfortable with the darkened shadows looming all around.

"Angus I need you to round up the men and let them know we'll be forming a search party. I'm going to visit Teenabe and his family. I'll explain the situation and beg they help. Their skill would be a major asset right now. I should have hired an Indian tracker long before this but I know how the Indians feel about the white people. Especially the law and military. Have the fellas meet me tomorrow morn at sunrise on the North side of the river. I picked up Randall Hurley's tracks there and then lost them near the water."

"Sure thing Sheriff." Angus nodded then straightened his back and left.

Christian was a little nervous knocking on the door to the cabin housing. Teenabe and his family. Quickly he shook off his apprehension and reminded himself that Teenabe knew he was there before he even knocked on the door. Indians were strange in that manner. They were much more spiritual and bonded in an earthy manner than the white men.

When the door opened Christian became engulfed in the pleasant smelling aroma of tobacco and freshly cleaned hides. A young man about his own age waved him in and motioned for him to sit upon an empty pelt on the floor. Teenabe sat directly across from where he was placed and openly gazed at Christian with amusement dancing in the dark depth of his knowing eyes.

"What brings you to my home Sheriff?" Obviously Teenabe was not one to mesh words and waste time.

Christian explained the entire situation, telling the story from start to finish without missing a single detail, pausing only to accept a drink from Teenabe's wife before begging the elderly Indian for his help.

"I am old Sheriff. I do not move with the wind anymore. Many sunrises I find it hard to move. Pain fills my body on many days. But I am the last of my people in this region. For the sake of the Ottawa and the honor of my people, I will help. When do we leave and do you have provisions?"

"We leave at sunrise sir. Unless you think it better to make it a different time. I thought it best to show you where I lost the trail…while it is fresh. And yes, I have enough provisions for two days…maybe three at the most."

"Please do not call me sir. It is a white man's word. Sunrise is good."

"What shall I call you then?" Christian hoped he hadn't offended the Indian in any way as he took great comfort knowing the wise man was going to help. In a sense, Christian placed all faith in Teenabe's tracking abilities.

"You may call me friend or even better Teenabe. That is my name. My friends us it always."

Christian smiled instantly bonding to this older Indian. "You can call me Christian as my friends do too. Thank you Teenabe. I'm grateful for your help."

Millie woke with a splitting headache. Her hands were tied and she could barely breath. There was a piece of cloth shoved so deeply into her mouth that she had to concentrate on breathing evenly so as not to gag. Where on earth was she? Looking around all she could see were trees and branches overhead. She was in some kind of small clearing. There had to be water for she could hear the river flowing and the stench of fish was overpowering. Every bone in her body ached. Her throat was dry and raw. She was thirsty beyond belief and made to get up solely intent upon finding something to drink and remove whatever vial cloth was in her mouth. An unexpected thump in her side had her sprawled back on the ground gagging and reeling with pain. She tried hard to breath evenly again.

"Where's Josie?"

Millie first starred at the boot that had kicked her and then looked up into the face of a mean looking stranger. No, not exactly a stranger. He was familiar somehow. Suddenly she realized he looked just like the man she had served dinner to in the jail. This had to be his brother. The one everyone was looking for. Instantly a thought formed in her mind. How much would the Sheriff love her if she could help catch the outlaw? Maybe her abduction had happened for a reason.

The man jerked the cloth from her mouth and asked again "where's Josie?"

"I don't know."

"Horse shit!"

"Really I don't know but you and I may be able to help each other. You see, I hate Josie too. In fact, I want her dead."

"Why?"

"What kind of stupid question is that? Anyone that meets her wants her dead. She's aggravating that's why."

"Where is she?"

"I told you I don't know. I can guess but I'm not certain."

The man roughly yanked her to a standing position using her hair, bringing her face within inches of his own.

"This is the last time I'm going to ask. Next time I'll shoot ya dead. Where is the little bitch?" His breath on her skin was absolutely putrid.

"I'm guessing she'd be at the doctors office in town. I poisoned her. That's why I was in jail. Now unhand me this instant."

The night was young yet and the moon glowed brightly. A breeze blew softly enough to cool the air and steady enough to keep the dampness from settling on the ground. Although it seemed calm, an eerie quaver danced through the air.

Randy's mind whirled. Poison? Was she dead? He wanted revenge upon Josie. Nobody was going to take that opportunity from him. Certainly not the girl in front of him.

"Is she still alive?"

"What?" It took a moment for the question to register in Millie's mind, caught off guard as she was since she had been focusing on the mans' rotting teeth. "I really don't know."

"What the hell do you mean you don't know? What kind of horse shit answer is that? She's dead or she ain't. Which one is it?"

"I said I don't know. What's wrong with you? Don't you understand English? Not very smart for an outlaw."

Randy didn't like this woman any more than he liked Josie. He punched her square in the jaw and as she fell back onto the ground he examined her more closely. She wasn't bad to look at although someone else had already given her a black eye. Her mouth obviously aggravated more than just him. Her curly blond hair hung in rivulets framing a delicately soft heart shaped face. Her chest rose heavily up and down as she struggled to hold back tears of pain. He felt himself begin to harden. He could have this woman and still go back and snatch Josie. There was no reason he couldn't. Hunger filled his eyes with the thought.

He grabbed the rag that only moments before he had pulled from this lady's mouth. Gagging her with it once more he went a step farther and pulled a dirty handkerchief from his pocket. He wrapped that around her mouth to secure the gag and tied it tightly at the back of her head.

"Now listen here missy. You can make this easy for old Randy or you can make it hard but one way or the other…we're gonna have us some fun."

Millie could do nothing but shake her head back and forth. Tears ran freely down her face soaking the wrap around her mouth. This man was horrible. What did she ever do to deserve this? As soon as she asked herself the question, she knew the answer. She hadn't been the nicest person in the world. She swallowed the humility and squeezed her eyes tightly shut. She didn't want to see Randy's face. She just wanted to shut him out of her mind completely.

Randy grabbed her already bound hands and secured them to a stake in the ground. Then he roughly ripped the front of her gown wide open. Her breast lay bare and exposed. They were white and soft. He squeezed them hard bruising the delicate tissue and bringing more tears of pain to Millie's already wet eyes. Seeing her pain caused a tremor of excitement to course through his midsection stopping at the base of his penis, causing it to get harder. He loved hurting women. He so enjoyed seeing them in pain. He grew more and more aroused by the moment.

He continued to rip the rest of the garments from her body until she was completely naked and exposed to his dangerous gaze. Yeah she was a beauty. He'd break her like a wild horse. Before he was done with her, she'd be begging him for mercy. When the next time came, she'd voluntarily move the way he wanted her to. There'd be no need for ties and restraints. She'd learn her lesson the first time around. He'd make sure of that.

He squeezed her breast again before sticking a finger into her most private area. Millie gagged on the bile rising in her throat. She kept her eyes shut refusing to look at him. She would not acknowledge what he was doing. She just wouldn't. And if she made it through this alive, she'd be a different person. Quietly she began to pray. She prayed for the strength to make it through the night. She prayed for God to guide her. She prayed for forgiveness. She prayed for a future of healing and happiness. But most of all she prayed for a release from the pain this man was causing her. This terrible pain that now encompassed her entire being.

"Ahh." Randy growled. "A virgin. Now isn't that sweet?"

Hours later, when he was sated, Randy left Millie lying naked and bloodied. He knew she wouldn't be moving for a while. He'd hurt her badly. She'd be too sore to move for hours. Redressing, he untied his horse and left. While it was still dark, he'd go find Josie. He'd bring her back here and do the same to her as he did to Millie. Heck, maybe he'd go back and forth between the two girls, have some fun for a few days. This island of rock was a safe hide away. He felt certain that no one would ever search for him here. When he was through with the girls, when he finally grew bored with them, he'd leave. No one would find them for days. They'd most likely starve to death. The thought excited him anew and his urgency to find Josie was refreshed.

Trotting through the rivers cold flowing currant towards the bank, Randy and his steed were deep in water. It soaked into his boots as it grew higher and higher. The horses head was barely above the surface. This was the deepest part. In a few moments they'd be out and drying off. The woman had said Josie was at the doctor's office. He knew right where that was. A plan formed in his mind as he rode through the thick woods along the rivers edge.

"Damn mosquitoes." He smacked several as they bit him unremittingly. As he warred with the insects he grew angry and agitated. Damn it, he'd already done this once. Nothing like taking chances. As he rode he began to care less and less about getting his brother back. He'd done just fine without him for some time now. Hell Neb could take care of himself. And if not then it was his own damn fault. It was Neb's fault for whatever happened. It was Neb's fault for being weak. Yes, he thought less and less about Neb and more and more about the girls. His thoughts of the two girls and what he was going to do had him all hard again. He adjusted himself in the saddle and continued to ponder his luck.

Finally, he left the bank of the river and rode through the thickness of forest before breaking into the clearing that was the outskirts of Providence. Once again he tethered the horse and felt for the knife at his waist. Clinging to the shadows, he made his way to the small structure he was sure was the doctors office. He waited silently along the side of the building, listening for any sounds from inside. Nothing. He tried to peak in the window but the curtains were drawn. Damn. As quietly as he could he climbed the steps to the porch cursing his heavy footedness as he walked to the door. He tried the knob. It was locked. Double damn. Pulling the knife from his side pocket, he quickly popped the lock and made his way inside. There was no light to see by but he could hear breathing that wasn't his own.

"Stop right where you are." Came a raspy voice.

It must be the elderly doctor he had seen before. As his eyes adjusted to the darkness he saw the old man holding a rifle, apparently ready to shoot.

"Say goodbye old man. You've overstayed your welcome in the living world."

With that Randy grabbed the barrel of the gun and swung it quickly around knocking the butt of the gun into the old man's face. He could see the blood running freely from the man's nose. The old doctor was feeble and no match in strength for Randy. He grabbed the docs hair and pulled back his head exposing the wrinkled skin of the elders throat. Swiftly and with skill he sliced across the neck from ear to ear then let the limp body fall to the floor. That was easy, he thought as he wiped the blood from the knife onto his pants before tucking the weapon back into the leather strap attached to his side.

Walking toward the back of the office Randy looked for anyone else that might be there. Adrenaline raced through his veins, He felt pumped up enough to take on an army of men. This had been a good night so far.

In the rear corner he found Josie securely tucked beneath a pile of blankets and wrappings. He wrinkled his nose as he got closer. She smelled of goose grease and kerosene. He ripped off strips of sheeting then tied her hands and feet. Next he gagged her mouth. Oddly enough, Josie was limp and didn't struggle an ounce. Perhaps the other lady really did poison her. Well she was alive. That's all that really mattered for now. To have her alive and writhing beneath him would be better but for now he would settle for a successful kidnapping.

Later, back on the island he'd been hiding out on, he plopped Josie's body down next to Millie's beaten form. He kicked Millie in the side and dumped some whiskey over her face to revive her.

"What the hell's wrong with her? Why won't she move?" He barked impatiently.

Millie had to look around for a moment trying to understand what he was talking about. Seeing the still body lying next to her was shocking, yet she wasn't surprised. She groaned knowing it was Josie.

"God forgive me." She begged and began to cry again.

"I asked you a question woman. What's wrong with her?"

"I told you earlier I poisoned her. If she's alive it's a miracle."

CHAPTER ELEVEN

The heart wrenching screams coming from outside jerked Christian from a peaceful slumber and tossed him into a panicked state of frenzy. He could only guess at what was happening now. It seemed his entire life had been in complete disarray for weeks on end. Between Millie, Randall Hurley and Josie, he hadn't slept but a few scant restless hours in weeks. That hadn't kept his exhausted self from sleeping soundly last night. Apparently his lack of slumber had finally caught up with him for he slept clean through the night and now, adrenaline pumped through his body since the screaming outside had yanked him from such a profound sleep.

He skipped on one foot across the dusty floor as he slid the opposite leg into stiffly wrinkled trousers in an attempt to make it to the door and get dressed at the same time. The screams were coming from Old Doc's office just across the way. On that realization Christian began to worry while a peculiar sense of foreboding washed over him. Josie was in trouble. He knew it, could sense it without stepping one foot outside the door. He could perceive with his entire being that all was not right. This surreal sensation was overpowering. His stomach clenched tightly and he staggered momentarily struggling with his boots.

It was early morning as the sun had yet to rise, around 5:00a.m. as best as he could tell. The smell of pine was refreshing and he inhaled deeply. Too bad he didn't have time to enjoy it as he had always loved the outdoors. The crickets continued to spurn their songs of mystery as drops of dew blanketed the grass. Now why on earth would someone be at Old Doc's place at this ungodly hour? Asking himself answered nothing. He was somewhat abashed for he was eager to meet with Teenabe as planned and be on his way. He was certain that the old Indian had the ability to locate the outlaw.

He found Hanna on the porch with tears rolling freely, eyes bleak and haunted, swollen from crying. She was trembling uncontrollably, her color flushed and pale. Instead of asking questions, Christian laid one hand upon her shoulder, gave a

supportive squeeze, nodded and then stepped over the threshold. He was so taken aback by the gruesome brutality that greeted him he could do little but stand frozen in place, absorbing the scene before him.

Oh poor Hanna; having walked into this must have been an awful shock to her, but he knew she was a strong woman and would soon be taking charge of what needed to be done. She'd be okay in time.

A large pool of blood covered the entire parlor. The smell of it was unnerving as he could not only smell it but taste its metallic touch on his tongue just by breathing the air. Christian wondered briefly if it was only the blood he smelled or was it death as well? Old Doc lie limp and lifeless, right smack dab in the middle of the mess. Some small ray of hope had him checking for a pulse even though he already knew in his heart it was futile. He also knew without looking that Josie was gone. Yet clinging to another small ray of hope, he checked anyway. He prayed his instincts would prove incorrect just this once. God please let her be there, he begged silently, safe and sound. I promise I'll be a better person. I'll follow your word forever. Please just let her be there unharmed...of coarse she wasn't.

His worst fears confirmed, he quit the room and stepped back outside for a breath of badly needed air. Holding Hanna he allowed her to sob stridently on his shoulder. As tears flowed from her, he found difficulty in keeping his own at bay. He blinked several times. It would do no one any good to see him fall apart at a time when his strength and commandeering would be needed most. Damn it. Where had he gone wrong? Didn't the Doc keep the door latched at night? In fact, he distinctly remembered giving firm instructions to do just that. Why hadn't he insisted on sleeping there himself instead of putting the old man in charge of Josie's safe keeping? Why had he been so fickle with the entire situation? After all, Old Doc wasn't the first casualty of this whole mess.

Question after question piled upon him along with guilt and his shoulders sagged visibly as if the burden was too much for him to carry. Angus approached with a questioning look. Christian shook his head sadly. Townsfolk began to gather quietly in the street. Many of them still wore robes, pajamas and night caps. Few among them had taken the time to dress properly. All of them wondering what had occurred and waited patiently for an explanation. However, they didn't dare press or invade as they were a tightly knit group and supported themselves from the comfort of friendship. Screams in the early morning hours were not a normal occurrence in Providence, and they knew that their valuable ladder of friendship and family had been damaged somehow.

Christian squeezed Hanna's shoulder with encouragement before placing his hat atop his ruffled head and addressed the crowd.

"Folks, we have a very sad situation here. I'm sorry to have to tell you that Old Doc is gone. He's passed on to be with the good Lord himself." Gasps and mummers of shock rippled through the crowd.

"That makes that the second murder in this town this summer. Both have happened in the same way. I can't say as to how sorry I am." Here he paused and took a deep breath. "Josie's been kidnapped. Now I know some of you harbor hard feelings for her and feel that she's responsible for all this. But she's not. She's one of ours now and she's a victim just as much as Old Doc was. She didn't ask for any of this nor did she hold the knife that killed two of ours. I've planned to form a search party this morning. Teenabe has agreed to help. Originally, I was only looking for Randall Hurley. Now it seems there's much more at stake here."

"Sheriff. Sheriff!" Joey ran up the porch interrupting the sheriff in a panicked and breathless state of frenzy. He had obviously run as fast as his young legs would take him.

"What is it Joey?" Christian bent down to meet the young man eye to eye.

"Sir, Millie is gone. Someone broke into the jail and took her. I swear it so sir, went right through the roof. The Judge is there. He sent me here to fetch you right quick sir, as he's a sprig upset."

Christian stood and looked to Hanna. "Can you organize some of the women to clean Old Doc up? I'd see we give him a proper burial." Several women stepped forward just on hearing his request. Hanna nodded.

"Any of you men that care to help out can meet me in front of the jailhouse as soon as you can get ready Bring your firearms."

Christian did one more walk through of the scene at Old Doc's office before moving down to the jail. He took quick note of the busted latch and blood covered rifle. The Doc had apparently tried to fend off the intruder.

At the jail house he was stunned to find the roof completely open above the one cell. The Judge sat silently upon the bench once occupied by his daughter. When he looked up Christian could see a world of hurt in his eyes. Although he could offer no encouragement to the Judge, he mentally put the scene together, fitting the pieces of each act of brutality like a puzzle, knowing that although Randall Hurley hadn't meant to take Millie and most likely had to back track to get Josie, Millie's life as well as Josie's were in grave danger. But, if Randall Hurley had time to return twice in one night, he couldn't be too far away. That thought alone was a gift of encouragement but at the same time, offered little comfort.

Approaching a large party of men, Christian quickly instructed a few men to stay behind. Repairs needed to be made right away to both structures. A coffin needed to be built and a new grave dug. That in itself was a back breaking chore, not one to be left to the women of which had enough to do already.

Hanna stepped quietly to his side awaiting a few words.

"Sheriff, the women have made a few decisions, to ease your mind before you go." She wrung her hands together fretfully and fidgeted back and forth from heal to toe in an attempt to calm her nerves. "We will clean up and prep Old Doc for a proper service as you requested. We'll clean the jail and the office as well. We'll also be closing all local business today, mainly the restaurant. We'll be using it to prepare a proper feast, a feast to celebrate two things—the passing of Old Doc's soul into the hands of the Almighty God and—the safe return of all our men, Millie and Josie. Both of which are good friends. We expect you to deliver. God speed."

"Thank you Hanna." Christian swallowed the lump of worry in his throat and prayed with all his heart he could deliver their request. God forbid if another life was lost. He'd never forgive himself. These people deserved much more that what they'd gotten so far.

"I have one more thing to do right quick if you men will honor one more request." At their nods Christian disappeared into the jail returning scant moments later with Neb Hurley in tow.

The group stood in astonished silence, jaws dropped and fist clenched.

"Angus, find Neb a rifle please." It was a curt order but none questioned the Sheriff's judgment. If they were to stick together and succeed in this endeavor, they'd have to start now. The men made quick work of loading their rifles, packing saddlebags, saddling two spare horses and accepting offerings of jerky, bread and berries from wives and friends.

As soon as the sun rose fully, it was evident the day would be hot and muggy. Even though the bright orb in the sky still hung to the west, the men were plastered with sweat. Trotting through patches of overhung trees brought a small semblance of shade but they mostly followed the banks of the river.

Teenabe had insisted on examining the happenings at Old Doc's office and at the jail before heading out. He now sat silently astride his stallion, old but proud. He looked wise and surreal, stopping often, searching for signs that were invisible to Christian's eyes.

Christian repeatedly sent up silent prayers of help and guidance in this endeavour. He had put all his faith into a red skinned man he hardly even knew. A man that had every right to hate white men and wish them dead for they had done nothing but disgrace and dishonor the Ottawa Indians. Christian repetitively implored that Teenabe lead them to Josie and that she and Millie be alive. That thought caused a steel resolve to go through him like a blade of folded steel, it settled in the depths of his heart. Anger enveloped that steel resolve. He swore on Josie's life and the happiness of his future, he'd kill Randall Hurley. God forbid anyone who ever tried to hurt her again. He was a man of the law but the law be damned if it came right down to it. He'd throw in his badge. The smell of dead fish brought his thoughts back to the present. This day was bound to be long.

Millie awoke to the sound of Randy relieving himself upon a dry patch of ground. The stench of him nauseated her. In fact, just looking at him caused her stomach to toss and turn like churned butter. The man was a fool to think he could get away with this. Why her father would see him hanged whether she lived or not. She shut her eyes and concentrated on not moving, not that she really could. Her body was terribly bruised and abused but she didn't want Randy to know she was awake. Perhaps he'd leave her be for a while longer.

"Get up woman." The bellow was accompanied by his boot scuffing the earth, sending dirt everywhere. It pattered across her face and pain assailed her tender scalp as he pulled her off the ground with a fist full of curly hair.

"Make some breakfast."

"Ok." She responded meekly. "What is there to make?"

He threw a sack of food supplies at her. Dumbfounded she stood and starred at the bag.

"What the hell's wrong with you woman?"

Looking up with tears in her eyes and a tight ball of fright in the pit of her belly she replied in a shaky voice. "I don't know how to cook."

"You're jesting."

"No. I really don't know how to cook. I can clean the mess but I'm afraid I can't prepare it."

Growling, he was up and at her before she could bat an eyelash. He snatched the bag from her hands and with another swift move had her landing with a thump upon the ground, her cheek throbbing from the force of the blow.

"I'll make my own damn breakfast but you ain't gettin' any. You hear me?"

Millie shook her head and stood to gather what little dignity she had left. Without further direction, she began to get out the cookware needed for his breakfast. Once the food began to sizzle her stomach rolled and growled loudly from hunger. It was just awful to smell such divine odors such as sizzling bacon and fresh coffee and not be able to have any. Her throat was dry and scratchy.

"I beg a boon of you Randy."

"What's that?" He talked with food in his mouth, smacking loudly yet growling at the same time. Millie thought it amazing that someone could do such things all at once without thought.

"I'd like some water." Realizing he wasn't going to give her any she meekly added, "please."

"Well now that's better. A little more submissive this morning ain't ya?"

Her cheeks burned with embarrassment but it was worth it for he tossed her a rugged looking canteen. "One chug is all you git. Any more en' that and I'll backhand you. Got it?"

She nodded before savoring her one chug. It was the best sip of water she'd ever had, even if it was old and warm.

Opening her eyes Josie lay very still trying to desperately absorb her surroundings and decipher her current situation. An onslaught of questions ran through her mind. Where was she? What had happened? How long had she been asleep? Why did she hurt so badly? Depressingly, she had no answers. Suddenly she realized that she missed Christian terribly. Not only did she miss him, she needed him. She wanted nothing more than to be held in his arms right now. Where was he? Shivering with a chill she turned slowly on her side, trying to see where she was. Her shivering increased when she witnessed Randy Hurley tossing hot bacon grease onto non other then Millie McQuade. Oh, she thought, this couldn't be good.

Millie screamed as grease burned her arms and midsection. Now there was no reason for this. She hadn't done a darn thing wrong. Randall Hurley was just plain wicked. She swore he just liked to see others in pain, more so if *he* caused the pain. Well she wouldn't show him anymore hurt. The only thing he was bound to get out of her was trouble. Without asking permission, because surely she didn't care, she walked painfully to the waters edge and dunked her arms into the river. The coolness of the water diminished the worst of the burning. "Oh" she moaned closing her eyes. She could just sink down into this river and loose herself in it. Give up the battle. Certainly it would be much better than what awaited her here on this rock of an island. This fish smelling, bug infested, God forsaken place that she had so desperately wanted to visit just a few short months ago. Usually the Maumee River looked beautiful and calmed her, today it did nothing but aid her thoughts of suicide. She thought to herself how foolish she had been, imagining herself in love with Sheriff C. Love. Her mind stuck on that word. She wondered if she ever really knew what love was. Everything had been merely a possession to her before. Nothing more than a ranking, a symbol or status of wealth and authority. But, never had she loved. She realized now as clearly as the sun would rise each morning and set each evening. Was there something wrong with her? And right now, what did she have to live for? Her father? Maybe. Herself? Humbled, she noted that "herself" wasn't worth all that much. So lost in thought was she that she didn't even realize she was crying. Real tears. She had cried quite a few tears last night and today. It was most likely the first time ever she cried from hurt rather than a means to get her way. But why was she wasting tears on self pity and an awful man? No more. After all, she was a McQuade. She had dignity and pride. She would survive...persevere. It was hard not too. Lifting her chin, holding her head high, she walked back to the campsite. The soul searching complete, she returned a stronger, better person.

"Get up Josie. I know you're awake." Randy kicked her side.

"I'm trying you big ox. Can't you see?"

Choosing not to say anything to the smart remark, Randy grabbed a good handful of the night shirt Josie wore and yanked her up roughly. He effortlessly flung her over the saddle. Now Josie, she had spunk. She had a mouth but she had a streak of fire in her that had Randy's groin tighten just thinking about it. In time, he thought. Not much longer.

Josie lay limply looking at the ground below her. She could barely breath as it was. Golly how had she gotten into this pickle? Chewing her bottom lip with worry she presumed to be better off than what poor Millie was at this point in time. Her heart went out to the girl. It was funny how you could hate so deeply one day and feel entirely different the next. There were a lot of thoughts running through her head and yet she suddenly lost them all as blackness overtook her once again.

Millie gathered the rest of the supplies and loaded them into the packs. She knew only that they were moving to a new location. How...she couldn't fathom for there were three of them and only one horse, fully loaded right now with Josie and supplies, and a heck of a large river to cross. She did the best she could to tie her torn clothes together and cover most of her skin.

"Come on woman!" Randy bellowed as he slipped a knotted rope around her neck and tied another around her wrists.

"Wha...what are you doing?"

"You and I are crossing on foot. You try anything, or slip and fall, this rope will tighten like a noose. Now move damn it." With that he smacked her behind surly leaving another bruise.

Millie almost choked on fear as Randy tied the other end of the rope around his waist. "What if you fall?"

"You better pray that I don't sweetheart."

The water wasn't unbearably cold, nor was it extremely deep, at first. It was however, full with currant and slippery as all get up. Randy walked on one side of the horse leading it by the bridle. Millie followed on the opposite side flanking the horse, the rope slung over the top of the saddle, intertwined with Josie's seemingly unconscious form. Guilt washed over Millie for the hundredth time for what she had done to Josie.

Randy was in fact the first to fall. Luckily he got himself up without incident. However, it caused Millie's heart to falter as one hand automatically went to her throat as if to form a barrier between the rope and her neck.

The currant pulled more forcibly as they got further from the island. They were no where near the shore. Millie grasped the straps of the saddle with a death grip fighting just to stay upright. Slowly the water grew deeper and deeper. Even the horse was unsettled as it's eyes rolled upward. The water began to cover Josie's forehead as she hung limply over the horses saddle, belly down and unconscious. Millie tried desperately to walk, hang on to the horse and hold Josie's head above water in an attempt to keep her from drowning. The task was neigh impossible and a most tiresome struggle. Thankfully the horse did most of the work as her weight was indivertibly added to the load.

They trudged on painstakingly slow. Their progress seemingly getting them nowhere yet bore every ounce of endurance she had. Millie wondered why they didn't cross over on the other side of Roach De Buff, that had to be where they were, that had to be the island. On the other side the water would be shallow and less treacherous. Why didn't they leave the same way they came? Apprehension filled the hollow pit of her being as she answered her own questions. There would be no tracks to follow should someone come looking for them. Once again tears flowed freely down her face as she struggled to find some hint of hope. Some desperate way of getting out of this terrible situation. If only Josie would wake up. Another mind sure couldn't hurt. The odds would be better: two against one.

Come nightfall, a fire was burning brightly, a sure sign that Randy was fairly confident they hadn't been followed or discovered. Least ways he felt sure no one would be able to pick up their trail. Josie woke shivering and cold as her clothes and hair were damp. She didn't see any sign of Randy within the campsite. Daylight was quickly fading and the air hung heavy with humidity. She could hear a dog barking in the distance and silently wondered if they had neared another town.

Millie was a short distance away, huddled into herself in a crouched position. The forlorn look upon her face as well as all the cuts and bruises tore at Josie's heartstrings. At closer approach Josie made eye contact.

"Oh, my lord!" Josie uttered the curse as a daunting understanding of all that had transpired sank in. She heartedly embraced Millie. Her hands smoothed curly wisps of hair from Millie's face as tears rolled down both their cheeks. Not another word was spoken out loud yet a silent conversation ensued. It was a conversation of love, faith and strength, a conversation of re-birth and encouragement. A compelling beginning to a silent bond of sisterhood that would help both girls to sustain the hurdles that life, as unfair as it was, had currently thrown at them. Together they would face the morning and somehow, someway, they would get away from Randy. They would find freedom and appreciate living all the more because of what was happening now. Josie reminded herself of what her Mama always said. "God wouldn't give you more than what you could handle". Well, he sure was pushing it this time.

The moment was roughly stolen when Randy grabbed both girls by the hair and smashed their heads together. They were so absorbed in their thoughts and feelings that neither girl heard his approach from behind. The shock took away some of the pain but Josie's forehead smarted something fierce. She inwardly acknowledged that Randy had in fact won one battle. Normally she would have smart mouthed a comment to him, now however, she was reluctant to do so for fear that he would retaliate by hurting either her or Millie. It would be smartest, she thought, not to rile him too much. If she and Millie were to break away, they would need their wits about them as well as their strength. Randy's blows had a tendency to rob a person of both.

"I want supper Josie. Since this dimwit can't cook…" he looked at Millie, kicked dirt in her face, then pushed her over, "you better." After spitting on the ground he barked "Now!"

Josie jumped as the thunder of his voice clapped ricochets of pain through her head. She began to rifle through the supply bag, searching not only for food but for something that could aid in escape. She tried desperately to ignore the continued pain throbbing at her temples.

Millie lay upon the ground glaring at Randy when an idea suddenly took root. It was a marvelous, wonderful idea. How amazing it was…this idea. The answer had been right in front of her face all along and she hadn't seen it. "I'll help," she told Josie, "by gathering some roots. Perhaps you can boil them into a poultice for our wounds." It was a statement that bellied a world of promise. Millie's heart beat fast with anticipation and worry. Was her voice too loud? Could Randy guess that she was up to something?

As if on cue to her silent concern, Randy nodded his consent. "If you're not back in five minutes, I'm coming to find you. I'll hunt you down like wild game." The grin on his face and the excitement dancing in his eye assured her of what exactly would happen when he did find her.

She shuddered inwardly and responded meekly "I'll be back before that."

Josie worked efficiently at putting supper together. There were potatoes, that was the extent of it. She plopped lard into a frying pan and busied herself with cleaning and cutting up the hearty vegetables, all the while worrying and fretting about Millie. She prayed that Millie wasn't doing anything foolish. Josie could only imagine how Millie must be feeling right now. She wasn't certain how she would feel herself, kept hostage in a violent situation, the future looking bleak at every cross-road, if she had been violated the way that Millie had. Josie felt guilty. She considered that she had faired better through this ordeal so far than what Millie had. A small selfish part of her prayed that Millie didn't run away or escape, for that would leave Josie by herself with Randy. Look at what he had done to Millie. She couldn't blame the girl for trying if she did. Yet at the same time she prayed that Millie would get away. It would be best, she thought, if it were only herself facing Randy's wrath—kind of like damage control.

Millie sprung up behind Josie before she was able to dump the cut up potatoes into the pan. "Here Josie…I gathered these. I'm not sure if they'll help at all…but I tried."

"I'm sure these will work just fine Millie." Josie responded raising a questioning eyebrow when finding poison ivy leaves wrapped in a torn piece of Millie's skirt and scouring rush in the palm of one clenched hand.

"While you cook, I'll lay out Randy's bed roll. I'll work something up for us to pass the night on as well." Millie's offer was kind and sincere. Josie knew however, what she was up to and had to stifle a chuckle. It wasn't hard to figure out and in a small way was refreshing. As she cooked she discretely sprinkled the rush atop a large portion of the potatoes, scooting a smaller portion to one side of the pan for her and Millie. She couldn't help thinking that the vindictiveness in her actions felt good and in a way…reviving.

Randy hovered close by, listening to every word the girls exchanged and keeping and eye on Josie as she used a knife and various other utensils to prepare the meal. He thought about allowing her to wash in the river. She smelled something awful. The stench nauseated his stomach, yet he wanted her something fierce. He would have his way with her and make sure that Josie learned who was boss. Millie apparently had learned her lesson, Josie would too, to his way of thinking. In time, it might not be so bad traveling with two young women. They could attend to his every need. Eventually, he'd have to find a new partner and most likely share the girls…but that was in time. For now, he wasn't even sure he needed Neb anymore. He sure wasn't worth the hassle he caused. But Neb was the only kin Randy had left. If you couldn't rely on kin—then who could you rely on?

Josie laid the meal out then fetched water to boil for both drinking and for coffee. She urged Millie to eat. Neither girl had eaten much the past 24-hours, as they hadn't much of an appetite. Yet they both knew they needed to gather and conserve their strength. Randy didn't begrudge them the meal, although he ate the majority of what was prepared. Josie watched him from across the cook fire and wondered if some people were just born mean or if bad things happened to make them mean. Josie could see herself not liking men after this.

Between her Daddy and Randy, she'd had her fill of life's lessons regarding the opposite sex. Then she thought of Christian and her stance softened completely. Her body warmed and a grip of longing squeezed at her heart. She took comfort in thinking about Christian. He was out there somewhere tracking them. Surely he'd be to their rescue soon. She just had to hang in and take things one moment at a time. She could make Christian's job easier by leaving a trail for him to find and follow. She'd figure out a way to leave signs and markings that Randy wouldn't be able to see or figure out—no matter how attentive he was. She'd start now by accidentally spilling the grease in the frying pan. When Josie picked up the pan, Millie leapt up from her seated position and offered "I'll take that Josie. You cooked, I'll clean."

"Thanks again Millie." Josie acted like she was handing the pan to Millie but tripped instead. The grease went everywhere, leaving a good three foot span of dirt soaked with lard as evidence of their visit upon the land.

Randy was quick to respond pulling Josie up by the hair and barking at Mille to clean the pan and put fresh dirt over the ground right away. Millie shuffled to do as was bid while Randy yanked Josie painfully to the river. There he unmercifully ripped the night dress from her and tossed her roughly into the water.

The chill of the water felt good but at the same time took her breath away. Josie stood waist deep covering her breast with her arms…stupefied.

Randy threw a bar of soap at her. "Wash for God's sake. You stink to high heaven."

"I stink?" She shouted the question at the top of her lungs. Anger washed over her emotions like a gigantic wave of fury. "You stink you big ox!"

Randy didn't rise to the bait. He just sat back and devoured her with his eyes. Josie backed further into the river never taking her eyes from his. She swallowed the lump in her throat. Shivers of dread danced along her flesh bumped skin.

Then Randy adjusted the crotch of his pants and sat back. He obviously wasn't in any hurry to go anywhere. He didn't say a word but that sinister silent stare said it all. Josie felt she was riding a crest of fear like nothing she had ever faced before. It was her turn and she knew in her heart of hearts that if it wasn't her, it would be Millie. She had no weapon. What on earth could she do to keep a man the size of an ox away from her? What could she do to avoid what she knew was going to happen? "Oh, God," she prayed. "Please help me." She willed Christian to find her now. Perhaps in situations such as this, every minute mattered. She slowly and methodically began to clean herself. She very slowly washed her hair…twice. She washed every part of her body…twice. At the onset of the third washing, Randy rose and stood near the waters edge. It appeared he wouldn't hesitate to come in and get her.

"Come Josie." Randy's voice portrayed his eagerness to get his hands on her. His eyes danced and glared with wicked thoughts as each moment brought him closer to what he had been waiting for.

"No." She backed further into the water. Although her night dress was torn and on the shore, she still remained in undergarments, and had no qualms about making a run for it. Not since she saw the excitement in his eyes. She truly didn't know if she would survive whatever it was that Randy wanted to do to her. Whatever it was that had him looking so evil and dangerous.

"Don't make me come in there." His nostrils flared with anger. The shade of his skin burned red as the boundaries of his anger expanded. Damn the twit. If he had to go into that water—he'd strangle her.

"You need a bath too Randy. You stink."

"I don't bathe in rivers."

"Why?"

"Get over here damn it."

"I said no. You need a bath Randy. Please make this easier on me and clean yourself up." She pleaded with him in an attempt to buy some time.

"Git out of the water girl. Now!"

"You can't swim." Even though she said it out loud, that realization brought her power and courage. She stepped deeper into the water. "If you want me, come and get me." With that challenge, Josie turned and began making her way to the other side of the river. Trying to run through water was like trying to push a train through the mud. Every step she took, every move she made was bogged down by the waters depth and current. She made little progress and was already breathless when she heard the splash of Randy entering the water behind her.

Second guessing herself, she wondered if she was wrong to presume that Randy couldn't swim. He certainly didn't' hesitate to jump in and chase her. Perhaps she just needed to go deeper, where swimming would be required. The bad thing was she didn't know where the deeper areas of the river were. She fought to move a tangled wet mass of hair from her eyes and spent a few desperate seconds scanning the river. Over to her right she saw ripples and waves in the water. Surly that meant depth. In a split second she made the decision to let the current carry her in that direction rather than fight for the shore. Escape was the only thing on her mind, not Millie, not the risk she was taking with her life, just getting away from Randy. Escape was all she thought about as she fought for freedom, praying the water would give it to her. The moment her feet no longer reached the bottom of the river, Josie relaxed her body and let the river carry her. She focused on staying afloat, keeping her head above water. Every now and then she would glance around in an attempt to locate Randy. Across the water, for as far as she could tell, he was no where to be seen. She let herself float a while longer, praying that her strength would hold as her limbs grew weaker with each passing rock. She scanned for Randy again and felt her spirit soar when she failed to locate him. Heaving a sigh of relief she struggled to drift closer to shore while desperately trying to feel for the bottom and gain footing. Just when she thought she couldn't fight anymore, she gained ground and boosted herself onto the river bank. She lay there panting for air, exhausted, cold and numb. How far had she drifted? It felt like miles although she new that concept was erroneous. She couldn't have gone too far. She shut her eyes and instantly began concocting a plan on how to rescue Millie. Then they had to get back to town. One step at a time. Golly, she still couldn't seem to catch her breath.

Suddenly her senses were assailed by a familiar odor. By the time her brain registered the fowl smell of Randy, it was too late. He stood above her looking down with the most evil eyes she had ever seen. Satan himself would have a tough time topping that ominous expression. She struggled to squirm away from him to no avail. Randy was on top of her before she could gasp a full breath of air. He had knocked the wind right from her as he pinned her wrist above her head, then landed a wallop of a punch smack dab in the middle of her face. She heard the sickening crunch and snap of her nose a brief second before she began to choke on the blood that was freely flowing into her mouth as she was still on her backside upon the ground. She couldn't breath. That was the immediate concern, not the pain. Between the broken nose, her exhausted plight, and the heavy weight of Randy upon her chest, she was quickly loosing her grip on life. As she coughed and sputtered, Randy began ripping at the undergarments, the only covering she had left. The fierce panic that overcame her led to a burst of energy as insanity took over. She fought and actually landed a few good blows herself. Randy would not be unmarked by his ugliness. The harder she fought, the rougher he became trying frantically to control her flying fist, squirming body and ear piercing screams. When Randy tried to squelch the screams by covering her mouth with a filthy hand, Josie bit hard enough to remove flesh. When he let go of her mouth to control her hands again, she kneed him in the groin. He felt ribs break as he placed his knees atop her chest and began squeezing around her throat with every intention of steeling the life from her flailing body. He couldn't be sure because of all the blood, but he thought her lips were turning a nice shade of purple. She began to weaken her struggle and he felt excitement stir as her eyes rolled towards the back of her head.

"That's enough" he murmured. Although she wasn't lifeless, she was on the brink and would no longer struggle. He removed the rest of the torn garments and spread her legs butterfly style, degrading to Josie had she been conscious, yet revealing to him. He studied her body while unzipping his trousers. The bruises enhanced his libido and he dreamed up more torturous things to do to her. He loved to hear her screams and pleas, begging him to stop hurting her.

He brought his arousal to the soft folds between her legs and wondered if she would be a virgin like the other one was. Lifting her legs to rest on his shoulders he paused another moment to adjust his fingers around her throat again. He could see the shallow rise and fall of her chest indicating she was still alive. At the moment he was to gain entry, he heard a fierce growl. Turning he looked into the eyes of an animal that must have been a mix between dog and horse. The animal growled and inched closer displaying teeth that could damage a mans flesh and rip it to shreds in no time at all.

"Git" he ground out, slowly losing the arousal that ruled his actions only moments before.

The animal inched closer and snarled even more ferociously. Randy began to remove Josie's legs and reach for his gun when the animal attacked. It was on top of him before he could blink, tearing flesh from his hands and arms as he used his limbs to protect his face and neck. Adrenaline rushed through his veins as he fought to locate his gun. It was if he watched the attack from afar. He could see what was happening, he could see the large dark colored animal with it's teeth barred, he could see the gun, yet he couldn't move an arm to reach for it as that simple action would leave one side of his face unprotected.

Amidst the growling and struggling, there came a strangled cough from Josie. The animal turned it's attention offering a brief respite and enough time for Randy to grasp the colt five shooter laying close by. The animal must have sensed this defeat as it took off running for cover in the murky greenery lining the riverbank. Randy shot a full round of bullet and powder towards it anyways. He wasn't sure if he'd hit the critter or not, but he did hear a painful yelp as bullet number five must have met its mark.

Randy glanced at his arms which burned painfully. They were torn to shreds. Josie was awake and blinking back tears while trying to cover herself. He grabbed her hair and yanked her mercilessly to her feet.

"Back to the camp site, now!" He barked the order yet felt his voice wasn't as rough as it should be. It must be the pain. "What the hell was that thing?"

Josie could barely talk but managed to state in a raspy voice, "That was the dog you kicked around when you first captured me. He's grown a bit don't you think?" She didn't intend to be so contrite in response. The words just came out that way and she stiffened, awaiting a physical attack as punishment.

Anger flowed through Randy, but oddly enough, it only exhausted him. He just needed to clean up and rest. Some whisky and a good nights sleep was sure to fix what ailed him. He'd have another go of Josie tomorrow, when he could think straight again. Next time, he'd tie her up. That would make it a lot easier. He'd be keeping an eye out for that dog too. If it was still alive, it wouldn't be the next time it tried to attack him.

CHAPTER TWELVE

Once back at the camp site Josie gained a small amount of comfort from Millie's presence yet felt instant exposure when Millie's eyes raked over her beaten body. Millie did her best to comfort her friend and the girls carried on a silent conversation of compassion as Randy huddled near the fire drinking whiskey and cursing loudly. Josie decided to wait until a later time to explain about Hops and the attack, although she knew Millie thought the worst had happened; just like with her. She didn't think she could talk about it now without crying anyways. Just thinking about Hops laying out there, either dead or needing help made her chest ache and brought tears to her eyes. Then she remembered hearing a barking noise earlier. She didn't really think much about it then, but barking dogs along the river weren't a normal occurrence.

Her shoulders shook again as she heaved a sigh. Dwelling on what had already happened to Millie and what had almost happened to her didn't help matters at all. Did people ever run fresh out of tears? She seemed to suddenly have an over abundance of them. She searched for her nightdress by the river bank. It was torn terribly but would have to do considering the situation. Her feet were cold and she couldn't stop shaking even when she willed her body to be calm. It was summer and many considered it a blessing if the evenings grew cool. Why was she feeling like it was ten degrees out? Again her thoughts wondered to Christian, then to her Daddy. She missed her Daddy terribly. Perhaps it was because she was hurting so badly right now. It was similar to when she caught a cold. Every time she took ill, she missed her Momma dreadfully. She had thought it a smart idea to run away. Ironically, she had run smack dab into even more trouble than what she would have if she'd stayed home. How was Daddy? Was he eating? She couldn't just shake off the love and family bond that used to be there. She hoped her good memories of her family would last forever for right at this moment she felt so forlorn, that those memories seemed to be all she had.

Josie had a difficult time moving and breathing, not only was she still getting over being sick, but Randy had done a good job on breaking and cracking ribs. She wondered how long it took broken bones to heal. She acquired some comfort in the pain as she thanked God she was still alive. And, if Hops had followed their trail and found her, surly Christian would. When Christian did find her, he'd take her to see the Old Doc and all would be well. Believing in their rescue required a lot of faith, something she had difficulty creating at this particular moment.

The silence was broken as Randy hurled an empty whisky bottle into the fire and barked at Millie to fetch another. The bottle whooshed in a burning response. The girls looked at each other, then both fetched the whiskey. There was a silent pact between them, as there was safety in numbers; they would stick together from here on out. Randy indicated without words that he wanted the whiskey poured onto his wounds. Knowing that act would cause him pain gave both girls a boost in spirits. Add that to the fact that there was ivy spread in Randy's bed roll and scouring rush mixed into his food earlier, the girls almost became downright giddy. They had to suppress their excitement.

Millie was too afraid to pour the whiskey, so Josie bravely stepped forward to perform the task, placing an arm in front of her ribs for protection should Randy do as he always did and take a swing at her. He was however, surprisingly calm about it. It was as if he'd had whiskey poured on open wounds many a times. The cuts were deep in some areas but for the most part were flesh wounds. Even with the whiskey treatment, Randy would be lucky if an infection failed to develop. He was dirty, the dog was dirty, and their living arrangements currently weren't the greatest, not to mention the insects that landed and bit on a regular basis.

The girls voluntarily bedded down together in hopes that Randy wouldn't suspect anything. They were both exhausted, beaten and struggling to stay upright. Once their bodies spread flat upon the ground, they fell asleep in no time.

The sun was hot this morning as Christian peered along the river. A feeling of unease seemed to settle not only over him and his group, but the land as well. He didn't like it one bit. Most of the frustration was caused by the river. Every time they'd pick up the trail, they would lose it again in the flowing water. On a positive note, they had enough men to spread along each side of the bank to search for disturbances within the overgrown beds of brush, bushes, trees and soil. But it continued to be a maddening puzzle as they would pick the trail up, lose it again, pick it up, lose it again. He felt like screaming and probably would if he thought it would help.

The dark cluster of thunder clouds hanging low threatened to wash away what little evidence they could find. Then, Christian's worst fears were brought to surface as Teenabe dismounted and validated by nose the markings on the ground. Blood. This was the kind of trail that no one in the search party wanted to find. It was an ominous confirmation of bad news. It appeared to route away from the river bank but Teenabe went in the opposite direction. A stone's throw away were markings near the water, a clear sign of struggle and a larger stain of blood. Thank goodness for the Indian's skills as Christian and his men would have followed the trail immediately and missed the other area completely. If men swooned, Christian would have done so right then and there. As it was, his stomach clenched painfully when the Indian removed a clump of hair from a rock. It was long, brown and caked with blood and mud. Josie's.

This time Christian couldn't hold back the feral growl that formed in his throat. Could a little sprig of a girl like Josie lose that much blood and still survive? He didn't think it was possible.

The Indian remained low to the ground, speaking quietly in a tongue that the white folks couldn't comprehend. Mere moments passed but to Christian, every moment felt like an hour. It was as if he had a sixth sense. This extra sense measured how much time Josie had left and flowed like and hour glass. He hoped and prayed that his assumptions were correct. Because, even though he was panicked right now, the anxiety he felt confirmed that Josie was still alive. Alive that is, if his senses were intact. He couldn't bring himself to think of the alternative.

Teenabe waved Christian closer. "There is blood of three here."

Christian felt a wave of relief wash over him. If this was the blood of three people, then conceivably, not much of it was Josie's. Perhaps she wasn't as bad off as he thought. Anger boiled over and he fought to control his rage. Blood was blood. Josie had been hurt and lord only knew what else she had been through. "What next?" he asked while looking to Teenabe for guidance.

"We follow the blood trail then double back." The response was clipped and unfriendly. Apparently, Teenabe had some reservations about who he was dealing with and was struggling to hold his anger in check as well. "Sorry friend. I am riding on the heals of evil. This man we chase, makes me feel scared inside. I fear for those who cross his path. I fear the reckoning."

Christian growled. "Don't you worry none. I'll take care of the reckoning."

The blood trail led away from the river and kept low, under several low hanging trees. Teenabe confirmed his suspicions that the blood came from an animal rather than a human when the group finally caught up with the injured dog laying snug against a boulder, panting and whimpering with pain.

Christian fell to his knees and took inventory of the animals injuries. His hands were steady as he felt the dogs body and whispered soothing words to keep him calm. The yelp that ensued assured Christian of where the injury was. One of Hop's hind legs was torn up pretty badly from a bullet. The only saving grace it appeared, was that the shot was long range, coming from some distance away, but damaging none the less. There were several areas around the main wound that had penetrating damage as well. All in all, the leg was mangled.

One of the men in the party cautiously ambled up to the dog and aimed his gun at the animals head. It was customary to put an animal out of its misery rather than have it suffer. But this dog belonged to Josie and Christian wasn't sure he could do that. With a gesture he stayed Angus's actions. "Does anybody know what to do to save this dogs life?"

Teenabe bent low and examined the dog. "The leg must go. It's the only way. The dog will suffer much. You should put him down."

"I can't. This dog may be all I have left of Josie. Plus, if she does make it through this, I don't want her hating me for not offering the dog a chance."

The Judge, who had been silently traversing along, piped in with the idea of having one of the men take the dog back to Teenabe's Indian wife, whom had an excellent reputation of healing injured animals. "There's been enough loss already. Most likely, more to come. We should minimize and keep what friends we have. Apparently this dog did something to help our girls. He should be treated like a king for the rest of his days." The Judge's words were final.

They lost the trail again at the waterway but picked it up a few hundred feet up river and followed it to an area that must have been a camp-site. Remaining traces of abuse were everywhere. It was easy to see shuffling and struggle marks left upon the ground. It was also easy to spot blood drops and spatter amongst several different surfaces such as rocks, dirt, trees and one localized area near the fire pit. At these signs, Teenabe announced that they were close as the earth was still warm where the fire had burned. This news was a relief to a certain extent. The closer they were, the sooner Josie and Millie would be safe. On the other hand, every moment counted as frustration and urgency compiled in all their minds. Finding more evidence of blood and apparent abuse did not bode well with any of them and fear of what they would find settled in all their hearts.

"Millie." Josie shook her shoulder gently so as to not scare the daylights out of her. "Wake up. Come on, we've got to get moving." Her soft whispers echoed in the cave like crevice where they had set up camp for the night, disturbing the blanket of silence.

Randy lay upon his bed roll, deathly white, unresponsive and covered in poison ivy. He must have scratched the itch all night long as his arms were almost raw. His wounds from the dog bites appeared to be festering already. The girls cautiously took inventory of his illness.

"Millie, I almost feel bad for doing this. He was probably going to come down with fever from infection anyways. Maybe we caused a burden his body can't handle. His death will be on our hands."

"Don't you dare feel sorry for that man Josie Edwards. This is simply his come around. I had mine. Now he gets his. That's what happens when you do wrong by folks. That's what happens when you're down right mean. Besides, we can't undo what we've done. We can pray for forgiveness and guidance, but it's too late to go back now."

Josie knew that Millie was right. "I know, but it still feels wrong."

"That man raped me!" Millie's chin quivered as she spoke. "He has taken my virginity Josie. No man will ever want me now. He tried to do the same to you!" She spoke with such vehemence that she spat as her lips moved. "He has beaten us, starved us, and degraded us in ways we will never forget. The rest of our lives will be spent trying to get over the damage the past few days have caused. And, if given the chance, he would continue to do so until it killed us. It's either him or us Josie. Whose lives do you value most?"

"You're absolutely correct." Josie was now fixed with determination and back in control of her emotions. "I'm sorry Millie. I think I'm feeling a bit out of sorts today."

"That's ok. We'll get through this." The girls squeezed hands briefly.

"What are we standing around for? Let's restrain that big oaf so that he can't chase after us if he does feel better later. We'll take his gun, the food and the horse. Should he wake up and feel better, there's water all around. He can fend for himself."

"What about the wolves? He'll fall prey to them." Millie was deathly scarred of the wolves in the area. She had heard numerous stories with horrible endings."

Millie had just chastised Josie for feeling sorry for Randy and now, she herself felt badly and somewhat bereft at what they were doing. Was there such a thing as a humane death? Could they leave Randy there to die in a fashion that wouldn't make them feel guilty for the rest of their lives? Somehow she didn't think it was possible. It was odd she thought, that if he stood trial and hung from the end of a rope, she wouldn't carry an ounce of guilt but instead feel justified.

"I don't think they like rotten meat." The barb went unacknowledged. "But, we'll place some rocks at the entrance for protection before we head out. Hopefully, we can find our way back to town. Randy sure did a good job at getting us lost in these woods. I'm not sure *he* even knows where we're at. Like you said Millie, this is our way of staying alive and intact. We must do what we have to. Besides, the wolves have plenty of natural game to hunt. It's not as if they are starving. I think that would be the only reason they would come after us, if they were absolutely dying of hunger."

The evening before, they had left the river and traveled for hours through the swamp. It was difficult to see then because it had grown dark and the trees were thick as molasses. Now, in the daylight, it remained dark and disorienting, only a shadows difference from the night before. Josie couldn't even use the sun as a directional guide since the blanket of branches covered the area like a large canopy. Even though it was a warm day, the morning chill was enhanced by the vastness of shade offered freely within the forest as dew droplets could be heard falling from leaves and landing softly on the carpet of pine needles they rode upon.

The horse trotted along carrying both girls. They were famished and Josie searched as they rode for edible berries and nuts. When they did finally spot some, it felt as if they were having a feast. Even the horse enjoyed the sweet morsels. Josie felt bad for the horse too. She cold tell by looking into it's eyes, that they were full of sadness. Randy most likely treated his steed the same way he did them. Compassion filled her heart for this animal. That thought led her to think of Hops. She wondered again how he was doing. Most likely he had died out here in the wilderness, alone and hurting. On that thought, she began to cry. And cry she did. Millie joined in and they cried together. Slowly the wracking sobs turned into tears of joy. Joy for being alive, joy for getting away from Randy, joy for the sustenance they had just found and joy for the very air they breathed.

"Come Millie. Let's go further today. In a few hours, we'll watch for a good place to bed down. Then, I'll try to shoot a rabbit. Lord knows, we need something healthy to eat."

"Yum" was Millie's only reply other than the rumble of her stomach in response to such succulent thoughts of roasted meat on a spit over open flame.

Nick Edwards swatted at the mosquitoes swarming all about. He was in a foul mood as he hadn't had a drink in more than a month. Although he thought the worst was over, he still shook uncontrollably from time to time. His appetite hadn't yet returned to normal either and he had lost a lot of weight lately. He was ashamed that he had made such a debauchery of his life. He had learned all about humility throughout his withdraw from the bottle. Too many days and nights had passed where he could do nothing but lay in pain, sick to his stomach and feeling like he was delusional. Now, each day was slowly getting better. As each day passed he felt a little more in control of his life again…and a little more able to handle the pain and sorrow of loosing his wife. The grief was no longer unbearable. He didn't feel so bad about the baby. He was sad about the baby dying and that sure did hurt something fierce. But, the loss of his wife, his companion for near 20 years was unbearable. He had felt as if every ounce of life had been sucked right out of him. He lost his own will to live and had thought terrible things for the longest time. His weakness and inability to deal with the yearning for his wife after she passed had caused him to turn to the bottle. That same weakness had aided his neglecting the relationship with his only daughter, Josie. Josie. When she needed him most, he had failed her. He felt just awful. The one goal he had in life now was to find her. He would spend the rest of his life looking for her if needed. And when he did find her, he would spend the rest of his life making sure she knew that her Daddy had made a terrible mistake. Her Daddy loved her with all his heart.

Randy roused to a state that he considered mostly dead. He knew the girls were gone before he managed to crack one eye open to a slit. He also knew he was sicker than a dog that drank turpentine. He saw the bottle of whisky laying near the dying embers of the fire. He couldn't tell how long he'd been out. By the glow of the embers, it had to have been hours. The girls had quite a lead on him. He noted the missing supplies, gun and horse. Fire burned within his core heating every nerve with the fury of flames. Grinding his teeth did nothing but hurt his head. Grunting with pain he rolled onto all four limbs and crawled to the whiskey bottle. Spit dripped from his mouth as he slowly and painfully made his way nearer the fire. A burning pain lanced through every fiber of his being.

He was in a sorry state. He grabbed the bottle and drank deeply, then poured some liquor over his hands and began to rub it on his arms, neck and face. The burning sensation only added fuel to the fire of anger. When he did catch up with those girls, he'd waste no time in killing them. Thinking of how sweet revenge would be was a pleasing thought as he drifted into the darkness of unconsciousness.

"Josie I'm starving."

"I know hon. Me too." She had tried twice to shoot a rabbit. All she had managed to do was miss the target, fall some branches which she wasn't aiming for, and scare away any other form of life. Now, they had empty tummies and both girls were weak, cold and tired. She couldn't imagine they'd feel any better come sunrise since malnutrition was the biggest part of their problems. Even though they had eaten while with Randy, it had been few left over morsels, not enough to keep a person alive. The berries they had eaten earlier in the day had gone right through them and both girls had suffered bowel problems late in the afternoon.

"I'll boil some water and add some hickory bark to it. That will help us feel a little better. Maybe it will ease the soreness throughout our bodies."

Millie moaned. "I don't think I can even move to do that much. Maybe I'll feel better in the morning."

"Aye. Perhaps when we return to town Old Doc will fuss up a storm due to our condition, swaddle and baby us until we're like new. Wouldn't that be nice?"

"Mmm…that would be heavenly. Josie, I can't help but wonder…that tree overhead, looks just like the large tulip tree we passed earlier this morn. See the bark at the bottom. It's been rubbed by something. The markings are similar don't you think?"

"I had noticed that and I'm praying we are wrong. I pray God we haven't gone in circles. That would only give Randy a gained chance of finding us wouldn't it?"

"I can't help but shake just thinking of it."

"Then let's not think about it. Right now, we have to conserve our strength and think positively. We will be just fine as soon as we either get back to town, or your Daddy and the Sheriff finds us. I'm certain they are looking and won't give up until we are found. Let's think about what good can come from this. First there is our friendship. I feel as if you are the sister I've never had. Our friendship shall last for years and years. That is definitely something good that has come from this. And, perhaps we have stopped Randy from hurting anyone else in the future. Who can fathom what crimes he's committed and how many folks have suffered from his meanness?"

"You're right you know. Our friendship is something I shall cherish for all my days. And, I think I've changed for the better. Before I was so cold and jealous of you. Actually, I was jealous of any lady prettier than I. I thought I wanted the Sheriff. Now I realize, I only wanted attention. And, I think…to better you. I am shamed by my actions. I will spend the rest of my life trying to be a better person. Lord knows there are things more important than sleeping in and powdering my face. I was a spoiled brat. I had no good cause to be that way either. I was mean to people that didn't deserve to be treated badly. I was no better than Randy."

"Millie I think you've always been a good person if not a bit ornery and thank you for the compliment. But I must confess, I would give anything to have your golden curls and thick lashes."

"I only hope God has plans for me beyond this day. Isn't it funny how one moment we take life for granted and don't appreciate it, then the next moment we are fighting hard to preserve it? Golden locks or no, I will fight to live another day."

The horse whined next to them and the girls both froze mid sip of the heated water. Darkness was fully upon them, the only light given from the fire burning fresh made from hemlock branches.

"It's only the wind." Millie prayed out loud.

"Nay. The last time a horse made a noise like that for me, I got sprayed by a skunk." She shuddered remembering the gagging stench that had stayed with her for days. "We must trust the horse's instincts. Something is amiss." Josie grabbed a branch and wrapped the edge with a torn piece of fabric from her already shredded night dress. Then she dipped it in the fire causing flames to dance from the end. "Here Millie. Hold this. I will tie the horse so he doesn't run off…"

"Don't tether him too close. I would hate to get trampled should he spook."

Josie calmed the horse the best she could while peering into the shadows. The piercing stare of eyes glowing silver in the moonlight froze the blood in her veins. Several pair of eyes were scattered around the circumference of the clearing where they had bedded down. Josie quickly grabbed more branches, wrapped them with material then stabbed them into the ground. She placed several to outline the clearing then proceeded to start them all on fire. It would be a full time job keeping the flames burning, likely they would run out of material. But hopefully the dancing flames would help keep the wolves away. "Wolves."

Millie sat up instantly panic etched her voice. "Are they man eating wolves? I've heard many stories about man eating wolves."

"That's ridiculous. They are only curious. I don't see them barring any teeth. They're watching us. The flames should keep them away until morning. How about we take turns tonight. I'll keep first watch and wake you in a few hours. Then you can take over. We have to keep the fire burning. If we do, we will be fine I'm sure."

"I don't think I can fall asleep now. Not when there are wolves waiting to eat me! Could you sleep now?"

"No. I dare not even try, but you should refrain from thinking nonsense. We've been told stories by our parents to keep us from wondering off into the woods. It was tactic that's all. They are not going to eat us. Have you looked at us lately? We are skin and bone. The wolves would continue to be hungry and gain no nourishment at all. I'm sure they can sense that. I hope."

"Oh blast it! We'll both keep watch for now. Where's that darned gun?"

"Awe, shame on your mouth. I have the gun. But we only have three shots left far as I can tell. I can't aim the darned thing. It's frustrating as all get up."

"Looks like it's lye soap for both of us. Your mouth is as pottied as mine." At that they both giggled, sat next to the fire, clasped hands and held branches. Their vigilance at keeping the wolves at bay was won out by fatigue a few hours later.

Randy was sure he'd been out of it for a while. An entire day at a minimum. He ached all over and his gut wouldn't stop clenching tight every time he moved. He was hungry but afraid to eat anything. He itched something fierce and felt as if he was going to pass out each time he tried to stand and walk. But hatred fueled his body. Hatred for Josie and Millie and the need for revenge got him to his feet. He would find them and when he did, he'd slit their throats just like he did that fellow back in Providence. Excitement at the thought caused a flutter of anxiety to ripple through his body. He watered his gut with more whiskey. He could follow a trail well enough. The girls' had been dumb enough to leave one. A clear one. Any two year old could follow this trail. Obviously the bitches weren't very smart.

CHAPTER THIRTEEN

Both girls felt even weaker in the morning. Lack of proper nutrition, sleep and exposure to the elements had taken it's toll on their bodies. The ordeal they had been through and the abuse they had sustained left them with little strength and gloomy spirits. They traveled in silence. Josie sat mounted while Millie walked leading the horse by it's reins. The horse was in bad shape too. It's had been abused for much longer than the girls had. And both girls felt badly about it. So badly that they were taking turns riding the creature as they felt it too was lacking in strength. If their spirits were down, the horse's were much worse. Josie couldn't wait to get back to town, give this steed some tender loving care and then introduce it to Buster. She hoped they would get along. She really didn't know what happened when horses didn't get along or if that was even an element she had to fret about.

For the time being, neither girl had any sense of direction and both were clueless as to which way to travel. Giving the horse the lead wasn't an option as this horse was so worn out that if Millie did pull the reins, it would just stand still looking sadly around as if waiting for something.

Both girls were lost in their own thoughts when Randy jumped out from behind a tulip tree spooking the horse as well as the girls. Josie held on for dear life and screamed for Millie to run. As soon as the horse calmed, she reached behind her to pull out the gun. She had never shot a man before, but was fully prepared to do so now. Each moment passed in a blur of confusion as she tried to still the horse and take aim. Randy waltzed bravely towards her.

"You can't shoot me Josie. You're a Christian woman. You will burn in hell if you kill me." He took another step closer.

"Actually Randy, I will pray that you meet the devil, and that he gives you your due you cold hearted piece of shit."

Randy had never heard her talk like that before and somehow sensed that she was fully prepared to pull that trigger. In that same instant, he heard the sound of the shot and the echo that reverberated throughout the woods. The bulled hit him square in the chest and he gasped for air before falling to his knees. The wind had been knocked right out of him and the burning sensation spread to his neck and abdomen in mere seconds. So this was what if felt like to be shot. He grew excited for a brief moment at the painful sensations fluttering throughout his body. His heartbeat was erratic and he could hear his blood pulsating through his veins. He wondered if Neb felt this way when he had shot him. Of course he didn't intend to shoot his brother, but he did none the less. Did he feel like this? He caught his breath again and looked directly into Josie's eyes.

"That one was for Millie. This one is for me!" With that she shot again and the bullet hit him in the neck. He was struggling to breath before. Now he was gasping as he felt the life force slowly leave his body. He fell face first into the mud and lay unmoving.

Josie watched for several minutes. Yet she refused to dismount. Tears ran down her face. They were not tears of sadness, but tears of relief for she knew without a doubt that Randall Hurley would never hurt anyone ever again. Especially not Millie, her or anyone else she loved and cared for. With that thought she spun the horse around and looked for Millie. Gone. She was no where to be seen.

"Millie!" She yelled as loud as she could. "Millie..." She was met with silences and suddenly felt very alone. "Millie...please...where are you?"

There was no trace of Millie anywhere. Well she was just here Josie thought with frustration. She searched the ground for signs of tracks to which way Millie had run. At least she had obeyed and took off, fleeing to safety, away from Randy. The markings on the ground from the horse being spooked threw Josie off and she was confused as to what markings came from what source. She couldn't tell where Millie had gone, so she took a guess and began looking for her friend.

Within an hour she located the river. The horse drank freely at the much needed nourishment. Millie dismounted and leaned over the waters edge to wash her face and hands. The water felt refreshing and cool.

"Hello."

Although the voice was meek Josie nearly jumped out of her skin. She spun and faced a little girl that was more bedraggled and filthy than she was. She appeared to be weak, malnourished and ready to collapse. "Hi."

"I'm lost. Can you help me find my mommy and daddy?"

"I'll try. I'm lost too. We can look for help together. Would you like that?"

In answer the little girl felt into her arms and Josie hugged her fiercely. What on earth had happened to this little one to strand her out in the wilderness like this? "Here sweety, drink some water and wash your face and hands. It will make you feel better."

The little girl obeyed. "My name is Henrietta. Etta for short. I'm named after my grandmamma." The little girls voice quivered as she spoke. She was close to tears.

"Well Etta, how did you come to be lost in the wilderness?"

"I was playing outside out camp. My ball went into the woods. I looked and looked but couldn't find it. Now I can't find camp either."

"How old are you Etta?"

"Six." But my Pa says I'm a smart six.

Josie chuckled. "I bet you are." I don't have much for food. But I did spot some berries over there a ways." Josie pointed in the right directions. "You can ride with me until I find my friend and get back to town. Does that sound ok?"

"Is your friend pretty like you?"

"She's prettier." Josie smiled and lifted the girl into the saddle. "In fact, you look a lot like her. Beautiful blond curls, big blue eyes."

"My mommy's got blond hair. My daddy says it's like the spun silk. I don't know what that is. Do you?" And this began a long conversation that followed a line of questions from Etta that kept Josie entertained for hours. She realized that she had not followed Millie's trail, and in fact had ended up near the cave they had slept in the night they poisoned Randy. She had inadvertently followed Randy's tracks instead of Millie's and tried desperately to hide her frustration from her new companion. The good thing was there was still plenty of daylight left to keep trying. Millie couldn't have gone far.

Millie sat beneath a tree and broke down crying. She didn't know what had happened to Josie. She had heard the shots while running and was terrified that Randy had somehow killed Josie and was on her trail right now. But she was exhausted and felt ready to give up. She just couldn't do this anymore. She didn't have the strength to run anymore. She wasn't even sure she could go on living much longer in this harsh reality of wilderness and swamp infested territory. Those thoughts soon had her sobbing into her knees. Her entire body shook as she cried wholeheartedly. How would she die? Would it be the wolves? Starvation? Randy? She preferred none of them but felt utterly helpless to ward off any of them any longer. She prayed for help and guidance from the Lord. She prayed for a sign of safety, or a clue on how to get back to town safely. She prayed for life, for food and comfort. "Please God. Help me."

Nick Edwards couldn't believe what he was seeing. An angel smack dab in the middle of nowhere. She was crying, beaten and appeared to be a mess but she was beautiful. He approached slowly. "Are you ok Miss?"

Millie nearly jumped clear out of her skin he had startled her so. She spun around and looked at him. A man. It was a man. Fear filled her eyes as she gripped at the torn garments covering her chest and cautiously backed away from him.

Nick read the fear in her eyes. She had been mistreated. "I'm not going to hurt you I promise. You have my word on it."

"And whose word may that be?"

"I apologize ma'am, for not introducing myself properly sooner. I'm Nicholas Edwards. Friends call me Nick. It would please me if you would do so as well."

He was met with silence so he continued forlornly. "I'm searching for my daughter Josie. She ran away. I miss her terribly and have been searching for over a month now, with no luck unfortunately."

"Why did she run away?" Millie knew the answer but needed to test this stranger to see if he was fibbing, dangerous or who he really claimed to be. She suspected he really was Josie's father as the resemblance was uncanny.

"I was a drunken fool after her Mamma died. I'm afraid I wasn't a very good father."

"Oh!" Millie gasped and flew into his arms. "You won't hurt me will you? You are a good man. I know your Josie. She is my best friend ever! She misses you terribly. She does. I swear it."

Nick couldn't believe his ears. First he finds and angel and then she knows Josie. God must be watching over him. "Come with me. Well get you fed and you can tell me how you met her. Does that sound okay with you?"

She nodded and began to cry again. Soon Nick had her fed, cleaned up and somewhat warm. She felt extremely tired but had promised her savior the story on how she came to know Josie. Nick wanted nothing more than to hear how this young beauty knew his daughter. But, she was badly beaten and worn out. He wrapped her in blankets and told her to sleep as he nestled her in front of him while saddled on his mount. Perhaps latter, when they bedded down for the night in front of a burning fire she would be better able to talk and share her story. For now, this young lady needed care, protection, and a doctor. A fierce sense of longing enveloped him. This girl couldn't be any older than his daughter yet he craved her. It had been a long time since he was with a woman. Perhaps that was why this need felt so overwhelming. More than that, he felt a connection, some familiar closeness. It was as if they were meant to be together. He shook the feeling. She was too young and had obviously been hurt. He was not the type of man to have enough patience to work through something like that. He would just take care of her for now. Until they got this all sorted out and he knew exactly what had happened to her and where she came from, he was only watching over her. Hell, he could be her father! It she were his daughter, he'd kill whomever had hurt her like this. He'd also kill any man who thought the kind of thoughts he was thinking right now! He was irritated with himself and tried to take deep calming breaths of the dampening air that blanketed the forest. The scent of pine and hemlock soothed him and he silently willed the tremors and shakes away.

Latter that evening, before a warm fire, Millie told Nick everything. Everything from the first moment she stepped off the stagecoach to the moment he found her. She left out nothing. Included was every brutal detail of her treatment as well as Josie's. Nick learned about the town, the Judge, Millie, the Sheriff and how Josie had fallen deeply in love with him. The deaths, brutality and friends his daughter had made. He felt helpless and confused. He didn't know if he should be happy or upset. He decided that all emotions were acceptable at a time like this and that he would just deal with one at a time. He was most unsettled by the fact that his daughter was out here somewhere, in the dark, alone or with a very bad man. Nick was beside himself with worry. It would have been easier if he hadn't known in a way. He was also angry that Millie didn't tell him as soon as they met. They may have been close to Josie and he could have tried to pick up her trail, but no, Millie didn't have that kind of foresight. He was more than a little upset as he paced back and forth, ran agitated fingers through his hair and cracked his knuckles several times. His anger with her dissipated however when he looked at her. The poor girl had been through a lot and was in very bad shape. Both eyes were black and swollen, her hair was a knotted mess, her dress was torn and hardly covered her body, of which had bruises of many colors everywhere. Her lips were so swollen that it had to hurt when she talked, one whole side of her face was black as could be and she babied her wrist as if perhaps it was broken.

"You know Millie, you went through a bad experience with Randy Hurly. It's not supposed to be like that. When a man and woman love each other, it's not brutal."

"I don't need the lecture. I know how it's supposed to be, and how its not." She snapped her words out in a heated twist of anger and resentment. "I don't deserve love anyways. I was a very bad person before all this happened. I'm ashamed and have to pay my penance. This may have been part of that penance."

"Bullshit!" Nick stood up and flicked the remainder of his coffee into the fire. "God doesn't deal out penance like that. That kind of pain is purely evil Millie. You are a beautiful woman and good at heart. Someday some man will be very fortunate to have you. And this whole experience will only make you a stronger person. Things always happen for a reason. I don't know what the reason for this was anymore than I know the reasons why my wife and child died. But there is one. We just have to search and find it."

Millie watched him. The stricken look upon his face and the raw truth of his words had her staring dumbfounded into the flickering flames of the dancing fire. She knew that he desperately wanted to find his daughter, especially after hearing her story. Josie could be in a lot of trouble or worse yet, lying dead in the wilderness. Yes this man was staying put for her sake because she was weak and needed the rest. She knew that without asking. His concern filled her with gratitude. She felt as if she could talk to this man. Really talk to him. She sensed something about him that offered her a strong comforting feeling of security and she relished it.

"What if I am with child? How can I love and raise something that came from such a brutal experience? That child would have it's fathers evil blood and wickedness running through its veins. Furthermore, I would be unable to find a husband and... I would never be accepted into polite society again. This would just make raising the child even more difficult. I can't help but be afraid of what the future might bring."

"Millie, you have to remember that if, and that's a strong if, there is a child, it will be made of you too. It will have your features, your kindness and your blood running through its veins. How can you not love that? Plus, you do have friends and family that love you very much. I'm sure they wouldn't turn their backs on you in your time of need."

"I suppose it's something to think about. Either way, the worst is over. I'm sorry to lay my worries upon your shoulders. I thank you for listening Nick

Edwards. I also thank you for your kindness this evening in taking care of me."

"You're welcome Millie. Maybe you should sleep. You certainly need to recoup your strength."

"Good night then."

"Good night angel. Sweet dreams."

Josie and Etta were woken in the early hours of morning by the trumping thunder and booming echoes of horses hooves beating upon the sodden ground. The earth shook and rumbled in a way that told Josie there were several horses not just one or two. They had bedded down in the middle of a clearing and Josie was hoping to get her bearings come morning when she wasn't so exhausted. Now, she wondered if they would see the dawn.

Approaching the midst of the clearing, Christian searched for signs of Josie and Millie. Teenabe had assured him they were close and now held up a hand, slowing his horse and shushing the darkness. All others followed his leadership. Teenabe motioned for Christian to dismount and walk with him. The others stayed where they were. Christian could hardly see in the darkness and cursed his lack of night vision. The Indian seemed to be able to see for miles in the dark.

"Careful friend." The Indian stated. "They are directly in front of us. One has a gun pointed to your chest."

Christian was so relieved he could barely breath. The night air was damp and musty. It suddenly filled his lungs and held him hostage. Swallowing he spoke softly. "Josie girl, is that you?"

An audible cry of relief was heard and the next thing he knew, Josie came at him full force, hugging him tightly and almost knocking him off his feet. Christian had never cried in front of folks before, but he did now. Tears rolled down his face as he held Josie close and clutched a hand full of hair briefly taking in her scent. He heard her gasp in pain as he squeezed her tight. "Are you ok?"

Josie couldn't talk. She simply nodded then began to cry. All she could think about was the fact that it was over. She was safe in Christian's arms again. Every bone in her body ached. Her ribs hurt to no end. Her nose was broke, she was filthy, hardly clothed, beaten and starving, but it was all better right now. This moment was the first moment of the rest of her life. She cherished it.

The Judge came running. "Where's my Millie?" Teenabe held a little girl who appeared to be scared senseless. Millie was no where to be seen.

"I lost her. Randy tried to attack again and I shot him. But Millie ran to get away. It was only a few moments, but I couldn't find her. I've searched all day. Randy did her in a real bad way Christian. I hurt more for her than for me. Oh God." Josie gulped and began crying again.

"Let's stoke the fire, have coffee and clean up. Josie can tell us the entire story and this young one can have flap-jacks and syrup." Teenabe bounced little Etta in his arms as he spoke. "Then we will re-trace Josie's steps, go back to where she and Millie split up and start over. We will find her. It will be very soon. I can sense that she is alive and safe. I will ask for guidance from my God. He will show me the way."

The Judge sat down, clearly stricken and worried. He was as pale as goose down. His tears glimmered in the moonlight. For his sake, Josie wanted to leave out the worst details yet she had to tell the tale in its entirety. The nightmare was over for her, but Millie was still in trouble. The more information she provided, the better the chances the group had of finding her. And, once she began to open up, she couldn't seem to stop herself. It felt as if the words tumbled out on their own accord. In a way, it made her feel better about the whole ordeal. Talking always had a way of doing that for her. She paused at the part where Hops was shot, and sent up a prayer. Then she went on to explain how they escaped thanks to Millie's quick whit and how she shot Randy, then she looked directly at Neb and said "I'm sorry."

Neb nodded. Then he walked over to Josie and gave her a gentle hug. "My brother is the one that shot me. I tried to forget that, but I can't. I get better each day. He is dead. He will now get what he deserves. There will be no mercy on his soul."

When they broke camp, Etta rode with Angus who had quickly taken a liking to the little girl. She kept messing with his beard and he constantly swatted her little hands away, but he never complained. Soon, she was asleep in the saddle and Angus looked bewildered. "Why does she like me?" Angus asked Josie in a voice that was more than a little perplexed.

"It's that teddy bear look. Women can't resist." She winked in the darkness as Angus grumble before riding ahead.

Christian had promised that once they got back to town, he would send posting notices to all the settlements in the immediate area as well as up and down the river. Hopefully the little girls parents would see it and come to collect their daughter. Until then, she'd have a loving place to stay with them and they would try to make her happy and content while waiting. There was a good possibility though, that they would never locate the parents. This area led to harsh living. The land took more lives than not. They agreed to think positively and together, they would cross that bridge if and when they got there.

Josie sat behind Christian in the saddle and was soon lulled to sleep by the bounce of the horse. The horse she had been riding was being led by a rope and following the pack. There were two pack horses being led in the same way. The horse however had been feed, watered and given a good brushing during the short respite. But even after all that the poor animal was too weak and under nourished to carry any riders. Teenabe did assure Josie that the horse would be fine with a little care and that she was in fact pregnant. This explained the sadness in the horses eyes all the time. Josie made a mental note to talk with Christian and see if they could keep the horse and her foul when it was born. She would love nothing more and the experience of a foul entering this world would be a great memory for Etta.

As the sun rose, Teenabe called for a rest. All riders dismounted, relieved themselves, drank heavily from the canteens and stretched the aches and pains from their stiff bodies. Josie stirred and focused. She tried to dismount but could not. Her body was too sore and suddenly unresponsive to what she was telling it to do. Christian seemed to understand her dilemma. He slide off the horse carefully then reached up to help her down. This was his first chance to look at her in the daylight and what he saw took his breath away and had his blood boiling in no time. He lifted her into his arms and gently placed her under a tree. "I am so sorry baby. Oh God. I am so sorry."

"I'm all right. Honestly. It looks worse than what it is I'm sure. I'm with you again. That's all that matters."

He held her while holding back his tears. "I wish you wouldn't have shot and killed Randy."

"Why?"

"Because I would love to kill him with my bare hands. Shooting was too easy for that bastard."

"He's were he belongs now. You have to trust in that."

"Can I get a blanket over here?" Christian yelled at no one in particular. Josie was in nothing more than torn rags and was hardly decent to be viewed by anyone in the group. Plus, she was shivering almost uncontrollably. "As soon as we find Millie, we will get you to Rapids and find a doctor."

"Why not Old Doc?"

"Oh, Josie I'm so sorry. I didn't realize that you didn't know. When Randy broke into the doctors office to take you, he killed Old Doc."

"I should have shot him three times." Tears rolled down her cheeks at this revelation. She was once again consumed with anger towards Randall Hurley and began to shake.

"What do you mean?"

"I told him the first shot was for me, the second was for Millie. I should have shot him in the gut for Old Doc. Darn it all."

"Well if Randy had a hole in him for every person he killed or hurt, he'd look like a human pin cushion." He wrapped a blanket around her and placed her in front of him when they remounted. She soon leaned into him and fell asleep. Christian worried that she was hurt worse than she let on. It didn't seem feasible that a human body could take that much abuse, be that beat up, and still survive. He held her close and peered at her sleeping face often, continuously checking for the shallow rise and fall of her chest. He feared that at any moment, she would stop breathing.

It wasn't long before they found the area where Randy was shot and lay face down on the ground. All the riders were silent as the led their mounts to circle the body. All weapons were drawn and pointing to Randy even though he lay unmoving. Neb dismounted and cautiously approached the body while the other riders stayed atop their steeds. Josie hugged Christian tightly and refused to look at first. But like a magnet, she was drawn to the scene and couldn't not see for herself what the outcome was. Then she bravely slid off the horse and walked towards where Randy lay. She needed to see what she had done to him. She needed to verify that he was in fact dead.

Neb rolled the still body over with one booted foot, keeping a hand ready to grab for his gun. Randy lay looking blankly into the sky. His eyes were clouded and unfocused. Bubbles of blood gurgled in his neck as he gasped for air through the bullet hole in his throat. He was still alive, but barely. He no longer appeared to be evil and threatening. Instead he was pale and deathly. Anyone that didn't know him might take pity on him, but not Josie, not the Judge, not any man in that circle right then. Josie peered into the faces of everyone present, slowly turning in a circle. Each face was tightly composed and grim. She made eye contact with Neb and what she saw there shook her deeply. Neb features portrayed years of hate, love and betrayal. He was trying to sort through it all as he peered down at his dying brother.

But, there was no hesitation in Josie's movements as she snatched the gun from Neb's holster so quickly Neb had no time to react, and shot Randy between the eyes. "That one is from Old Doc." Pivoting on one heal, she replaced the gun while Neb stood speechless. Then she went back to Christian and stood silently waiting for the reprimand that was sure to come. None did. Not from Christian, not from the Judge, not from anyone. As she glanced over at Neb, a single tear trailed down his face.

Neb and Angus dug a shallow grave to bury Randy before the group moved on. They covered the mound with rocks. No grave marker was placed. No cross was displayed. No prayers were said. Teenabe issued a warning that the ground would soak up all the evil as it left Randy's body. The area should be avoided for it now harbored a bad spirit and would be dangerous ground for all who passed over it in the future.

For Josie, seeing Randy get buried had a lifting effect upon her. It was a closure of a sort and she was glad that she was able to view the burial. She would share every aspect of Randy's demise with Millie as soon as they found her.

About mid day they came upon the smothered remains of a fire. But there was evidence of two people, not just Millie.

"Are we following the wrong trail?" Josie wondered out loud.

"No." Replied Teenabe. "She has met up with someone." He looked at the coffee grounds on the soil and the grease that still sizzled when he poked into the embers with a stick. "She has been fed well. I don't see any signs of struggle."

"I wonder who it could be out here in the middle of nowhere." Josie was very afraid again. "It could be another outlaw. He could hurt her." Her voice rose as she spoke. Panic was taking root.

"Calm down now Josie. We don't know who it is. For all we know it could be Etta's Daddy looking for her."

"That's a nice thought." Josie swallowed.

"They can't be more than four hours ahead of us. If we stay steady, we should catch up with them by supper time." Christian was hoping for the best. He prayed that whomever Millie was with, he or she was taking good care of her and treating her nicely.

Josie continued to shiver no matter how closely Christian held her and how tightly he kept her swaddled in the blanket. She shivered while she was sleeping, which was every time they were mounted and riding. He knew she must be exhausted, but he couldn't understand the shivers. He prayed silently and wished there was a doctor here with them now. He felt helpless to make her better and furthermore he had discovered a gash on the back of her head that should have been stitched. Since he had first viewed her injuries this morning, her forehead and both eyes had darkened to black and gray shades. He knew she hadn't been injured any further while he was with her and couldn't understand why the markings were getting worse by the hour. He didn't like feeling so helpless and determined that he would never let her out of his sight again. Lovingly he hugged her close and inhaled deeply fighting to keep tears and frustration at bay.

Neb rode up next to him. "How is she?"

"I don't know." Christian replied. "Her face is discoloring worse and worse by the hour. I don't know how to fix it or what is causing it."

"Head wound. It is still bleeding on the inside. I've seen it before. My mother died from my father hitting her on the head with a wooden board. She died two days after she was hit. Until she died, Randy and I thought she was fine. She cooked and cleaned like normal. She cried just like normal too. My father was a mean son of a bitch. That's partly why Randy was the way he was. When we were kids, we were knocked around and beaten often." He was silent for a few moments. "We must watch Josie carefully. When I think about my mother, I think that if she had stayed in bed, it might have helped. But I'm not a doctor."

Christian nodded in silent agreement and thought about what Neb had just said. His few words had revealed a lot about the man. What a horrible life. What kind of hell had he lived through during his childhood? Then Christian thought back to his own carefree childhood and almost felt guilty because it had been so wholesome and fun. He certainly would never do anything abusive like that to his wife or children. Some men did though. He could never understand why. And one time, he even saw a family where the wife was the one that was abusive. He looked down at Josie. Try as he might, he couldn't imagine her being abusive in any way. In fact, he was proud of the guts she displayed in finishing Randy off. She, more than anyone, deserved the justification of his death. It took a lot of courage to stand there and do that. She had faced her fears and come out the winner. Then he realized, he never doubted her strength and courage. It was his he questioned.

A few hours later a strong wind brought the smell of cooking meat towards them. It was supper time after all and they were close to finding Millie. Christian's stomach growled loudly, the Judge sat up straighter on his horse and Angus whispered a childhood story into Etta's ear as they rode. Everyone seemed to suddenly become rejuvenated with energy. Josie opened her eyes and clutched Christians shirt. She didn't talk but he could tell something was wrong.

"What is it Josie girl?" She didn't reply but began to squirm indicating she needed to dismount. "Hold up fellas."

Neb was right next to him as he quickly dismounted and stood next to Christians horse. "Hand her down."

Christian carefully complied. Josie's feet hit ground but she couldn't stand by herself. Her head was spinning out of control and she needed very badly to throw up. She tried to walk by herself to a bush, but almost fell instead. Neb caught her. She pointed to where she wanted to go and together both Neb and Christian got her there. In no time, she had emptied the contents of her stomach and was heaving dryly. She was once more sweating and shaking from expending what little energy she had. She meant to stand but again, her head spun and she passed out. Christian nimbly caught her.

"It's her head." Neb's remark was ominous given the story he had relayed about his mother.

Teenabe watched the scene before him unfold. Josie was in great danger. The spirit of death was close. "We will go to where the food is cooking and camp there for the night. Josie cannot go on without rest. Being bounced around on the back of a horse is making her worse. Her injuries are grave. When we find Millie, we will return to my Indian wife. She will care for the girls as no white man doctor can. You have my word."

When they were close enough to the camp-site to hear voices they decide to hold back and yell a warning. That way, the horses wouldn't get spooked, the people wouldn't get spooked and they could from a distance evaluate the situation to see if it was in fact Millie that was there, and if so who else was with her. If she was in any danger, they would be able to respond better from a distance rather than ride into some type of trap.

"Millie?" The Judge hollered. "Millie honey are you there?"

"Daddy?" Millie's sweet voice carried to the men on the breeze. "Oh Daddy you found me!" Tears of joy spilled from Millie as she ambled weakly to the edge of the brush. "Daddy I'm here and I'm ok. Come closer and see for yourself. Josie's Daddy is with me. He's been searching for her and came across me instead. It's ok, join us, all of you."

The party inched closer and got a better look at Nick Edwards who stood silently by the fire. He scanning face searched for signs of his daughter. "Is Josie with you? Is she okay?"

"There are many questions and many answers." Teenabe replied as the rode into the clearing. "We will get to them all soon enough. We must camp here if it is ok with you. Josie's injuries are grave and she must rest."

With those words, everyone began dismounting, talking and hugging at once. Introductions were made all around and the Judge was overwhelmed with a great feeling of relief when he hugged his daughter. He too began to cry. "I thought I had lost you."

"I'm here Daddy. I'm here." Millie sobbed into his coat. "Oh Daddy I've been so terrible and childish. Please forgive me. I promise to be better. I promise."

"Now there's no need to be talking nonsense. Let me look at you." The Judge held her back with straightened arms. She looked just as bad as Josie did. "What did that bastard do to you?" His hands shook and his knees felt weak. For the first time in his life he doubted the legal system. Rightfully, Josie should be prosecuted for shooting Randy Hurley. The outlaw should have been brought to trial and judged by a jury. The old him would have stood by the old adage— no two wrongs make a right. But, he conceded that he was happy Josie did what she did. In fact, he was relieved. He couldn't blame Josie for killing Randy Hurley. If Randy were still alive, the Judge felt as if he could murder him with bare hands. This wasn't a good feeling and certainly not one he was familiar with. Realizing that he was capable of such violence if given the opportunity shook him to the core. "Perhaps we both need to do some soul searching." With those words he thought about the possibility of retiring. What would happen if he didn't work anymore? He was tired of traveling as a circuit judge. He was tired of the elements but he was mostly just tired. He wanted to spend time with friends and family. He wanted to be there for Millie as she recovered from this horrible ordeal. And he suddenly realized, he wanted to have grandchildren to spoil rotten. He looked intently at Millie and silently acknowledged that that may not happen for a long time yet. He continued to look her over and was most concerned with her wrist.

"Daddy, it's ok. Really. I'm fine. A little beat up. I sure could use a bath." She laughed lightly. "My innocence is gone Daddy. I'm so sorry about that." She broke down then and sobbed loudly as the Judge held her close. He whispered soothing words in her ear and told her it would be all right. They would handle it, come what may. At first Millie didn't seem to hear the words, but after a while, they penetrated her sobs and calmed her broken spirit. She felt better. She had spit out the worst and gotten through it. "I love you Daddy."

"Oh baby I love you too. It's going to be ok. I promise. I will be with you until you are better. I won't leave your side."

"I want you to meet Mr. Edwards." She pulled him by the hand to where Nick hung back. "Mr. Edwards, meet my father, Isaac McQuade."

CHAPTER FOURTEEN

Josie opened her eyes. It seemed to take a long time before she could focus. She felt so warm and cozy she didn't want to move but the view overhead was unfamiliar. Her nostrils burned from inhaling some medicinal scent yet oddly it was comforting. She turned her head and would have bolted to a standing position if she hadn't been swaddled like and infant in animal pelts and quilts. Seated next to her, sitting side by side, was her Daddy and Christian. Her two favorite men in the whole wide world. Both men must have been with her for a long time since they snoozed in unison. It was almost comical and one corner of Josie's mouth lifted into what could have been a smile if it hadn't taken so much effort to move those few facial muscles.

Then she took inventory of her surroundings. Everything within the cabin appeared to be primitive and useful. There were pelts and hides on the walls serving as a blanket, enveloping the cabin, helping to keep the inside temperature moderate with little effort from the firepit or open hatch along one wall. Hand spun rugs layered the floor. Boned utensils sat atop a table along with some herbs that had been crushed in a bowl with a stone. There were arrows leaning at an angle in one corner by the door and the accompanying bow hung on a hook just above them. The place was clean but different. She couldn't quite place it. It was welcoming and she had no fears as she surmised, it must be a safe place to be since both her Daddy and Christian were there. They wouldn't be sleeping peacefully if danger lurked nearby.

"Daddy?" Although her voice was small and soft both men jumped, sat up straight and looked at her as if she had two heads. She couldn't help but crack a smile. "Daddy, how did you get here?"

"It's a long story doll. But I'd be glad to tell you. We have plenty of time."

"Where am I?"

"We are at the home of Teenabe, the Indian tracker that helped us to find you. His wife has been nurturing both you and Millie. You've both done well under her care."

"Is Millie ok? Please tell me she's doing well. Oh I want to see her. She's like a sister to me now. I love her that much, I do."

Christian chuckled. "Why don't I leave you and your Daddy here to talk for awhile. I'll be back later with Millie in tow and then you can visit with her if you're up to it. Right now, you and your Daddy have some catchin' up to do." He bent down and kissed her softly on the forehead.

"Christian." Fear had her choked up and she suddenly found it difficult to talk. Then she calmed. "Don't go far. I need you. I love you."

"Well see, I knew you were crazy from the first moment I laid eyes on you. Now you bonked your head and have become delusional!"

"Am I delusional?"

"If you think I'm ever going to leave you again, or let you out of my sight, then yes, you are delusional. I'll be right outside the door and I love you too." He squeezed her hand gently then left. Josie felt his absence. It was as if a cold draft had settled over her heart. She wanted him back in the room but tried to settle her nerves and overcome the feeling. If this was how her Daddy felt when her Momma died, no wonder he had a hard time dealing with it. Compassion and understanding filled her.

Nick Edwards cleared his throat. It was hard for him to admit and accept the fact that he wasn't the most important man in her life anymore. He wondered if all fathers felt like he did at this moment, lost, bereft and saddened. "How about that talk?" His voice came out gruffer than he meant it to be. Then he cleared his throat.

Josie and her Daddy talked for hours. The time went by quickly and she felt better of a sudden. At supper time, Christian returned with Millie as promised and both girls got lost in their own conversation until Christian reminded them that their food was getting cold.

The soup was delicious and filling. Josie ate three bowls before declaring herself stuffed. She sat back against a fully stuffed feather pillow. She was growing tired but was content.

"Tomorrow we will cross the river and return to Providence." Christian was excited to get home. "We have horses to take care of, company to keep; since your Daddy and Etta will be staying with us," he winked at Josie "and a dog to feed."

"A dog to feed?" Clearly he was confused. Didn't he know that Hops had been shot and was probably laying out in the wilderness dead somewhere? "Christian I…"

He didn't let her finish. Instead he stayed her statement with a hand and rushed over to the door. When he opened it, Hops bounced in and was lapping licks upon Josie's face before she could bat an eyelash.

"Hops! Oh you're alright! Oh I love you too." Tears rolled down her cheeks as she hugged and kissed the dog.

"We thought the dog might not make it. His injury was bad Josie. We should have put him down, but I couldn't." Christian's eyes were full of unshed tears. "Teenabe's wife treated him too. Good thing you named him Hops. It's actually kind of ironic. Now he only has three legs and can do nothing but hop."

The dog barked loudly then went to Christian and began licking his hands. As Christian petted him, Josie took in the bandage on the dogs hind stump and the awarkwardness with which the dog moved. More the half the leg had been removed but the dog already seemed to have mastered getting around on three legs. He was still in pain as evidenced by little yelps and whimpers here and there but clearly happy to be alive. "Hops saved my life. I am glad that you spared his. Come here boy." She patted her leg signaling the animal to come to her. "I will love him always." More hugs and petting ensued. "How will we ever thank Teenabe and his wife?"

"I'm not sure. But we will be indebted to them forever." Christian realized that he couldn't put a price on the value of what Teenabe and his wife had done for him. Josie was priceless. Hops was priceless. Millie was priceless. His future would have been completely different and bleak if Teenabe hadn't been willing to help a stranger that had come knocking on his door begging for help. For the rest of his days, he would be thankful to the Indian family. "We will have to think of something."

The next day, when they returned to Providence there was a feast waiting. The townsfolk had erected a barn near the river. The packed earthen floor was covered with straw. A variety of makeshift tables held food from one end to the other. Three men were in one corner playing their fiddles and a small group of young couples were dancing and twirling about. They were celebrating the safe return of the men, Josie, Mille, Hops and the demise of the named outlaw.

Josie wasn't able to attend and remained in bed but listened to the music through the open window with Hops and Christian by her side smelling the delicious aroma of the food as it wafted in. Little Etta had been carried off to join the festivities on Angus's shoulders. He had also promised the little one a dance if she behaved and a big piece of apple pie.

Millie promised to attend for a short while only because Nick Edwards had asked if she would. She knew she had been through a lot and shouldn't be thinking the thoughts that she was thinking. But she couldn't help it. Nick Edwards was very handsome and she was very attracted to him. He was a strong man, with a wondering soul. It was as if he had a hole in his heart. She wanted to fill it. He was the strongest man she had ever seen even if he was a little older. But she didn't think of his age as old. She thought of it as defining. Thinking about his chiseled features and the tiny specks of gray in his dark hair had her heart beating rapidly. She almost felt childish as she waited for him to collect her. Her wrist was in a splint and because of it, she wasn't able to wear her prettiest dress. But she made do with what she had and improvised. She pinched her cheeks when she heard the knock on the door and a genuine smile lit her face.

Nick took in Millie's burgundy gown with a low cut bodice and snug waistline. White lace trimmed the sleeves and hem in the newest style. Her chest had been brushed lightly with powder and she smelled faintly of roses. She looked stunning yet he grumbled in dismay. "You shouldn't be allowed to go out wearing something so low cut. Everyone can see what you have to offer."

Millie's smile froze. Was he implying that she was a woman lacking in morals? Just because she had lost her virginity didn't mean that she was careless with her heart. Suddenly she felt cheap and shamed. She had been looking forward to spending some time with a very nice man. Now she felt guilty for those feelings. In an instant he had put her in her place and disappointment hung heavy upon her shoulders. Tears sprung to her eyes and she began to shut the door in Nick's face. "Perhaps you should attend alone Mr. Edwards. I am no longer in the mood to go out this evening. Good night." Her voice was short and clipped. She wanted him to leave and closed the door that served as a barrier, shielding her face, her heart and her feelings from his view. He mustn't see her cry. She'd not cry over any man ever again!

Nick realized an instant too late that his harsh words had hurt her. Surly she was overly emotional right now and extremely sensitive because of the rape. Then it dawned on him exactly how his words had been interpreted. "Oh. Millie please open the door. I didn't mean for it to come out that way." He waited. Nothing happened. "Millie please. I'm begging. Open the door and look into my eyes when I apologize to you. Then you can see for yourself that these words are coming from the heart, if I have one that is. There's not much left of it. There's a hole in it the size of the moon. That happened when my wife died. But I am well…"

The door squeaked open an inch and she peered through the crack with one eye. Even though that eye was blackened, Nick thought it beautiful. "I'm sorry." He put his hand on the door and pushed it open further taking a step towards her. "I honestly didn't mean for it to come out that way."

"How did you mean it then? Were you speaking in fatherly terms?" Her voice was still clipped. If he wasn't looking at her he'd have no idea that she was about to cry. But unshed tears clouded her eyes and her chin quivered just slightly, symptoms that were traitorous to her voice.

"No." He placed a hand on her waist and drew her closer to him. "God forgive me but my feelings for you are far from fatherly. I know it's wrong but I want you Millie. I want you and I don't want other guys to see what you have. That's what I meant to say." She smelled like flowers and soap. He was enticed by the aromas and the cut of the dress. Damn the festivities. If he had his way, he'd have her right now. "I find it very difficult to be honorable in your presence. I think of things I know I shouldn't."

She looked plaintively into his eyes. Questioning him silently.

"I'm old enough to be your father and I've lost my soul mate, my wife. I keep telling myself that. But here you are, desirable, sweet…" As his words cut off his mouth covered hers in a gentle explorative kiss.

At first Millie wanted to pull away and run in fear. But before she knew what was happening, her body betrayed her. She felt sensitive to the touch and reeled with a sensation she'd never experienced before as it bloomed in the deepest regions of her womanhood. She leaned into him and began to kiss him back with an urgency she didn't quite understand.

Nick knew the moment she gave in. He felt her body lean heavily into him and become compliant. He hardened with need. "Millie, we have to stop now. If we don't, I'm afraid I won't be able to control myself. I won't be able to stop. Do you understand what I'm saying?"

In response Millie pulled him further into the room, kicked the door shut and hooked the latch behind her. "Please love me."

Nick was lost. She had him, hook, line and sinker. He was drowning in a sea of need. He felt as if she needed to be loved, but he did too. It had been so long that he had gone without. He'd been alone in more ways than one. He'd had no one to share his life with, no one to love physically, challenge mentally and serve as a companion. He desperately wanted all that now. He missed it something fierce. He knew without a doubt that if he gave in to Millie now and loved her like he wanted, she'd have to be his for life. "Millie do you understand what you are committing to? If I have you now, you will be mine for always."

"I'm yours in heart already. My body is just another facet. What I feel right now isn't some childish young girl fantasy. It's real. I need you to love me. Don't just take me like Randy did, but love me Nick. If you love me, I will give freely and I promise to love you back."

It was in that room, during those dark delicious hours, during that hot and smoldering night that Millie learned how wonderful it was to be loved. She learned what desire truly was and began the process of healing. She would gladly spend the rest of her days loving Nick Edwards. They never made it to the party. They never left the room and Nick never regretted any of it. He was committed and suddenly looking forward to the future. It had a lot to offer and he was filled with a contentment that he hadn't felt in more than a year. Life felt right again. He had a reason to live, someone to love and his daughter back in his life again. His only worry now was answering to the Judge.

The Judge had quickly gotten to work sending notices to higher up officials that he was resigning his position. He had thought about it all night and day. He was determined that this was what he wanted to do and requested a replacement be sent forthright so that he could spend some time showing the new judge the circuit. He also pardoned Neb for his association with the crimes that Randall Hurley had committed. Currently the only way he could pardon the man was if he did it before a trial was called to order. If it was after that, Governor Bartley would have to get involved. He wrote a missive to Bartley explaining everything and requesting a visit from his old friend. He felt that Neb Hurley had been a victim just as much as what Josie and Mille had been and was justified in these actions. He made the pardon official with a wax seal and his imprint. While he was at it, he drew up papers that pardoned Millie for her attempt on Josie's life. Next he pardoned Josie for her assault on Millie. Even though these crimes had never been officially drawn up, he felt it necessary in order to give closure to the entire ordeal.

Before leaving his office, he went to the desk, peered out the window then leaned over to blow out the oil lamp. He took note that Nick Edwards was collecting Millie from her room at the hotel across the street. In the darkness he watched as words were exchanged. Something was amiss. Then he saw Nick advance into the room and caught a glimpse of Millie's clutched fist pulling him in. Nick Edwards was a fine man but he still wanted to march over there and interrupt the interlude. Then he chastised himself. His daughter would not partake in an interlude. Especially considering what she had just gone through. No, if this was truly what it appeared to be then he would have to trust in Millie's good judgment and sensibility. The only way that girl would give herself to another right now is if she were in love. Love. He prayed that was it and that she would hurt no more. Perhaps those grandchildren would come sooner rather than later. He smiled to himself before joining the merrymaking.

The Judge worked the cider table for a while and once plenty of cups were filled, he danced with Hanna. He was quickly out of breath and forced to acknowledge his age. Then he realized he was fine with the fact that he was getting on in years. Yes, he was getting old...but wasn't life grand? In the middle of the gathering, the music was halted and everyone stood in silence while the Judge announced his plans to retire and aid the community as best he could as a permanent resident. Then he announced the unexpected pardons. The unanimous response was remarkable.

"There is one exception to these pardons that I must announce and I regret that Millie isn't here to hear it, but she'll be fine with it I'm sure. She is otherwise disposed at this moment, so I'll explain it to her personally in the morning. She did start the fire to the restaurant. I say so regretfully and I cannot pardon that. She has been working at the restaurant and performing remarkably I am told. So if the owners will agree...I will have her work off the debt to the community. She will serve a community sentence, working at the restaurant full-time until her debt has been paid in full. The papers have been drawn up and are already in the hands of the owners."

Loud cheers and congratulations filled the room. Hanna stood quietly next to Neb hoping that he would ask her to dance. When Neb heard the pardon, he was uncertain what to think and how to feel. He was still dimwitted from time to time and had to really think about what he wanted to say before he said it. He had a lot of difficulty pronouncing words that had multiple syllables and became frustrated very easily. When the Judge approached him and handed him his pardon, Neb was speechless. He shook the mans hand and gave him a quick hug slapping him firmly on the back. "Thank you."

He walked outside to get a breath of fresh air. Hanna followed close on his heals. Neb stood looking across the street seemingly staring into nothingness. Hanna knew he was deep in thought yet sensed that he needed her. "I'll give you a penny for your thoughts." Her eyes sparkled in the moonlight. She thought she glimpsed a star shooting of to the right but didn't chance a look.

"I'm feeling very humble." He was quiet again for a few more moments and then continued. "I like it here. I like it very much. I don't want to leave. I have friends for the first time in my life and more importantly, I'm in love."

Hanna backed away a step and took a deep breath. She couldn't believe what she was hearing. He was in love. She clasped her hands together and breathed deeply once more. Luckily she hadn't told him how she felt. She would have looked the fool and been so embarrassed. Did he fall for Millie while searching for the girls? Oh…she so badly wanted to be happy for him, but was hit with a viscous wave of jealousy. Tears formed in her eyes and she blinked quickly to hold them at bay.

Suddenly Neb turned to her. She was startled and yelped in response.

"Hanna. Will you marry me? I don't have much to offer as I don't even have a job. But I know I love you and I want to be with you. I want to be here, in this town, with you forever."

In answer she flew into his arms. Their lips locked in a heated kiss that spoke volumes of their love for each other and the promise of what was to come later, after the vows were spoken. When she pulled away she looked lovingly into his eyes, wiped the lipstick from his mouth with her thumb and answered. "I would love to be your wife. Yes. Yes I will marry you Neb Hurley. I thought you'd never ask!"

"I guess we better collect the minister from the church in Rapids. Here. Here!" The Judge yelled and cheers went up again. Hanna turned a shade of red, realizing that their conversation and kiss had been witnessed by many.

Etta squealed in the distance and Angus made a toast to the prosperity of the community. Providence and it's people were thriving. The fiddlers played tune after tune as the moon shimmered over the gently flowing water casting dim shadows and moonlight over the main street of town. The evening was peaceful and one that everyone would remember for the rest of their days.

Josie ventured towards the lean-to intending to visit the horses and sneak a few carrots to them as treats. About a week had gone by and she felt much improved. Most of her strength had returned as she had hardly been allowed out of bed, between Christian, her Daddy and Etta all watching over her, how could a person do anything other than heal? She followed Teenabe's wife's directions explicitly and was surely on the mend. Her heart had mended some too. She forgave her Daddy whole heartedly and in a way that seemed to patch up some of the pain she had felt at losing her Mamma and baby brother. She thought pensively at the lessons she had learned over the past several weeks. Love seemed to be a mighty thing. It healed all wounds but if misused, had the potential to be very blunt and painful. She smiled then thinking of Christian.

The horses were happy to see her. She gave them each a carrot, rubbed their noses and spoke softly to them. As their line of vision focused they looked down their noses to see her better and nodded their heads, an animated response to her visit. She was pleased to see that the animals got along nicely. She was also very excited for the foal to be born in just a few weeks.

Christian approached quietly from behind and slipped his arms around her mid-section then nipped her ear and kissed her neck. "Hey beautiful. What are you doing out here by yourself?"

"What are you doing out here? You are supposed to be at work."

"Didn't I tell you I would never let you out of my sight again?"

She turned to face him and giggled. "That's going to be impossible. Don't you think? Three hundred and sixty five days in a year, twenty four hours a day, one thousand four hundred forty minutes a day...and how many years to you think we will be married? Hmm...I will have to figure out how many minutes that is exactly." She tapped her chin with one delicate finger and looked heavenward with a silly expression upon her face.

"Mmm. That is something to think about. I wonder how many of those minutes can be spent in bed." He kissed her neck again and felt himself harden just from being close to her. It was getting more and more difficult to behave with each day that passed. "Where is everyone?"

"Etta is with Mrs. Hayward getting fitted for new outfits, eating candy and being spoiled. My Daddy took Millie out for a picnic lunch and a walk. I'm all alone for a little while. Just me, Hops, Buster and the new horse. We have to give her a name you know."

"You'll have to name her. I know you'll come up with something significant." He picked her up and kissed her soundly. She snuggled her nose into his chest as he carried her back to the house.

"I can walk Christian. You don't have to carry me."

"I know."

"Where are we going?"

"To bed. That's where you belong my dear. In bed."

"I'm tired of being in bed all the time."

"You had best get used to it. You're going to be there a lot in the future." He looked down at her and winked. "You still need more rest. The wedding is on Saturday. Just a few days away. Mrs. Hayward received your gown today. That's why I'm home. I brought it to you."

"Oh Christian. I'm so excited!" She clapped her hands together as he put her down in the rocking chair. "I really can walk you know." He was over-reacting a little. She was dizzy for a few days after returning to providence and managed to only fall once while attempting to reach the outhouse. Unfortunately for her, Christian was right there and now he wouldn't let her do anything until the day of the wedding. That was what the Indian woman had told him was best.

"Hanna has already collected her dress. She and Millie will be over this evening to try everything on and do whatever it is that you women do when kicking us men out of the house."

"That sounds absolutely wonderful. Imagine, all three of us getting married on the same day! What a party we're going to have. And, just think, we will always remember each others anniversary's." She laughed out loud and smiled even wider. "You are going to look so handsome."

At that he grumbled.

"Hey." She whispered. "Come here. I have a secret to tell you."

Bending before her he looked at her expectantly. "Well, what is it?"

She bent forward and whispered in his ear. He turned beet red. His jaw dropped. Getting the response she expected, she boldly slid one arm around his neck and began trailing kisses from the side of his face down to his neck. She let her other hand massage his side and when he stood, she daringly stood too. She pushed close and cupped a hand over the bulge in his pants. Let him try to resist her this time. She wouldn't have it. They were alone and she intended to make the best of it. She intended to drive him absolutely mad with desire. She had been talking to Hanna and Millie a lot lately. She had a fairly good idea of how this worked and what she could do. She rubbed up and down, not soft, but not hard. His size increased and she marveled at how that worked. It was amazing to her and she wanted to look upon his member and watch it change. Lucky for Christian, she felt loved enough to be brazen with him. He made her feel attractive and desirable. She didn't think she'd ever need that, but she did. It was important to a woman. Then she realized that the harder he got, the more he responded, the stronger the feeling she had in the core of her being. It was a burning desire to be touched. She wanted to explore his body, and have him explore hers. And, the more he responded, the braver she felt. She also felt empowered in some small way. It excited her even more.

Reaching down she began to fumble with the buttons on his trousers. When he made to pull away she stepped into him, refusing to ease up, and began to stroke his member through the material of his pants. He groaned audibly. "Josie."

She pulled him by the shirt while undoing the buttons, towards the bedroom they ambled, where she kicked the door shut. When the front of his shirt was open she began to trail kisses along his chest, down his stomach, over the trail of hair to the undone button of his pants. There she hesitated long enough to wrestle his garments down. His member bounced in front of her. A long hard shaft. It wasn't like anything she'd seen before yet she was more curious than anything. She placed her hand around it and gently kissed the tip. She had been told that doing this was the thing that men desired most. It was supposed to be special. And Josie, wanted her first time with Christian to be very special. She wanted to please him in a way that no one else ever had. His hands rested atop her head as if he was undecided on what to do.

Then he moaned and she was sanctioned as the burning sensation within her expanded. Her legs felt weak as she got down on her knees. Her flesh became overly sensitized. She liked this. Millie had said it would hurt. This sure didn't. It felt nice. She ventured further and began to lick his shaft like a lollipop. He groaned again. Josie took that as a good sign and feasted upon him putting the whole thing in her mouth. She bounced back and forth. Christian clutched her hair with both hands forming fists of barely contained desire. He guided her back and forth, forcing her to stop a few times lest he lose control. She was driving him absolutely crazy. Where did she learn this? Was he wrong to think she was a virgin? He'd never come right out and asked. Oh, but he didn't care. Not at this moment he didn't. Her tongue was expert in its manipulation as it glided up and down, gentle then rough, circling the tip and then disappearing as her entire mouth engulfed him once again before she'd come up for air and repeat the process. He was going to blow soon if he didn't stop her.

He tore off his shirt and pulled her to her feet and then proceeded to tear her clothes off, not even caring about the buttons that flew every which way. He was ravenous for her. He wanted to taste her body, every morsel of it. When they were both completely naked, he lay her upon the bed and looked over every inch of her essence. He wanted to taste every inch of bare flesh. Her eyes smoldered with desire. "Don't move." He commanded. "Don't you dare move a muscle."

"Why?" She asked sweetly.

"Paybacks." He kissed her lips quickly and then began to suckle upon her breast. Her nipples grew hard and puckered instantly and yet he sucked until the nubs were little peaks of flesh that he could twirl his tongue around. While he was doing that, his member was rubbing the top of her abdomen. It felt wonderful. She was craving something but couldn't quite place what it was. Her body instinctively began to move and rub opposite his movements. She liked this. She liked it a lot and she grew wet and wanton with desire.

Christian trailed kisses down her rib cage to the patch of hair between her legs. He softly rubbed his hands along the inside of her thighs so lightly that it almost tickled. Then he pressed her legs apart and gave her a staying look when she made to question him. With his fingers he separated her womanly flesh and began to kiss, suckle, lick and taste her. Oh she tasted good. He couldn't get enough. She was so sweet and compliant. She was purely enjoying his ministrations as little moans and mummers came from her lips constantly. She turned her head from side to side and wiggled unknowingly in an attempt to reach that climax they were both working towards. Every now and then he would hit a spot and she would spasm and moan. It felt marvelous. She was wet and open. She had to be ready for him. He couldn't wait another minute.

Her legs were splayed wide open as he kissed his way back up her body before covering her mouth and placing his manhood at the entrance of her womanly core. She was so warm, so wet, he could hardly think straight anymore.

She could taste herself on his lips when he kissed her and the tip of his member touching her nether lips felt absolutely divine. She arched upwards trying to get closer to it his shaft, wanting to feel it there. She wanted him inside her, deep inside her. She knew instinctively that that was where he belonged. She grasped his shoulders. "Now."

He deepened the kiss and plunged in with one swift stroke. He felt her maidenhead tear and paused momentarily to monitor Josie's response but she was tight around his shaft and the need to move back and forth was overpowering. He stroked in and out slowly at first, trying to be careful not to hurt her. Now wasn't the time to be selfish, but God help him, he couldn't stop. It felt too good to hold still. But then something wonderful happened. He realized that she was moaning with pleasure. He increased his rhythm. She lifted her legs, met him thrust for thrust and begged him not to stop.

"Oh, Josie. You feel so good." He squeezed her breast as she clutched the pillows. Then he placed one of her hands on her breast. She took his lead and began to feel her nipples with both hands. Watching her feel herself was so pleasing, he would remember how she looked at this moment forever. He held her legs up farther allowing him deeper access and the bed began to bang against the wall. "Look at me Josie."

She did, she looked right into his eyes as he requested but she had a difficult time in doing so. He was making her feel so good she was about to explode. She wanted to thrash about, not just look at him. Then they both looked away as their desire exploded. She practically screamed as her orgasm clutched his shaft in rapid contractions sending tingling sensations throughout her mid-section and down her thighs. "Oh. Oh. Ummm."

He clenched his teeth as he emptied every ounce of seaman he had into her. Little contractions were still squeezing him so he remained still, enjoying the after effects of her climax. Watching her reaction the entire time. "Are you okay?"

"Mmmhmm." She had her eyes shut and lay limp upon the pillows.

"I didn't hurt you did I?"

"Ummumm." She moved her pelvis in a circular motion. "Do we have to wait long to do it again?"

He threw his head back and laughed out loud. "For God's sake woman, you're going to be the death of me."

EPILOGUE

"Hurry Josie. We have to leave now!" Christian was irritated and anxious to get moving. Every minute was critical. Hanna and Neb had already left, taking nothing but the horses they were riding on. Etta sat in front of him, running her fingers through Buster's tresses, pouting but quiet. She was worried about her baby horse of which she loved dearly. He was strung behind them and would fare out just fine. But Etta was too young to comprehend what was happening to her and her new found family. She was more upset by the fact that she couldn't ride atop the little horse and couldn't understand why. Christian would explain later.

Joey sat atop his own horse. He was an added member of their family as well. It was an unspoken but accepted pact made in silence. Nobody really knew what happened to his real parents but Josie loved him to pieces and the two were now inseparable.

"I forgot to grab the smudge pot. We'll need it." She swung herself into the saddle a little awkwardly since she was several months into her pregnancy. Her back ached and surely wouldn't get any better during a long trek atop a horse. The air was acrid with smoke as many people had set their homes aflame before abandoning them. "Where are the others?"

"They've left. They'll be meeting us in a little town called Swanton. It's a days ride from here. We'll ride a little slower. Don't worry, your dad, Millie and baby Nicholas are fine. Are you going to be ok?"

"Do I have a choice? We have to do what we must."

"I'm sorry we have to leave our home and belongings behind. We'll get more. I promise. Next time around will be even better."

"My home is where you and Etta are. Everything else is just geography. It's the death of so many friends that upsets me. I can't not think of them and my heart is broken for those that are left behind." Her tears were flowing already. She wanted to be strong for both Etta and her unborn child but she was even more emotional than normal and felt as if she had no control over her body, thoughts and emotions at times.

He smiled. "I love you. You can have a good cry while we ride. But we can't belay leaving any longer. I'm sorry."

Christian felt bad for her having to leave and ride while so heavy with child. He worried something fierce, especially since her mother had died during childbirth. He wouldn't have chosen to travel, but staying would be deadly. The town of Providence had survived a lot. It had grown and prospered with a surplus of produce, pelts, grain and many other goods that flowed through the village thanks to the Erie canal. Travelers came and went every day, hence the reason they were fleeing their homes now. Travelers conversing through the village had infested it with cholera. The only chance they had of surviving, was to leave Providence as quickly as they could. Every second they remained behind posed a risk that one of them would become violently ill.

They had lost many of their friends. Cholera was a horrible sickness. It affected the bowels and many folks died within a few hours. Cholera's attach left behind corpses that resembled prunes. The body fluids were gone, leaving a sunken cavity of what once was. It seemed there was nothing anyone could do for it. No one that got it survived. It was made famous by the press since President James K. Polk, the eleventh president of the United States had died from it.

So far, they lost Angus, the Judge, Hank, Mr. and Mrs. Hayward, and many others. It was a terrible tragedy and Christian prayed that his family remain free from the curse. He did more than pray, he begged God to spare them as his family was precious to him.

Several hours went by and Christian felt relieved. None of them had been sick as of yet, and they had traveled approximately twelve miles. "Let's make camp for the night Josie."

She heaved a sigh of releif then dismounted slowly, groaning on the way down. "I feel like a big burlap sack full of grain. Pretty soon you'll have to hull me over your shoulder to take me anywhere."

Etta began to giggle as Josie made an show of wobbling around in a circle, exaggerating her sway as if she were as big as a house.

"Come on you old bag. I'll help with supper." He grinned as she swatted playfully at him.

"That's not nice Mr. Coy. Do you know what bad boys get?" She wiggled her eyebrows up and down waiting for his response.

"No. What do bad boys get?"

"Denied." She spoke in a loud drawn out voice. Then squealed as he chased her down and landed a kiss atop her head.

"I will not be denied. I'd rather die first."

"Well, you keep saying I'll be the death of you."

"We're going to be okay Josie. I promise. We'll be okay." And they would be. As long as they had each other, everything would be fine. They were living in difficult times and consistently prayed for the best. But their family was growing. And their love was strong. They would persevere.

HAWALA
By Leo Teohari

December 1989: The world watched and accepted a lie while one of the most highly trained political machines assassinated its dictator. Yet the assassins, the dictator's inner circle, rise from genocide promising to lead a torn nation to better times while creating diversion to hide their own crimes: selling arms, housing terrorists' training camps, laundering money, selling children and stealing the country's assets.

Alec Popescu, defector from his birth country, returns in the post-Iron Curtain era bringing millions in investment for the new "Democratic" Romania. Yet, unknown to Popescu, his newfound stature and success threaten the power of the political elite. Blind-sided, he's caught in a treacherous web. Framed by the government, arrest warrants are issued, Interpol notified. Newspapers carry the headlines. Popescu's family members turn their backs and he finds himself a fugitive.

Paperback, 302 pages
6" x 9"
ISBN 1-4137-2723-9

Risking his life to clear his name, Alec uncovers bigger political crimes as he battles against the fierce KGB-educated Communists, Romania's Central Bank and the Italian mafia.

About the author:

Leo Teohari holds both a law degree and a degree in international economics. He defected from Communist Romania in 1980. Helped by the Catholic Church, Teohari settled with his family in Toronto, Canada, and became a successful businessman. Today he writes about his experiences and runs an international trade consulting business.